The Goblins had closed to fifty meters when a stiff wind blew up, casually throwing the tiny band's scent at them. Halting, the lead Goblin tipped his head back to sniff the wind with a wide, flat nose. Drool escaped from between twisted and cracked teeth. Humans. More scouts caught the scent and a cry rose up through their ranks. Weapons were raised. Natural pack hunters, Goblins had muddy grey-green skin and stood close to five feet. Most were heavily muscled and overly armored. They weren't exceptional fighters, often relying on strength of numbers. They knew they had the advantage and prepared to attack.

They halted immediately when a huge man emerged from hiding to confront them. He taunted them. Mocking them with his defiance. The Goblin whip master pushed his way to the front ranks. He had one eye and a long, white scar running the length of his face where the other had been.

"What's this?" he snapped.

Grelic placed the tip of his broadsword into the dirt and waited. His feet were spread a comfortable distance apart. His body language suggested he was calm, relaxed. Goblins spit and yelled insults in their foul language. Grelic didn't blink. The whip master cracked his leather and the mob quieted.

"Where there's one, there's more," he snarled. "Move slow, dogs. It's man flesh for supper!"

THE DRAGON HUNTERS

The Histories of Malweir Book Two

CHRISTIAN WARREN FREED

Copyright © 2020 by Christian Warren Freed

Excerpt from *Armies of the Silver Mage* 2021 Christian Warren Freed
Cover design by Warren Design
Cover copyright 2021 by Warfighter Books
Author Photograph by Anicie Freed

Warfighter Books
Holly Springs, North Carolina 27540
https://www.christianfreed

Second Edition: January 2021

Library of Congress Cataloging-in-Publication Data
Name: Freed, Christian Warren, 1973- author.
Title: The Dragon Hunters/ Christian Warren Freed
Description: Second Edition | Holly Springs, NC: Warfighter Books, 2021.
Identifiers: LCCN 2021930764 | ISBN 9781734907537 (trade paperback)
ISBN: 9781735700083 (ebook)
Subjects: Epic fantasy | Fantasy

Printed in the United States of America

10 9 8 7 6 5 4 3 2 1

"Armies of the Silver Mage was a great read...any fan of Lord of the Rings or Game of Thrones will love this book. I'm looking forward to next book."

"The book is almost an homage to the great classics like Sword of Shanara and the Lord of the Rings. The author has cleverly used his past military and combat experience to make the battle scenes more realistic."

The Northern Crusade
Hammers in the Wind
Tides of Blood and Steel
A Whisper After Midnight
Empire of Bones
The Madness of Gods and Kings
Even Gods Must Fall

The Histories of Malweir
Armies of the Silver Mage
The Dragon Hunters
Beyond the Edge of Dawn

Forgotten Gods
Dreams of Winter
The Madman on the Rocks
Anguish Once Possessed
Through Darkness Besieged
Under Tattered Banners
A Time For Tyrants
A Good Day For Crows

Where Have All the Elves Gone?
One of Our Elves is Missing
From Whence It Came
The Lazarus Men
Repercussions: A Lazarus Men Agenda
Tomorrow's Demise: The Extinction Campaign
Tomorrow's Demise: Paths of Salvation*
Coward's Truth: A Novel of the Heart Eternal

A Long Way From Home: Memories and Observations
From Iraq and Afghanistan+

Immortality Shattered
Law of the Heretic
The Bitter War of Always
Land of Wicked Shadows
Storm Upon the Dawn

War Priests of Andrak Saga
The Children of Never*

SO, You Want to Write a Book? +
SO, You Wrote a Book. Now What?+*

*Forthcoming   + Nonfiction

Acknowledgments

I would like to thank those who helped contribute to this novel. Writing it proved slightly problematic since I was in Baghdad in 2005. Silly things like war kept getting in the way. Still, much of this story wouldn't have been possible without the feedback and support of my friends: Gina Grey, Jurgen Kote and Ardjan Balla of the Albanian Army, and Charlotte Brock. You guys were my anchor throughout the process. None of this would have been possible without the drive given to me by my parents, however. To them I express eternal gratitude.

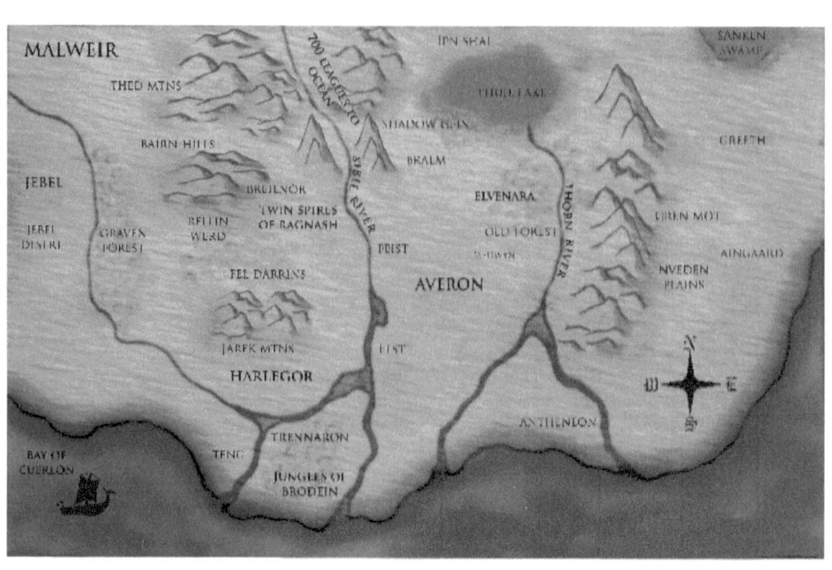

MALWEIR
SANKEN SWAMP
IPN SHAI
THED MTNS
700 LEAGUES TO OCEAN
THULE LAKE
SHADOW PLAIN
BAIRN HILLS
GREFTH
BRALM
JEBEL
BREILNOR
ELVENARA
SHIEL RIVER
THORN RIVER
RELTIN WERD
TWIN SPIRES OF RAGNASH
OLD FOREST
CIREN MOT
JEBEL DESERT
GRAVEN FOREST
DITWEN
AINGAARD
NVEDEN PLAINS
FEL DARRINS
FEIST
AVERON
JAREK MTNS
EIST
HARLEGOR
N
E
ANTHENEON
TRENNARON
TENG
W
BAY OF CUERLON
JUNGLES OF BRODEIN
S

A Foul Wind

A pale wind kissed the fading winter day. Spring was but a few weeks away and the lands were still being assailed by an unexpected blizzard coming down from the Darkwall Mountains to the north. Massive snowdrifts dotted the lightly forested plains. Trees drooped under the weight of gathering ice. Winds howled and screamed in tortured agony from canyon to valley. Even the skies, normally pale blue by this time, were sickened in a mottle of grey and black. Winter refused to let go.

Normally Fitch Iane would be nestled in his favorite chair built by his great grandfather, in front of the fireplace, but this winter had been especially harsh on hunting and fishing. A record six storms all but crippled the lands, making it next to impossible for most to gather food or firewood. As he tramped through the woods on the way home, Fitch wished for the thousandth time that he'd been born some sort of royalty. Living in a warm, toasty palace with marble floors and dozens of waiting servants seemed the life. A sudden gust of wind sent ice and snow down the back of his heavy coat, forcing Fitch back to grim reality.

Still, it wasn't all bad. His knapsack was filled with three cleaned and quartered hares and a handful of plucked grouse. Not too bad considering it was just for him and his wife. The thought of Shar, with her warming smile and long, flowing golden hair stirred his passions. How much he'd give to be lying next to her supple body under the down blankets right now. Fitch shook his head. That sort of thinking would leave a man dead quicker than getting cut wrong. Besides, he still had too far to go to get distracted with thoughts of what came next.

Fitch sighed and continued his trek across the darkening landscape. He couldn't help but shiver at the unseasonable cold. The snow should be nearly gone by now and the land was soggy from the additional moisture. A quick glance around and he figured it would be another six weeks before things got right. Six whole weeks. Fitch wondered how this year's harvest would turn out. The farmers were all but panicking by now. As it was, this part of Thrae wasn't known for outstanding crops or heavy farming. Most of the residents of Gend, Fitch's home since birth, were miners. The kingdom of Thrae won ownership of the jewel mines after a fierce war with the Dwarves of the Bairn Hills nearly a generation ago.

It was left to those like Fitch to provide for their homes and right now all he wanted was to get out of the insufferable cold. He could almost taste the stew and freshly baked dark bread. A pint of heavy ale would do nicely too. Fitch stumbled, his foot snagging on a buried root. A tremendous roar shook the very ground as he dropped. His heart froze as a blast of freezing wind sliced into him. Fitch looked around but couldn't spot the source of the fury in the gathering darkness.

"What?" he asked himself, hoping his mind could rationalize the moment.

Fitch looked up just then and noticed the entire eastern sky seemed as if it was on fire. He smelled ash and burnt meat. He wanted to believe it was just an illusion played by the setting sun. The first flicker of flames shooting up over the treetops changed his mind. He looked around. Everywhere he looked trees were blackened and dead. Fresh snow was dusty, charcoal splashed. *What nightmare could have done such a thing*? A tiny whisper in the back of his mind warned that the answers were much closer than he wished.

Then it hit him. A horrible, sickening thought all but crippling him. Fire. Smoke. Distance. Gend! His village was burning. Fitch dropped his sack and started running. The need to get home, to find Shar, overpowered all other thoughts and emotions. A nightmarish roar frightened the world. Fitch covered his ears and ran. Blood began to trickle from his nose.

When he got closer he could hear new sounds, sickening sounds of steel ripping human flesh. Women screaming. Children crying. Fitch suddenly grew very afraid. His body became lethargic. He found it difficult just to move. *Shar*. Thinking of her kept him going, but he was so afraid. A warm feeling ran down his leg. Sweat turned cold. His body shivered and trembled. He was no great hero, but neither was he a coward. *What manner of demon can make me so?* Fitch Iane gave in to his fears and collapsed. He used what strength remained to crawl under the boughs of a snow-laden fir and cried.

The screaming quickly drowned out his sorrow. Fitch tried covering his ears. Tears streaked his frozen cheeks. Strength abandoned him. Fear dug deeper, gaining strength and crushing him. Jagged pieces of ice fell from the pine needles and cut his face. He didn't care. His only concern was staying alive. *Just to stay alive!*

What must have been hundreds of booted feet crunching through the ice-covered snow inspired new terror. Fitch reluctantly opened his eyes and had to cover his mouth to keep the gasp from escaping. He barely made out the huge, barrel-bodied figures marching by. Watching the shadows move so stealthily through the forest reminded him of the ghost and ghoul stories his mother used to tell him and his three brothers when they were growing up. These apparitions were much more real. Fitch got a good look as they marched closer.

Garbed in black and grey, they had massive bodies and spoke in a gnarled tongue. The sound of their boots crunching made him cringe. Stomp, stomp, stomp. He wanted to break and run but couldn't. The demons wore armor and had flowing capes of the purest black. Spikes jutted up from their helmets. Axe and sword rested in their mailed hands. Some sang songs which were cruel and wicked. Fitch saw hundreds of them moving through the forest. He'd never believed in demons before. They seemed so dire, menacing. Then he noticed the tiny rivers of crimson staining their armor. Blood! Demons or not, they were pure killers. Struggling to control his sobs, Fitch watched them as they merrily went about slaughtering every last man, woman, and child in his village.

A pair of demons halted nearby, close enough for him to hear part of their conversation.

"...much longer?" snarled the first.

The second spit a wad of bloody phlegm. "Maggots take too long to kill. No honor. They run instead of fight."

"The king's army will come soon. We must hurry. Ramulus wants them all dead but we aren't strong enough to fight an army."

"One hour," the second confirmed.

The demons stalked off, going their separate ways and leaving Fitch more frightened than before. He didn't want to die. The thought replayed in his head over and over. He knew it was shameful to be so selfish but he couldn't help it. Gradually, the slaughter abated and the demons returned to the shadows. Fitch was alone. The flames of Gend slowly faded. Night crawled back into the world. He nearly summoned the strength to crawl out of his self-imposed prison when that horrible roar shattered the calm. A fierce gust of wind shook most of the snow from the branches. Fitch pulled his knees up as an immense presence sailed overhead. Wrapping his arms around his knees, he cried himself to sleep.

Dawn crawled across Malweir with eerie casualness. Fitch reluctantly wiped the crust from his sore and bloodshot eyes. He was damp from melting snow and frozen to the bone. His body shivered uncontrollably in a desperate attempt to find warmth. The overwhelming sense of fear was gone but he was still loath to leave his hiding place. Some of the demons might have stayed behind.

Shar. The thought of her brought tears to his eyes. He couldn't help but feel she might still be alive if only he'd been there. If only he'd...no, he would be dead as well if he hadn't hid. Shame and disgrace competed for his soul. Fitch Iane was a shell of a man. He held on to the sliver of hope that Shar managed to find a place to hide. That she had somehow made it out of this nightmare alive. It was all he had left.

Summoning what little strength remained, Fitch crawled out into the open. He made his way through the smoldering ruins in search of his wife. He had to know. An hour later he stood in front of the ruin that was his home. Their home. He looked at the desperate pile of burnt timber, searching for the one thing he didn't want to find. Fitch sank to his knees as waves of raw emotion burst free. He had let her die. He let them all die.

"I'm sorry, Shar. I am so very sorry," he whispered through heaving sobs. "I should have come back. I should have helped."

Half a day passed before he remembered he was alone and had nowhere to go. Fear kept him alive last night. The coming night was another matter. Fitch needed to find some food and shelter before he froze to death. He retraced his tracks to his pack and contemplated returning to Gend for the night. Much of the residual heat had worn off but there was enough to keep him alive until dawn. *No. The demons might return.* Fitch gave in, knowing he had to get as far away from Gend as possible.

With heavy heart, he turned his back on what had been his whole world. Fitch Iane walked away with horror that would forever dominate his life. Shar's face haunted him every time he closed his eyes. It wasn't long before he realized he hated himself. Hated how he cowered and hid while everyone he had ever known died. It didn't matter that one man couldn't make a difference. Fitch was a coward.

He wandered aimlessly for most of the day before finally deciding on a plan. The capital city of Kelis Dur and King Rentor needed to be warned of the growing darkness. Fitch may not have been able to save his loved ones but he couldn't allow the same fate to befall the rest of Thrae. Kelis Dur was more than five days away by foot, but with a little luck he might hitch a ride with a passing wagon or caravan once he made it to the major trade lanes.

First things first. You need rest or they'll be finding your corpse once the snow melts. Fitch found a suitable campsite under a small rock outcropping and set about making a fire. After filling up on cooked grouse and melted snow, he wrapped up in his thick bearskin hunting coat and let sleep claim him. Nightmares toyed with him and he tossed and turned long into the dark hours. The fire died out just shy of midnight, right when winter decided to throw its final blast across the world.

TWO

Grelic

The world shuddered and groaned under the pounding late winter storm. Few dared to brave the elements, even tucked away in the comparative safety of the major cities. Life in the kingdom of Thrae all but halted. The citizens of Kelis Dur huddled in their homes, eagerly awaiting the return of the sun. Yet no matter how difficult the times, there were always those who never stopped. Mercenaries and bounty hunters seldom found the time to pause. A winter storm was certainly no reason.

The roaring fire in the common room of the Battering Ram constantly attracted the wrong kinds of crowds no matter what nature threw in the way. Dozens of potential heroes and more than a few villains milled about, drinking and bragging. A bard sang tales of greatness off in the far corner as serving maids kept a steady stream of fresh mugs flowing to the paying customers. Many a pipe was lit, coating the ceiling with a thick layer of smoke.

"Damned strange happenings this winter I say," old Bartus told the men at his table. His one eye scanned each for signs of what they might be thinking.

Helf laughed and drained his pint in a long gulp followed by a hearty belch. Foam dripped from his moustache. "You always say that, old man. Sometimes I think you want strange things to happen!"

Bartus jabbed an accusatory finger at him. "Says you! I know what I know. People talk."

"Most have nothing useful to say," Helf countered. "I didn't come here to argue with you. I just want some more ale to take the chill off."

"Judging from the size of your belly I'd say you been keeping warm often," young Nurlen grinned. Unlike the others, time and age hadn't begun to sink their teeth into him.

"Mind you, boy," Bartus snarled. "We both be veterans of the Dwarf War. Back when you was suckling on your mother's tit. You'd do well to hush yourself and listen."

Nurlen stayed quiet. He'd been around them long enough to know they meant no ill. Helf watched the exchange, mindful of the hurt Bartus continued to carry. Losing his eye had cost him his job at the chandlery as well as his wife. He'd never been the same.

"You heard tell of that man they found a week ago? Near dead and half mad," Bartus asked knowingly. "Says he keeps talking about demons in the night."

"Faw!" Nurlen snorted. Youth didn't necessarily involve naivety. "Demons and monsters don't exist. All them are stories my ma used to tell me to keep me in line when I was getting out of hand."

Bartus leaned forward, so close his drunken breath made Nurlen grimace. "Just where do you think them stories come from, boy? There's many a strange thing that goes bump in the night round these parts. Many I don't care to remember." His voice trailed off. Bartus sat quietly, wishing some memories would fade.

Helf was about to break the unnerving silence when a table on the far side of the room suddenly flipped up. Mugs and dishes flew, sending beer, food, and worse across a large portion of patrons. Angered shouts were quickly drowned out when a beast of a man rose from the commotion. A heavy fist lashed out to catch the nearest city guard in the jaw. The sharp crack was unmistakable. The guard's head twisted and he dropped. The big man roared and struck again. Another man fell. The crowd started easing back by the time the fourth man dropped.

He moved with lightning quickness. Snatching up the nearest man, he hefted him overhead and threw him into the crowd. Another man dropped his ale with a squeak and bumped into Bartus. The old man started to lash out when he caught a glimpse of the giant's face. *I know you. Yes, I do.*

"Are you all right?" Helf asked, seeing the confusion in the old man's eye.

A fresh squad of city guards burst through the front door, bringing chill, winds, snow, and legal fury with them. Their dark blue cloaks concealed boiled leather body armor and the standard truncheon of the city guard. The raven feather painted on the armor gave them purpose and a sense of pride.

"What's all this?" bellowed the sergeant of the guard. His thick, black moustache had flakes of melting snow still clinging to it.

The big man bellowed with fresh challenge. Sergeant Phaes was no fool. He'd been in the city guard for nearly twenty years and had dealt with his share of drunken fools. He'd also seen enough to know when a man was so drunk he became dangerous. *Look at the size of this bastard. I'll need a ballista to take him down.* Worse, he knew the man.

Phaes took a step forward and held up empty hands. "Take it easy, Grelic. It's just your old pal, Phaes."

Grelic's eyes narrowed. Rage distorted his features and his face burned the color of fire. Regardless of anything the guard said, he was too drunk and angry to calm down now.

Shit. "You don't want to hurt anyone, Grelic. I know you. We've been friends a long time. Come sit with me and have a drink. Talk to me about what's bothering you."

Phaes felt his stomach cramp with the knowledge there was no way Grelic would fall for it. Instinct told him a fight was coming. He hoped no one got killed. His doubts nearly disappeared as Grelic took a quiet step forward. The big man's face calmed just before his huge fist crashed into a guard's head.

"Take him down!" Phaes cursed.

His men ran forward, swords drawn.

"Don't make me do this, you big, dumb bastard," Phaes shouted. "The king doesn't want to see you back in the dungeons."

Grelic didn't care. Raising his fists above his head, he roared defiance. Phaes sidestepped the rushing man and gave a quick signal. A pair of guards dropped their swords and cast a heavy mesh net over Grelic before he could change his path. His momentum slowed. The rest of the guards closed in and beat Grelic to the floor. Only when he was unconscious and snoring did they stop. He didn't stop fighting the entire way down. Another three men were taken out, the last being kicked so hard it dented his helmet. Phaes groggily regained his feet, swearing more than a few teeth were knocked out. He looked around the common room and was relieved to see everyone at least breathing. He'd once seen Grelic take out almost an entire Averonian infantry platoon singlehandedly. A hard man for hard time. Peace had no room for men like Grelic. And men like Grelic didn't understand peace.

"Are you all right Sergeant?" one of the uninjured guards asked with a sly grin. Like Phaes, he too had been involved in more than one of Grelic's episodes.

Phaes scowled. "How is it you never seem to get a scratch whenever we do this?"

The guard shrugged innocently. "I could say luck, but I don't believe in it."

Phaes rubbed his aching jaw. "Next time you go first."

"Speaking of next time, what do we do with him?"

"Take him back to the outpost. Hopefully he'll sober up and we can get him released." Phaes knew King Rentor would find out quickly and he'd already threatened to take the old warrior's head the next time he did something like this.

"Let's hope the king doesn't find out."

Phaes agreed. *At least not until Grelic is sober and gone.*

It had been a long time since Grelic felt pain this intense. His entire body throbbed from the thorough beating at the hands of the city guard. Head swooning, he attempted to sit up but found the effort not worth the reward and collapsed back onto the stale mattress. Had he been more aware he would have realized at least one of his ribs was broken and his body a mass of bruises.

"Hurts doesn't it?" a familiar voice said from somewhere nearby.

Grelic rolled over to his uninjured side and peered into the murky light. "Be better with some ale."

"I'm afraid not, old friend. Ale's what got you here in the first place."

The giant warrior shook his head. Sobriety slowly filtered through his system. "Phaes? That you?"

"Aye," answered the sergeant. "And it's no ale for you. Rentor already wants your head for the last time. You almost killed poor Dagola."

"He shouldn't have gotten in the way. That was a private conversation," Grelic protested.

Phaes laughed. "A private conversation between you and half of the common room at the Stag. As I recall it all started when someone told you to be quiet."

"Says you," Grelic snorted. "He insulted me."

Phaes rose and grabbed the pitcher of water sitting on the table beside him. Even though Grelic hadn't asked, Phaes knew it was what the big man needed. Locked in the same room as always, the big man watched Phaes stroll to the door and pass the pitcher. They both knew the cage wasn't built strong enough to keep Grelic locked up for long. Plenty of times Phaes worried that the bars were about to break while Grelic raged. Grelic nodded his appreciation, took the water, and drained half of it in one gulp.

"Are you going to let me out or is the king's personal guard on the way to take me to the gallows?" he asked when the iron bars finally came into focus. "Seems being behind bars is becoming a habit for me. Although, free room and board does a man good on occasion."

"On occasion," Phaes agreed. "I doubt the king will be so nice as to allow you the opportunity to swing from one of his ropes. I'm guessing he'll send the executioner in here to get it done. You're not a liked man in the royal court."

Grelic paused to consider this, rubbing his chin thoughtfully. "How much time?"

Phaes shrugged. "A few hours at most. Not as long as a man of your stature needs to blend back in and become a decent member of society. Still, there's enough time to escape Rentor's wrath. Head back to the mountains and wait out the winter. He'll forget this one soon enough."

"The mountains? In this storm?" Grelic asked. "I'd never make it. Don't care how strong I used to be."

Phaes slipped the key into the lock and opened the grate, iron door. "A few weeks of fresh air will do you good. You've been through more than any other man I've known. If anyone has it in them to survive a few weeks of winter it's you."

Grelic offered a sheepish grin. "There was a time when I believed those stories. I'm not a young man anymore, Phaes. Four decades have come and gone and what have I to show for it?" He held up his hands, scarred and leathered from a lifetime of toil. "Just these. My entire life's story is trapped in these hands. But you, my friend, you have a wife and children. A home. That is the true test of a man. A legacy. When I'm gone, who will remember my name?"

Phaes recognized the speech. He'd heard it a dozen times. Grelic tended to grow sentimental, almost fatalistic, after a hard night's drinking. "Another night like this and I might not be able to forget. You hit very hard."

Grelic laughed. Phaes looked at him closely. The big man wasn't actually a giant, but damned near close enough for these parts. He stood close to seven feet tall and had a massive, heavily muscled frame. Phaes guessed he was close to three hundred pounds with very little fat. His hair was turning grey and thinning. Scars crisscrossed most of his body. Thick eyebrows gave him a fierce look, almost concealing his ice-blue eyes. Three days' worth of growth covered his lower face. His nose had been broken at least a dozen times. Any sane man would rightfully stay away, but Phaes valued friendship in any form. It certainly made his job easier.

Heavy knocking interrupted his thoughts. Phaes started towards the door when a deep voice bellowed, "Open in the name of the king!"

THREE

King Rentor

Broken rays of light punched down through the endless banks of dull grey clouds. A murder of crows launched from nearby treetops. Townsfolk considered them ill omens. Rumors of mystics and hedge sorcerers using the birds as familiars and for casting spells had been passed down through the generations. Whenever crows flew, windows were shut and children shooed inside. Even bad was happening across Kelis Dur without the crows.

King Rentor met the dawn with a dour expression. Well past the prime of his life, Rentor was a staunch man of immense stature. Near six feet tall and a great, barrel chest, he bore an imposing figure. His arms and legs were thickly muscled, resembling small tree trunks. A graying beard hung down to his steadily rounding stomach. Much of the hair on his head was gone. Rentor had been a great man, fitting of ruling the mountain kingdom of Thrae.

What comforts he usually found in the first rays of light were absent this day. His quiet moments of reflection and preparation lost to the vagaries of his troubles. Brow furrowed, he clasped his hands behind his back and frowned at the world. Word had already reached him that Grelic was at it again, busting up the Battering Ram this time and injuring many for no reason other than the fact that he couldn't handle his drink. Rentor sighed. He actually liked the man. They had fought together during the Dwarf Wars. The big man had even saved Rentor's life. If it were up to him alone, he would send him on his way. But the kingdom's councilors were braying for blood.

Common wisdom said to exile Grelic. Regency warned otherwise. A king couldn't allow himself to be ruled by emotion or personal feelings. At the very least Grelic would be transferred to the dungeons and held long enough for him to realize there were no more chances forthcoming. Long enough for Rentor to figure out what to do. The aging king sighed and pulled his bearskin cloak tight. *One week past spring and winter continues. Curse my luck for being born the heir to the frozen throne.* Reluctantly, he went back inside. The day was beginning.

Rentor strode down marble corridors, hands clasped behind. As much as he enjoyed governing his people, he was in no hurry to pick up the task today. Grelic was a nuisance but far from his only problem. Rumors of something sinister in the Thed Mountains plagued his informants. Miners were disappearing. Not enough to cause a stir, but enough to send trembles through the local communities. His initial fears were the Dwarves were starting up again and military action would be necessary. Dwarves were a fierce and hearty foe, but they fought with unparalleled honor. Rentor ruled them out. Something dark was brewing in the south.

His tired green eyes looked up at the sound of hurried footsteps. He struggled to keep them from rolling. Prime Minister Codel Mres always seemed to be in a hurry. He was also in the thin minority that thought what he had to say was important. Nine times from ten he carried some obscure bit of intelligence Rentor already knew. If they hadn't been boyhood friends Rentor would have replaced Codel already.

"Good morning, sire," Codel said with a smile. "A word?"

The king slapped a hard hand down on Codel's shoulder. "It wouldn't be a morning if we didn't find the time for a word. What troubles do you bring me today?"

Codel's eyes shifted nervously across the hall. "It is best left said behind closed doors."

His hushed tone was enough to convince Rentor. They shuffled into a quiet room where the prime minister could voice his concerns. Rentor went to the desk and poured two glasses of fresh water. "Tell me this involves a harem of the most beautiful women running loose in the palace," he joked.

"To be so fortunate, though I doubt the queen would approve," Codel said and smiled thinly. "There is trouble in the east."

"I already know this."

Codel shook his head. "Not this, sire. Word has come that the Silver Mage has conquered the kingdom of Gren. Strange creatures are now spotted in the night. Evil days are upon us."

Rentor frowned. It was no secret the order of Mages had disintegrated and all but destroyed themselves, but those events were nearly three hundred years before he was born. The Silver Mage hadn't been seen in almost all those years, prompting Rentor's suspicions of whether Codel's reports were accurate. Besides, Gren was very far away and the least of his concerns. He voiced that to Codel.

"Distance does not matter. The Bairn Hills are hundreds of leagues from here yet their armies came to war with us."

"Point taken," he said, his cheeks flushing at the rebuke. "What does a Mage have to do with our quaint little kingdom? There must be something you are missing."

Codel wore a knowing smirk, as if he finally held the upper hand in a long standing duel. "There is. We have a man who claims to have seen the nightmares plaguing us. He's half mad and recovering from severe trauma but I have every reason to believe his accounts."

"How so?"

"Riders were dispatched to his village to validate his claims. They returned late last night and confirmed that the village of Gend has been burned to the ground. Blood stained the snow and there were hundreds of partially digested corpses. Men, women, and children."

Rentor pinched his nose with his thumb and index finger in disgust. "Where is this man now?"

"Monks from the Order of Harr are tending him."

"Codel, my friend, tonight you and I shall visit this man and hear his tale for ourselves. Until then we have the usual. Keep this under wraps. I don't want panic spreading throughout the kingdom. It's hard enough running Thrae on a normal day."

Codel smiled outwardly, knowing the contempt he inwardly felt wouldn't do him any good just yet.

The Order of Harr was one of the dying breeds. One of the oldest religious sects in all Malweir, their society was slowly being washed away by the basic lack of faith that set in most civilizations over time. Less people felt the need to prostrate themselves to the old gods. It was a new world, full of possibilities and individual realizations. Men simply didn't care the way their ancestors did. The old gods were being replaced by industry and massive population centers.

Yet the monks persisted. They continued to wear the traditional grey robes and kept their heads shaved but for a sliver of a beard. Many were converted ex-convicts pardoned by the kings of Malweir. Harr was not so choosey when it came to proper followers. All it took was that moment of clarity when faith was professed and the brotherhood accepted with open arms.

Harr monastery rested on the edge of a mountainside. A single land road was the only entry and exit point. Peaceful as the monks were, they were none the fool. Too many times in their storied past they'd been prey to bandits or mobs of people whipped into fervor. A drawbridge spanned the narrow ravine leading to the main buildings. It was rigged to collapse, promising a long fall before a painful death on the jagged rocks below. The buildings were from an ancient time, carved out of the mountain itself. Statues of men and women lined the paths of the inner courtyard, their faces were worn away in the dimness of time.

The monastery had the look of contempt for the outside world. It was not warm. Not inviting. Everything was drab grey. The color signified their relationship to the ordinary. The belief that no man was better than the next. The philosophy of their god. Several walls had cracks and whole chunks of ledges and balconies had crumbled away. Empty windows peered out like haunting eyes. A lone sentry was always on duty in the bell tower to alert the monks of visitors. Faith alone wasn't enough to protect them during hard times.

The bell started ringing an hour before midnight. Word spread quickly. A column of riders was approaching. A well-drilled reaction force of twelve monks marched to the walls, each wielding a short range crossbow and short sword. Though trained and drilled for such an event, the monks of Harr weren't warriors. Few among them thought they stood even the slightest chance of repelling an assault if the enemy had their minds set. The bravest of them saw death moments away.

Father Seldis eased his way through the aging walls, helped by his trusted servant and acolyte, Phic. There were days when Seldis felt as old as the decrepit buildings he maintained. Already ancient, he felt every day of it. So much so that the flesh was already wasting from his bones.

"Damned cold night for visitors," Seldis said as freezing winds lashed him.

Phic shook his head for the hundredth time that day. "Father, you shouldn't swear so much. You know Harr looks down on such behavior."

"You're too young to know better, young Phic," Seldis reminded him sternly. "As far as what Harr thinks, well, I'll let you know when I go see him. It won't be too much longer. We both know that. So stop your fussing and get to the gate to greet our visitors."

"Yes, Father," Phic said and hurried about his task.

Seldis admired the youth. Taken from a broken home as a mere babe, Phic had been groomed and trained to become a valuable member of the Order. It didn't take much for Seldis to imagine the boy wearing the head monk robes one day.

The gates opened with an aggravated groan. Golden torchlight invaded the blackened courtyard. Seldis smiled as King Rentor's imposing figure came into view. Monks bowed and whispered astonished greetings at the surprise visit. It had been a long time since the king of Thrae bothered to grace them with his presence. Seldis, however, remained wary. Rentor was a good man but there was no mystery as to the purpose of his visit. He'd come to see their guest.

Rentor graciously accepted his hand. "Well met, old man," he said with a heartfelt smile.

"King Rentor. What an unexpected pleasure, and on so cold a winter night," Seldis smiled back.

Rentor feigned a shiver. "Damned unseasonable, even for your mountain retreat."

"Come inside. There is hot soup and ale for your men in the kitchens and I believe I might have just the thing to ease the cold from our bones in my private study."

The king laughed. "Father Seldis, you are a very insightful man."

"Amazing what a lifetime of enlightenment will do for you," he said and waved off the compliment. "Brother Phic, be so good as to see to the king's men. And get our brothers back inside. We don't need any more statues out here."

Phic bowed and went about his takes. The courtyard quickly filled with warriors, monks, and horses. The men of the Order of Harr left their frigid positions, most eager to get back to sleep and forget how close they'd stumbled towards getting killed. Only Brother Ibram stayed in the midnight cold. His youthful eyes absorbed every detail about the soldiers milling below. How many nights had he wasted lying awake on his meager cot thinking of quests and crusades? Oh how he longed to be the hero rescuing the kidnapped princess from unspeakable evil! But such was not his lot. He was a monk in the Order of Harr. The quest he served was not one of heroism and grateful women, but of self-deprivations and eternal enlightenment. Even so, Brother Ibram went to sleep with visions of battles raging in his mind.

Seldis poured a tall goblet of mulled wine and relaxed in his favorite chair. A small fire cackled softly, casting a warm glow over the old furniture and shelves of dust-covered books. Rolled up scrolls lay scattered about the room, some in organized piles, others left wherever he finished reading them. Tidiness wasn't overly important at this stage in his life.

"I suppose I should ask why you've come, for formality's sake," Seldis said after a few uncomfortable moments of silence.

Rentor gave a knowing look. "We both know why I'm here. Besides, I know of your talents towards mind reading."

"Don't be ashamed of that, Rentor. My gift extends to everyone if I choose."

"Is he still alive?" asked the king, leaning forward slightly to betray his nervousness. "He may be the only link I have in figuring out what is happening in my kingdom."

Seldis smiled and drank deeply. "There is much more going on than you can imagine. I feel great evil stirring. Dark times are ahead."

"Your words are cold," Rentor scowled.

"I offer neither hope nor doom."

"What can you give me?" He drained the rest of his wine.

Seldis did the same and answered, "A chance."

"I don't like the sound of that. Failure may also be implied."

"Indeed, but you'll come to find that a great many truths we cling to are simple fabrications of something greater. Success or failure. Who are we to question the will of Harr, or any of the other gods?"

Rentor finally leaned back. "I prefer cold steel in my hand and an enemy I can fight. Win or lose. Not the whim of a half-forgotten deity I'll never meet. Offer me a chance at closing battle with this new threat and I'll take your odds."

"As I said, Rentor, all I can offer is a chance. What you do along the way will determine your destiny."

Increasingly uncomfortable, Rentor set his empty goblet down and stretched. "Your fire burns low. It needs more wood."

Seldis folded his arms across his thin chest and watched Rentor add another log. He knew the king was a superstitious man, careful never to cross the gods despite all of his bluster. He also knew a difficult journey lay ahead.

Seldis was old but his eyes were as sharp as a hawk's. Visions told him of the coming ordeal though the outcome remained veiled. Seldis didn't doubt Rentor had the strength to carry through; he'd seen the man in battle. It wasn't strength that worried him.

"Shall I take you to him?" he asked quietly.

Rentor turned to Seldis. He seemed almost reluctant. "I need to know what I'm facing. The kingdom may be in jeopardy."

If you only knew. "Come. He was near death when we found him. Delirium had already set in. I doubt he knew where he'd stumbled to."

"How long has he been here?"

"Less than a week. The Brothers have slowly been nurturing him back to health."

Rentor nodded, absorbing every word. "His mind?"

"I've been seeing to that," Seldis replied as they made their way through the main building.

The king offered a half-hearted laugh. "Some might consider you a Mage."

"That order destroyed itself long ago. Greed often leads to such misconception. The Mages got to greedy and suffered for it. I, however, lack hubris. Or so I've been told."

"The histories say they could have ruled the world," Rentor said, making idle conversation.

Seldis agreed. "No army in Malweir could have withstood their assault. They weren't always corrupt. The Mages began with the purest intentions. They protected Malweir and her peoples. Who knows how many wars were avoided thanks to them. But as in all, men hide greed. They destroyed themselves to save us."

A shiver ran down Rentor's spine. People had been raised in fear since the end of the Mage War. Though the orders of Mages were gone, Rentor had long believed normal men were especially susceptible to cruel acts. "You're aware of the rumors coming out of Gren?"

"It is much more than a rumor. Not every Mage was killed and many of their dark creations continue to live. They wait in the shadows for the right moment."

"How can such creatures be defeated?" *And how can I link Gren to my troubles?*

Seldis stopped outside a door at the end of the torch-lit hall. "Not even I can tell. My sight is blocked. The man you seek is within this room. I must warn you, his mind is still fractured. You may not discover the answers you seek."

"I must make the effort."

The door creaked open, revealing a portly monk sitting in a rocking chair beside the sleeping man. Brother Arabub nodded to Father Seldis.

"How is our guest?"

"He fades in and out. He's also beginning to speak in full sentences. We had a lovely conversation about a woman named Shar. I believe she was his wife," Arabub said. His eyes never left the king.

"Thank you, Brother Arabub. You may leave us now. The king would like a private word with our guest. I will come get you when we're finished," Seldis told him with a fatherly tone.

Arabub pulled the blanket from his legs, rose, and bowed before excusing himself.

"This is a sad state for a man to be in," Rentor said, looking down on Fitch.

Seldis agreed. "His name is Fitch Iane, from Gend. His soul has been gravely wounded. Worse, I have seen glimpses of his darkest thoughts. Seen some of what he witnessed."

Rentor's eyebrow rose. "Tell me."

"It is not my place. That is something he must tell you for himself. Ah, he's awake."

Rentor stared down on the shell of man. Indescribable emotions conflicted. Fitch was malnourished and needed a shave but otherwise looked well enough. It was the eyes that told the story. Fitch's eyes were wild, betraying raw fear. Rentor sighed. He doubted he'd be able to glean any useful information from questioning this man.

The experience was vastly different for Fitch. He stared up at Rentor and, instead of a king, saw only dark shapes. Dreadful memories of monsters and fire immediately rushed forward to embrace him tightly. The smell of roasting flesh sickened his nostrils. Wicked flames stretched towards the heavens. Tears welled in his eyes. His chest racked with sobs. *Shar*.

"No more, please," he whispered and tried to hide his face beneath the blankets. "No more."

Seldis reached down and placed a comforting hand on Fitch's arm. "Be at peace, my son. You are safe in these walls. There are no demons here."

"No. This is one of them! He must leave," Fitch hissed, suddenly cruel, spiteful.

Rentor's cheeks flushed. Any other man might already be dead for spewing false accusations. He had no pity for Fitch, that much was certain. Rentor wasn't the sort who believed in pity. Men were dealt the hand the gods wanted.

"No, no. This is the king of Thrae," Seldis soothed. He moved his hand to Fitch's forehead and whispered, "See through the veil."

A pale yellow glow spread from his fingers, blanketing Fitch's head. The darkness fell away and Fitch looked upon his king for the first time. His mouth dropped open.

"Sire," he mouthed.

Rentor eased into the chair vacated by Brother Arabub and put on his best sentimental face. "There is no need for formality here, Master Iane. I need to know what happened in Gend, if you can tell me."

Fitch suddenly focused. His eyes lost their hazy, wild look. Rentor watched his face contort as he tried fighting the rising fear. Tried to conquer his emotions. The terror was too strong.

"Relax. Peace be upon you, Fitch Iane. The fear is your ally. Fear is our reason for carrying on when reason demands otherwise. Fear is the most powerful emotion we have. Fight it. Fight it and you will be free," Seldis chanted.

Slowly Fitch ceased struggling. His eyes fluttered and closed. The king fought back the aggravated sigh tickling his throat.

"I am not a patient man, Seldis. There must be something else you can do."

"Such are the times we live in. You must learn patience if you wish to see our kingdom through the coming darkness," the monk replied.

Rentor wished he could solve the riddle with his sword. All he needed was the right target to attack. War was a simple thing. Ruling a kingdom, however, was much different. Rentor knew he wasn't going to make progress by sitting and waiting. He decided it was time to leave.

"I was returning home from hunting," Fitch's voice filled the room.

Seldis removed his hand and sidled towards the door. Fitch's tale spilled out in an uncontrollable wave, forcing Rentor to lean forward and hinge on every word.

FOUR

Captain Cron

The ancient walls of the monastery groaned under the weight of an unusually strong wind. Loose snowflakes choked the air. King Rentor exhaled a plume of breath. Any apprehensions he felt before speaking with Fitch were horrifyingly amplified. Visions of terrible monsters and unimaginable hatred played out in his mind despite common sense assuring him none of those things existed. Not in the modern world. Rentor was an old man and knew where reality and imagination crossed was a dark road. Nightmares lurked on that road. Inescapable. Slip a little and the night would claim him. It was a private fear he'd held since first taking up the crown from his father's dying hand. A good king should be afraid. Fear allowed him to rule better.

The half-moon cast a haunting, pale glow over the snow-covered lands. The effect was amplified by the low cloud cover. Rentor looked out to the mountainsides. Crooked tree branches looked like so many wicked fingers stretching out for him. He shivered, though from the image or the cold he was unsure.

"His words speak ill of our future," he said once Seldis joined him. "What manner of creature can so carelessly slaughter women and children?"

Seldis breathed deeply, enjoying the crisp winter night. "I've always liked this time of year. The air feels good in my bones."

Barren branches rubbed together in an eerie screech.

"You're avoiding my question."

"I know."

Rentor frowned. "Why does that trouble me further?"

Seldis offered a thin smile. "We don't always want to hear the truth, Rentor, despite our protests. Truth can be as evil and malicious as the past. Darkness will always try to quench the light. Will you stand against the weight of the night?"

"What choice do I have?"

"Sometimes it is better that way."

Rentor wasn't convinced. "How can I prepare if I don't know what to expect?"

"Trust your heart. It will tell you the true path. Not all of us walk in shadows. There is a light, Rentor. Finding it will be your hardest task. Treachery and betrayal lay along the way, but take heart. Great friendship and heroism also await."

"Betrayal? By whom?"

Seldis paused to think. "I cannot see. That knowledge remains hidden to me. Tell me, what would you do if you knew ahead of time?"

It was Rentor's turn to smile. "I think we both know that answer."

"Precisely! Kill the traitor before the appointed time and you disrupt the balance. Events that should happen won't, thus changing the outcome. Many wish to know the future and that in itself is a doom."

"I can't live by looking over my shoulder, Seldis. There must be a better way."

"Be the king, Rentor. Look to faith. Aid will arrive from many sources though your biggest ally will be the least expected."

"You frighten me sometimes," Rentor admitted after it became clear Seldis would say no more. "Very well. I will return to Kelis Dur and prepare for war. The day will soon come when I will call on you again, my friend."

"We shall be there when you need us," Seldis confirmed.

Rentor swung his gaze back to the night. "A shame winter lasts so long. I might enjoy the view otherwise. Take care of yourself, Father."

They embraced and Seldis watched the king stalk back to the courtyard. His mind already raced ahead to what needed doing. The more he tried to look into the future the more troubled he grew. Seldis closed his eyes. *How could I tell Rentor that Fitch Iane will play one of the greatest roles in this drama?* He had much to do in order to prepare Fitch for the coming trials. Much of the torment had faded but Fitch remained in a foul place. Seldis nodded and went inside as the last horse left the courtyard.

Codel Mres was waiting in the stables when Rentor's party returned. His face had a blue tinge. Never fond of the cold, winter's additional fury left him in a soured mood. More and more lately his thoughts turned towards moving south to warmer climes. Starting a new life where the weather wasn't so aggressive. The youth of his time were taught to embrace the rugged nature of their environment, but Codel was never the outdoors type. He preferred a warm fire and the accompanying amenities. Let others stalk the harsh winters.

"Blue is a good color on you, Codel," Rentor announced with a deep laugh.

Codel hid a scowl. "I can't feel my ears or nose. Did you learn anything from the monks?"

"Some and not enough."

"A riddle?" Codel asked. He despised riddles.

"Speak with Father Seldis long enough and you will begin to understand. Come. It is time to go home. I have much to think on and we could both use a warm bed with warmer women."

Rentor didn't bother looking back. He knew Seldis was still there watching.

He awoke with a start. Sweat beaded across his brow. Heart pounded in his chest. Already fading shadows of nightmares haunted the darkened corners of his bed chamber. Melena groaned softly and rolled over. Rentor gave her a quick glance before sliding out of bed and going to the door-sized mirror hanging on the wall. Heavy rings hallowed his eyes. He couldn't remember being this tired. Body worn down, Rentor had to laugh. *All part of the price of being king. I need a new job.*

Splashing cold water on his face, Rentor dressed in a heavy robe of crimson with gold trim and went to watch the dawn. He made a quick stop in the kitchens and enjoyed a meal of fruits, cheese, and freshly baked rolls washed down with ice water. He normally liked some sort of meat with his meals but the recent nightmares left him without much of an appetite. Faint rays of sunlight began to seep through the curtained windows. This was the only time of the day that belonged solely to him.

He left the already forming lines of petitioners to the court appointed clerks. He ignored most of the staff and did his best to avoid Codel. Heavier matters weighed him down and he needed clarity. Rentor hoped the dawn offered more than night tried to steal. Closing his eyes, he lost himself in thoughts and harebrained schemes. It didn't take long for one idea to outshine the others. Rentor grinned. He knew what to do.

Captain Cron stood looking out the window of his second floor office, hands clasped sharply behind his back. He was a young man for his rank, hardly entering middle age. Rich black hair was closely cropped. His moustache was heavy and long. His body was rigid the way a soldier should be, muscled and disciplined. Cron's uniform and boots were spotless. Thin creases ran the length of his trousers, ending in polished boots. Everything about him whispered professional soldier.

One of the youngest captains in the army, Cron entered his position trying to prove himself. He drilled his men mercilessly. They were the best looking unit, to his knowledge, and the best disciplined and trained. Pride forced Cron to push harder and it paid off. His soldiers collectively had more decorations and awards than any other unit. They performed their tasks with flawless enthusiasm. It was no surprise when a runner came bounding up the stairs to report the arrival of a troop of the king's own guard. Cron returned the salute and grabbed his winter jacket.

Seeing the king himself shocked him with uncertainty. Normally such matters were left to diplomats and couriers. Wondering why or how being pointless, Cron went to meet his king. Worry didn't profit him. A twenty-year career put him in the perfect position. He was the senior-most field commander and, despite the protestations of the generals and crusty old veterans, commanded a hefty portion of the fighting strength. He surmised that if rebellion ever broke out many would turn to him before making their decisions.

"Do you ever relax?" Rentor asked.

Cron nearly let the smile break his stern facade. "Sire, such activities often lead to a warrior's untimely death. A man needs an edge. Besides, my men have been chosen for enough of your special assignments to know when alertness is required."

King Rentor merely smiled. He liked a man who wasn't afraid to speak his mind. Too many others told him what they thought he wanted to hear rather than what he needed to. Cron always told him the truth in no uncertain terms. That, more than anything, was cause for respect.

"Precisely why I am here now, in person. Come, let us get back in your office. Some matters are best left unheard by the wind."

Cron asked nothing and led them back to his office.

"No questions?" Rentor asked along the way.

"Sire, you haven't given me anything relevant to ask questions on."

The king eased himself in the comfortable leather-covered chair opposite of the desk. "Tell me again why I haven't made you a general?"

Cron mirrored the king, leaning forward on the desk and steeping his hands. "You and I both know I am more useful at this level. Leave a sword in its scabbard too long and it rusts. What do you require of me?"

"The village of Gend was attacked and destroyed a week ago. I want you to have a company go and investigate. Find out what you can and report directly to me. No one is to know of this."

Cron felt his collar tighten. "Do we have any ideas who did this?"

"You wouldn't want me to take out all of the fun, would you?" Rentor asked.

The slight hesitation in his voice told Cron all he needed to know. Rentor had suspicions but couldn't act without evidence. Nor could he freely give away the data, not yet. A danger crept into Cron's mind. This was unlike the king. He broke his own rule and asked himself a double-edged question. *What is he hiding?*

"Sire, I trust you understand that the security of my men must come first. If they're to give their lives I would like to know it is worth it."

"Some circumstances even a king may not discuss, Captain. Doing so now would tip our hand and give our enemies time to react. See what you can find out. I'm not asking you to fight a battle. I'm not asking much nor can I give much. Your trust and usual professionalism are all I ask. We don't know who did it and I don't want to go to war with the wrong people."

Cron rose slowly. "I'll see to it personally, sire."

"Nonsense. This is a task for normal field commanders. Your position is irreplaceable, Cron. I need you to stay in Kelis Dur and prepare the army."

Cron wasn't convinced. "Sire, you and I have both been on enough campaigns to know there are times when a true leader must be in front of his troops. I feel this is one of those times. If we're about to go to war I need to have firsthand intel of the situation. What better way for me to get that than by going to Gend myself?"

Rentor threw up his hands in surrender. "You are a very hardheaded man, Captain. Very well. The captain of Kelis Dur will ride forth but do not engage anyone. We're not ready to go to war. Oh and Cron, remember this, for there are times when a king must also be in front of his people to lead."

Rentor viewed Cron as a son. Losing him would not only hurt the kingdom, but the army and his own feelings. Slowly the king rose and left the young captain to his planning. There were times even a king wasn't welcome.

Cron waited until Rentor was gone before fixing his adjutant with a menacing glare. "Come in here, Resh. I want to speak with you about the importance of early warning and etiquette."

Swallowing hard, the teen slipped in and shut the door behind him.

Thirty riders waited in two lines. Cron, at the head of the column, looked over each man. All three squads had been personally selected. He knew each of the riders but two, those being fresh replacements for two retiring veterans. A stiff wind shuffled their forest green cloaks. Swords and shields, axes and bows were all strapped in place. Each squad had enough combat power to equal an entire infantry company. Cron left nothing to chance. Better men had died for less.

Their faces were stern, betraying no hint of their true emotions. This was their duty. Though Cron hadn't briefed them on the possibilities for violence, danger was a constant companion. Seasoned professionals, they understood the cost of leaving their base. Each man was prepared and willing to die for Cron and kingdom.

Leaning down, Cron gave his horse a soft pat on the neck. "Column, forward!"

FIVE

Alfen

The sharp crack of the whip echoed down through the dark tunnels and caves. Young Alfen Bew cringed with each subsequent scream. Only six years old, he was the youngest prisoner. No one knew where they'd been taken to, nor why they were captured. Alfen couldn't remember much of his home. Endless days in near total darkness dulled his senses. He never saw any of the others. Their screams kept him up with an endless string of nightmares. Alfen wasn't sure he wanted to meet the others.

Time quickly became irrelevant. He'd tried to keep track at first but his captors beat any hope of escape out of him. Kept in caves and forced to work underground, Alfen had seen too many fall under the lash and not rise. The bodies were taken away and burned in huge fire pits that never went out. He'd also seen what happened to those caught trying to escape. Their screams lasted the longest.

The ground constantly shook. Distant rumbling from the bowels of the world filled him with dread. Alfen and the others were forced to dig, and he was certain they were going to reach the center of the planet before long. His captors came from a massive castle carved into the back of the mountain, staying only long enough to oversee their slaves before returning. Alfen feared them the most. They blended with the dark, making it next to impossible to spy. The rare glimpses he got of their faces were sheer horror. Demons from the blackest night. Alfen quickly became thankful for the night. Any little bit to help keep their grotesque features and sickly grey skin hidden became a blessing.

The heavy tramp of booted feet marched closer. Alfen instinctively hid behind a small boulder at the back of his cell and whispered prayers that they weren't coming for him.

"Next one," growled a foul voice. "The Master wants a new whore tonight."

Both monsters laughed. A horrible, gurgling sound that suggested suffering. Alfen closed his eyes but the darkness only amplified the grating teeth and heavy drooling. The hairs on his arms rose every time he heard one speak. Fighting back tears, Alfen tried not to think when the rusted iron door on the next cell screeched open. A woman screamed, pleaded. He heard the sounds of laughter, followed by clothing ripping. The rough slap of angry hands and the guttural groan of someone being punched. Naked, the woman was pulled from her cell and dragged away. He knew she'd never be seen again.

One of the monsters kicked his door, making him jump. "Back to sleep, maggots! Work comes early."

Laughing, the monsters ambled off with their prey. Alfen put the moment from his mind. He lay back down and hoped to find sleep. The ground was cold and covered with a thin layer of slime. He couldn't shake the images of the woman. Too many times he wondered if he was next. The crunch of dull steel striking flesh sickened him. He hid but wasn't foolish enough to think it would help. Six years old and Alfen was growing immune to the horrors. The sight of bodies didn't upset him much anymore. Neither did the smell.

He heard another woman scream. Perhaps it was the same one. There was no way to tell. People were always screaming down here. No one bothered learning anyone's name. People simply didn't last long enough. Every few weeks another group was brought in to replace the dead. He'd seen Elves, Dwarves, and even a few Gnomes. He never knew who had captured all of these people or why. It didn't matter. They were brought in to work the mines.

Alfen didn't know much of anything to be fair. He kept to himself as much as possible. The only interesting fact he'd learned from his time in the mines was a single name. Ramulus. Even the monsters seemed afraid. Alfen wondered what could inspire fear in the most fearsome. He hoped to never find out.

SIX

Suspicions

Cron titled his head back and let the cold wind kiss his face. He'd been stuck in an office for so long he nearly forgot the simple pleasures of being in the field. Rentor's scouting mission provided the perfect excuse to abandon the endless piles of reports and command issues and return to the simpler life as a field soldier. Cron was a warrior. It was important to not only remind himself but his men as well. Winds slipped down into his tunic and he shivered at the delicious feeling.

The call of a crow turned his head to the barren branches of a nearby stand of ash trees. Unsure why, Cron called for a halt and nudged his horse closer. They were four days out of Kelis Dur and in the wilds. Any trace of civilization was lost out here. The high country was as close to pure wilderness as possible. To Cron it was a familiar friend. He'd grown up out here, learning the ways of the wild as soon as he could walk. Hunting, fishing, trapping, and, most importantly, tracking became his skills. His favorite pastime was learning how to read the forest. He and his friends spent endless hours wandering the forests while other children played games and stayed indoors. Other lands named men like that rangers. Cron was just a soldier.

The crow looked down on him with mocking indifference. Considered ill omens by the upland folk, most of Cron's men shied away from the dark bird lest bad times befell them. Some made protective signs while others furtively glanced around. Cron scoffed at the nonsense. Crows were just birds but he never once admonished his men for their beliefs.

"What do you know?" he whispered, staring up into the crow's cold, black eyes.

The crow cocked its head and cawed. Cron didn't like it. He understood birds, even respected them. The crow launched into the drab grey sky and disappeared. Watching it go, Cron took careful note of the direction. The air suddenly grew colder. One crow. Only one. Cron took that as a bad sign.

Sergeant Notam pulled up alongside his commander. A permanent scowl crossed his face, influenced by the scars running from his left cheek down to his collarbone. He liked to tell people it was an old battle wound though truthfully it was a bad run-in with a bear when he was a child.

"What's on your mind, sir?" he asked in a scratchy voice.

Cron continued to watch the bird. "I don't know. Something feels amiss."

The same uneasy feeling continued to grow the deeper into the wild they went.

"Snow's starting to melt. About damned time too," Notam observed. He knew better than to pry too deeply. "The cold never did sit right with me."

"You are the master of understatement. Plus you're getting old," Cron smiled. "I have a bad feeling about what we are getting into."

"The crow?"

Cron nodded. "Keep the men alert. I want them ready should any surprises pop up."

"The men are always ready, sir. Maybe if you left that big fancy desk more often," Notam snarled.

"I'd what, Sergeant?" Cron demanded.

Notam broke out in laughter. "It's nice to see your sense of humor hasn't dimmed. What are your orders? It'll be dark soon."

"There should be an old way station not far from here. It'll provide enough shelter for the men. I think after that we need to go in the same direction as the crow."

The veteran sergeant wheeled back towards the column barking orders. Riders formed ranks and pushed on to the dilapidated way station just as the sun dropped below the horizon.

Winter may have finally decided to release Thrae from its grip but the nights remained close to freezing. Cron's men huddled together under heavy riding blankets and cloaks. They had one small fire to provide warmth, despite it being against Cron's better judgment. A watch was set and those not on duty struggled to find sleep on the bitter, frozen ground. Most of the soldiers stayed just far enough away from the fire so as not to sweat during the night. Otherwise they'd freeze come the morning.

Notam and Cron sat off to one side quietly talking.

"Are you going to tell me what's going on or do I need to keep second guessing you?" Notam asked once he saw the last man fall asleep.

Cron immediately felt at ease. He and Notam had been working together for nearly a decade. They knew how the other operated and could think ahead. Very few sergeant and captain relationships worked so well.

"We're being watched," Cron finally admitted.

Notam bit back his laugh. "Aye. We've been tracked since leaving Kelis Dur. A scout?"

"More like a spy. I've been sending the rear guard back every league or so. They haven't found a single track that wasn't ours." He ran a hand through his thick black hair, hoping they had more time. "If we wait and try to catch him we'll lose."

"Or walk into an ambush," Notam added thoughtfully.

"I don't think so. There've been hundreds of places for ambushes along our route. I think whoever it is wants to know what we're going to find in Gend."

He poked a stick around in the fire. A burned-through log collapsed in a pile of heated coals. Neither soldier noticed the pale yellow eyes watching them from the safety of the night.

"What's your plan?" Notam asked.

"We can't armor up or we give away our hand. It's possible the enemy doesn't know what we do. I say we keep riding as is, throw an extra eye on the tree line from time to time. Whoever it is seems content with watching."

"For now."

"For now," Cron agreed. "Rouse the watch at dawn. We break camp and strike for Gend. I don't want to spend any more time there than necessary."

"Is it that bad?"

A nod confirmed his fears. Cron went on to explain everything he'd been told. The tale was brief and grim. Notam felt his stomach churn.

"An entire village gone. And people celebrate we've been at peace for so long. You don't think it's the Dwarves again do you?"

Cron didn't know. "I doubt it. They are above killing innocent civilians."

Both men remembered how a handful of sturdy Dwarf warriors ambushed an entire company, one hundred twenty riders, and slaughtered them to the man. All Cron's company found the next day were shredded corpses and blood stains. Not one of the enemy had fallen. The incident quickly sent panic rippling through the ranks and nearly turned the tide of battle against Thrae. It wasn't until Rentor made his stand at Kressel Tine did men take hope and turn the Dwarves back. Neither Cron nor Notam remembered the battle as victory. The war ended when both kings met and agreed that enough had already died. The mines in the Thed Mountains lay abandoned ever since.

"Goblins then?" Notam asked in bored speculation.

Cron did his best to steer away from the conversation. He didn't want to spend the night wondering who was going to attack or when. Sleep was rare enough for troops in the field. Notam didn't suffer from such delicacies. All he needed was a place to lay his head. Sleep found him.

"There haven't been any Goblins in Thrae for hundreds of years. If it is their work we need to know why now. Why here? There's something about this whole affair that doesn't feel right. Something sinister."

Notam spit into the fire. "You've spent too much time around politicians and their games. This could just be the prelude to a good old-fashioned war. We'll do the fighting. Let the people in Kelis Dur worry about the rest. Soldiers shouldn't care about making nice. Kill them all and be done with the matter. Get some sleep, Captain. You'll need your wits about you on the morrow."

Cron wormed his way through the snoring bodies and found his spot. His eyes closed but sleep was a long time coming. The pale yellow eyes blinked and disappeared.

"Do you smell that?" Notam asked shortly before midday.

He reigned in his roan mare. Experienced eyes shifted slowly across his field of vision. Nothing moved. Not even the wind. Any tracks were lost in the slop of melting snow and mud. Notam felt uneasy for the first time. *Curse you, Cron. Your stories have me jumping at shadows.* Several times already he thought he heard strange bird calls. Heard bushes rustle that shouldn't have. He sniffed again, catching the faint aromas of acrid smoke and sulfur. Notam instinctively drew his sword.

"Fire. Somewhere in that direction," he said and pointed across the lightly forested hills.

Cron paused to study the map. "Gend should be just ahead."

The veteran would have replied if he wasn't already barking out orders.

"Weapons out! Battle ready! Form ranks for village search!"

That baleful sound of steel leaving leather, familiar as an old friend, sang through the trees and underbrush. Axe and sword, lance and pike. The soldiers of Thrae adjusted their helmets and body armor one final time. Each squad dispersed into a loose arrowhead formation. Squad leaders took point. Cron and Notam assumed their positions between the first and second squads and ordered the advance.

Decay choked the forest air. Though the flames had long since died, the heavy odor of smoke and ash seemed fresh. Miniscule rays of sunlight filtered down through the clouded sky. Blackened branches stretched out in agony, scratching against each other when the wind blew. Every footstep sounded sickly and diseased in the sucking mud. A horse snorted. A boot clanged against the lower edge of a shield. The entire forest looked dead the closer they got to the village. Ash mixed with forming puddles of melted snow to make a thick paste. A flight of fattened vultures burst into flight at the sound of approaching horses.

Cron looked down at the heaps of gnarled bones and scraps of flesh still clinging to a human arm. Steeling himself up for what was yet to come, he mentally prepared for the brutality of his expectations. More than one man lost strength when they entered Gend. Horses were reluctant to press on. Soldiers leaned right and left to vomit.

The column halted at the rubble that had been Gend's temple. Not even grizzled, old Notam kept his food down. Arranged neatly in double rows were the impaled heads of the villagers. The parts scavengers hadn't already eaten.

SEVEN

Gend

It was well past midnight by the time they finished burying what remained of the villagers and washed the blood from their hands. Cron had never seen such a horrible mess. The smell of death permeated the air so badly he wondered if this part of Thrae would ever recover. Body parts, what they could find, were thrown into a large pit and burned before the plague could take hold. Wolves and other predators had already reduced the workload. Some of the blood covering the ground was already washing away with the melting snow. What Gend needed was a good, long rain to cleanse the land.

Cron finally led the column away just before dawn. Blood-red fingers of sunlight crept into the world. He quickly looked away. The riders moved through the fading shadows, towards the flickering glow of torches in the night. Forward scouts halted the column and were sent to investigate. Notam went with them while Cron had the rest form a defensive circle and wait.

The smell of rotting flesh unsettled the horses. Notam gently stroke his roan's neck. Peering through the trees, he managed to see a row of severed heads surrounding by torches. Whoever had committed the atrocities at Gend was still in the area and leading them on. Notam spared a glance at the heads, disturbed to find every eye open and staring back at him.

"Damnation," he muttered. "Captain's going to want to see this. You wait here. I'm going back to bring the rest of the patrol up."

Notam spurred his horse to a gallop and disappeared from view. Neither of the two scouts noticed the pale eyes malevolently glaring at them from either side of the trail. By the time Notam returned there wasn't a sign of either man. It was as if the forest came alive and took them. Cron deployed the squads and conducted a thorough search of the surrounding area. They spent six hours desperately looking for their comrades and never found a single track. With great reluctance, he called an end to their search just before dusk. The patrol returned to Kelis Dur with two less men.

Reben didn't know how he wound up in the cave. He didn't know why he was bleeding from three different wounds or how he'd gotten wounded. The first thing he remembered was watching a battered sword plunge through Ele's chest. Deep red blood bubbled across Ele's lips and his eyes rolled mercifully back into his head. The corpse hit the ground with the sound of wet meat. Reben stared down into his friend's lifeless eyes.

That's when he started to struggle. To find a way to escape. Others needed to be warned. If he could only find Notam or Captain Cron. Sharp pain exploded from the back of his head suddenly. His vision blackened with speckled lights. Grotesque laughter echoed around the chamber. Rough hands shoved him forward. His chin struck the slime-covered ground and he blacked out.

Three sets of eyes glared down on him when he awoke. Two were pale yellow. A low hiss called from the darkness of the cave.

"He's awake."

A deeper, more wicked voice rumbled in response, "Go and get Scourd. He wants to see this man suffer."

Hissing laughter followed and one of the sets of eyes disappeared. The hatred clinging to the voice was unmistakable. Reben started to lose hope. There were plenty of races in Malweir that hated men but none so bitter as Goblins. Ancient legend suggested that men and Goblins once shared the same lands and enjoyed the prosperity of peace. Then the trouble began and war engulfed both races. Man was victorious. Goblins and their kin hadn't enjoyed the kiss of the sun or the embrace of the summer wind since. Courage fled Reben as he realized what his captors were. There would be no dawn for him. Hope crashed around him like so many shattered icicles on stone.

"Look at him! Squirming like he can escape. Don't you worry, Scourd knows what to do with you."

Rough fingers gripped his hair, pushing him away. Reben quivered but stayed quiet. Anything he had to say would only give his enemy more power. The best he could hope for was a quick death. He looked around, trying to get a better view of his surroundings. The cave was small; walls were covered in greenish slime. Rusted chains hung in no apparent order. Bits of rotted flesh and more than a few bones still clung to several. Reben thought the wretched odor of Gend was bad, but this went far beyond. Soiled straw was strewn across the uneven floor. Dark stains, probably blood, ran up to his body.

Reben looked up and stared into the third set of eyes. Unlike the other two, these eyes didn't glow yellow. They were cold, calculating. If he didn't know better he'd have sworn he'd seen them before. The figure slipped back into the shadows after noticing Reben staring. Exhausted, the scout dropped his head and tried hard not to weep. He didn't know where he was or how he got here. The last thing he remembered was Notam leaving him and Ele at the strange ritual site. A dark fog rolled in the moment Notam turned and left. Reben tried to scream, to shout out at his sergeant for help. Darkness took him and he awoke to Ele being speared.

"Has he spoken?" asked a voice laden with centuries of pure hatred.

A more human voice replied, "We haven't asked him anything yet."

Reben heard bones cracking.

"Good. We begin."

A smaller figure bowed and knelt in front of the prone scout. "What were you looking for in Gend?"

Reben's eyes widened. That voice. Those eyes. He cringed in shock, knowing he had met this man once before.

"I know you," he said. His parched throat burned. "Traitor!"

The man rocked closer, giving Reben a long, hard look at his face. "Traitor? That depends on which point of view you take. So you can't say that I'm not a generous man, I'm going to ask you one time. Forsake your allegiance to Rentor and join us." He held out his empty palms. "In this hand I can give you life. A kingdom of riches and wealth. The freedom and debauchery that comes with owning your own lands. This hand brings only death. You will die without anyone ever finding you. Lost to the vagaries of time and forgotten by history. What is your answer?"

Reben spit in his face. The man didn't even blink. Calmly wiping his face, he tucked the rag back into his tunic pocket, smiled, and stood. He turned to the yellow-eyed Goblin and said, "Cut his hands off. Perhaps he'll be more reasonable afterwards."

The Goblin snarled and drew a rusted sword. The same one used to kill Ele. Reben screamed as the jagged steel hacked down through flesh and bone. Rivers of blood poured onto the straw and stone.

"It doesn't need to be this way. Tell us what we want to know and I promise to kill you quickly. Why did Rentor send you to Gend? What does he know?"

Reben could barely cry. Pain threatened to steal his consciousness. His body already felt cooler. It takes a grown man roughly five minutes to bleed out. Time was not in his favor. If he could only last long enough without answering questions.

"Last chance. Tell us now," the man barked sharply.

Reben lost himself in the pain. Tears cleansed his cheeks. He wet himself. His bowels emptied. Unexpected calmness spread through him, making the experience almost peaceful. His eyes drooped.

The man looked down at the blood-spattered hem of his robes in disgust. He had no qualms with ordering someone's execution though the actual deed was revolting. Blood never washed out, staining clothes and soul equally. "Send his head to Rentor. I'm leaving for Kelis Dur."

Scourd, the Goblin, snarled, "What do we tell Ramulus?"

"Tell him the king knows nothing. Ride back to Druem and find the shard. I'll keep the king busy long enough so he won't become a problem. The sooner we find the shard the sooner Ramulus can make his war on men."

He pulled his hood up and left the Goblins to their murder. Reben was so close to death he barely felt the cold blade sawing through his neck. Even if he had, it would have been a welcomed relief.

Rage consumed Cron. He'd lost men before, more than he cared to remember. But that was in battle. Men were supposed to die in battle. Reben and Ele were the first he'd lost on a routine patrol. Not killed. Lost. Disappeared without a trace. Cron took personal responsibility and went to inform the next of kin for both men. He'd offered his resignation to King Rentor. The king waved him off, saying there'd be a time soon enough when brave men would lay down their lives under the auspice of war. Cron knew Rentor still wasn't telling him everything. When he stopped to consider it, he didn't think he wanted to know the full truth.

He stood looking out his window, barely noticing the fresh spring morning. Blooms were popping out along the branches. The snow was nearly gone. Song birds had come back, filling the courtyard with joyous melody. Days were gradually warming up. The sun was shining. Cron cared less. His every waking thought was dedicated to his missing men. Nightmares plagued his dreams, often waking him in a cold sweat. He swore on the gods of his forefathers to discover the truth.

Weeks went by without any clues. Numerous patrols were sent back to Gend without proper authorization. Every one of them returned without anything to report. Cron decided to step up the training schedule. Several junior officers agreed that battle was coming. When it arrived, there would be little time to prepare. Cron needed to be ready for the storm to strike. Finally, after nearly a month of agonizing over Reben and Ele, Rentor summoned him.

Stewards escorted Cron to the king's private quarters. None of them spoke once Cron announced himself. Their slippered feet stole over the gold-streaked marble. His own footsteps were heavy and cumbersome by comparison. Statues of past kings and heroes lined the entrance halls. All seemed to glare down on him accusingly. Cron ignored the statues and marched on. The stewards escorted to a door twice as tall as a man and made of rich mahogany. They bowed and left the captain to find his own way inside.

Scowling with contempt, Cron turned the gold handle and pushed the door open. The sight nearly stole his breath. Six pairs of black marble pillars supported the vaulted ceiling. Stained glass windows stretched nearly ten meters high. A hung, many tiered chandelier hung from the ceiling. The wooden framework lined panes of lightly colored blue. Reflected sunlight filtered through the windows, producing a star-like effect. Cron had never seen such a sight. Potted trees and various plants from the southern jungles of Brodein lined the walls of the circular chamber. Flowered vines crawled up the pillars and a light mist was in the air. So taken by the sight, Cron failed to notice Rentor's imposing figure standing beside a bubbling fountain, feeding ornamental fish.

"Impressive, is it not?" Rentor asked. "I had it built after my first year as king. Even then the stress of leadership was more hassle than it was worth. I needed a place to relax where I could come to be alone and reflect upon my decisions."

Cron went to the position of attention and stayed silent.

"Perhaps you need such a place," Renter suggested with a sad smile. "The disappearance of those two men…"

"Reben and Ele, sire," Cron firmly said.

Rentor nodded. "Reben and Ele. It still bothers you?"

A scarlet bird with dark purple tail feathers chirped from atop a pillar.

"Our enemy has finally deemed it necessary to tell us what happened."

Cron's throat tightened for reasons he wasn't sure. Deep in his heart he knew both men were long dead. He stared at the king with bitter apprehension, not daring to hope.

"A constable discovered the bag outside of one of the taverns in the middle of the street. He brought it straight to the palace after inspecting the contents. Reben and Ele are both dead, Cron."

"I'd like to see for myself, sire," Cron whispered.

The sack sat atop a ceramic pedestal on the far side of the room. He smelled the rot and decay from where he stood. Visions of Gend sickened him. Cron knew what was in the sack. He didn't want to look in, to see what remained of his scouts. But he had to. He'd never forgive himself if he didn't. First step unsteady, he pushed forward lest the demons plague him further.

Cron cursed himself for the foolishness of it. He was in the presence of king and friend, the garrison commander of Kelis Dur. Righting himself back to the proud warrior he was, Captain Cron purposefully strode to the pedestal and opened the sack. A swarm of tiny gnats flew up in his face. The smell of raw death assaulted his senses. Cron caught the glint of sunlight reflecting off of a glazed-over eye. He closed the sack and exhaled a long, slow breath.

"Do we know who did this?" Cron asked.

Rentor's face darkened. "Whispers. Shadows in the dark, but nothing substantial enough to chase. Whoever it is doesn't want us snooping around Gend. That makes me want to know what happened more. I've noticed you have patrols routinely going out there now and your training exercises have increased. What do you know you're not telling me?"

Cron cleared his throat, eyes never leaving Rentor. "What we both know, sire. War is coming. I understand your hesitancy but I am a military commander, not the king of a land. When the call does come, your army will be prepared to fight."

"All the more reason for me not to involve the army any more than necessary."

"What do you have in mind?" Cron let curiosity get the better.

"A king must always have contingency plans."

Cron wasn't sure he wanted to know. He bowed once and excused himself, taking the sack with him. Rentor excused him and stayed in the chamber. The song of the scarlet thornbill soothed his raw nerves.

EIGHT

Council

"Exactly where do you propose I send the army, General Huor?" Rentor asked, agitation grinding through his tone. "Shall we invade the Dwarves? Just in case? Or is Averon more to your liking? It's been a long time since they last went to war. Tell me, Huor. Whom do we bring the hammer of justice down upon?"

The gaunt Huor flustered. His face speckled red with embarrassment. Veins pulsed on his temples. "Cordon the area. Reinforce the border stations and bring the army to full alert. Personally, I doubt this is the work of an organized enemy, sire. The people need to be our primary concern. When word of this reaches the ears of the general public there will be panic and fear in unmanageable amounts."

Cron gently cleared his throat, hoping to stop the argument from escalating. "Mobilizing the army can also have a negative effect, sir. We move too soon and risk giving ourselves away."

"Smart words from the man responsible for losing two men without a battle," Huor snapped. "You are the garrison commander for a reason."

"Pointing fingers is hardly useful," Codel Mres said and smiled. "This is time for us to band together, not fragment."

"Prime Minister, when was the last time you swung a sword in battle?" Huor asked with a sharp glare lesser men shied from.

Codel's face flushed but he refused to look away.

"Politicians make laws, not fight wars. My troops are constantly defending Thrae against raiders and insurrectionists. Most of the time this information never makes it back to Kelis Dur. Malweir is not as safe as you'd like to think, safe here in the palace. Leave the war making to the soldiers."

"No one is arguing the diligence of your men, Huor. I, however, am questioning your reasoning for alerting the entire army," Rentor said with a calm, steady voice. "Please don't misdirect your ire to the Prime Minister."

He missed, or ignored, the heated look Mres shot him.

Some of the color left Huor's face. "Let me mobilize my men and deploy them to forward positions. Should the enemy strike again we will be in position to react."

"Unless they attack where the army isn't. How many of your precious civilians will perish then, General?" Codel asked.

"React is the key word, Huor," Rentor interrupted.

All bickering ceased and eyes turned to the king.

Cron asked, "Sire?"

"I don't intend on reacting, gentlemen."

Huor shook his head, confused. "I don't understand."

Rentor offered a devious smile that only a king could get away with. "As I said, plain and simple. We're going to force our enemy's hand. Make him react to our plans."

"Are you sure that is wise, sire?" Codel asked.

Rentor barked a laugh. "Who said anything about being wise? I'm going to strike and make the enemy so angry he can't help but fight back but it will be at a time and place of our choosing, not his. Take the advantage away and make him fight on our terms."

"I'm in," Cron said quickly. Anything to reduce his seething sense of self-hatred since the incident at Gend. "When do we leave?"

Huor snorted.

"Not so fast," Rentor said and held up his hand. "I'll need my commanders here, planning the offensive. You stay in Kelis Dur."

"They were my men, sire. Could you sit back and watch?" Cron asked, barely managing to control the anger in his voice. "Honor deserves no less."

"Could a king sacrifice one of his top military men for petty revenge? We have all lost men, Cron. Make no mistake about what I tell you. We are at war. Thrae will have need of our combined military genius before this is done."

"But I…"

Rentor cut him off before he could finish protesting. "Good soldiers follow orders, Captain."

Cron clamped his mouth shut.

"Sire, perhaps you weren't listening to your own arguments. Who exactly are we going to attack?" Codel asked.

"The hand behind the blow. We're going to flush him out with a small group of men, make him so nervous he makes mistakes. Then we send in the army and end this foolishness. I seriously doubt we're about to fight demons or other nonsense," Rentor said. "More like Goblins or Trolls. Evil men at the very least."

His piercing gaze unsettled Codel.

General Huor scratched the stubble on his chin. "This could work. Who do you have in mind?"

Rentor offered his most kingly smile. "I have the person created for such a quest and no, his name remains mine until he is well away from the capital."

"Surely you don't have one of us in mind," Codel protested and instantly regretted making the remark.

"No. Not one of us. Neither do I think the enemy is patiently waiting for us to make a move. Whoever it was knew Cron was coming."

Silence gripped the room. Rentor used the break to fill his empty goblet with white wine specially imported from Harlegor twice a year. A content sigh rushed out once the cool liquid hit his lips.

"Any more questions?" he asked.

Codel Mres and General Huor slowly shook their heads, still reeling from the unspoken implication. Cron stood with a look of utter contempt. He lacked the experience of concealing his emotions and was notorious throughout the kingdom for having a terrible temper when matters worked against him. Rentor followed suit, dwarfing everyone else in the room.

"If you'll excuse me, I have other kingly duties to perform."

They bowed and filed out of the private study, leaving Rentor alone among the expressionless statues and endless shelves of leather-bound books. He stared deeply into the marble face of the first king of Thrae. What he faced was insignificant to the first king. A man who faced Goblins and Trolls and won a kingdom.

"If only a sword could solve my problem," Rentor sighed.

He retired to his private chambers and changed from the formal dress to a more subtle ensemble of leather boots, trousers, and a loose-fitting dark green shirt. The rings and necklaces went back in their box beside the heavy crown. He'd often wondered why kings needed such accoutrements. *Damned things are more cumbersome and gaudy than practical.* Leaving his shirt partially unbuttoned to enjoy the warm spring day, he took a last look in the mirror to convince himself he wasn't old and headed out the door.

Grelic slept on a cot far too narrow to support his massive frame. A half-eaten tray of rations sat on the simple wooden stand beside the bed. Most of it was the rangy grey meat that didn't look appetizing when the jailor brought it in. He'd eaten his share of rotten food over the years but even this gave him a bad feeling. Maybe if he had a flagon of ale or wine to wash it down, but that was the reason he was locked in this cell.

Breaking out was a viable option. He'd studied the walls and bars intently as soon as he sobered. The task wouldn't prove overly difficult but that wasn't the message he wanted to send Rentor. The first few weeks went by before his mood soured. This was the longest he'd been kept and that worried him. Even if he did escape he had no idea as to where he was. Rentor's soldiers bound and blindfolded him before Phaes managed to protest. So the days fled with Grelic becoming more convinced Rentor's executioners were coming for his head.

He awoke with a sigh. Warriors. He'd been one once. Spent his entire life fighting in one campaign after the other. His mother abandoned him when he was barely five years old. Winter and packs of wolves nearly saw him done but Grelic was a natural fighter. He escaped his tormentors and grew to be a giant of a man. He went east, spending years as a student in a gladiator school in Harlegor. There he learned the finer arts of weapons and unarmed combat. He left at the age of thirteen without suffering a defeat. A roving band of mercenaries took him in not long after and he continued to enjoy the spoils of victory.

He was sixteen when they went up against a patrol led by the future king of Thrae. Rentor was an unassuming soldier, barely a leader, but he was wily. The boy king disguised his caravan as a pay unit to lure the mercenaries into a trap. Grelic alone survived. Not because he ran, but because Rentor watched too many men fall under his blade. It would have been a shame to kill such a warrior. They formed an uneasy alliance. Rentor offered Grelic his life back if the giant agreed to join the army and train it how to fight. He'd even offered a steady salary. Grelic smiled at the memories. *What fool would waste the chance for a steady life doing what he enjoyed after so many years wandering?*

The army became a good home for young Grelic. He excelled in every aspect of training and soon found himself being groomed for a leadership position. With age and experience he became a man and one of the most feared combatants in northern Malweir. Unfortunately, becoming a man led to the discovery of drink and women. Grelic played as hard as he trained. His excesses became the talk of the barracks, ultimately proving his downfall. Discipline slipped and he lost everything.

Grelic slipped from his cot and stared out the small circular window at the pale sun. Great sadness filled him.

"One more day in the sun," he whispered. "One more chance to prove my worth."

A deep voice behind him replied, "Be careful what you wish for."

Grelic turned. He knew the voice almost as well as his own. He looked back at Rentor. Neither blinked. Grelic showed no fear. Either Rentor had come to finally finish the job or he hadn't. It was that simple.

"Come to do the job personally eh?" Grelic said with a smile. "I expected no less."

"Think what you will of me but I saved your life more times than you know. For the life of me I can't figure out why. You've cost me more in hospital expenses and tavern upkeep than the rest of the army combined."

Grelic's cheeks flushed. "You've no need to justify yourself to me, King Rentor. I know what I've done."

"Damn you, Grelic," Rentor cursed. "The ministers want to see you finished. They're tired of punishing you and think having you banished or executed will send a clear message to other lawbreakers. If I could find a way to put them on the front lines of a battlefield I would. Then again I don't care to lose a battle."

"You mentioned about being careful what I wished for?"

Grelic wasn't in the mood to bandy with the king. There wasn't any point in aimless pondering or supposition for a man trapped in a dungeon with death hanging around his neck. That made the whole conversation terribly frustrating.

"You want a war, to feel the power of the blade one final time before Lord Death comes to claim you," Rentor stated.

"I'm listening," Grelic replied.

"I'm offering you the chance."

"Against who?" Grelic asked, mirroring the king's movements. "There is no war that I know of."

"I'm trying to keep it that way."

Grelic laughed. "By involving me?"

The king nodded. "As odd as that sounds, yes. We're already under attack. An unknown enemy has been raiding small towns and villages outside of the protective blanket of the army."

"You want me to find out who's doing it and stop them?"

"More or less."

Grelic slowly reached up and wrapped his curiously strong fingers around the slightly rusted bars. "Tell me why I should care."

Rentor wasn't sure what he'd been expecting but selfishness was certainly on the list. Still, he nearly walked out before realizing Grelic was testing him. "It gives you back your neck. Or perhaps you'd prefer the enjoyment of the ministers while your neck snaps after the drop. Take your pick. Go on the hunt one last time or inspect the gallows. The choice is yours."

"Not much of a choice when you think about it," Grelic replied without thinking. "It's too drafty down here for me anyway. Who do I have to kill?"

"That's what I need you to figure out. Once you get released, come to the rose gardens behind the palace. Make use of the back gates. Climb the wall if you need to. Just don't get caught. The last thing I need is to be seen consorting with you."

Grelic nodded, finally noticing Rentor's casual attire. He didn't come dressed as a king. If it weren't for his naturally imposing stature, people might not recognize him. He wondered what game the king of Thrae played at. Grelic praised the decisions though doubted the reaction of the public once they discovered he'd set himself free. *Or is it escaped?* It didn't take much to imagine betrayal at the end of this foolishness.

"You trust me to do this alone? What's to keep me from grabbing a horse and heading south? I think I've had enough of cold winters and jail cells," he said.

Rentor stifled a small laugh. "Don't be absurd. No other land will take you and you know it. As for going alone, let me be perfectly honest. I think you are the best chance we have at avoiding a war. We lose if you fail. No, I'm not sending you alone. I need you but don't trust you a lick. The others chosen will have just as much experience as you. Perhaps in different arenas but skilled nonetheless. Grelic, you and I may not see eye to eye any longer but you're the finest warrior this land has seen in a hundred years. Thrae needs you. I need you. If ever a man had a calling it is you."

Grelic pretended to give the matter some thought. He'd known his answer the moment Rentor gave his proposal. Truthfully he couldn't wait to have a purpose again. Too many aimless nights were spent getting drunk and whoring. The chance to swing a blade again was almost a dream. A violent demise was something he'd planned for a long time. Rentor almost offered him one. As a youth he'd gone to see a shaman. The wizened old man confirmed he was going to die in battle.

He casually turned from the king and went back to his window. His one outlet to the real world. A flock of brown geese honked nearby, returning to their spring roosts. "Battle is all I've ever known. War. Duels. There is thrill in swinging the blade. I want to have some say in the men coming with me. Battles are won by men who live, breathe, and die together. The people you send will just get in my way and probably won't return. This is my only demand."

His words were slow, calculated. Rentor immediately recognized the underlying threat. He was being warned not to send anyone along that was going to betray Grelic once the mission was complete. If suspicion kept the giant on his toes, so be it. Ever so slowly, Rentor closed his mouth and turned. He'd done what he set out to do. The rest was on Grelic.

The giant didn't bother turning back around until after the king was long gone. That's when he noticed the key placed expertly in the lock and an empty hallway beyond.

NINE

Secrets

Fitch Iane shot up from a troubled sleep. Sweat pooled in the grooves of his forehead. His eyes were streaked through with red. Dark bags circled around his eyes gave him a haunted look. Lightning crashed outside. Fitch jumped. His heart pounded. Fragments of the dream infiltrated his waking self. It had been the same one since the monks of Harr first revived him. Since then he hadn't awoke on his own, until now. Brother Arabub, half asleep himself, nearly jumped at the commotion and excitedly ran to find Father Seldis. The old man had requested to know the moment anything important happened.

The aged oak door groaned closed, leaving Fitch alone again. Panic threatened to set in. He struggled to slow his breath, quietly battling the demons leaping up from the darkness. He tossed back the bearskin blankets and eased his feet to the cold, stone floor for the first time in weeks. Fitch wanted to stand but not even the magic worked by the monks of Harr was enough to give him back his previous strength.

Fitch breathed the strange air and looked around. He was clean and shaved. The monks were adamant about taking care of him as much as possible. His bedding was fresh and scented candles burned softly against the far wall. Appreciating everything the monks had done for him, Fitch knew there was no way he could ever repay their hospitality. He used to frown upon the Order. The monks of Harr were often persecuted through primal fear and a lack of understanding. After this he intended on being an ardent supporter until the day he died.

Father Seldis entered the room and smiled warmly. "I hear you've recovered, my boy. Congratulations. You had us worried for a while."

Seldis buried his doubts. He'd figured Fitch for a dead man from the moment he was brought in. There was an unmistakable darkness in the man's heart. A decay so deep and hurtful no amount of healing could help. That darkness was eventually going to claim him. It was just a matter of time. Seldis wept inwardly. No man deserved such torments before going to join his forefathers.

It was all Fitch could do not to laugh. "Father! I've never felt so alive. It's almost as if I've been reborn. What have I done to deserve such treasures?"

Seldis returned his smile with equal enthusiasm. "Perhaps the gods decided they have need of you. Perhaps the pain in your soul is finally healing. We could spend the rest of our lives discussing the finer points of theology and still not come close to the true answer. The world is strange and mysterious. Who are we to contradict the will of the gods?"

"I've never been a believer in the old gods," Fitch admitted almost ashamedly. "A farmer's life is practical more often than not. Praying doesn't grow crops or put food on the table. My people, my family, saw little need for the gods. We struggled through life on the merits of our own hard work and determination. I've never seen proof of a god."

Seldis remained silent, content with letting him vent.

"I have seen darkness. Pure, uncontrollable darkness. I was lost, Father. I saw demons ruin my home and life. They stole the only person I have ever loved and laughed as they walked away. No, I've never seen a god but I have seen what the lack of faith rewards. Will others suffer equal fates?"

Drawing a deep breath, Seldis replied, "I'm afraid men and women go through such dilemmas every day. Malweir is full of creatures and certain powers we know almost nothing about. I have seen many in my time. I've been to where bad gods lurk and fields where gods go to die. Marvelous and dangerous. Darkness is falling on us, as you have guessed. King Rentor tries to stop it though I suspect it may already be too late. More villages will suffer Gend's fate. War is coming, Fitch."

Fitch seemed horrified. "Is Thrae really going to war? With demons?"

"Difficult to answer. I suspect the king feels the need to defend his lands and people. I would do the same if I were king."

"Your words scare me, Father, more than seeing the demons. Are there no good men to step forward? As a child I always listened to the tales of Mages and heroic quests. Now should be such a time for brave men to take the sword and save us all."

"I agree, Fitch, but there will be plenty of time to ponder the course of the future. Let us find something to eat and drink. It will be a joy watching you feed yourself for a change," laughed Seldis.

Fitch agreed and took his first unsteady steps out of bed. To his surprise it wasn't as painful as he'd expected. In fact, it was almost as if he'd never been stuck in bed for three weeks. Seldis kept his mind busy through the meal with simple stories and lackluster tales of the Order of Harr. They both liked to think of themselves as simple men trying to make the best out of life. Fitch agreed the monastery was a peaceful place that seemed to have an individual feel of serenity for each of them. He went on to comment how, while he'd never had use for gods or prayers, he'd always respected priests for answering the calling. Just as he believed he was meant to be a farmer and take care of his family.

Tears flowed freely at the thought. Images of Shar's soft face mocked him from death. The pain was still too near. Seldis managed to convince him all had happened for a greater purpose. He too had a calling to answer. When Fitch asked what, Seldis simply placed a hand on his forearm and told him all would be revealed when he finally opened his eyes. Fitch had no idea what that meant. His eyes started to droop. He needed sleep, real sleep, not the troubled manifestations of what had happened.

Seldis noticed his slowing pace. "I can see my conversation is boring you. Perhaps some rest will do you good."

Fitch moved to protest, sputtering how Seldis was anything but boring, but he was tired. The nightmares left him perpetually drained. "Perhaps you're right, Father. I can barely keep my eyes open, though no fault of yours. It's just…" He left the sentence unfinished.

"I know, my boy. I know. Come, let's get you some rest so you can tackle the coming challenges full of vigor and renewed."

The weight of knowing Fitch's fate was nearly unbearable. Seldis wanted to tell him. Wanted him to know he'd been told in a dream what role Fitch was meant to play in shaping events. He wanted him to know he was going to die. But if Seldis so much as hinted at it there was the possibility Fitch might turn his back on the people who needed him the most. Ruin would wash the world. With heavy heart, Seldis helped the drowsy young man back to bed. He blew out the candles and retired to his private study.

Fitch Iane dreamed of glory and battle.

Across the monastery in the simple monk quarters, Brother Ibram struggled with his own troubled dreams. Not nightmares. His visions were of quests and heroes. In the dream he wore the royal blue of Thrae. He fought for the kingdom, for every man, woman, and child incapable of defending themselves. Ibram saw himself swinging his sword against great and terrible enemies. Against a wave of violence so strong it threatened the foundations of the world. He was a hero. Just like Phledian and Mour, the legendary warriors who defended the Order of Harr against the dark creations of the Mages. Men would learn of his deeds and sing praise.

Despite the pleasing nature of his dreams, Ibram found them a curse. They haunted his waking moments in ways no nightmare possibly could. Monks were peaceful, having washed their hands of armed conflicts long ago. He'd been selected as a youth to heed the calling and take the robes. Violence of any sort was frowned upon. Infractions often resulted in expulsion. Ibram felt his vows were constraining him more and more, keeping him from achieving his true potential. Just once he wanted to feel the grip of leather tongs wrapped around a sword hilt. He doubted he could take a life. The thought proved disturbing.

The Order of Harr maintained that all men were inherently good natured. When Ibram argued how that could be, especially after the devastation of the Mage War, he was met with disdainful looks and muttered prayers. The old gods still had a strong presence despite most people having stopped believing. Light or dark, the gods still clung to hope. Ibram was no fool. While he didn't want to offend any deity, he knew there had to be more than what the monks taught. The wisdom of Harr wasn't enough.

Ibram awoke sometime in the middle of the night. The now familiar gleam hungered through his dark brown eyes. He'd had the dream again. There was an ancient myth about a sword made from a fallen star by Elven smiths. No one ever knew what happened with the Elves, only that they kept to themselves whenever possible. The thought that Phaelor, the Star Silver sword, might come to rest in Ibram's hand enthused him to great ends.

An unseen force guided his thoughts, desires. Ibram wasn't tired of the robes or the daily toil in the monastery. He found it peaceful and solitary. There was tranquility that he could only find here. The monks were his friends, his family. They were the one group of people he could trust without worry. But Ibram knew his heart. There was only one way to make the dreams stop. He dressed and headed for Father Seldis' private chambers.

The dust-covered tome was remarkably thick and well written considering how old it was. Seldis carefully thumbed the pages like a loving father. Most of the pages were worn and cracked. Time and age slowly wore the book down. He sighed. Even treasures such as this book succumbed to age. Seldis carefully rewrote every single letter once a decade. The process took nearly a year to complete, but as far as he was concerned, this book was the single most valuable possession in all of Malweir.

He leaned back in his favorite, worn chair and rubbed his tired eyes. The candle in the middle of the desk was already burning low. It was time for bed. Seldis wasn't as young or spry as he used to be, a reluctant admittance that took far too long to accept. Now time was against him. He took another look at the image in the book before moving his chair near a window. An almost pale-gold light came down from the half moon. Seldis swirled the spiced wine before drinking. It was a weakness from a previous life, but every man had weaknesses. Besides, he never drank in excess and Antheneon made the best wine on the continent. He savored the warm sensation as it passed down his throat.

He had been expecting the light knocks on his door and glided almost effortlessly across the room to present his sincerest smile upon opening the door. Brother Ibram bowed politely and entered with a flurry of apologies.

"Awfully late for a random stroll about the monastery," Seldis said once they were both seated.

Ibram couldn't look him in the eyes. "I've had trouble sleeping of late."

"Bad dreams?"

"My dreams make me question myself."

Seldis narrowed his eyes. "You doubt your faith?"

"I doubt my ability to follow it through. Father Seldis, I dream of wars and battle. Glory and honor. These are not our ways. Why do I dream such?" Ibram's voice bordered on frantic. His eyes held a cagey look.

"Who knows what lurks in our hearts, my son?" Seldis asked. "Long have I been in this position and even longer have I lived as a monk. Harr teaches us that everyone has a place in this world. A purpose. Perhaps we are not so fortunate as to decide for ourselves."

"That would mean my life has been a sham thus far," Ibram protested.

Seldis leaned closer and said in a deep voice, "Tell me your heart, Ibram."

Ibram exhaled a deep breath. "I want to know what it's like to swing a sword. I want to be that man riding out on grand quests and saving the helpless. I want to feel the camaraderie only brothers in arms can feel."

He nearly smiled. Saying it wasn't half as bad as he feared. The long days spent contemplating how best to approach the subject seemed for naught. Endless hours of torment shattered like glass once he said the words. He realized there was hope. Harr might damn him for his decisions, but Ibram knew he couldn't go back. Not now. He trembled as he waited for Seldis to react.

Seldis eased back into the cushions of his chair, folding his hands in a well-rehearsed move. "Brother Ibram, I may have just the tool to test your desires. What do you know of Thrae?"

TEN

Kialla

The light drizzle felt good on Grelic's head. He turned his face up to the clouds and let the rain wash the fatigue from his face. A crisp wind blew just hard enough to feel good, almost refreshing. He'd never enjoyed the stench of civilization. Kelis Dur wasn't as bad as some of the other cities but it was enough to keep the wind out. Grelic hated the confinement of the walls. Organized society wasn't for him. He didn't enjoy crowds or seeing your neighbor as soon as you stepped out the front door.

He needed forests and streams. The smell of grass after early morning dew. He needed the thrill of the hunt. The sight of a stag bounding away. No city offered that. Perhaps that's what made him so different. He'd never felt the need to huddle next to his fellow man for comfort or security. Never needed constant companionship to justify his existence. He was a child of the world, born and bred for the ultimate freedom.

Grelic lowered his face and stared thoughtfully at the open world. The urge was growing. Part of him, that wild, untamable part, wanted to turn his back on humanity and run off. Primal and seething, the wild side whispered to him. He often wondered how easy it would be to abandon the kingdom of Thrae and his promise to the king. Forget the troubles and hardships. Certainly better men who actually cared were willing and available to fill his place. Let them save the world. Grelic wondered, but not for long.

"Damnation," he cursed and headed back towards Kelis Dur.

Loyalty and honor were his strongest principles. He'd been raised to believe a man was nothing without his word. Too often that mantra became a bane. A curse for him to battle through while lesser men turned and fled from their responsibilities. Grelic wandered aimlessly for a time, uncertain in which direction to go. He knew she was here, or at least she had been the last he heard. If he had any chance of success he was going to need her help. Finding her was going to be the problem.

Grelic wound up on the main avenue in the center of the town. Kelis Dur wasn't overly spectacular for a capital city. The Sibit River ran in a long loop through the old city. Most of the palaces and gardens had been rebuilt once the rulers decided to clear out that part of town. The buildings were all the same lonely grey or rustic brown. Occasionally he spied a green or blue to break the monotony. Grelic suspected the drabness was due to the true mountain and stone traditions of the founders. Early settlers of Thrae were as hard as the environment they chose to live in.

Thrae was a land of constant storms and bad weather. There was so much rock in the soil it was almost untamable. Farmers had the worst of it. The land had broken too many men. Not even their iron toughness was enough to keep many alive during the hard times. Grelic knew he'd make a miserable farmer. He was too headstrong. Too set in his ways. Farmers required patience and his barely lasted the duration of a battle.

Sickly clouds began rolling in, promising a nasty storm. Grelic had nowhere to go and no real idea where to begin looking. Out of the thousands of faces in Kelis Dur he could think of only one capable of helping. Whistling an old childhood tune, the giant shoved his hands in his pockets and ambled off in search of Phaes.

"Are you out of your mind? Rentor's entire cabinet wants you dead and you're going to help them?" Phaes shouted with disbelief. "This is madness!"

Grelic smiled in response. "What choice do I have?"

"Do what you first wanted. Head south and find a new place to get into trouble," Phaes told him. A look of utter disgust crossed his face.

"They'll just hunt me down and never stop until too many are dead. How hard would it be for one of those weasels to hire another assassin team? I'm not going through that again." He paused to pass the violent memory. "This is my chance to finally be free."

"How long have we known each other, Grelic? Twenty years? Thirty? The men opposed to Rentor won't stop until you and he are both gone. You do realize you're not just a random target?"

The giant held up his hands. "I don't blend well in a crowd either, Phaes."

The old sergeant grumbled something incoherent and stormed off to the other room. Grelic stood patiently in front of the fire, drying off from the heavy rain he'd been caught in. Despite a powerful thirst, he wisely passed up the proffered flagon of wine Phaes offered. He already dreaded his initial confrontation with her and getting drunk now would only make it worse. Phaes eventually returned with a pot of cold stew and a loaf of fresh, dark bread. He placed the pot on the iron hook and swung it into the fireplace. Being cold and wet was bad enough. Cold food was downright insufferable.

"Damned miserable day," he said. "Tell me again why we don't already live down south?"

"Who'd take us? I'm not changing my mind, Phaes. I'm tired of constantly being on the defensive. Now is the time to put pressure on the ones responsible for putting me in chains. This is the best chance I'm going to have. Maybe the only one."

"If you'd just..." he dropped it, realizing there wasn't much point in arguing with a headstrong man almost as wild as the mountains themselves. "What makes you think she'll join you?"

Grelic tested the stew. It was starting to bubble.

"Not sure she will," he replied. "But Kialla does like a fight. Sometimes I think she's too much like me."

"That spells trouble for all of us. The last thing Thrae needs is another you drunk and fighting. Too damned much trouble," Phaes grumbled. "My head still hurts from the last time you hit me."

"I apologized for that, and I was drunk," Grelic protested.

"Still doesn't take away the pain."

Grelic scowled. "Will you help me or not?"

Phaes served them both healthy portions of stew and bread. The food was hot but bland. Spices and seasonings were always rare this time of year and Phaes was a horrible cook. "Let me do some checking. Last I heard she was over working the room at the Ram. Looking for a hire no doubt."

"Been a long time since I was last there," Grelic said between mouthfuls.

Phaes struggled to hold back the snort. "Been a long time since you last busted the place up. Do you have any idea how much you've cost the innkeepers here?"

"About as much as I am tired of hearing about it," he replied angrily. "How soon can you find her?"

"Give me until sundown. Oh and try not to smash anything while I'm gone. If trouble does show up please take it outside."

Grelic grinned. "Would I let anyone destroy your house?"

Phaes didn't want to answer.

Kialla sat up and ran her fingers through her shoulder-length, auburn hair. A sheen of sweat covered her naked body and she was still breathing hard. Her dark brown eyes held the gleam of lust, a rare look enhancing her natural beauty. She was lithe and very athletic. In her late twenties, she was childless and never married. Not for lack of suitors. Kialla was the object of several men's affections. She ran her hand down her lover's stomach, finally resting on his hardening member. There was a mischievous twinkle in her eye.

"Looks to me like someone wants more," she said with a sultry voice.

His hand gently curled around her neck and pulled her down.

"The things you do to me," he whispered right before her lips touched his.

Kialla sat at her usual corner table in the Battering Ram's common room, nursing a pint of bitter ale. Her chair was tipped back enough to allow her long legs to prop up on the table. Faded brown boots went up to her knees. Her blouse and trousers were different shades of green and brown, in stark contrast to the vibrant city folk colors. Her clothing suggested she was a hunter. Few were so foolish as to ask what. Her steeled gaze kept most people at bay. She was anything but the tender kitten she appeared.

Staring through the clouds of smoke and heavy crowd, she searched for potential employers and assassins alike. Kialla had never been the drinking sort. She generally had one before getting bored and finding either a job or entertainment. She didn't know why she still hung around Kelis Dur. There wasn't anything special about the city or the kingdom. Her adventures had run her across the vast northern kingdoms and beyond. She'd seen things no living soul should ever witness and walked away to tell of it. Kialla was a survivor.

Today's heavy storm left half the common room empty. She failed to understand how bad weather could dampen spirits so. After all, Thrae only had bad weather. Most people chose to stay warm and dry in the boredom of their homes than come out and enjoy good food and halfway decent company. Considering she had a reserved room upstairs, she failed to see the problem. So Kialla sat and sipped her drink, trusting something was bound to turn up.

The corner was the safest, most naturally defensible position in the room. She had a clear view of everyone coming and going out both the front and kitchen doors. Most of her weapons were locked in her room, but she never went anywhere without Lady Killer. The slender dagger had one jewel encrusted in the pommel: an amethyst. She'd never seen a jewel that shade of purple before. Kialla won the dagger from a drunk in a card game years ago. He'd tried to reclaim it later that night. She left him lying face down in an alley drowning in his own blood. Lady Killer never left her side.

Her eyes flashed as they paused on a familiar face. Kialla forced herself to remain calm as the giant seemed to pick her out of the crowd deliberately.

"I was wondering how long it was going to take you to show up," she said with a tight, utterly false smile.

Grelic took a seat opposite of her and motioned for the barmaid.

"Oh no you don't," Kialla warned. "I'm not going down with you when Rentor's men come to take you away."

He groaned. "You too? Can't a man enjoy one drink in peace without the rest of the world coming down on his head? One drink! Damnation!"

"The way you drink? Doubtful," Kialla said and couldn't help but giggle. Grelic still had a way of making her laugh, even after all their years knowing each other. She was young enough to be his daughter and just as nasty. "Why are you here? Last I heard you were going to be hanged."

"That was the plan. They let me go on good behavior."

She braced for the hammer strike.

"I need your help, Kialla."

Bam! There it was.

Slowly, she swung her legs down off of the table and sat up. "Why don't you just stop by to say hello?"

"Too many words. By the time we finish with pleasantries I'd already know your answer. My way gets to the point quicker."

She shook her head in mock disbelief. "Flattery, Grelic. One day you'll learn how to talk to a lady."

He smiled. There'd been plenty of women in his life but the thought of having a committed relationship was too restrictive. Confining. He revolted at the thought of abandoning his freedoms for anyone. Men like him weren't meant to sire children and live ordinary lives. Born while his father was away at war, Grelic was meant to die with sword in hand.

Grelic waggled an accusatory finger. "Don't sweet talk me, lass. I've seen you use your tongue as sharp as a blade. It may work on most men but not this one. Bat your eyes or flick your hair, it won't work on me."

They both laughed a little. Grelic gave the barmaid a playful slap on her rump after she set his drink down. She offered a sly, knowing look and sauntered off. He never would have done it if he didn't already know her.

"What do you need me for?" Kialla asked. Odd, but she found herself almost jealous.

He spent the next fifteen minutes explaining his deal with Rentor and what it might potentially mean to the future of all involved. She was skeptical toward anything dealing with the king. Rentor wasn't a bad man but he didn't seem the sort to forgive grudges. Still, his people loved him, which was more than could be said about people like her and Grelic. Warriors without a war. They were of the sort most folk frowned down on when peace reigned.

"It doesn't exactly sound like much fun," she said when he finished. "Personally I'd rather sit here and enjoy the view. Who are we trying not to fight again?"

"I'm sure we'll find a willing opponent," he replied. "We always do."

"What happens if we take on more than we can handle?"

"When has that ever happened?"

Her smile was brief. "More times than I care to remember. If I do this, and I'm not saying I will, what difference will it make to the future? Wars are one thing. I don't feel the need to be a hero and I don't want to be one. All I want is to make my way through the world unnoticed until death comes to claim me. Can you offer me that?"

"Sometimes we don't get the choice. Fate decides what we're meant to be. You and I are fighters, Kialla. From the day we were born. No amount of wishing or hoping can change that."

She stood, smoothing the wrinkles from her blouse in such a way he had to notice the supple curves beneath. "I'll let you know."

"By dawn. I'm staying with Phaes."

Her hand gently stroked his stubble-covered cheek. It was soft, lingering. Grelic watched her leave, admiring her shape and sway. Only when the door closed behind her did he frown. *This might be harder than I thought.* Grelic downed the rest of his ale and motioned for another.

Kialla went back to her room with a smile. She hadn't seen Grelic in months and was glad to know he wasn't dead yet. Despite all of her protests and casual disregard she realized she really did care what happened to Thrae. Not that she ever had many friends. She cared more about what happened to Grelic and why he felt so obligated to do this.

ELEVEN

Of Dragons and Mages

Cool spring breeze danced across the peaks and towers of Kelis Dur. The half-moon lurked directly overhead, offering shafts of haunting light through the thin layer of intermittent clouds. The rains had stopped hours ago, leaving Thrae waterlogged. Thick clay-like soil prevented the water from draining properly, even with the major river running through the city. The air held a semi-permanent chill slight enough to keep most men inside.

Codel Mres wasn't most men. He wasn't imposing. Wasn't even brave or particularly strong. He was cunning and manipulative and he was tired of standing in Rentor's shadow. Tired of the endless jests on his character. Tired of perpetual embarrassment in front of lords and nobles. There was a time when Codel aimed to please his childhood friend. He'd dedicated much of his life to the kingdom and had nothing substantial to show for it. Codel had better, bigger designs for his world and those didn't include the current monarchy. That's when they came to him, promising riches and power unimaginable until it blossomed in his mind.

He cursed as he stepped in a puddle. Even from atop his private tower he found it impossible to escape the near perpetual deluge. Codel had been promised Thrae for his subversive efforts. At this moment he doubted very much he wanted it. A raven cawed from the small cage resting on a stone table. Beads of water frosted the purple-black feathers.

"You don't like the rain either, eh?" Codel chuckled.

Reaching inside, Codel made a quick chirping sound. The raven hopped down from its perch and onto Codel's arm. The prime minister removed his one true friend and stroked the wet feathers. The bird watched him with curiously dark eyes. Codel fumbled slightly as he attached the small leather case to the raven's leg.

"Fly true and fast, my friend. The world is against us," he whispered for no reason.

The depths of his treachery were only eclipsed by his own desires. He launched the bird and watched as it headed north. Paranoia always gripped him for those first few moments. Would an alert guard notice and shoot it down? Or would hawks be sent to hunt the raven? His head would be on a pike should Rentor ever discover the truth. Drawing his cloak tighter to keep out the chill, Codel carefully avoided the puddles on the way back inside. Thunder rumbled in the distance, promising more rain.

Less than one hundred leagues separated the Darkwall Mountains, the far northern border of Thrae, and the Great Northern Sea. Early spring was no different from late winter. Weather seldom improved until midsummer and then only for a handful of weeks. There were few settlements in this part of Malweir. Jagged cliffs filled with caves reached forever down the coasts.

A day's ride from everywhere, right in the middle of nowhere, stood the mountain Druem. Ancient legend whispered of a war between gods being fought here, forever ruining this part of the world. They spoke of a curse placed here by the dark gods. Any man brave, or foolish, enough to enter Druem returned changed. Malweir was full of stranger creatures and mystic places. Druem was recognized as the most powerful. Hatred dwelled within the heart of the mountain.

Skies laden grey and black from perpetual storms wreathed the mountaintop. Small foothills spread out for miles around the base, turning the land into a massive lesion. Blackened forests ringed Druem, though from a distance. Only scrub brush grew nearby. Smoke was often seen weeping from cracks in the mountain. No one knew for sure what evil dwelled within and none felt the need to know so badly as to risk their lives.

Druem stood in the center of the kingdom known only as the Deadlands. Abandoned by Dwarf, Elf, and man, the Deadlands became home for Goblins. The foul race burrowed into the mountains and spread their brand of filth until the kingdom had become so corrupted no life thrived. They built their city, Mordrun Bal, at the base of the mountain. Mud and rock huts half buried in the rotting ground held thousands of Goblins, Gnomes, and other foul creatures. Most had already left, marching south for the great war against the other races of Malweir. Darkness crept back into the world. It was only a matter of time before the storm broke. The dark gods wanted to return and would stop at nothing to reclaim Malweir and plunge everyone into eternal torment.

Scourd watched a column of Goblin soldiers march through the spiked gates of Mordrun Bal and snarled. They'd taken losses. Ramulus would not be pleased. The Goblin commander left his balcony and headed back inside Druem. Worming his way through dimly lit corridors, the Goblin dreaded the coming conversation. He hated living underground. The air was too thin for torches to burn. The only light came from bored-out shafts made by Dwarf slaves. The sound of hammers and picks reverberated sharply off the bleak rock face. Slaves of every race toiled endlessly in the mountain for reasons they died without ever knowing.

Mountain Trolls in slightly rusted chain mail stood guard over the massive stone doors built deep in the heart of Druem. Scourd ignored them, intent on getting this task finished and coming out alive. No easy task. Already his legs quivered from the waves of fear pulsating up the corridors. He didn't understand how the Trolls managed to withstand such raw power. Their skin was thicker than any other race and they appeared to know no fear.

Dressed only in knee-length leather kilts and their armor, the Trolls were armed with tulwars the size of a grown man. They stared down at Scourd impassively. One of the reasons they guarded the chamber was for their lack of individualism. Trolls were community creatures. They needed to be told what to do. Only once in all of history had a Troll army been defeated. Their king fell, run through with pikes, and the army crumbled. Scourd didn't care about Trolls so long as he found they were on the same side. Otherwise…

He halted a safe distance away. "Open the gate. I must see Ramulus."

"Ramulus no bother," grunted the Troll on the right. It was the sound of crushing boulders.

The tulwar rose menacingly. Scourd held his ground, knowing it was all for show and honor. The heat down here was the worst part. He felt like he was trapped in a furnace. Scourd stared up at the dim-witted Troll. They knew him, in fact they'd seen him nearly every day since being brought in, and still they gave him problems. He suspected it stemmed from being conquered and used as either slaves or heavy assault troops. Unspoken contempt sat on the air between them.

"Open now," Scourd growled in reply. "I have work to do."

The Troll took a step closer. The ground trembled. "One day not need you," he threatened before turning back to his partner. "Open door."

The massive door opened with a groan, trails of dust and pebbles running down the walls. Scourd brushed past the Trolls, careful to not touch one. That was instant death and he was no fool. The door closed behind him, trapping him in the mighty cavern where Ramulus slept. The cavern was easily larger than Mordrun Bal. Fires burned hotly at random spots. The walls were stained black and sanded smooth. A fetid odor clung to the rock outcroppings littering the cavern. It reeked of pure death.

"Why have you come now?" asked a voice so deep it shook the foundations of the world. "I have not sent for you."

Scourd swallowed hard. His eyes searched the quasi darkness for Ramulus but it was a wasted effort. He'd only seen Ramulus once. The great wyrm was among the last of his kind in Malweir. Every other time he was left with fleeting shadows and imagined glimpses. But always there were the eyes. Pale globes of frozen blue glared menacingly from the dark. Scourd recoiled from the intense hatred of the glare.

"There is word from Thrae." He tried hard not to stammer.

Gouts of flame licked up from a nearby pit.

"Thrae is of no concern to me." A scathing hiss echoed throughout the cavern.

"Rentor suspects us, Ramulus. Soldiers will come," Scourd continued.

He caught the brief flicker of a spiked tail.

"Rentor's soldiers are your problem. You and your kind serve me for that one purpose. Deal with them when the time comes."

"And the traitor?"

The sound of tons of flesh moving assaulted his ears. The devilish eyes disappeared briefly before opening much closer. Scourd knew Ramulus would devour him in a single bite if he said the wrong thing, but he needed to voice his concerns.

"Leave him to me. Examples must be made if we are to maintain order. Ready your armies should Rentor prove too inquisitive. Do not let this distract our operations. Proceed with attack on Thim. The men of Thrae need to be reminded of their place," Ramulus grated in a strained, serpentine hiss.

Scourd's flesh tingled with every word. A steady chill ran through the shadows of his soul when the dragon spoke. It whispered dread and the death of the future. Scourd blinked rapidly. *Was that a man I saw walking off?* He wanted to caution against attacking Thrae. Rentor was already deploying his elite forces and Scourd already had so many forces moving south he feared Mordrun Bal would be indefensible.

"You question me, Goblin? I, who roamed the skies when your kind first crawled from the mud? I've toppled mountains with the flap of my wings and ruined nations with my songs of flame. Worm! I am this world. I'm immortal. An eternal reminder of your casual frailty. Leave me before I rethink your importance," Ramulus roared.

Each word threatened to split the ground, rattling Scourd's bones. The Goblin commander bowed curtly and spun on his heels. A single thought ran through his mind. *No one is immortal. Not even dragons.*

The blue-bellied song bird landed just out of reach, watching the approaching man with fading curiosity. It was about to fly away when the sudden high-pitched shrill caught its attention. Cocking its head, the bird returned the call. The old man smiled. Satisfied, the bird stayed in place and watched the man amble past.

Dakeb laughed quietly to himself. Long, grey hair framed his face, concealing thin cheekbones and a pointed chin. His smile was warm and kind. Nature was a much better friend than any man. He'd spent his long life protecting the innocent and preserving wildlife. Malweir was a better place when left untouched, he believed. Too often did an ignorance lead to the wanton destruction of life. Too few men realized the importance of their deeds.

He sighed. Perhaps that's what happened to the Mages. Their foundations went back thousands of years to a wilder, less civilized time. They worked for hundreds of years in the quest to better Malweir. Then, as in all things, corruption set in. Greed overtook members of the council and the orders were plunged into turmoil. The great war that followed consumed the Mages and nearly ended all life on Malweir. The races of the world picked sides and met on the lush fields of Averon.

A secret coven of dark Mages left the battle and returned to Ipn Shal, their ancient palace and source of knowledge. Led by Sidian, the Silver Mage, they attempted to turn the crystal of Tol Shere into a weapon to destroy their enemies and free the dark gods from their eternal imprisonment in the process. The world nearly died that day. A handful of Mages, Dakeb included, realized something wasn't right and followed the coven back to Ipn Shal. They ended the threat and destroyed the crystal. *Only it wasn't destroyed, was it? No. We killed our wicked brothers and broke the crystal into four shards. We should have destroyed it entirely back then.* The battle in Averon was won, if barely, and the Mages passed into obscurity.

Dakeb remembered those days jadedly. He remembered nightmares and how the sun never shined. He'd seen and done horrible things no living thing should ever experience. Life lost its luster then. The Mage War ended with the destruction of the crystal and the deaths of nearly all of the Mages. For Dakeb it was a personal failure. He'd been there in Ipn Shal when the dark Mages lost the war. He was there when the world stopped caring.

The old man sighed and passed a final, carefree glance at the blue bird. The bird chirped merrily to him as if to say it was all going to be fine. Only it wasn't. Dakeb was no fool. Old wounds lingered in his heart. His thoughts reverted to his lost brothers and sisters and the handful still alive. It was hard not to ask the precious few for help, but he knew this was a task best done alone.

How many are going to pay for our hubris this time? For as surely as the sun sets there will be war. It's happening all over again. This time, however, he recognized the signs in advance. Spring may have come to Thrae, but darkness rode the evening tide. Hope for tomorrow quietly began to fade.

Dakeb the Mage walked on.

TWELVE

Doubts

The crisp sound of clashing swords echoed across the training ground. Cron ducked a blow aimed at his head and rolled. His attacker cried out and stabbed down. Cron barely managed to parry as he rose to one knee. A roar went up through the assembled spectators. Frustration flashed across his attacker's face. Cron struggled to his feet and tried to catch his breath before the next assault. There wasn't time.

Sparks danced as their blades met three times. Both men spun. The attacker swung a backhanded riposte towards Cron's ribs. Still in mid turn, Cron dropped the sword behind his back to block the blow. He was drenched in sweat, face flushed from exertion. Cron wasn't sure he could win. Then it happened. His attacker parried a glancing blow and lunged. His boot caught on a half-buried rock and he pitched forward. Off balance, Cron took advantage. A string of quick upper body blows drove his opponent to his knees. Cron continued to strike, hitting so hard he knocked the other's sword away. Exhausted, the beaten man slumped forward.

"Winner!" declared Sergeant Notam as he stumped across the training field.

Cron stabbed his sword down into the ground and offered his hand. "You're getting better, Prial."

"Not good enough to best you."

"Between you and I, you nearly had me," Cron said and smiled.

Prial suspected as much. "Damned rock."

"That's war, lad. You can be the fanciest swordsman in the kingdom and lose to a rock," Notam said.

Prial didn't know how to take that. The trouble with Notam was no one was really sure whether he was praising or condemning them. Not even Cron had figured it out.

Slapping Prial on the shoulder, Cron said, "Go on, Prial. Towel off and watch the next duel. Maybe you'll find the right move to beat me."

He watched the lad move off, silently appraising him. They were going to need more men like him before the end.

"Something's troubling you. Holding it in doesn't help anyone," Notam noticed, handing Cron his sword.

Cron looked at his sergeant, his friend. He wanted to tell him to butt out and forget about it. That this was his problem. He'd taken a week's leave to personally inform Ele and Reben's families. Their fathers understood while the mothers collapsed in tears, unwilling to believe their sons were stolen from them during peace. It broke Cron's heart to see them kneeling with tear-stained faces. It hurt worse knowing he couldn't warn them that worse was approaching.

"We did everything we could. Thinking about it won't bring them back. Put it to rest and drive on. Worse came from our mission than their deaths," Notam said.

"Such as?"

"I want to know who put those heads on display. That's not the work of bandits or raiders. We've fought them and it was a damned, dirty business but not their style. Worse, what burned Gend? The men are already whispering about dragons."

Notam never ceased to surprise him. Every time he figured the grizzled old man for just another hardcore sergeant with no heart, Notam cleared his throat and forced him to change his mind.

"There hasn't been a dragon spotted east of the Jebel Desert in generations. Not since the Mage War. I can't believe one would be hounding us," Cron replied.

"Believe it or not, something very large destroyed that village and murdered the villagers," Notam said, stern-faced and dour.

Cron kept his mouth shut. Speculating didn't help when Rentor was trying to plan a war against a faceless enemy.

Notam scowled. "I know that look."

Cron offered a false smile. "I have a lot of thinking to do."

"Will you be staying to watch the final rounds?"

Cron shook his head. "I have too much work. Make Prial the winner in my place and let him continue fighting. The extra practice will do him good. Besides, I wouldn't want a rock to be the cause of a grudge between us. Oh and Notam, the winner gets a four-day pass beginning tomorrow morning. Give them something worth competing for."

Notam knew their men didn't require bribes through prizes. A combat soldier is one of the simplest creatures. He eats, sleeps, trains, and drinks. When it is time to go to war he goes without complaint. When it came to competition, every last one wants to be the best, if for no other reason than to brag to his comrades. Notam suspected it was the same in every army across Malweir. The gods knew he'd run into enough of them. He grimly watched Cron stalk off. Tensions surrounded the captain. Notam saw it in the way he walked. How stiff his conversation had grown. *One day I'm going to have a talk with that lad.*

"All right, boys," he growled at the hundred-odd men still assembled. "Who's next?"

Two men stepped forward. The air sang with clashing steel.

"Come back to bed, husband. I'm getting lonely," the queen purred.

Rentor stood looking at his reflection in the mirror. His image almost laughed back, mocking him with disdain. Taunting him for his failures and misgivings. Rentor watched the image laugh every time he thought of the future. What future, it cried. *Your complacency has damned this world! Had you bothered paying a little more attention the enemy wouldn't be moving against us.* Rentor studied his reflection and cursed.

"I feel old, Melena," he finally admitted. "Tired. My bones ache though the winter chill is long faded. What's happening to us?"

Concern flushed her features. "What's wrong? I've never heard you speak like this."

He gave a halfhearted laugh. "I never have had to. Do you remember when we first took the throne? Those were grand times! We were unstoppable. Malweir stood in awe of what we were meant to achieve."

"You're scaring me."

"Love, I scare myself. What happens if I've made the wrong decision by sending Grelic on his task? All of Thrae will be doomed and it will be my fault."

Melena slid from bed and into a light robe. Rentor watched, that familiar stirring in his loins from seeing her shapely naked form. Even after decades of getting to know every inch of her body, she still managed to arouse him. Melena wrapped her arms around his massive waist and rested her head on his shoulder.

"I remember long nights under the stars with your arms around me. I remember the look in your eyes when our son was born. I've never seen you more proud. I love you, Rentor. I am beside you the entire way, no matter what awaits us at the end."

He gently kissed her forehead.

Father Seldis bent to smell the first bloom of the year. The white jasmine was always his favorite. The sweet smell was fragrant and reminded him of gentle times with his long deceased wife. Hypnotic as it was, the smell always managed to make him cry. *If only the rest of the world understood the simplicity of beauty. Would there be wars?* Seldis doubted it. More leaders needed to stop and smell the grass after a light spring rain. He sighed. If only was a haunting epitaph. A blue and purple butterfly landed on the back of his hand a moment before Rentor entered the royal gardens.

"I hadn't expected to find you here, Father," Rentor announced. "Welcome, as it should be, my home is yours." His eyes flicked over to the monk standing in the corner, beside Fitch Iane. "I see you've brought a guest."

"Master Iane practically insisted," Seldis replied.

Rentor doubted that. "He seems much improved. A month has made quite the difference. Perhaps I could use a short stay at the monastery."

"Time heals, King," Seldis said.

Time and a little magic, no doubt.

"The mountain jasmine is beautiful. My own garden is ripe with it, though not to this magnitude," Seldis said and gestured across the enormity of the gardens. Draping vines of white climbed trees for as far as the eye could see. "It is good to be king at times like this."

"At times," Rentor agreed. "Tell me, Father, what do the monks of Harr have for me this fine morning? Can't a king enjoy a quiet stroll in his solitude?"

Seldis leaned closer and said, "With no guards? Alone? A king asks for death that way. Any king, no matter how well liked."

"I don't care for your tone, Father. You make the future sound bleaker than I care to dream."

"A king should be afraid. Treason is never far away. Ware the long knives in the dark, as they used to say."

Rentor raised an eyebrow. "Surely you didn't come here for subtle warnings? I've known you long enough. Why are you here?"

"The Order of Harr is offering you our assistance," Seldis said simply.

"Assistance for what?"

Seldis chuckled. "Come now, King Rentor, I may be old but my mind is as sharp as it has ever been. Grelic is a strong man. A proud warrior but he is headstrong and rarely listens. He needs balance."

For a moment only Rentor was surprised. Then he remembered Seldis knew things impossible for normal men to know. He suspected the elder monk dabbled in magic or, at a stretch, was one of the last remaining Mages in Malweir. "You're getting a little too old for adventures, don't you think?"

"My questing days are long behind me. All I require is a good fire, mulled wine, and a book. But young Fitch here, his task is yet to be undertaken. I believe he is destined to go on this quest," Seldis replied.

The king stepped away. Fitch Iane was half a man at best, more liability than help. "You ask me to entrust the lives of every man, woman, and child in this kingdom to the will of a broken man? A difficult proposition, Father."

Rentor knew Seldis had reasons he wasn't going to give. That was the monk's way. Give just enough information to entice, leave you wanting.

"Normally I'd caution against such a move, but here I can only ask, what does your heart say?" he finally said. A queer look crossed his face, as if he already knew the answer.

"Grelic's not going to like this. I hope he doesn't kill the boy before they leave the gardens."

Seldis grinned. "I doubt anything so drastic. In fact, I believe Fitch and Grelic will get along just fine."

Rentor had his doubts. He'd seen plenty of wonders in the world, but evidence of Grelic's kindness wasn't one. The giant was a warrior through and through with little use for men like Fitch. Rentor wanted to laugh, knowing he had no use for broken men either. *If only I weren't king and twenty years younger.*

"One day you're going to tell me how it is you can remain so optimistic when darkness falls around us," he told Seldis. "More around here need your attitude."

Shadows crept into his memories like dust on forgotten bones. A time of reckoning was approaching.

"It's not difficult, once you figure life out."

They stood in silence for a time, staring at the tiger-patterned orchids coming into bloom. Rentor had much to think on.

"What are they talking about?" Fitch asked quietly.

He didn't know, but Brother Ibram felt just as nervous, if not more, than Fitch was. Memories were slurred. Fitch barely recalled being visited by the king. In fact, he barely remembered anything of his time with the monks. How he got to the mountains was a mystery equal to why he now stood in the royal gardens of Kelis Dur.

"I don't know, but Father Seldis is a wise man. If anyone knows what he is doing, it's him," Ibram replied, hoping to instill confidence in them both.

Fitch had already stopped paying attention and allowed his mind to wander off in the sheer amount of rare plants and trees surrounding them. Flowers of every color came into bloom, filling the gardens with almost intoxicating scents. The wonder and beauty trapped within the stone walls brightened his heart.

"I never imagined such a place could exist this far north," he breathed.

Ibram agreed. "Father Seldis says there is equal beauty in all things. For myself I seldom see it."

He was about to say more, revealing a darker part of his character, when a giant of a man strode past. Ibram's mouth dropped. The man was unmistakable. Everything suggested confidence and strength. Ibram stood in awe as Grelic presented himself to the king. An old fear crept back into Fitch. Flashes of demons and nightmares stabbed at him. He feared he wasn't ready to accept the task Seldis seemed so sure of.

"Who is he?"

Ibram balked. "One of the greatest warriors to have ever lived."

Rentor appraised his guests. He hadn't expected a young woman when Grelic demanded the right to choose his own people. She was quite attractive, though he doubted he'd want to cross blades with her. That same intensity lingered in her eyes. Grelic wouldn't have brought her if she wasn't dangerous.

"I see today holds many surprises," Rentor said. "There are a lot of people who think you've already fled south."

"I don't run from a fight." Grelic barred his teeth.

"The true mark of a man," Seldis said with enough sarcasm to rouse Grelic's ire.

"You are?"

"Of no concern for the moment," Rentor stepped in. The last thing he needed was a murder in his gardens.

It didn't take long for Grelic to roll his eyes and notice the two men standing in the background. His eyes narrowed angrily. "We had a deal."

The king held up his hands, attempting to calm him. "The deal stands, but you need to hear me out. There are forces at work much more powerful than either of us knew. It's going to take more than you and this girl to resolve our problems."

"This girl," he ground through clenched teeth. "Is worth more than fifty of your best."

Rentor's skin crawled as Grelic's entire body tensed, preparing to fight. "We can leave now."

"That won't be necessary, Grelic," Seldis said in his calming tone. "Times are trying enough without friends abandoning one another. Hear him out, please."

For reasons he couldn't explain, Grelic almost felt compelled to listen. Odd feelings resonated off of the old man. Some whispered danger, others content. Either way, Seldis was a man to be wary of.

"Your tongue has a strange bite, but I know when I am up against power. I will hear you out, old man, just this once."

They stared at each other for a moment, each testing the measure of conviction.

"Enough of this. I let you out of prison for a reason, Grelic," Rentor scolded.

The giant squinted as sunlight struck his eye. "Aye, and I accepted for reasons of my own. Remember that, King."

Kialla had had enough of their bravado. Her words were sharp and hostile. There was business to conduct. More importantly, she wanted to know what could instill such latent fear in so many powerful people. "It is extremely rude not to introduce a lady."

Their banter stopped as all three men turned to Kialla. Seldis wore a charming smile, as if he'd been waiting for her. Grelic seemed at a loss for words and Rentor's face flushed with mild discomfort.

Grelic spoke first. "King Rentor, this is Kialla. She's a tracker without equal and the closest friend I have. And as I said, she is worth fifty of your best."

Kialla curtseyed awkwardly and flashed a dazzling smile. "Sire."

Rentor returned the smile. *She just might be more dangerous than Grelic. No doubt her tongue is as sharp as her blades. At least something is going right.*

THIRTEEN

Deals Struck

They stared at Father Seldis with incredulous looks. No one believed what he'd just said or how he casually mentioned the one place people in Thrae purposefully shunned. The Deadlands. Mothers warned their children of darkness and pain. Even Rentor kept his men far south of the Darkwall Mountains, the border between Thrae and the Deadlands. Ancient texts suggested Thrae once went from the Thed Mountains to the south, up past the great forest of Qail Werd and the Darkwall mountains to the edge of the Great Northern Sea. But that was before the darkness settled in the far north. Now Rentor's patrols barely went as far as Qail Werd.

Rentor spoke first. "Father, we all know the Deadlands are a place of growing despair, but no one has gone there in decades, at least not during my time as king. What cause is there to send men now?"

"Some of what you speak is true. The Deadlands are void of life. No plants grow. No animals make their home in the dead forests or barren plains. As you say, I cannot recall the last time I saw the peaks of mighty Druem for myself. Evil now gathers under the great mountain because we allowed it. Our enemies know our natural reluctance to enter the Deadlands, making it the perfect place for them to build and grow strong. War is coming, King Rentor, as you accurately predicted. A war so fierce it threatens the security of all Malweir, not just Thrae."

Ibram felt a perverse excitement building. The war of all wars! A war unlike any other in all of Thrae's history and he was going to be a part of it. Ibram started having delusions of being a hero. Reality shook him when he noticed Seldis glaring at him.

"So we are going into the Deadlands?" Grelic asked. "I've roamed Qail Werd and even the lower foothills of the Darkwall. Many strange creatures lurk within. Some without name. I've also heard rumors of the Deadlands from the Pell Darga. The mountain folk warn of great evil at work in the north. If all this is true, we cannot hope to defeat it with a handful of fools."

Rentor was impressed. He hadn't expected caution out of Grelic. *Maybe we have a chance after all.*

Kialla cocked her hips aggressively. "What are we waiting for? Let's get packed and head out. There's no point in wasting time if the monk's predictions are accurate."

"I'm afraid it's not so simple, my dear," Seldis cautioned. "There are many forces at work here. Some for evil, others for good. We must trust to the east wind. I have seen things, images in my dreams. The Deadlands are not the place to go."

Grelic snorted. He grew tired of the double talk. "Then where?"

Seldis leveled his gaze on Fitch. "The beginning. Gend holds many secrets we haven't yet unlocked. Go to Gend. There you will find the clues to your long journey."

"My men tell me there is nothing left in Gend but ash and bitter memories. What secrets can there possibly be?" Rentor asked. He failed to see Seldis' logic. "The dead are buried. Nothing remains."

Tears welled in Fitch's eyes. Shar. His heart cried out. Brother Ibram saw and placed a comforting hand on his shoulder to steady him.

"The words may sting, but I know no other way to speak them," Rentor said after seeing the reaction they caused in the villager.

Seldis added, "Your family has moved on to a better world, Fitch. The troubles of this one are forgotten. They await you. You will see them again when it is time."

Grelic shifted balance to his other leg. "This one is weak. Taking him is wrong. No matter what the monk says, he is a liability."

Ibram stepped forward, compelled to defend Fitch. "He'll do his part, as will I."

The words, spoken from the heart, only made Grelic laugh. "Your part? There's no need for priests on this adventure. Leave your gods behind. I need warriors."

Shame stung Ibram. His eyes bore the hurt and his fists were clenched in a useless gesture.

"I agreed to let you choose certain members for this quest. You bring one. One more to stand against the potential Goblin horde you are likely to face. Or worse. Don't argue with me on this, Grelic. Thrae is my kingdom and I have more to worry about than just your ego. Accept my will or find yourself back in irons," Rentor threatened.

"Fine. The monk and farmer come," Kialla said. "But understand this, sire, my life is now affected by their deeds. I'm not about to put myself at risk if they don't perform. I agreed to help Grelic because he is my friend. I'm not bound by oath or allegiance. If I feel I am in peril due to them I leave."

"Fair enough," Rentor said, though he suspected she was the sort to stay to the bitter end.

He watched them, studying each. There couldn't be four more distinct people. Grelic was the veteran warrior with too much pride and experience. The combination might very well work against him. Fitch Iane was shaky at best, a broken wreck of a man who struggled for dominance of his own soul. Ibram was as close to a defrocked monk as they came and suffered from his own delusions. Rentor wondered what made a man so unhappy with his life that he was willing to throw it away for causes he didn't understand. The only saving grace of the group was Kialla. She had a calm presence and a level head. He quietly picked her as the hinge on which success or failure depended. Rentor knew they weren't going to be enough.

"I'm not asking any of you to fight a war for me. All I ask is that you prevent the coming storm. If what Father Seldis says is true, there are dark times ahead. Find out who attacked Gend and report back to me. I'll have the army ready to strike as soon as I get word. You are all that stands between peace and the sheer destruction of our way of life. I wish there was more," Rentor said.

"Perhaps there is," called a youthful voice from the shadows under a stand of maple trees.

The garden exploded with the song of steel being drawn. Rentor spun, hand instinctively reaching for the short dagger hidden in the folds of his golden robes. Grelic and Kialla already had swords drawn and were crouched in defensive postures. The king strained into the shadows and was rewarded with the slightest flicker of movement. He stepped forward.

"That's far enough, King."

A black shaft raced by Rentor and split the chest of an alabaster statue ten feet behind him. Rentor froze. His guards were too far away to be of use, knowing this was a private meeting that never officially happened. "What do you want?"

He'd survived numerous assassination attempts in the past. None had been this close, leaving him unsure of how to proceed. Charging ahead would leave his feathered corpse on the ground just as standing helplessly would. He could hope for a distraction by Grelic or the others, though none of them seemed inclined to take the fight to the assassin.

"I should have thought that was obvious." There was an innocent charm in the tone.

Rentor lowered the dagger and spread his arms. "You'll never escape."

Laughter insulted him. "I got in. I'm sure getting back out won't be a problem."

The shadow moved. A man stepped into view. He was dressed in form-fitting black clothes and had enough weapons to start a small war. His face was painted black, leaving only his piercing eyes exposed. And he was grinning. "Killing you is not why I'm here."

Rentor startled at the sound of Grelic sheathing his sword, followed closely by Kialla. His eyes narrowed, assuming the giant had turned on him. Treachery for treachery. Rentor slowly dropped his hands and waited for the stranger to make his move. The man was slender and toned. His eyes were dark, almost black, and he was not afraid. He'd broken into the palace, threatened a king's life, and wasn't concerned with the consequences. Impressive, or incredibly stupid.

"Why have you come? Give me an answer good enough to let you live," Rentor demanded.

The man bowed. "Well said, King. Malweir needs more like you. My name is Pregen Chur. I am a master thief, part-time assassin, and all-around ladies' man. As to why I am here in your lovely garden, ask Grelic."

All eyes turned on the giant, who maintained his rock-hard composure.

"I need people I can trust. People who know how to operate with limited guidance and won't run from a fight. Pregen works alone by nature," Grelic answered.

Pregen smiled brightly.

That man has the brightest teeth I have ever seen. Rentor shook his head.

"Relax yourself, King Rentor. He is one of the best at what he does. Do not let youth or charm beguile you. Pregen Chur is needed for this task."

Fitch swooned as the power of a future vision wrenched his stomach. Ibram balked at the statement. Assassins weren't the heroes of tales. Only Father Seldis seemed unaffected by the revelation.

"What need have I for an assassin? You are not to make contact with the enemy," Rentor reinforced.

Pregen bore a hurt look.

Grelic stood his ground. "I was thinking more along the lines of thief. They come in handy in a pinch and we don't know what we're getting into."

"I don't like this."

The giant smiled. "There's nothing to like. This is war. You and I have both been there. Forced into situations against our choosing where no answer is right or wrong. The fancy dreams of monks and wizards can't help us." He tapped the hilt of his broadsword. "You've given me a want-to-be-warrior and a broken man. Fine. They'll come along though I suspect neither will return alive. They're not made for the kind of life you force upon them. Of course, there's the very real chance none of us will return."

"These men were handpicked by Father Seldis, a man I trust above all others. If he has faith then so do I. Come. If this is to be it, so be it. Time is wasting and I would see you leave before dusk."

Codel Mres watched the exchange intently from his hiding place. Anger trembled through him. He felt betrayed. How dare Rentor go against the council! He resisted the urge to strike down his childhood friend here and now. Demonic voices begged for release. He screamed back at them and collapsed. When he awoke, darkness surrounded him. Fitting, considering how close Thrae stood to utter annihilation. Codel smiled wickedly. Rentor's heroes didn't stand a chance.

Pregen Chur was the last to leave the private gardens, choosing to remain alone rather than muddle in the company of others. Too many people in one place made him nervous, stole his edge. His best work was done at night and alone. Here, in the late morning and amidst a host of strangers, Pregen was out of his element. His senses felt dulled, as if he'd forgotten a lifetime of training and rigid discipline. Still, a familiar sensation crept up his spine. Pregen turned slowly and methodically scanned the gardens. There was another person here. Watching them. He waited patiently as Minster Codel Mres stepped out of the shadows to confront him.

Grelic, the warrior: the legendary hero of many battles and part-time miscreant. He sat astride his massive horse looking down on the people who were about to follow him into doom or glory. Two were proven in the field and knew their way about the land. They'd both taken their share of lives and had extensive experience in the wild. He didn't trust them fully, knowing both would look after self-interests if things got too hairy. Grelic didn't mind. He knew exactly where they stood. There would be no surprises.

The other pair was going to prove problematic. Brother Ibram, now dressed in simple riding clothes, had cast aside everything he'd spent a lifetime to achieve for the vain ambition of glory. Grelic doubted he'd achieve anything worthy of song, much less remembering. History was full of fools. Fitch Iane simply shouldn't be here. Grelic looked at the man and saw only distress. He briefly contemplated finishing the man one night and putting him to rest. A foul taste filled his mouth. The man was a coward, but for reasons Grelic couldn't understand.

Rentor strode up to him and stroked the horse's neck softly. "Save this kingdom."

Grelic grinned, savage and demented, and kicked his horse into a trot. Rentor and Seldis watched the small party ride out into uncertainty. The old monk closed his eyes and wept. Not even his fervent prayers to Harr would be enough to save them when the dark rain finally broke.

FOURTEEN

Alone in the Dark

Mist covered the ground like a foul blanket. There was a slight chill to the air, a reminder that the night was dying. Kini Ar looked out the window of his guard tower and wondered what he was doing. The tower, if it could be called such, was more like a hunter's platform. Barely large enough to fit a man, it offered a stable platform to shoot a bow, but little else. The only advantage Kini found was it allowed him to see a goodly distance, when the weather permitted.

Most of the villages in Thrae had erected similar defenses after word of Gend spread. Thim was no exception. Every man old enough took his turn during the nights in one of the four hastily constructed watch towers. The rest continued to build a palisade around the village. Last night had been Kini's turn at watch. It wasn't half as bad as he expected, considering none of them had any military experience. Kini was a simple baker. Breads and pastries were his specialty, not swords or a bow. He didn't mind doing his part for his home, though he failed to see the point. Kini was convinced there wasn't anything out there that needed to be defended against. Gend was either inflated due to the story being passed down or just made up to begin with. He scoffed at the notion of monsters attacking Thim.

The zip of an arrow and the wet thump of it striking his chest, piercing through his heart, were the last things Kini heard before his corpse tumbled from the platform.

Hundreds of bulky, dark shapes emerged from the mist and casually surrounded the sleeping village. Scourd walked among them, careful to keep silent as his Goblins executed their task just like they'd done a dozen times before. He impatiently waited until four pillars of flames rose above the village. All defending guards had been dispatched and their towers set ablaze. Thim was helpless. Scourd finally grinned savagely, a visage of utter malice and contempt for humankind.

He turned to the Goblin closest to him and ordered, "Unleash the Dwim."

The Goblin stalked off, his grey barrel shape quickly being lost in the mist. Scourd felt the temperature drop sharply as scores of Dwim sidled through the Goblin ranks. He was careful to avoid their touch. Dwim were powerful creatures and certain death to anything they came in contact with. Their lidless, opaque eyes stared at the buildings and homes of Thim. Their mouths were locked in a rictus of agony, twisted by the dark powers of the netherworld. Dark Mages once delved too deep into the black arts and the Dwim were the result.

They'd been human once. Men and women stolen in the night and transformed through unspeakable nightmares.

The Dwim struck with voracity seldom seen. Crashing through windows and doors, breaking through walls as if they were naught but curtains blowing in a soft wind. The Dwim fell on their prey with undisguised maliciousness. They killed without thought, sucking the very souls from their victims with a harrowing silent scream. Scourd listened to the utter silence gripping Thim and shivered. Such things simply should not be allowed to exist. He despised the mindless creatures. Most had been women or children. Dark Mages quickly discovered the value of twisting women. Through some foul comedy, the Mages tore the fabric of the world. Bred for the singular purpose of killing, Dwim were incapable of individual thought. They obeyed his orders without question but could easily be turned against Scourd should Ramulus decree.

Scourd watched and listened to the growing symphony of chaos. The Dwim had been instructed to capture another hundred villagers and kill the rest. Personally, Scourd thought his Goblins were more effective on the battlefield. He'd tried arguing the point with Ramulus but the dragon seldom listened, leading Scourd to believe a more nefarious character was pulling the strings in Druem. Dragons were revered for their ability to make war. They killed and slept. Hailing from the islands far to the west, Ramulus was one of the few winged beasts that actually made it this far. Scourd wondered why, and how.

"The Dwim are nearly finished," hissed one of the Goblin captains.

Scourd snarled, the deep rumbling sound coming from his barrel chest. "Burn everything. Have the scum take the prisoners back to Mordrun Bal. Ramulus wants his army ready soon."

"At once."

The smell of burnt flesh soon choked the predawn air. Scourd inhaled deeply, relished the scent. His mouth watered.

"What of the bodies? We are hungry, Scourd," an impish Goblin asked.

Scourd lashed out. The back of his hand crushed the imp's skull with a sickening crunch. "Leave them where they died. Back to the Deadlands! Soldiers will come soon."

The Goblin commander stalked off, leaving the dead Goblin in a spreading pool of blood and brain matter. Energy revitalized him. It had been so long since he last killed for pleasure, Scourd nearly forgot the sensation. Packs of Dwim started leaving the village, dragging half-senseless victims. Three wagons waited just beyond the tree line to carry the prisoners back to the laboratories of Mordrun Bal. Once the last prisoner was loaded, the Dwim disappeared. Scourd watched their wood-colored bodies dissolve into the mist with a tremor of disgust.

"Move out! We are out of time!" he ordered, suddenly eager to get as far away from the Dwim as possible.

Alfen Bew covered his ears and started singing to drown out the fresh chorus of screams. He hated the night. Especially those when more prisoners were brought in. It never occurred to him that they were all women or children. Alfen figured the men were sent down to work the mines. He watched a seemingly endless train of fresh prisoners being shoved into cages. He didn't know any of them.

Alfen normally spent his time ignoring the others. He'd made the mistake of befriending others in the beginning. One by one they were taken away, never to be seen again. He was the last. Back then Alfen harbored hope of being rescued. Surely his parents, Rena and Bors, must be out searching the countryside with their dog Asha. They would be worried to death, not knowing where he was or even if he was still alive. That fear of unknowing kept Alfen going for only so long. Now he merely tried to not think about home. His family. His friends. He was six years old and more than likely going to die without ever seeing the sun again.

What Alfen couldn't have known was his father was already dead, murdered by the same raiding party that captured him. His mother was gone as well, turned into one of the lifeless Dwim, one of the very creatures she used to warn him about in her tales of monsters and gobbledygook. Alfen Bew was as alone as he would ever be. Better men grew desperate and tried to escape. He was six. Escaping wasn't very realistic. So Alfen spent his days avoiding others and trying to hide.

The screams grew closer. He couldn't block them out any longer. Alfen gave in and crept closer to the bars of his cell to look. Shock rippled across his face. He knew the woman screaming! She'd always been kind to him, slipping him extra scraps of bread or rotted meat. She was one of the few who actually cared for him. While he never spoke very much with her, Alfen considered her a friend. Now she was being taken away just like all of the others. Sadness gripped him when she passed. Goblins sneered, ignoring the other prisoners. Alfen cowered with that old fear.

He suddenly lunged for the bars and shouted, "Let her go!"

The Goblin barked laughter and kept walking as the woman turned her head to give Alfen a final glance. Her soft eyes pleaded with him not to say anything else. The way her golden hair framed her face reminded him of his mother.

"Wait your turn, little one," the second Goblin hissed.

Alfen gripped the bars so hard his hands hurt. He felt helpless, but what could he do? He sat down and tried to think. The only thing he could do for her was to never forget her name. He vowed to say it every night before he went to sleep. Shar.

FIFTEEN

A Bad Start

It began raining just before dawn. An unexpected cold front turned the mid-spring drizzle into cold, punishing rain. Grelic wiped the water from his brow in a useless gesture and kept riding. The foul tempered look etched into his face said what they were all feeling. He turned every so often to see if any of the others had given up and gone home yet. They'd only been on the road for a few days and misery set in. Ibram was the first to protest. Brave, but Grelic only laughed in his face. Monks were too soft if a little rain threatened to break him.

"Perfect way to start the quest," Kialla smiled.

Grelic ignored the minor lust growing inside. Her auburn hair clung to her soft cheeks, enhancing her natural beauty. A heavy riding cloak managed to keep her from being thoroughly soaked. She told him it was a gift from the Elves of the Old Forest. He didn't bother asking for what. Things just were.

"Mmm. I'm not sure who's more uncomfortable, the monk or Pregen," he replied.

Kialla laughed. It was a glorious sound to the older warrior, akin to song birds on the first true day of spring. A small part of him almost wished he had settled down and raised a family. A son. Sadly, Grelic knew he lacked the ability to keep women happy. There were times when he failed to keep himself happy. The thought of having others depend on him every day without fail frightened him.

She turned back to enjoy the thief's discomfort. Pregen was the sort to willingly travel on long, dangerous journeys in unknown lands. She suspected he seldom left the major cities. "Master thief and part-time assassin! I hope you're not taking him for his word, Grelic."

"Relax. I've known him for a few years. He should do what I need him to."

An uneasy thought dawned on her. "His deeds are seldom talked about. I never heard of him until the gardens. Grelic, he's younger than me! He can get us all killed. Hells, he might even be working for the enemy."

The painful slap of wet flesh echoed through the group. Grelic turned to watch Fitch pull a dead mosquito from his face. If he weren't a naturally confident man, Grelic might start to lose hope. "At least we know his charming side is true."

Kialla shot him a dirty look, though she reluctantly admitted Pregen did have a certain quality about him. And he was attractive. She guessed he came from wealth, given the softness of his hands and his smooth words. "Has he actually killed anyone?"

Grelic refused to answer.

Fitch cursed after killing yet another mosquito. He'd already lost count of how many times he'd been bitten. It was certainly more than everyone else combined. He was used to being miserable, or so he thought. Small village living offered everyday misery, whether from food or farming. At least he had Shar to keep him happy when he returned home. He sighed. That life seemed like so long ago. He changed the subject before that old wound reopened.

"They could have picked a better day," he griped to Ibram.

Ibram didn't care. He rode without focus, wishing for the bad weather to pass. Destiny had summoned and he knew he was about to become a great hero, an immortal legend passed down through generations. The rain threatened to dampen his spirits enough to make him reconsider.

"This isn't so bad. Consider it a cleansing by Harr before we truly begin the quest," Ibram replied. He held up a cupped hand, letting the water fill it before drinking quickly. "This is the life, Fitch! We're practically kings of our world."

Fitch was fairly positive Ibram was ready to draw his sword and start hacking away at imaginary heroes like children do. He had an odd suspicion of the real reason Ibram left the order. Fitch started to think the man was borderline psychotic.

"If this is what being a king is like I'll have no part in it."

Ibram was stunned. He failed to see how any man wouldn't enjoy the freedom of doing whatever he wanted or where. After all, heroes didn't answer to others. "Why did you let Father Seldis convince you to come along?"

Fitch shrugged, the answer lost in the jumble of broken thoughts and unfinished memories. "To help the kingdom I suppose."

Ibram fell silent, so coldly were the words spoken.

Grelic finally called a halt around midday. They'd come upon an abandoned hunting lodge and decided to break for a quick meal and the chance to dry out a little before continuing. They fixed a hasty meal of dried meat and cheese while sitting around the small campfire. Grelic warned against anything larger despite it being the middle of the day. They couldn't afford to take chances.

He noticed they sat divided. Standing in the doorway, he paused from looking up into the dismal skies to study his group. The rains lightened enough to offer the false promise of hope but there wasn't any sign Grelic found that the storms were going to abate. He saw how Ibram sulked off to one side. Fitch seemed desperate to escape Pregen's boasts and sordid tales. Kialla caught his eye and she rose.

She walked softly to the giant and offered a cup of steaming tea, which he drank quickly. The warm feeling spread through his chilled body.

"Thank you," he told her and handed the cup back.

She took a moment to look at the weather before replying. Storm clouds grew darker to the east, promising more rain. She stuck her hand outside, watching the droplets roll down the back of her hand.

"Quite the odd collection we have, eh?" he said.

"What's bothering you? I've heard all of your stories," she teased. "Seems there were plenty of times you managed more with worse."

"Some stories are only meant to build the legends. You should know that."

"So the hero of Kressel Tine didn't exist?"

He shot her a menacing glare. "You damned well know that's true."

"Lighten up. I was just kidding," she spat back. "What's wrong with you? Talk to me, Grelic."

He watched the rain. Lightning danced through the murky sky. "None of this makes any sense. Something sinister is behind our problems. Dark times are approaching. Don't trust any of these people, Kialla. One of them is a spy."

She immediately thought of Pregen. His mercenary ways could easily have been compromised for the right price.

"How do you know?"

"We're being followed."

She resisted the urge to reach for her sword. Grelic gave her a knowing glance before he walked off into the rain. Her instincts took over. She scanned the tree line for any sign of their pursuer. She could feel it. That gnawing presence growing in the back of her mind. Danger called to her, whispering her name like a jaded lover. The warnings were subtle enough not to raise alarms. Yet. She looked up in time to see Grelic fade into the ground-clinging mist.

"Where is he going?" asked Ibram. The look on his face was the same as a child's pride at sneaking up on his father.

"To scout the land," she replied simply.

"By himself? What if something is out there? He shouldn't be alone," he exclaimed.

Grelic was a legend but even heroes needed help from time to time.

Kialla barred the door as Ibram made to follow. "No. He works better alone. Right now you'll just get in the way and draw attention to him. Let him work. Grelic knows what he's doing."

Mild rage flushed his face. "Why should I listen to a woman? What do you know of war?"

Kialla leveled her most menacing glare, cool and deadly. "Tell me, monk, what do you? How many hours have you spent on your knees praying while better men shed their blood in your defense? Don't speak to me of war."

Ibram clenched his teeth and stormed back to the fire. He stayed silent for the longest time, letting the flames lick up his hatred. When he couldn't stand it any longer he made to get up and confront her.

"She probably just saved your life," Pregen said calmly in a low voice. Ibram spun. "I can take care of myself, thief."

Pregen shrugged. "I'm sure you can. I'm also sure Grelic could kill you before you even knew he was near. There's no complacency among people like us. This isn't your precious Order of Harr. Even that young lady in the doorway has killed men. You don't really think you're a match for her, do you? We were each picked for a reason, Ibram. Let the warriors fight the battles."

"I'm just as good as any of you," Ibram mumbled, much of the fire drained from his voice. He slumped down. The absence of anger left him cold.

Kialla winced from the hurt tone in his voice. Part of her wanted to say something. To let him know it wasn't personal. The rest, the vast majority, knew his inexperience and brashness was going to get one of them hurt or worse. She wasn't about to let that happen.

The storm picked up.

Grelic returned shortly. He was soaked to the bone. The dangerous look in his eyes was enough to keep any question unasked. He took a seat in front of the fire and made a futile attempt at getting warm. Chills wracked his massive body. Dirty water dribbled down his face and neck. It made an evil hiss whenever it struck the hungry flames. His face was sour. The quiet reminder of why he didn't like living in Thrae. Only Kialla noticed the speckle of blood on the cuff of his sleeve.

They waited just long enough for Grelic to lose the chill and change into dry clothes before heading back out. His mood darkened with the sky, as if the trek through the forest had wrought an undeniable change in him. The giant let his horse stretch his legs. Together they led the company down the winding forest road.

"What did you find?" Kialla asked him once she was sure they wouldn't be overheard.

Grelic's eyes flittered across his field of vision. "We are being followed. There were horse tracks running parallel to our course. I tracked them back for a while. Whoever it may be, they're no pathfinders. There were too many signs. Broken branches. Footprints in the mud. I searched as long as I dared and then doubled back."

She knew him better. "The blood?"

Grelic laughed. "I thought it had all washed away. That is all that was left of a Goblin scout."

Kialla frowned. "Goblins don't ride horses and there are no werebeasts in Thrae the last I knew. Who's on the horse?"

"A good question," Grelic replied. "I found the Goblin about a hundred meters into the trees. I think he was watching both us and the rider. He never saw my dagger though. I never found the rider or any other Goblin."

An uneasy feeling was growing inside her. "Goblins never travel alone. It looks like the spy Rentor warned us about already knows our route. Do you still think it's one of us?"

He frowned. "I don't trust a single one of them if that's what you mean."

"Should we try to catch him?" she asked. The idea of being pursued all the way to Gend troubled her greatly.

"No. I want to get to Eline as soon as possible and out of this weather. A good night's rest will do us all some good. From there we strike for Gend and discover the truth to this madness."

They rode west, each lost in vastly different and disturbing thoughts.

Three full days and nights it rained. The mood of the quest worsened, spoiled by foul weather and constant unspoken hostility. By dusk of the third day they arrived at the small city of Eline. Farm houses and freshly plowed fields alerted the group and soon the outlying areas turned to houses and shops. Smoke columned up from chimneys, suggesting warmth and a place to rest. Grelic had been here before, only the last time there hadn't been a crude wall or towers. He halted them just outside of range for the archers standing guard.

"Mind your tongues here. These people are spooked by what happened in Gend. Don't mention our quest or where we're from," he said and his iron gaze fell on Fitch. "It's going to be hard enough trying to blend in for the short time we're here. Stay in your rooms as much as you can."

Ibram's face tightened as if to speak but he stayed quiet.

"Let's go," Grelic ordered.

The tiny band hailed the guards and rode to the gates of Eline.

Notam cursed himself for letting Cron drink so much. The sun was almost at its peak before he groaned out of bed. Seldom the heavy drinker, he found the taste heavy and bitter. Though it fit the generally dour people of Thrae, he preferred a light berry-flavored wine. That alone made him a rarity amongst the ranks.

Head pounding, Notam felt his stomach lurch. The color drained from his face as his body revolted against the alcohol forced into it. He walked across the courtyard on unsteady legs to the steps of the command building. The semi-light of the sun trying to break through the ever-present veil of grey clouds sent lightning bolts into his eyes. He dreaded climbing the short flight of steps leading up to the front doors. Twin lion statues flanking the steps were uncharacteristically intimidating this afternoon. Notam tried to ignore their unflinching glare and climbed.

The sentry on duty snapped to attention. Notam winced as the steel-capped spear butt crashed onto the grey slate floor. He waved off the guard's diligence with an aggravated grimace and struggled on. As much as a stickler as he was for drill and ceremony, Notam clutched his aching head from the reverberations. He despised the guard now almost as much as Cron. Each footstep inside was as harsh as a thunderclap, turning the brightness in the hall into coffin nails.

Damn you, Cron. He winced again. Even thinking bad thoughts hurt. Notam slowly wound his way down the corridors until he reached the commander's quarters. He had every intention of giving the younger man a royal chewing. At least it sounded good. The sad reality was he allowed himself to succumb to temptation and peer pressure. Cron wasn't to blame. It was all his fault. *Water. I need water and a pot to vomit in.*

He entered without knocking and felt his mouth drop. He came in expecting to find the captain behind his desk going over reports, patiently awaiting his arrival. Instead Notam noted the thin coat of dust on the polished maple chair. The desk was completely cleared except for a small parchment. Notam hesitantly unrolled it and read. His strength fled as he dropped down into Cron's chair and stared blankly out of the window. The parchment crumbled in his hand.

"Damned fool, what have you done?" he whispered to the walls.

SIXTEEN

Eline

The ambience of the Stag and Bow's common room left much to be desired. After three miserable days on the road west, they gained the sleepy village of Eline and were shocked by the lack of reception. People avoided making eye contact, instead shifting glances out of the corner of their eyes. Grelic and the others were met with open hostility and disdain, as if they were responsible for the bad times falling on Thrae.

They stumbled on a drunken Gnome who pointed them to the stables for a silver penny. The owner was a burly man who'd seen better days. He asked an exuberant amount to store the horses overnight, backing down only after Grelic rolled his shoulders and confronted the man. He even offered the Stag and Bow as the best tavern in town.

"Food's not so good but it's the kind of place folks go to avoid questions," he'd told them.

Pregen, of all of them, immediately complained of the lack of standards once they entered. Grelic held up a finger and scowled. The discussion ended abruptly. They paid for their rooms, price of dinner included, and changed into dry clothes. Baths were made available to each, for an additional fee of course, but they were able to wash the last three days worth of misery off before Grelic collected them to head downstairs.

The serving maid, an older woman slightly overweight and with a rosy complexion, brought them a platter of roast fowl, day-old dark bread, and a quarter wedge of white cheese. Ale and water were brought in large pewter mugs. Kialla was most appreciative for the table close to the fireplace. As much as she liked to present the toughened image, she still enjoyed being spoiled by the simple pleasures in life. They ate in relative silence. Spirits were too dampened for much banter. Then she noticed something peculiar.

"You're not drinking?" she asked Grelic.

The giant shook his head, so slight it barely moved. His eyes never stopped scanning the gathered crowds. "Not until we see this task finished. It is too dangerous now. Besides, a few weeks without ale will only make it taste better when that golden liquid hits my lips again!"

"I was thinking more that it would do you some good to stay away," she said as a not-so-subtle reminder that his drinking was what landed them in this situation in the first place.

Ibram finished his meal and wiped his mouth with a satisfying grin. The monks of the Order lived well enough but there was something to be said for a properly cooked meal in a proper tavern. Belly filled, sleep threatened to consume him. He frowned. Such behavior would have been acceptable for a monk but not for a warrior in the defense of Thrae. He owed it to himself to prove his worth. Ibram concealed a knowing smirk. Soon Grelic would understand his value and start treating him like an equal.

He stifled a yawn and stretched. "Where do we go now?"

Grelic eyed him questioningly. "To bed. We've a long journey ahead and will have need of strength before the end."

Pregen laughed. The pleasant sound was quickly subsumed by the disorganized clamor from the rest of the crowds. Embarrassed and frustrated by the continual lack of respect, Ibram angered quickly. He only wanted to make a positive addition to the group, why couldn't they understand?

"Don't be so quick to anger," Grelic cautioned. "You'll have plenty of chances to get yourself killed. Patience, boy."

Ibram looked to Fitch for support but the broken villager had already passed out.

Kialla intervened, recognizing the foolishness in Ibram's eyes. "Look at it from our point of view, Ibram. We face an unknown enemy and you haven't been tested in battle. The only way for this quest to succeed is by each of us doing our parts. We cannot afford to jump into a situation blind, no matter how eager we are."

He tried his best to listen, to ignore the sting and implications of her words.

Grelic wasn't going to wait for him to argue further. "Look, boy, I'm going to lay it out clear. Up until last week you were a monk, a peacekeeper for lack of anything else. I've killed more men than years you've lived. This isn't a game and no one is going to hold your hand. But I will not let you bring us down in ruin simply because you want to make a statement. There is a fine line between heroic and just plain stupid. Wait. Be patient and learn from what we can teach you. Blood and death are coming."

Ibram finally gave in. Tears soaked his eyes. His pride stung. His feelings were battered. Doubt crept in as he struggled to maintain some semblance of control. Inner demons mocked his rationale. Ibram's private war threatened to tear him apart yet he didn't know who he could trust to go to. He closed his eyes and whispered a prayer to Harr, hoping his god would forgive his ignorance and transgressions.

"Entertaining as this is," Pregen cut into the awkward silence, "I would like to know why we're just going to sit in this drab, out-of-the-way tavern instead of pushing forward. Brother Ibram had the right of it. Time is against us. We should move while the enemy is off guard. Waiting will only work against us."

Grelic ignored his initial instinct to crush the man's pretty face. "We are going to wait. In the morning I want you and Fitch to buy enough supplies for two weeks. Ibram will see to the horses. Make sure they are ready to go quickly. Kialla, see if you can find a small wagon. An extra mount to carry additional supplies at the least."

Pregen shot him a bored look. "Exactly what will you be doing?"

"I don't know yet."

The room erupted in song and cheer before the argument could develop. Dozens of well wishers poured through the doors to celebrate the spring wedding of the local crofter. Kialla smiled, forgetting the brewing mistrust between the group. The image of the bride quickly flashed by. She sighed, wondering when it would be her turn. No one noticed Ibram slip off during the confusion. Not even Pregen, with his deceptively shifting gaze, at least he never admitted it later. Nor did they notice the pair of uncomfortably familiar eyes staring at them from across the room.

Ibram breathed in the damp night air and felt refreshed. It stopped raining hours ago but the sky remained foul under a blanket of angry clouds. Darkness crowded in around the flickering street lights. He was reminded of the terrible power of the night, barely noticing he was the only one out. Smaller villages often thrived on the fear of the dark, a trait he found unhealthy at best. Monsters and such truly did roam the night.

He walked for a time, content in his solitude. Skipping mud holes and puddles occupied his thoughts, blissfully stealing him from his ordeals. The sword tapping his thigh after each step was both reassuring and troublesome. His deepest heart told him he was meant to be a warrior. His mind, however, refused to let Grelic's words go. They weren't spoken in anger or meant to belittle him, but the bite went deep. Ibram sucked in a deep breath and continued on with reinforced determination. He wasn't going to let the giant beat him back.

"Oh thank the gods! Sir, please help!" an old lady cried, hobbling out from a twisting alley. "Please sir. Be kind. It's my daughter. She's in trouble."

A fire sparked. Ibram saw purpose. A chance to prove his worth. "Look at me," he soothed. "I can't help you until you calm down and give me details."

She trembled beneath the frayed, grey cloak. He noticed how frail she was, as if time was slowly chipping away at her very being. Deep lines crisscrossed her hands and face. Dirty, stringy hair clung to her cheeks, reminding him of a wet dog. Broken nails turned her hands into claws. She had an odd odor about her, as if she enjoyed living in filth. Warnings went off in his head. This woman wasn't right. But before he could disengage she was half dragging him down the alley.

"Come, come. She is this way," the woman urged.

Ibram felt a liking to his own grandmother. She walked with hunched shoulders, her back threatening to break any second. Soon he was lost in the daunting corridors of Eline. While nothing like Kelis Dur, everything in Eline looked exactly the same. An odd sensation tickled the back of his neck. He felt like he was being watched.

"Slow down, old one. It's too dark here and I don't know my way," he called out just as her robed figure disappeared into the shadows.

Ibram's hand drifted to his sword. His senses screamed.

"Where are you?" he called out. "I can't see you. Come back!"

The odd hissing noise was so subtle he nearly missed it.

"You'll see soon enough," her voice crooned from the night.

Ibram swore the voice came from directly above. He took one cautious step though instinct warned to walk away. The crisp, metallic sound of his sword being jerked from the scabbard was virtually swallowed by the night. Thunder rumbled in the distance, menacing and threatening. His palms felt slick, insecure. Ibram envisioned dropping his sword at the wrong moment. He tightened his grip to compensate, so hard his knuckles bled white. Doubt and fear rose from the night to assail his composure.

Ibram had spent what felt like years secretly practicing his love for the sword. It was only against wooden obstacles or in play with some of the younger monks with a passion for adventure. Grelic had the right of it. He'd never faced another opponent in combat. Didn't know the feeling of his steel plunging into flesh or the reliving of that moment every time he closed his eyes. The true test of a nightmare was living through it. Ibram was about to begin his walk down the hard path of a warrior.

He muttered a soft prayer to Harr and dropped into a fighting stance. Shadows stirred to his left and right. The enemy leapt at him. Grey-brown figures lashed out, driving him back. Pain lanced across his lower ribs. He'd been cut. A venomous hiss burned his ears. Hot blood trickled down his flank. Ibram barely made out the shapes of his attackers. A blow from the right caught him across the thigh, gouging a small chunk of flesh away. He lashed out, desperate to strike back. The air whistled from the strength of an empty blow.

Overextended, he pitched forward. An attacker jumped and planted both feet in the small of his back. Ibram crashed down on broken rocks and old tree bark. The force of the impact knocked his sword loose. Struggling to catch his breath, he wiped the blood from his eyes and drew his dagger. Ibram managed to roll away a split second before a second attacker landed where his head had been. With no time, Ibram heaved his dagger and was rewarded with a fleshy thud. The attacker screamed an unholy sound and flashed palely. Ibram stared into the empty eyes of his foe and reeled from shock.

Shriveled brown skin crawled in the glow. Long arms and legs gave the creature a gangly appearance. The stench of decomposing flesh choked the air. Ibram swallowed his fears and dashed to his sword. He rose slowly, as if every muscle threatened rebellion. His breath came in ragged gasps from the strange combination of fear and excitement. Back against the wall of the closest building, he waited for what promised to be agonizing death.

The Dwim ripped the dagger from its chest and wailed with a mournful hiss. Others emerged from the night, slowly creeping towards Ibram. He gagged from the overpowering stench. Death had come. Ibram knew he lacked the skill to fight the undead. His heart cried out at the injustice. The Dwim closed in. They smelled his fear. The scent of his blood awakened primal urges buried deep within. Sickly ichors dripped from thousands of wounds. Vapors clung to them in miasmic clouds.

Ibram found no consolation from wounding one. The monster kept coming, ignorant of the fact it wept puss and foul liquids. His eyes shifted from wall to wall. Four Dwim lurched in, penning him against the slime-slickened wall. There was no way he could defeat so many. He considered praying again, though Harr hadn't listened to his earlier pleas. Father Seldis once suggested he prayed for the wrong reasons. It seemed ridiculous at the time. What god ignored the cries of his followers? Ibram frowned, knowing the answer he refused to admit. He raised his sword and prepared to die.

Violent green light, bright and filled with vibrancy, exploded the darkness with the arrogance of unnatural fire. Two of the Dwim were incinerated instantly. Ibram threw up his arm to protect his eyes as the very strength fled his body. For a moment he stood dazed in the after effects of the blast. His hearing felt muted, muffled. Tiny spots danced behind his eyelids. The sound of steel tearing tortured flesh became crisp. As did the ensuing guttural groan. Another Dwim, eviscerated from neck to groin, fell dead at his feet. Darkness reclaimed the alley.

Ibram awoke with a low groan. He tried to move but the amount of physical pain wracking his body changed his mind. He swore a group of Dwarves were slamming his skull with their hammers while singing a baleful dirge. Ibram passed back into unconsciousness, waking several times during the night. Each time lasted but a moment, hardly enough for him to look through the fog at the group of concerned faces staring worriedly back.

He became lost in the dark, wandering down empty paths leading to an obscure dream. Reality danced away as if fearful to his touch. His nightmares became so violent only a god could withstand them. Strange and deadly beasts intent on rendering Malweir to ashes struggled to break loose. Ibram watched helplessly as the world barreled towards oblivion. Malevolent forces battled for his soul, desperately trying to rip it from his flesh. He resisted, but at great cost.

Good and evil surrounded him to wage war. Ibram lay in stupor, unable to defend himself. A shadow stole his gaze, hovering over him protectively. The outline of a man took shape, bathed in an almost imperceptible blue tinge. He reached out for Ibram's hand. The monk faded as their hands touched.

Ibram awoke fully, eyes searching for his savior. He knew the man was Father Seldis but he couldn't find him. Finally his gaze fell on a very old man with a sad face.

"Alive I see," the old man commented. "Good. Malweir has need of men like you in these troubled times. Rest now. Old Dakeb will take care of everything."

Unconsciousness prevented Ibram from replying.

SEVENTEEN

Dakeb

"Much about your quest is not what it appears," Dakeb said to the anxious group. "The attack on your friend tells me much and I fear you have the right of it. Time is now your enemy."

Grelic rubbed his chin thoughtfully. "Time was never in our favor, but what new ill can possibly befall us? We know of the treachery in the palace. We've been followed since leaving Kelis Dur and now these monsters have come out of some childhood nightmare to haunt us. What do you know of the future you're not telling?"

"The future or the past? A very difficult topic. Both are forever linked, inescapable of each other. Tell me, Grelic," he paused to smile at the big man's shock. "Where does good end and evil begin? Is there resolution or just an odd, grey matter? Even the most evil deeds can be wreathed with good intentions."

Pregen slapped an aggravated palm to his forehead. "That's all well and fine, old man. Now explain to us what your little diatribe has to do with our quest. We want to know what attacked Ibram."

Dakeb looked hurt. "It has everything to do with the future. Dark armies are preparing for war. Listen closely and you can hear the drumbeats. The creatures that attacked your friend are the first sign of an old power rising. They are the Dwim, a twisted ruin of human flesh created in the charnel pits of the dark Mages. The Dwim have but one purpose, to kill. They revel in the feel of fresh blood and the vibrancy of fear. They will not stop until their prey is destroyed."

"I thought all of the dark Mages were killed long ago," Kialla said. Not even her normal rugged façade masked her growing fear.

Dakeb slowly shook his head. "No. One remains. His name I shall not speak here for the enemy has many eyes and ears."

Fitch stared nervously at the old man. That familiar sadness, ever present since the night Gend was destroyed, threatened to consume him. He wanted to find a cold place to hide.

"You make it sound as if there is no hope," Grelic said.

Dakeb smiled. "There is always hope so long as the heart remains true. That's the reason I've come. Yes. To bring you hope."

Pregen bit back a laugh. "What hope can you bring, grandfather? You've seen too many winters and not enough sun."

Dakeb closed his eyes and began muttering in the old tongues. He stamped a heavy foot and the fire in the room went out. Darkness stretched out to consume them. Then a blinding flash, forcing them to shy away and shield their eyes. When their vision cleared, Dakeb stood in the center of a ball of blue light. His eyes were red and foreboding, almost lost in the centuries of wrinkles and wild-looking hair. He had become power. Slowly the magic faded, leaving him simply Dakeb.

"Now that I have your undivided attention I will introduce myself. My name is long and old like the wind blowing across the Jebel Desert. Those who know me call me Dakeb."

From places he didn't know existed, Fitch asked, "Dakeb the Mage?"

Dakeb stared at Fitch, an unreadable look quickly turning into a smile. "The same. There was a time when I was the head of my order. Much has changed since then. Dark times have fallen upon Malweir."

"You speak of hope and doom in the same context," Grelic said suspiciously.

"The eye of the beholder," Dakeb said and shrugged.

He looked old again, an unassuming grandfather trying to see another winter. Heavy lines crackled his face. Shoulder-length grey hair fell loosely from his thinning scalp. He had the look of a man unaccustomed to eating. Not very tall, Dakeb was well known across the face of the world. From Averon to the dragon kingdoms across the sea.

"Where am I?" Ibram asked unexpectedly from the small cot across the room.

Dakeb grinned and ambled over. "Fear not, young follower of Harr. The world is yet in order. Your mind heals and the poison of the Dwim has left your body. Rest now."

Ibram stared up at the half-crazed man and felt calm. *Could it be the same man from my dreams?* "Who are you?"

His throat was dry, his voice hoarse and scratchy.

"Rest now," Dakeb insisted. "We shall speak later."

Ibram nodded, finding the similarities between this stranger and Father Seldis uncanny. When he dreamed, he was back in the monastery.

"Why did the Dwim attack him?" Grelic demanded.

"A good question. Perhaps they sensed something significant about him. I don't know. The more pertinent question would be whom do they serve? My mind is clouded of late. Whatever brews remains just past the edge of my vision."

"Perhaps they saw an opportunity and took it," Kialla suggested.

"Either way we must be cautious in the coming days," Dakeb replied.

Pregen jerked his head out of his hands. "We?"

"Maybe he can help," Kialla offered before Dakeb had the chance to reply.

"Or maybe he's one of the enemy. Am I the only one who finds this entire scenario too convenient? We barely trust each other and this old man wanders into Ibram precisely at the moment he's being attacked by supernatural forces? Let's not forget his claim of being the last of the Mages."

Realizing his point, they turned and faced Dakeb.

"He has a point," the old man said.

"That's it?" Kialla asked.

"What else needs to be said? If you recall, Mage-kind did their best to help all of the races of Malweir."

Pregen muttered, "Before nearly killing them all."

A flicker of annoyance passed his face like fast-moving clouds. "I am the last man who needs to be reminded of the past, thief. Oh yes. I know you all as surely as I know myself. I have been drawn here for reasons I have yet to discover. Forget the Mage Wars. Ipn Shal is in ruins. The grandeur and elegance of that time has long faded. What you see is all that remains of a better age." Sadness draped his words.

"I don't know or care about Ipn Shal unless the ghosts of your brethren plan on helping," Grelic cut in before matters escalated out of control. His patience was quickly waning.

Dakeb's eyes turned hostile. "You don't want that sort of help. The dead are best left to themselves. There is enough evil already at work here. Regardless, I can help. I know the secret ways and the ancient words. Young Ibram can attest to that. There is no promise I can give you of life, however. Such decisions are beyond my grasp. What I can offer is a better chance of success."

"You're not telling us everything," Kialla accused. "This is supposed to be a simple reconnaissance job. Even the king said…"

"King Rentor has no idea of the true danger he's in. Don't you see? The Dwim are being recreated after all these long years. Only a dark Mage has such power."

Pregen was tired of talk of Mages and their ilk. Valuing his life over the others, he threw up his hands. "I didn't sign on this adventure to fight magic or monsters. I'm leaving now."

No one moved to stop him. He swore the old man actually smirked. *No matter. I'm not going to throw my life away for a cause I don't believe in. Let the fools have their day. I want no part of it.*

"Leave or stay, the choice is yours. Though I will not guarantee you survive the night. The Dwim already know you are here. They will hunt you just as surely as they tried to kill young Ibram here," Dakeb cautioned.

Pregen scowled but sat back down.

"How many Dwim are there and where do they come from?" Grelic asked.

"Difficult to say. The furnaces of Druem have not been active very long."

"Druem?" Fitch asked, overcoming his fear. He'd heard that name before, but where?

"The dead mountain in the heart of the Deadlands."

Grelic frowned. "Men do not go into the Deadlands, Dakeb. Nor do they return."

"We must continue on to Gend first. The secrets we need to discover are there," Dakeb answered.

Grelic rose abruptly and reached for his riding cloak.

"Where do you think you're going?" Pregen asked with undisguised suspicion.

Grelic headed for the door. "There is someone I need to talk to."

The door slammed shut behind him.

By noon the poison was out of Ibram's system. The numbing sensation from being touched by the Dwim slowly faded. Color returned to his face and, after a hearty meal of lamb stew and bread, he was ready to ride again. The others went about their tasks, each eager to be off. No one went alone for fear of another Dwim attack. Dakeb sat alone in their room patiently awaiting their return.

Dusk arrived and there was still no sign of Grelic. They went down to the common room to eat their meal in awkward silence. The Mage watched each, studying their mannerisms and behavior. Mistrust threatened to ruin them. Disappointed, he recalled an earlier time when he was faced with similar divisions. He needed to find a way to bring them together quickly, before it was too late.

"I don't like this," Pregen said, breaking the silence. "He's been gone for too long."

Kialla wiped the drop of sauce from the corner of her mouth. "Don't worry about him. Grelic's been doing this for a long time. I trust him with my life."

"That's not what I doubt," he replied.

"Then what? Speak plainly, man," Grelic boomed from behind.

The thief dropped his gaze down to his cup of wine.

"Don't be shy now. I heard your words. Say them to my face."

Pregen slowly raised his gaze until he was staring directly into Grelic's steel eyes. "Fine. Where were you all day? We accomplished our tasks and returned yet you've been gone since dawn. Alone. We're being hunted and you disappear for an entire day. That doesn't sit right with me, Grelic."

He exhaled sharply. Pregen was a thief and assassin but no fool. Grelic, on the other hand, was the most dangerous man in Thrae, if not all of Malweir. Death rested in his massive hands for any foolish enough to invoke it.

Grelic laughed in response. "If that is your only fear you can relax. I was out getting information about recent happenings in the area."

"What did you find out?" Fitch asked.

"Strange tracks in the forests. Whispered movements in the night." He would say no more. Not here.

Dakeb leaned closer. "How long have they been going on?"

"Only a few days. It looks like they started the day we left Kelis Dur."

The Mage quickly recognized the implications. "I didn't know the situation was already so perilous. We must depart at once."

"Travel at night? With those things out there? You'll send us all to slaughter," Pregen protested.

"No," Ibram said. "I've seen his power. Dakeb can protect us."

"Protect? No. But I can certainly help. We must leave before dawn. I have a terrible sense of foreboding for this night," he replied.

"When?"

Dakeb glanced at the frosted window. "As soon as possible."

That was enough for Grelic. "Pack your things. We leave at the mid of night."

The thunder of hobnailed boots echoed angrily across the valley. Heavy undergrowth hindered the Goblin troop's march, forcing them to run to avoid being entangled. Whips cracked. Goblins snarled and spit. They uttered foul curses in their broken language as the whip master howled with delight. Soon enough they cleared the outer edges of Qail Werd, the lone mighty forest in northern Malweir and skirted the shores of Vorshir Lake. In ten days they would follow the Sibit River south and be at the gates of Kelis Dur. Their enemy wouldn't be able to react in time. But Kelis Dur wasn't their goal. Their master had another, better target in mind. Smaller, softer. The Goblins continued to run with murder in their hearts.

A rank odor gagged the night where they passed. Crows and buzzards followed their course, lusting for a fresh meal. Laughing at the birds, the Goblins ran faster. There'd be time enough for a feast of flesh, but not theirs. Somewhere to the south was the ripe and fertile flesh of a small group of men who needed to die.

"Faster, dogs! There's killing to be done," growled the whip master.

The sharp leather cracked again, lashing their armored backs. The Goblins picked up the pace.

EIGHTEEN

Gwarmoran

A bank of heavy clouds rolled in just past dusk and covered the northern kingdom in stifling darkness. Warm winds ground freshly budding branches together with a vile scratching sound. The Elves whispered how forests laughed at the arrogance of men. The trees had seen generations of mortals come and go without lasting effect. Fire and axe, malice and necessity drove the trees away from lands long theirs. Here, in the far north of Malweir, did they finally find a home.

Tonight they watched the small group of men and one woman steal between their trunks. The band moved with deliberate haste. The looks on their faces suggested fear, apprehension. Enemies could be anywhere. According to both Ibram and Dakeb, the Dwim moved like wraiths in the blackness. The horses snorted, feeling the wrong sensation lingering in the air. Grelic knew the game. He'd been a veteran player for decades. Tonight the giant warrior watched the darkness with mistrust. The hair on his arms stood on prickled flesh. He swore the trees were laughing.

Kialla pulled her cloak tighter to keep the chill out. Unease grew thick around her. Frowning, she asked Grelic, "Can you see anything?"

Grelic didn't respond. His eyes never stopped moving. The muscles on his chest tightened reflexively. One hand held the reins while the other danced over the hilt of his broadsword.

"They are close," he whispered after a time. "Yet when I think I'm about to find them I can feel them pulling back. Hiding in the night."

"I don't understand how they discovered us so quickly," she confessed through an exaggerated sigh.

Grelic paused to look back at the blackened shapes of his comrades. "One of us is a spy. I've been warning it from the beginning."

Which one? Kialla wasn't bothered so much by that as she was by the Dwim and whatever else Dakeb's tales of crafted monsters managed to plant in her psyche. Images of wicked claws stretching out from the night to steal her from the saddle mocked her. She saw her body being ripped apart, her flesh devoured. Kialla suppressed a shudder. Foul thoughts served no purpose. She needed a clear mind if she expected to retain her wits for the coming struggle.

"The enemy has many eyes. We must be cautious." Grelic stiffened. An unfamiliar scent caught his attention.

"I think it's past time for caution. We need to move faster and stick to the sunlight," she whispered.

He was about to respond when he heard it. The faint howling on a distant wind. Wolves! There was still time, for the call was yet far away.

Fitch immediately snapped awake. Growing up in the wilderness, he'd seen his share of wolves. By no means an expert, he knew enough to tell that this call was unlike any wolf he'd ever encountered. Fitch edged closer to Grelic, still unsure whether that would be any safer. The howling sang again, much closer and from the opposite direction. The group was being surrounded, the circle drawing tighter.

"Mage," Grelic called.

Dakeb came up alongside. A thoughtful look twisted his face. "They're not wolves. It's much worse."

"As long as they don't have Dwim with them," Kialla said bravely.

The old Mage half smiled. "Be careful what you ask for, dear. The night is full of many horrors. We're being stalked by Gwarmoran. Dark wolves from ancient Straedor."

"There are no dark wolves in Thrae," Grelic said.

Dakeb shook his head. "The way is closed to me. Something sinister drives the winds. I feel it coursing against us."

Another howl. This time from their right. One of the horses snorted in fear. The trap was ready. Grelic instinctively drew his sword, prompting the others into action. Danger prickled him like a long lost friend. Grelic felt the familiar rush of adrenaline spark to life and take hold. This was the single most defining moment of his life. When sword met flesh in the unmistakable test of wills. He could pick out massive shapes moving in the trees. The dark wolves were upon them.

"When I give the word, flee," Grelic ordered.

A shadow darted by, darker than the night itself. Then another. He heard the first snarl almost directly in front of him. Then he saw the eyes. Dark red and baleful, gleaming hatred from the night. The dark wolf leapt. Grelic's sword was faster, if barely. Hot blood splashed horse and rider as he sliced through the wolf's belly. Razor-sharp claws raked across the top of Grelic's thigh as the wolf dropped dead in a heap of dripping viscera.

He grunted in pain and bellowed, "RUN!"

The rest of the group dashed forward. Kialla took the lead. Her auburn hair flowed behind her, giving an eccentric wildness. A final cry rose from the surrounding darkness. Grelic wasn't sure but he counted at least a dozen echoes. The pack burst into action, rivaling the speed of horse. Fear drove both horse and wolf. A wolf darted past Kialla with an easy stride, forcing Grelic to frown. They were being herded.

Onward they ran, unable to stop without risking being torn to shreds. The wind picked up. Bloodlust boiled. Branches slapped riders while vines and underbrush tripped horses. Spider webs caught on their faces. They ran harder, lashing out at the wolves when one got too close. The terrain began to shift. Trees thinned out. The ground became rockier, threatening to hobble an unlucky horse. The remnants of last year's leaves crunched underfoot.

Grelic cursed his decision to leave at night. He was unfamiliar with this part of Thrae. A moment later he recognized what was happening. The dark wolves were forcing them into a steep ravine. Instinct screamed for him to stop and turn while there was still time. Dark wolves lined the ravine walls, prowling along the banks as the group kept running.

"Mage!" Grelic shouted again.

Dakeb urged his mount forward.

"This is a trap. Do something," Grelic ordered.

"We must stop running or I can do nothing!" Dakeb shouted back.

"If we stop we die!"

Left without choices, Grelic pushed them harder. He looked back, surprised to find the wolves with almost casual indifference. Gradually the dark wolves backed off, as if trying to catch their breath before the slaughter began. Grelic struggled to imagine what the others were thinking. Fitch was obviously scared to death. The thrumming bow string and successive scream broke his thoughts. A dark wolf dropped with one of Kialla's arrows in its heart. *Two down. But how many more are left?*

"Hold them back for as long as you can. I only need a few moments," Dakeb called once they came to a halt at the large bowl marking the end of the ravine.

Grelic wheeled about and prepared to attack just as another wolf knocked Pregen from his horse. Wolf and man landed in a bruised mass. Teeth, claws, and the occasional glint of steel in the moonlight could be seen. Two more wolves, easily the size of ponies, darted in to finish Pregen. Blood spattered their black fur. Another arrow feathered the nearest wolf's back as it ripped its muzzle out of Pregen's horse.

Unsure if Pregen was dead, Grelic slipped from his horse and entered the fight. His first blow nearly severed the first wolf in half. The smell gagged him, tears clouding his vision. Blinding pain lanced the side of his head. Grelic staggered. Three wolves moved in before he could recover. Grelic's horse bolted. He shook his head furiously in an attempt to reduce the pain and dropped into a fighting stance. His muscles loosened, fingers flexing on his sword. The three wolves circled at a distance, unsure of who was the true predator. Grelic shifted his weight and lunged. The nearest wolf shied away, giving him the opportunity he needed to attack.

Grelic dipped low and lashed out to his right. The second wolf charged and he stepped into it. Sword sliced through flesh and bone, hacking off one of the wolf's hind legs. The dark wolf's scream was high-pitched and long, reminiscent of a baby. The third wolf attacked before the rope of arterial blood splashed across the ground. Talon-like claws ripped through Grelic's cloak and tunic, slicing into his back. Grelic fell under the weight of the leaping wolf. Hot breath burned his neck. Saliva dripped like acid. He never saw the arrow whistle into the wolf's neck. The dead weight crushed him, knocking his breath away. It took all of his strength to throw the corpse off and rise on one knee.

Moonlight broke through the steadily thinning layer of clouds, illuminating the battlefield for the first time. Grelic's blood ran cold as he counted the number of wolves surrounding them. If the Mage didn't do something soon they were all dead. Dakeb had reined in his horse and dismounted. The old Mage drew his walking stick from the saddlebag and began tracing obscure patterns in the mud. The sounds of battle heightened, more ferocious. Dakeb worked faster.

Steam began to rise. A sulfuric odor tainted the night sky, mixing with the iron smell of blood. Dakeb chanted under his breath. He waved his arms in centuries' old rituals. Patterns and movements rehearsed, choreographed in a forgotten time. The ground beneath him took on a chilling glow. One by one the symbols charged to life, becoming lines of power. A throbbing hum vibrated the length of the ravine. High winds flared, instantly replaced with complete stillness. Malweir itself answered Dakeb's plea.

His eyes rolled over white. Dry lightning crackled across the horizon. A distant volcano spit ash and brimstone. Dakeb chanted louder. All around him the air dried. Moisture evaporated into artificial lifelessness. Fitch staggered under the raw feel of so much power, even as he managed to plunge his dagger into a dark wolf's eye. Dozens of wolves rushed across the valley towards the ravine. Nauseous yellow light enveloped the Mage.

And then, abruptly, the chanting stopped. Dead silence gripped the ravine. The Gwarmoran hesitated, recognizing the threat. They hadn't tasted Mage blood since the wars, when dark Mages used them to hunt down their enemies. The largest wolf howled in a mixture of pleasure and fury. It glared across the ravine at the Mage. The last Mage. The dark wolf snarled in unsuppressed delight. Dakeb opened his eyes when the wolves were fifty meters away. They ran hard and would be on him in seconds, ignoring all of the others. Dakeb smiled and raised his walking stick above his head.

Forty meters.

Lightning licked down to strike the stick. Dakeb didn't flinch. Flecks of saliva flung from the wolves' mouths.

Thirty meters.

Dakeb lowered his stick and pointed it towards the wolves. They howled in response.

Twenty meters.

Dakeb took a final breath. He could almost see himself in their eyes.

Ten.

"Melikali e abas!" he roared.

Thunder clapped and violence crashed down around him. Mage light spit from his stick, incinerating all of the wolves unable to twist away. Colorless ash and powder drifted lazily to the ground. Static electricity made Dakeb's hair stand on end, lending him a demonized look. He walked forward, lashing out at the great wolves. The ravine quickly changed, undulating and breaking from the raw power coursing through.

Gwarmoran paced uncertainly. Their leader had been incinerated. Pencil-thin lashes of bright yellow light continued to attack them. Some died. Others managed to duck behind a rock or thick tree. They snarled and spit, trying to decide whether to attack or flee. Dakeb didn't relent. Bolt after bolt crashed into the wolves. Trees exploded. Rocks melted. The sky filled with rage.

Halfway across the field, Ibram struggled for his life. Already bested by the Dwim, he needed to redeem himself or lose all good will in the others' eyes. Setting those thoughts aside proved more difficult than he had hoped. Doubt clung like shadows to his every move. Ibram struggled through it, using every move he had practiced in the lonely courtyards with less skilled monks. Slash, parry, block. None of his brethren fought like the Gwarmoran, however. He was hard pressed to stay on his feet as one of the larger wolves drove at him.

The wolf reared up on its hind legs and growled. Ibram took a step back and leveled his sword. A sudden whinny and charging horse snapped his concentration. The wolf turned its gaze on the larger target, affording Ibram the chance to duck in and drive his sword into the wolf's chest cavity. There was brief resistance before the combination of his weight and momentum pushed the blade in. The wolf's weight drove both of them to the ground.

And then it was over. Demoralized by the death of their leader, the surviving Gwarmoran backed away, disappearing into the night. A handful of bloodied corpses lay scattered across the ravine. Dozens of piles of ash lined the walls. Dakeb stalked through the middle of it, an ancient and reluctant warrior. Taking life, any life, sat ill with him. There was no pride in his deeds.

Decades of watching friends fall left him with an ever-present sense of grief and for a moment he feared the others were dead. His failure during the Mage War left him with too many ghosts and miserable dreams. He wasn't sure why, but his senses were at the point of overload. So much had happened, twisting and bending him to the point of breaking. Perhaps it all began with the eruption of Mount Zephues last autumn. That's when he first dreamed of the crystal of Tol Shere. The old Mage cursed his complacency. After all these long years he had almost come to believe the war was finally over. A body stirred, breaking his concentration.

Pregen groaned to his feet. Dried blood coated the side of his face. Leaning on his sword for support, the assassin looked around for the first time. His eyes strained to refocus in the pale afterglow of the Mage's assault. He'd been in his share of fights before, but nothing even remotely compared to the horror in the ravine. The very air stank of death.

"What did I miss?" he asked with a hoarse voice. "And why does it smell like burned dog?"

"Some questions are best left unasked. Leastwise while it's still dark. We have won a small victory but the Gwarmoran are not easily deterred. They will return, and in greater numbers," Dakeb cautioned.

Pregen rubbed his sore neck. "You've been a ball of joy from the moment we met, Mage. I can't wait to see what's next. Where are the others?"

Dakeb helped him up, once again leaning on his walking stick. "Come, let us find them and get out of here."

Together they set off through the ruined corpses and desiccated ground. Pregen was glad he'd been unconscious for most of the fight.

"No one man should have this power," he whispered when they passed a melted boulder. Clumps of charred flesh and fur stuck to it.

Dakeb sighed. "I agree. Which is why Mage-kind worked for generations to find new ways to detect and train potential magic wielders. Ultimately that power led to our ruin. We thought that by controlling it there would be less chaos in the land. Our arrogance led to blindness and eventual doom."

The thief knew better than to try and push the conversation. Besides, he had a healthy suspicion there would be plenty of time for such banter in the coming weeks. They finally stumbled upon Kialla climbing down from a fork in a great oak tree. Pregen smiled until he noticed the mangled corpse of a dark wolf hanging from the branches.

"They climb trees too?" he asked with a low whistle.

Kialla inspected the tear in her jerkin with a frown. She either didn't have an answer or didn't want to know. The others gradually came out of hiding. Fitch was his normal spasmodic self. He was the only one without a scratch, though his clothes were stained with dark blood and brain matter. Kialla spotted the stained dagger on the ground and smiled. Ibram was still alive. Blood and bits of roasted flesh clung to his face and chest. His eyes held a faraway look.

"Ibram!" Kialla exclaimed. "What happened to you?"

He turned slowly and gestured with his sword. They could discern five huge bodies lying in a crude circle where he just left. Dakeb reached him before he collapsed in the mud and placed a caring hand on his forehead.

"Thele bas I sanoo," he soothed.

Kialla leaned close. "Is he all right?"

"He's fine. I think the shock and exhaustion have finally caught up with him. It's not an easy transition from monk to warrior," Dakeb replied.

"It's not easy for anyone," she said. "Where's Grelic?"

The immediate area was clear of everything but bodies. They counted twenty of the Gwarmoran. The battle had been hard and they suffered from wounds and bruises. But there was no Grelic. Pregen felt his ire rising again. Kialla stalked the battlefield, stealing back those arrows that were salvageable.

It wasn't until Ibram groaned awake that Grelic came whistling back into the ravine, horses in tow.

"Grelic! We thought," she caught herself before making a fool.

Grelic forced a laugh. "Nonsense. Someone had to get the horses when the battle was ended. Wouldn't want to walk all the way to Druem, would you?"

He looked over the others, pleased to find them all alive. He gave the Mage a nod, expressing personal gratitude for the magic. Grelic had underestimated their situation, wrongly believing they had a chance at success. He now knew how wrong he was. There hadn't been any hope of surviving.

Grelic walked with an almost imperceptible limp. Another wound added to a growing list of scars and bumps. There were times, more often of late, when he wondered what kept him leading such a destructive lifestyle. The pains worsened and lasted longer with time. His memories were filled with foul deeds best left to fade away. He'd never chosen the life of a warrior. It was chosen for him. War was thrust upon him from childhood. What difference did it make if he *wanted* to or not? Most warriors died young, part of the unattainable dream of glory. Grelic preferred to pass with a head of grey hair. *More like stark white after tonight.*

"We must hurry," Dakeb urged.

The strain in his voice made Grelic believe him. The giant looked over his battered friends, stern eyes falling on Fitch Iane with suspicion. Was the unsuspecting villager the spy? Grelic grumbled softly. He just didn't know.

"Can everyone ride?" he asked, deciding brooding served no purpose.

Kialla wiped strands of blood and sweat-soaked hair from her face. "There is no choice. I feel others will come. Which direction?"

They stopped and stared at Dakeb. The old man offered a half smile. Much of his strength was gone, wasted during the battle. He was tired and needed to rest. Rest that, unfortunately, was a long time in coming. "West for now. When the sun rises we can adjust our course. If I recall correctly there are small hills filled with places to rest without worry from the Gwarmoran."

"How far?" Grelic asked as he climbed into his saddle.

The Mage thought for a moment. His recollection of Thrae was shaded at best. "Only a league or two I think."

That was good enough for the giant. "We move now."

Haggard and exhausted, the small band mounted and filed out of the ravine. The bodies of the dark wolves were already starting to rot. Grelic and Dakeb rode point until they entered the gently sloping hills the Mage had promised. It was well past midnight by the time Grelic called for a halt. He yawned mightily, cursing himself for getting so old so fast. Dakeb performed a hasty summoning spell to ensure the area was secure and the group took a thick copse of fir trees for shelter. One by one they drifted off. Grelic sat under the stars, watching the moon finally break free from the cloud cover. Pain wracked him, making it difficult to fall asleep. When sleep finally came it left him with one great, ponderous thought. What was yet to come?

NINETEEN

Bad Dreams

Howling winds kept screaming around him, growing stronger with each new gust. Rain poured down. The ground turned to thick mud. Water pooled around his ankles. Thunder and lightning dueled for control of the sky. Thick clouds of the purest black cloaked the night, choking off all life. Grelic stood his ground, pulling his cloak tighter to buffer what wind he could. His eyes were narrow, determined.

Grelic saw nothing of his surroundings. His senses were blinded and dulled. He didn't know where he was or how he'd gotten here. Lightning struck a few meters in front of him, knocking him down. Wiping the muck from his face, he briefly made out four obsidian monoliths spaced evenly in a circle around him. Each stone stood as tall as three men and was covered in strange symbols from a forgotten era. As quickly as he was allowed to view his surroundings, they dissolved back into darkness.

Swirling mists the color of disease emerged from nothing to lick at his ankles. Grelic balked and hastened to stand again. Brave as any man alive, he failed to understand how to combat what assailed him. Flesh and blood were one thing. This was entirely original. He tried to step back but his feet were rooted in place. Frustrated, Grelic drew his sword and waited. Perhaps death had finally come.

The mist reached up to touch him. It was cold, almost refreshing. Strange sensations spread through his body. An avid drinker, Grelic never once touched the lotus leaf or any other narcotic plant. This feeling was different, unlike anything he'd ever experienced or heard of. He felt relaxed. The sword suddenly felt heavy. He considered dropping it. His eyes struggled to stay open. Every time he blinked they stayed shut a little longer. Grelic swore he heard a woman's voice singing a soft lullaby on the wind.

Then he saw it. A slim figure moving towards him through the mist. He strained to make out who it was. Naked, the young woman stalked seductively up to him. Her slender hips swung provocatively with each step. Supple, firm breasts rose and fell with each breath. Grelic nodded in approval at her hardening nipples and patch of auburn hair between her legs. Only when her face came into view did he freeze with shock. Kialla. She smiled at him.

"Grelic, I've been waiting for this moment for so long," she cooed. "Come, make love to me. I need you, Grelic."

She was almost touching him now.

"I know you want me." Her finger traced the stubble on the curve of his jaw. "I've seen the way you look at me. Here I am. Take me. I'm yours."

He wanted to. Desires he hadn't felt in decades surged anew. His every secret passion ached to touch her smooth flesh. To inhale her womanly scent. To become one with her. Grelic's hand involuntarily inched towards her waist. She smiled. A flicker of something terrible lit her eyes. Grelic paused. The fog clouding his mind lifted slightly. Something sinister rippled beneath her golden-hued skin. He recoiled.

"What evil is this?"

She laughed as lightning raged. Heavier winds pelted him with rain and hail, forcing him to raise a hand to protect his face. Not a drop of rain touched her. Kialla stretched out her hands and tiny flames sprang to life in her palms. Grelic was sickened. He'd never been one to fear magic, until now. He doubled his grip on the comforting hilt of his sword and tensed in anticipation of the coming blow.

He had hardly moved when her skin began to change. Once a crisp golden brown, her skin was poisoned to the foulest shade of black. He watched with mute horror as her hair fell out in clumps and her scars cracked across her face and body. She transformed from supple and seductive to heavily muscled and threatening as lighting drove the sky light and dark. Her pleasant features dissolved into sheer evil.

Blinded suddenly by a nearby blast of lighting, Grelic wiped his eyes clear only to find her gone. In her place stood an enormous man with pale, grey skin. Coal black armor encased his torso, easily twice Grelic's size. Black pants and knee-high leather riding boots finished his ensemble. The hilt of a monstrous sword poked over his back even while he leaned on a crooked walking stick. Eyes of the coldest black stared back above a menacing smile.

"You know me," the stranger said. His voice was heavy and pronounced. The very ground trembled.

Grelic nodded. "Aye, Lord Death. Come to claim me already."

Lord Death threw back his bald head and laughed. A crow drifted down to perch on his shoulder and cawed. "No. This night I stalk another."

"Why have you come?" Grelic pressed, unready to give so easily.

"I come with warning. You are being used, hero. Dark forces drive you and your band. It was they who are responsible for summoning me." His visage darkened with anger. "As if I were a tool to be summoned at will. Fools. I, who has crushed worlds beneath my heel as if they were nothing more than dust."

Lord Death stalked away, pausing at the edge of vision, that blurred space where reality and dream mix. He pointed his crooked staff at Grelic and smiled. "We shall see one another soon, Grelic of Thrae."

Grelic awoke with a puzzled expression. His body was cold, as if death's presence lingered on his soul. A quick glance around the small camp showed the others were fast asleep. The sun was beginning to break, encasing the lands in that hazy blur of color and gloom. Grelic allowed himself to relax, if only a bit. There'd been no sign of the dark wolves since their battle early in the night though he doubted they'd given up the hunt so easily. Thoughts swirling through a thousand different scenarios, he pulled his sore body from his sleeping bag and stretched.

We'll see each other again soon enough.

He shuddered at the memory. "Damnation. I need a drink."

Trying to shake the disturbing images from his mind, he headed towards the nearby stream they'd crossed en route to the campsite. It seemed peaceful enough. The forested hills had an eerie calm to them, as if the world still slept. He stepped lightly over fallen branches and dead leaves, still crisp, hearing the stream before seeing it. Grelic sighed when he gazed upon the cool water. The area seemed peaceful enough. A large stag elk bowed to drink, pausing only to determine whether or not the big man was a threat.

Grelic ignored the elk and stripped his blood-stained jerkin before shoving his head in the water. It was ice cold, forcing him to catch his breath and keep his mouth shut before drinking half the stream. The water revived him, shaking loose old feelings of dread and leaving him cleansed. He jerked his head free. Water splashed and ran from his face and hair, dripping down his heavily muscled, scarred chest. He fondly traced a few of those scars, studying the white lines forever etched into his flesh. No time for nostalgia, Grelic tried to wash the blood from his jerkin.

"Mind if I join you?" Dakeb's tired voice sounded from behind.

Grelic frowned but kept working on his jerkin. "Feel free."

The old Mage sat with an exaggerated sigh. "An eventful evening, wouldn't you say?"

"You definitely proved your value. I don't know what would have happened without your magic," Grelic admitted after long moments of silence. He paused to skip a pebble across the undulating water.

"Magic I've not used in a long time. Mages aren't fondly remembered. We did nearly destroy the world after all."

Grelic shrugged. The Mage War was well before his time and of no consequence to his thinking. "If not you then it would have been someone else. Seems to be the way of things. I think we're bent on destroying each other."

"Aye. Sadly enough it is."

The giant sensed something important unsaid and wasn't sure if he wanted to know or not. Meddling with a Mage was bad enough, meddling with the past only led to trouble. Dakeb took the choice away from him.

"If last night is an indication, our path is filled with peril. Dark wolves don't hunt without a master guiding them. Whoever's stalking us sent them. But to what purpose?"

"Then we need to find their master," Grelic said without trying to think of what might be. Cold shivers ran down his spine.

"There is no time. I don't yet understand what is happening or why, though I have suspicions. What I do know is that war is coming to Thrae regardless of our task. We need to hurry."

Grelic's eyebrow rose sharply. "That doesn't sound good."

"It usually doesn't. Foul times have befallen us. Every generation has demons to fight, whether self created or not."

We'll see each other again soon enough.

"How's your thigh?" asked Dakeb in an attempt to relieve some of the growing tension.

They both examined the wound. Caked blood surrounded the gash and the interior was soft pink. Dakeb closed his eyes and sent invisible tendrils of power into the cut, searching for infection.

"I've had worse."

"I don't sense any poison, though it is difficult to tell with Gwarmoran. When we reach Gend remind me to make a poultice for it. For everyone. Dark wolves are no better than Dwim when it comes to pain and poison."

Grelic laughed. "What other foul creatures did you bring with you, old man?"

"I'm sure I can think up a few more," Dakeb said and chuckled. "Be fortunate there are no Gnaals on our trail yet. Nasty creatures made purely from hatred and magic. It would be nice to live in a simple world, wouldn't it? I can remember days, long before the veil of night fell on Mage-kind, filled with merriment and hope. Kingdoms strove towards common purpose and achieved wondrous achievements. Everyone prospered. Even the Goblins."

"What happened?"

Ancient pain flashed through his eyes. "The crystal of Tol Shere. Our council decided to forge the wealth of our knowledge into a single entity for generations to use as they saw fit. A noble idea but filled with flaws. The crystal allowed evil to return to the world after nearly a millennium. Several of the orders fell under the sway of darkness and used the crystal for unholy purposes. These we named dark Mage and our war began. With the crystal as a weapon they would be unstoppable."

"I assume they failed." Grelic knew very little history. The subject of Mages and their kind left his head swooning so he never bothered delving into that tragic past.

Dakeb nodded. His eyes bore a hollow, distant look. "A few of us managed to sneak back inside Ipn Shal, our fortress-temple, to stop the ceremony. The crystal shattered into four pieces. That's when I was forced to combat my best friend, Sidian. Darkness's hold on him was the greatest of all. We fought for a day and night, neither side gaining an advantage until I managed to pry the last shard of the crystal from his hands. When the dust settled there was no sign of him. I alone stood living. All of my brothers, both light and dark, were dead."

"It is a hard thing, killing a friend," Grelic said with empathy. The truth buried in his words ran too deep.

"If only that were so. There was no sign of Sidian whatsoever. I searched but never found a trace. What was left of the order tried to rebuild in the aftermath of the war, but we were few and the rage of the world stood against us. Some were killed in a great purge, others fled across the sea to distant shores. A handful of us went into hiding. As far as I know I am the last."

Grelic nodded solemnly, his mind wandering down strange roads. "What of the crystal? Could it still exist or hold power?"

"It does exist, though I took the four shards to different locations across Malweir. No one but I knows of their locations."

Grelic finally relaxed. Magical creatures were bad enough, but still killable, and he didn't want to think about the potential nightmare of an enemy with powers that nearly succeeded in destroying the world.

"Why are you up so early? It's not yet dawn," Dakeb said. "The others are too exhausted to rise."

Grelic passed a quick look back to the campsite. "They are young still. Too much emotion comes out when they fight. You and I have been around for a while. There's no emotion in battle left for me. I fight to stay alive, nothing more. Let them sleep. They will have need of such rest in the days to come."

"I started a stew a short while ago. Hopefully some of the herbs I added will give us a little extra strength. The road ahead is long and winding, filled with many dark places. We'll need all the help we can get. A little luck would be nice too," Dakeb said.

A small trout swam by. Grelic sighed. Life would be much simpler if he'd settled down and married. Images of Kialla naked and tempting danced in his head, despite knowing it hadn't been her. *Still, how can I look upon you the same?* "I don't believe in luck. Seen too much for it to be real."

"What do you believe in?"

"A good sword. The only thing I trust completely. A sword won't let you down."

Grelic saw Lord Death coming for him. *We'll see each other again soon enough.* He shivered again. Dakeb felt the wrongness of the moment but stayed quiet. He knew the big man would talk when he was ready.

"Perhaps Brother Ibram's Harr can help," Grelic finally said with a jovial tone. "Though I doubt he'll be too keen on one of his flock leaving the fold. Come, let's see if this stew of yours follows the rest of your reputation."

They ambled back into the campsite in slightly lighter spirits. The others were slowly getting up and doing their best to forget the night prior. Wounds hampered some, bleak memories the rest. Kialla flashed Grelic a smile and it was all he could do to return it without turning away and blushing. A naturally stubborn man seldom beaten in battle, Grelic struggled not to walk away from Kialla. It took his last measure of fortitude to sit down and ladle a large bowl of stew.

"How long before we reach Gend?" he asked Dakeb after the last bite of hard biscuit was chased out of his throat by a hearty belch.

"Tomorrow I'd say. I think it's safe to assume travelling at night is not viable."

"Damned well isn't. Neither is spending the night in the open," Pregen followed. The bandage covering most of his right bicep had bled through in the middle.

For once Grelic agreed with the thief. "Mage, you know this land better than myself. Is there sanctuary for us tonight? Somewhere safe this evil won't follow?"

Dakeb gave it a moment of thought. "There are caves in some of the hills. I'm sure young Fitch here can guide us better once we get closer."

Codel Mres sank back in his ebony chair. His face was paled, covered with perspiration. His muscles ached down to the bone. He was weak from exhaustion and failure. Not a natural Mage, magic came hard for him despite decades of training. At best, all he managed to perform were menial feats and party favors. His body threatening to rebel, he wondered what made him audacious enough to think he could handle performing such an intricate and brutal spell that could upset the balance of the world.

His arrogance, aided by lore from the Hooded Man, led him to believe he could control even death itself. So that's exactly what he tried to do. Lord Death would not be mastered by any man, however. None but the gods controlled him. Codel mired in failure and knew Lord Death would soon be stalking him. His only hope lay in the protection wards the Hooded Man gifted him with. He doubted they would. Life was just not that kind to men like him.

"What have I done?"

TWENTY

The Long Road to Gend

"I'm glad you're on our side, Dakeb," Fitch carefully said after an hour or so of internal deliberation.

It wasn't that he was afraid. The old Mage had a welcoming persona, like the men in Gend who'd always been around the tavern tables after a long day of hunting. Fitch respected and admired Dakeb. The Mage reminded him of Father Seldis and that in itself was comforting. They'd taken to riding together since the ambush after Grelic forced him to take the lead, reasoning they were close enough to Gend for Fitch to be able to get his bearings and guide them in.

Dakeb chuckled softly. "There are times when I wish I'd never learned such tricks and spells. Times have changed so much since the war."

"They must have been awful," Fitch replied, unsure what else to say.

A tear clouded Dakeb's eye. "Worse than you can possibly imagine. That's why I am here now. I don't want to see Malweir torn apart again."

"Do you really think this is going to come to war?"

"Difficult to answer. Sometimes a Mage can see the future. Not all of it, mind you, but enough to allow us a chance at preventing certain things. War among them. Ah, there are times when I wish I'd been born a plain, ordinary farmer."

This shocked Fitch. He didn't understand why anyone would give up a life of palaces and luxury for the daily toil and hardships associated with farming. He saw the way old Murray would go to the inn and drink his troubles away. Or the way Dettin looked after a season of poor crops. Farming just wasn't worth it from his point of view. As a hunter he took what he needed off of the land, rather than spent a lifetime of backbreaking work in the soil.

"Why would you want to be a farmer? There's no satisfaction in it. I've watched farmers all of my life and they're a miserable sort," Fitch said after a spell.

Dakeb replied, "Farming is the ultimate satisfaction, Master Iane. The power to create. Think of all of the families who are able to eat because of the selflessness of the farmers. Think of the gift Malweir bestows upon us as crops take root and fill the fields and gardens with bounty. Mankind's greatest success comes from our smallest achievements. To be so free is intoxicating."

"I suppose." Fitch really didn't understand what Dakeb was talking about.

Hunters provided just as much food, with equal variety. Of course there were days when the arrows went back to the quiver unbloodied. Fitch wasn't a dreamer by any means. He knew the limitations of his life all too well. Before demons robbed him of his future, he knew he was going to die an old man without much to show. Demons stole all of that and left him with dying embers. Not a vengeful man, he had no interest in finding the monsters responsible and hunting them across the face of Malweir. Killing them wouldn't bring Shar back and without her…

Dakeb hid a sad smile. "Just to feel the dirt beneath my fingernails I would trade all my long years of knowledge and wanderings. Life, Fitch. I'm talking about throwing off the shackles of responsibility and truly living."

Neither of them spoke for the rest of the morning. Too many old pains had resurfaced between them. Yet Dakeb never left his side. He found Fitch perplexing. There was an untouched emotion lurking deep within. An almost overpowering urge to do good hungered to be set free, as if seeking to make amends for past failures. Deeper, closer to the hidden areas behind Fitch's soul lurked a vicious hatred. Evil slept within Fitch Iane. Dakeb was frightened.

Grelic halted the beleaguered band shortly after midday. The sun was hot, too hot for the early spring weather. Looking skyward, he frowned at the bright blue sky. Not a cloud was in sight and the wind had stopped blowing. Grelic took it as an ill sign. Kialla rode up alongside him and slid from her saddle. Her grace made many men sigh over the years despite the rough edges she maintained.

"What's wrong?" she asked with a weary tone.

He avoided looking down into her eyes, just as he'd avoided getting too close to her since his dream. Whether from embarrassment or something else he wasn't sure. "I don't know. It doesn't feel right here. When have you known such heat in Thrae this early in the spring?"

"I hadn't thought about it. Winter was long this year. Spring is nearly finished. Perhaps it has something to do with the goings-on under Druem?"

It was an empty question. Without having been to the Deadlands there was no way to find a reasonable answer. So much had happened so quickly they were left almost numb. From the attack on Gend to their flight from the Gwarmoran, nothing had gone according to plan. Grelic felt like they were constantly one step behind their enemy. The implications proved unsettling.

"Grelic, why don't you look at me anymore? What have I done to you?" Kialla asked after a short time. She couldn't take the distance.

The giant turned away, not wanting her to see the hurt riddling his eyes. "I don't want to talk of it. Trust me when I say that you've done nothing, Kialla. I have personal demons to exorcise."

She closed on him, gently placing her slender hand on his muscled arm. "When you want to talk, I'll be here. Just like always."

Kialla walked heavily back to the others. Her shoulders sagged and her head hung just a bit low. She was beginning to wonder what it was going to take to get the giant to open up. Dwim and Gwarmoran. All the evils of the underworld were upon them and dissention threatened to tear the group apart.

Mistrust and blind hatred gnawed away at their resolve. She needed to know why.

Sitting on a small boulder half buried in the mud and weeds, Pregen Chur thumbed the edge of his sword. His casual demeanor remained, though shaken from recent events. It was almost as if nothing had happened back in the ravine. Kialla suspected he was in just as much pain as the rest but refused to admit it. They'd thought for sure he'd died when the dark wolf landed on him. Momentarily dazed, she found herself staring at his almost boyish charm and naturally handsome features, almost forgetting who he really was.

"How are you feeling?" she asked.

He gave her his best smile and lazily answered, "I've been better. The wounds are minor though. I'm flattered you care so much about me to ask. Hard times when a pretty lady doesn't see to her friends."

"Save it," she scolded. "I'm not in the mood for games. I was merely making my way through the group."

Kialla stomped off with him smiling.

"Besides," she called over her shoulder, "You're not my type. I prefer men who aren't afraid to get their hands dirty."

"I have no doubt, but you'll be begging me for a kiss before this is all said and done," he sang after her.

Kialla stormed away, cursing under her breath. Satisfied his sword was sharp enough, Pregen slid it back into the sheath and chuckled softly.

She marched past Ibram, who never bothered looking up. He numbly chewed on a piece of dried venison, staring back at the forest. When she finally found a place to sit and collect her thoughts she was surprised it was next to Dakeb. That's when she realized just how exhausted she was. Dakeb smiled and passed her a full canteen.

"Take heart, Kialla. All is not darkness," he said with a warm tone.

She drank deeply. "I'm afraid I can't let myself believe that. Not after what we've been through in such a short period of time."

"What really troubles you?" he asked suddenly.

She frowned, that feeling he already knew nagging at her, but she humored him anyway. "Everything. We're getting further into this quest and no one is bonding. I've been on shorter, less complicated jobs with more cohesion. Even after two attacks by creatures that should not exist we're still at odds. It feels hopeless."

Dakeb paused, taking a moment to look around their tiny campsite. "I can see your point but you needn't worry so. Sometimes it takes great tragedy to bring people together. Other times all it takes is patience and understanding. Not even the order of Mages had easy beginnings."

Considering how that order ended, she failed to find comfort. "Do we have that much time, I wonder?"

Dakeb only smiled in response.

They rode for the rest of the day. Fitch started drawing in to himself as old hunting grounds and deer trails became familiar. Gend wasn't far off. Just a few more hours, he assured them. A few more hours until he returned to his nightmares and the place where he left his wife to die. His confidence, what little that managed to scrape itself back together over the last few weeks, waned. He doubted he had the strength needed to see what remained of his home or the sun-bleached bones of Shar. Ghosts and nightmares waited to welcome him home.

Grelic reigned to a stop at dusk. After the events in Eline and the forest road he wasn't willing to risk their lives further by entering the village at night. Especially before the moonrise. Fitch couldn't have been happier. He had no desire to rush into his past, though part of him subconsciously wished to get it over with under the cover of darkness. He eagerly went about collecting wood and kindling while the others saw to the horses and patrolled the perimeter. Normally Grelic wouldn't have allowed a fire. They were in enemy territory as far as he was concerned and needed to treat every action as if it might give their presence away.

Grelic snatched up Pregen and they struck out into the lightly forested area to search for fresh meat. Thoughts of a nice rabbit stew entertained the giant as he fondly remembered what the Mage had done for them after the battle. He frowned. Dakeb troubled him. The Mage's sudden appearance bothered him deeply, leaving him with a growing sense of foreboding. Something very bad was coming their way. He figured he might as well have a full stomach to meet it.

Giant and assassin returned with smiles and hands full. Three large rabbits were skinned and quartered before being dropped into the already bubbling broth hanging over the fire. That night the group slept soundly. Grelic volunteered for the first guard shift, allowing the others a few more hours of rest while he tried to work out all of the pieces in an ever-deepening puzzle. When Ibram came to relieve him, the big man didn't say a word.

After a quick breakfast consisting of leftover stew, they broke camp and headed out. Dakeb cautioned before they got very far. Grelic seconded the warning. He kept them riding in a loose wedge similar to ranging cavalry units looking for the enemy. Fitch returned to the point.

The villager was surprised to find much of his old fears miniscule, almost casual. It was as if he wanted to head home, as if it were an inescapable conclusion. Father Seldis helped ease the suffering, working his mind in ways Fitch would never understand. Logically the only way for him to let go of the past was by returning to Gend and confronting his deepest fears.

They ran across the first burned-out hut an hour later. What remained was barely a meter high and covered with creeping vines. Gend died weeks ago yet a sickly, burnt smell permeated the air. Dark powers were at work to keep the world from reclaiming what had once been pristine wilderness.

"This was Lemis's place," Fitch told them. He'd known Lemis but never called the man a friend. Lemis was the village hermit: a crotchety old man who hated near everything and had no problem letting folks know it.

Grelic made out the curled bones of a hand jutting from the rubble. "What's the safest route into Gend?"

Fitch didn't understand. Gend was dead. There was no safe route. "What difference does it make? Everyone is dead."

The giant resisted the urge to strike him. "Which way can we get into Gend without being seen?"

"Down the creek bed and around the small mountain on the eastern road. None of the roads run near it," Fitch said after a moment.

Grelic grunted and forged ahead.

"Are you sure you are ready for this?" Dakeb asked Fitch quietly.

He shrugged. "What choice do I have? I'm already home. It's too late to turn back."

"Remember your faith, Fitch," said the Mage.

Confidence slightly bolstered, Fitch hurried to catch up to Grelic. The big man passed him a queer look but kept riding.

"I used to play in these woods growing up. My father taught me how to hunt here." He wasn't sure why, but he felt compelled to explain himself.

"You've got no need to explain, lad," Grelic replied. "We all need memories just for ourselves. Keep them locked away. Take strength from them when dark times strike."

He ducked under a thick oak branch spanning the game trail they started following. Fitch exhaled, feeling relieved at Grelic's acceptance.

"How many people lived here?"

"Just a few hundred. We were never a large village, but everyone knew each other and there were never any major troubles."

Grelic nodded. "I grew up in a village much the same. A long, long time ago."

Fitch found it difficult to believe he and the warrior had anything in common. They lived in such vastly different worlds. Fitch was a simple hunter with limited aspirations. Grelic was renowned across Malweir as a great warrior. What commonality could they possibly share? He decided to hold the question for another time.

Grelic didn't wait for another question. He much preferred a direct approach to issues or problems. "Fitch, I'm not going to lie to you. What you're about to go through is beyond me. I've never had to experience a deed so foul."

"You haven't? But you've been in countless battles," Fitch blurted out.

"All my life, aye. I've buried more friends than you've got people in your village but I've never seen anything comparable to what you endured. War is an easy task. Fight and live or fight and die. That's it. Losing all you know is much worse."

"I had a wife," Fitch told him.

"I know."

They formed up in a line at the edge of Gend. Here the stench was far worse than at Lemis's. Dakeb frowned. He couldn't be certain but he felt as if he knew the underlying spell that kept the land rancid. The problem gnawed at him, distracting him from what needed to be done. So much lately reminded him of the days following the Mage War.

Kialla, crossbow in hand, was the first to break cover and move into Gend. Her eyes danced over the blackened ground as she urged her mount into a trot. Snorting disapproval, her horse obeyed. Kialla tensed, expecting that initial startled cry to alert the other foul creatures lurking in the ruins. Yet for all of her appearances, she was remarkably calm. A disciple of the sword, she was in her element.

She gained the first set of ruins without incident. The smell turned her stomach. She almost threw up several times until she finally couldn't stand it any longer and covered her face with an old cloth. Reaching down, she gave her horse a reassuring pat on the neck and then motioned the others forward.

"What do you think?" Grelic asked after pulling up alongside her.

She shook her head. "Too hard to tell. There are too many tracks and they're going in every direction. But look here, these are made by men."

Grelic stared down at the footprints. The human ones didn't bother him nearly so much as the scores of hobnailed boot prints trampled over the top of them. "Goblins."

"And worse. Those were made by Gwarmoran. I think this was more than a mere raid. Something sinister is at work here, Grelic."

He looked around, hoping for more solid information. Broken spears stuck in the ground. Axe heads and a few swords and rusting daggers lay scattered randomly. The villagers managed to put up a small fight. Hardly worth the effort in all actuality.

"They were searching for something," he concluded.

"But what?"

An uneasy feeling bothered him. "I don't know. Push through to the far side of the village. We can figure out what happened once Gend is secure."

They moved quickly, despite the hampering lack of experience from Fitch and Ibram. Dakeb rode in to the village center and waited. Vermillion traces of magic lighted his fingertips. He closed his eyes and extended his senses across the immediate area. The heavy smell continued to bother him. A sudden disturbance, so faint it hardly registered, made him open his eyes. Dakeb spied the flicker of movement off to the right. He loosed a bolt of Mage fire. The explosion threw the lurker to the ground, where he rolled a few times to put out the hungry flames before regaining his feet and running for the safety of the trees.

"Grelic!" Dakeb shouted.

The giant emerged from behind a pile of rubble and charged.

"Don't kill him. We might be able to find out what happened!" the Mage shouted over the thunder of hooves.

He spurred his horse on, following Pregen and Kialla. Their quarry stumbled and almost fell. Grelic was already on him. Using the ruined buildings for cover, he evaded pursuit long enough to reach the trees. Both he and Grelic knew once the chase went into the forest it was all but over. A crossbow bolt zipped past, striking the bole of a maple tree near the man's head.

"Damnation," Grelic cursed.

The man didn't pause to look back but dashed into the trees. Grelic knew he only had one chance. Ducking right, he jabbed his heel into his horse's flank. They leapt over fallen trees, wheeled sharply around moss-covered boulders, and came up in front of their prey. Grelic slid to the ground and drew his steel.

"Drop your weapon and raise your hands," he ordered gruffly.

The man gently lowered his sword to the last of autumn's leaves and did as he was instructed. He lowered his hood and looked Grelic squarely in the eye. Shock rippled across the Grelic's face. He knew this man!

TWENTY-ONE

Old Friends

"You scared the wits out of me," Cron said after drinking deeply from Grelic's canteen.

The big man agreed. "You're lucky we didn't kill you. The gods know we've been attacked enough along the way already not to take chances."

"Damned near did. Between that crossbow bolt and whoever shot that fire at me I was close enough to death," Cron replied with an uneasy voice. "Just what was that fire anyway? I've never seen the like."

"That would be mine," Dakeb interrupted. "I sometimes forget my own powers. Too many years of privilege leaves me slightly delusional. My name is Dakeb."

Cron balked, instantly recognizing the name of one of Malweir's last remaining Mages. "When did you find such impressive friends, Grelic? The last I heard, you were up for a hanging in one of Rentor's private prisons."

"Sign of the times, lad. I'm not the one to turn down help. Not his kind leastwise."

The others joined them by Gend's ruined fountain in the old village center. Cron's initial assessment lowered considerably. He recognized Pregen Chur, though by a different name. Wanted posters of the thief were plastered throughout Kelis Dur. Cron shifted his gaze to the fragile man standing next to the obvious monk. He wasn't sure if Grelic or King Rentor chose those for the quest, but any optimism he had was slipping into despair. He was about to say so when one of the most beautiful women he'd ever seen rode up.

Cron was stunned. He'd never seen someone so gorgeous and was at odds trying to figure out why she was slumming with this motley assortment of characters. The boldness in her eyes enamored him the moment her gaze dropped on him. Perhaps Grelic had better taste than he'd taken the big man for. Either way, the desire to strike out on his own was dying. Grelic's voice brought him back to reality.

"What exactly brings you out here? And alone. This isn't the nicest place to find a captain of Thrae by himself."

The others crowded around the soldier to hear his tale. Grelic was more interested in his intentions.

"I was the one who led the patrol here once we learned of the attack. Nothing happened until two of my men were abducted. Their heads were delivered back to Kelis Dur shortly after I gave up the search. I begged, pleaded, and argued with the king to let me come back with a larger force. He said no. I decided to go against his wishes and come back on my own. I needed to know what happened to my men."

"A deserter," Pregen jabbed.

Cron shot a vehement glare. "Short words for a common criminal. I'm doing my duty to Thrae, thief. Why are you here?"

"Cron is a captain of Kelis Dur," Grelic intervened before matters grew heated. "The youngest ever chosen. You'd do well to remember that, Pregen."

The thief offered a soured look and fell silent as Grelic went about making introductions. He'd already made up his mind by the time it finished. Cron was an incredible asset, one he'd sorely need if there was any hope of surviving what was coming. The others were decent enough people but weak. They were the oddest group of adventurers he'd ever been a part of. Yet the entire kingdom of Thrae depended on them.

"I came here for revenge and to get answers," Cron admitted. "But now I believe I'm in over my head. There are signs and tracks of creatures I have no knowledge of. And now you show up in the company of a Mage. I'm thinking I'd be safer if I joined you."

Grelic listened emotionlessly. "I hear your words, Cron. You are a sure sword and honorable heart, but I warn you. We face more spawn of darkness than you could ever imagine possible."

"I thought King Rentor hired you for reconnaissance?"

"Aye," confirmed Grelic.

Pregen stared Cron dead in the eye. "I'm sure he thought so as well."

Cron held his retort. "You're not telling me everything."

"We're not sure what to tell," Kialla said.

To him her voice sounded like birds singing in early twilight. Cron didn't know what it was about her but she had strength he recognized. Even through streaks of dirt and sweat her high cheekbones beckoned.

Dakeb interrupted his lust with a quick slap on the knee. "The tale is long in telling but I'm almost positive it gets worse. Is that not so, Captain?"

"Speak plainly, Mage," Grelic asked. Dakeb's seemingly directionless babble continued to infuriate him.

"Very well, though I don't think this is the place for such conversation. I've finally figured out what this stench is."

Silence fell across them as they waited for Dakeb to continue. Obvious enjoyment painted on his face, he smiled.

"There are unusual amounts of sulfur and brimstone in the air. There is but one creature on Malweir capable of doing this. Fitch, do you remember seeing anything in the skies that night?"

Fitch sat quietly, unwilling to revisit his pain. Too often his nights were filled with the hollow echo of screams and ghostly figures storming through the mist and smoke. Demons. Fire. His eyes widened from sudden shock.

"I remember fire raining down from the sky."

Unable to stand it, he rose and walked off.

Ibram started to follow but Dakeb stopped him.

"Let him be, Ibram. He needs to face his own demons. He'll return when he's ready."

"The fires," Kialla reminded.

Dakeb smiled again. "Yes. The fires. The only creature on Malweir capable of doing this is a dragon. Nothing else is so powerful. It must be one of the great wyrms."

Eyes popped open. Mouths dropped. Going up against Goblins or even Gwarmoran was one thing. A dragon was something far, far worse. Pregen shifted nervously. He'd never fancied himself a particularly brave man. Facing down a dragon was not on his list of things to do. Doubts started growing. He considered leaving in the night and returning to his meager life.

"Are you sure? No one recalls the last time a dragon was seen in this part of the world," Grelic said.

"A dragon didn't kill my men, unless you know of one skilled enough to decapitate," Cron added.

"No," Dakeb replied. "Those murders were done by Goblins."

"This doesn't make sense," Kialla said. "What would a dragon want with Thrae?"

The Mage offered a thoughtful look. "A good question. I fear there is more going on we don't yet know. Something sinister brews in Thrae."

"Not for me," Pregen finally said. "I didn't come here to hunt dragons or any of the other monsters that have been hounding us since we left Kelis Dur. I'm being paid to find out what happened and report back to the king. Nothing more, Grelic."

"No one has decided anything yet," Grelic warned.

"Sounds like they have to me."

Kialla fumed. "He's right and you know it. We can't fight a dragon! If the Mage wants to risk his life against a dragon so be it. I say we leave now. We have our answers. Let's go tell Rentor and collect our pay."

"That won't solve anything. King Rentor will know but to what ends? There's nothing any army has that's capable of slaying one of the great wyrms," Cron said.

Pregen snorted. "And we do?"

"We have a Mage," Grelic added.

"What are you saying?" Kialla asked.

A gust of wind blew hair in Grelic's face. "We've reached the crossroads. Aye, it's true we did our job and the king specifically forbade us from taking further action. Rentor doesn't know about the dragon. A beast that strong can drive Thrae to her knees. The gods seemed to send Dakeb to us for a reason. I say that reason is to find this dragon and tame it."

"That is…a hard choice," Dakeb commented.

Pregen threw up his hands in frustration. "Count me out. This is ridiculous! How can a handful of rejects and misfits expect to succeed where an army won't? Mage or no, I'm going home to collect my pay."

"I'm in," Ibram told them. He walked off before he could change his mind or be talked out of it. His entire life had led him to this one point in time where he knew what the right decision was.

Grelic nodded. At least one other was on his side. *The boy may not be much of a fighter but at least he's got heart and that is something in rare commodity these days.* He turned towards Kialla, the one person he expected to have his back.

"I don't know, Grelic. I'm not one to shy away from danger, but I'm no fool either. I need time to think," she told him.

Cron rubbed the stubble on his chin. "I'm with her. I came here for personal reasons. Going head to head with a dragon isn't an easy decision to make."

"I stand alone, eh?"

"Give them time, Grelic. Even I'm not so sure we can win," Dakeb said. "Come, walk with me."

The Mage led them away from the village center. His casual smile and carefree demeanor were gone. Grelic swore the man looked far older than he actually was. They moved past the senseless destruction and into the forest. Life gradually beat through the death. Greens of every shade replaced the charcoal burns.

"Life should be so simple. Don't you agree?" Dakeb asked.

"What are you talking about?"

He gestured. "Look around you. There are no wars here. No dark dreams of power or conquest. Life goes on as it always has and everything exists together. Man could learn a great deal from trees if he only took the time to listen." Dakeb looked deeply into the giant's eyes, testing the measure of his resolve. "I have never fought a dragon. Not even during the war."

Mixed emotions rocked Grelic. He believed the Mage was capable of limitless power. Finding out otherwise shook his foundations of belief. He found a tree stump and took a seat, deflated suddenly.

"What then should we do? I'm no coward but if our strongest member is against this plan I will listen. Rentor needs to be warned, at any rate." He was surprised at how difficult the words were to say.

Dakeb nodded. "That must have burned your tongue."

"More than you know," he chuckled before breaking out into raw laughter.

"I never said I couldn't defeat one, merely that I haven't had the opportunity," Dakeb added after wiping a tear from his eye. It had been too long since he last laughed that hard.

Grelic raised an eyebrow. "Is there much difference?"

"In this case? Not really. But I feel obligated to try."

"What is it you're not telling me, Mage?"

That easy smile waned.

"You know something," Grelic pressed.

"Nothing concrete. I have suspicions but they belong solely to me until we can confirm them. Times are perilous enough and our enemy has spies everywhere. The Dwim and Gwarmoran attacks were no mere coincidence. We are being hunted, herded if you will, and until I discover the truths I need, my fears remain private."

Grelic conceded the point. "I won't argue with you. When the time comes don't forget to let the rest of us in on it."

"Agreed."

"That still leaves us with one issue," Grelic added.

"Who is going to warn the king."

Grelic sighed. "I can't say that I actually like doing deeds like this, but I'll be damned if peace makes sense to me. I've had a sword in my hands almost my entire life. Killing takes a special talent. A lot of men don't have the stomach for it. Part of me wishes I had been there during your war."

"Those were dark times, my friend. Too many lives were lost without purpose."

"Even so, every man lives for that one defining moment. I can't help but wonder, has mine already passed? Did I miss it? I've been in more wars than I can remember. Battles, places, friends I don't remember. Sometimes I think I should be there with them. Lost in the shadows of the past. Will history forget men like me?"

"History needs men like you," Dakeb replied.

They sat in silence for a time. Grelic absorbed what Dakeb had said. Strangely, it calmed him. Lessened his doubts and fortified his resolve.

"Let us get back to the others and see if we can convince them. I'm anxious to be away from here," Dakeb said after noticing the subtle change in Grelic's pose.

The warrior gave the area a final glance. Compared to the peaceful serenity of the forest, the ruins of Gend were a desecration to the world. A terrible blight was working in the north. It had somehow fallen on a handful of strangers to arrest the progress.

"Beauty should be preserved," Grelic said when they gained the edge of the ruins. "Where do we go from Gend?"

"I'm not sure. Thus far there has been no sign leading us in another direction. Our foe came from the Deadlands though. Of that I have no doubt."

"That means Druem."

Dakeb offered an appraising look. "Yes, I believe so."

A feeling close to fear nestled into Grelic's mind. He had no desire to see the long dead part of the world, nor the hordes of Goblins rumored to be festering within, but there were times when choice simply wasn't prudent. They walked on, surprised to find the others huddled in a group next to the fountain. Each bore a grim look. Grelic smiled to himself. He'd been in similar situations and knew the look well. It spoke of people who knew they were about to die.

"Welcome back," Pregen offered sarcastically. "We were starting to think the Goblins had taken you."

"Ain't a Goblin living that can best me," Grelic snorted to an assortment of laughter.

Kialla stepped forward. "We've been talking."

"And?"

"We're with you, whatever you decide," she answered. "Some of us are more reluctant than others, but we're all in."

Grelic finally exhaled that breath that had been trapped in his chest. "You do know we are heading into the Deadlands?"

"We know," Ibram said.

Cron half smiled. "There are better places to see. I've heard the Twin Spires of Ragnash are lovely in the summer. If it's the Deadlands so be it."

"When do we leave?" Pregen asked. He wanted nothing to do with any of it and quietly tried to figure out when best to abandon the others.

Grelic nodded and settled his gaze on Fitch. His respect for the villager returning to confront his past rose, but Fitch was no soldier. Still, he gave Grelic a shrug and was about to speak when Grelic silenced him with a hand. The warrior sprinted back to the tree line and crouched. A bird abruptly stopped whistling in the distance. Grelic narrowed his eyes and searched the forest, rewarded with several dark shapes stalking towards him. The faint brush of metal reached his ears. It was an all-too-familiar sound. Grelic drew his sword as quietly as possible and hurried back to the group.

Kialla noticed that familiar gleam in his eyes and went for her weapons. "What is it?" she asked in passing.

"Goblins."

TWENTY-TWO

The Aeldruin

A long, winding trail of mud and half-melted snow marked the passing column of horsemen through the eerily quiet forest. The midday sun was bright yet not quite hot enough to be a bother. Whispers of clouds hung randomly to the tranquil sky. Butterflies the mild colors of rainbows danced around the riders, inviting them to enjoy the peaceful mid-spring day. Bred for war and trained to endure long days, weeks even, on the hunt, horse and rider resisted the temptation to momentarily forget themselves.

The lead rider suddenly halted the column, rising in his stirrups. The others immediately fanned out in a wedge formation and searched the surrounding area for signs of danger. And they waited. No one spoke. A thin wind kicked up fresh pollen dropping from the pines. Horses snickered nervously, as if sensing something bad about to happen.

"Come out, Euorn," the leader called. His voice was light, carefree.

Each rider was dressed similarly in a camouflage pattern of light and dark forest colors. A trained eye had trouble discerning them from their surroundings. Their cloaks were light yet durable and waterproof. The ancient fabric kept them cool in the hot summers and warm through the depths of winter. An equal number of men and women filled the ranks, just as it had been for generations. People across Malweir knew them for their martial prowess and often sought them out to settle petty squabbles and civil wars. They were the Aeldruin. High Elf mercenaries grown bored with the teachings of the Sacred Tree.

Euorn emerged from the shadows and lowered his hood. Lustrous brown hair with a hint of red and blonde hung down past his thin shoulders, concealing all but the very tops of his pointed ears. He grinned.

"Lord Faeldrin, there is sign of battle," he reported without being asked.

Faeldrin also dropped his hood, revealing angular features centered around crisp eyes. "Where?"

Euorn gestured across the breadth of forest. "All over. The ambush happened here, or close by. It's hard to tell how many Gwarmoran but my guess is near two and a half score."

Even Faeldrin and his long centuries of mercenary work had never heard of so many attacking a singular target. "How many humans?"

"Six."

Faeldrin balked. "Six? Are you sure?"

He regretted asking the moment the words left his mouth. Euorn was the best scout and tracker in the company. He'd been recruited for that very reason. In fact, every one of Faeldrin's company was handpicked for the individual skills they brought. They had become his family and he cared for each dearly. Some took years, decades even, before relenting and joining him.

If Euorn took offense to being doubted he didn't show it. Even he had trouble believing so few stood against so many of the Gwarmoran. "Aye. The signs are muddled but I'm positive there were just six."

"Where are the bodies?"

Faeldrin looked over the battlefield, not looking forward to burying the remains.

"There are none. Leastwise none that aren't Gwarmoran."

The Elf Lord smiled. *This is getting intriguing, unless the remains are so horribly mangled the task proves overwhelming.* "Show me."

They rode through the copse of trees, leaving the rest of the Aeldruin behind. Faeldrin immediately noticed dark splotches of blood and ichor on bushes and tree trunks. Dark wolf corpses lay scattered across the ground in growing numbers the deeper they rode. Faeldrin was impressed. Whoever controlled the wolves knew exactly what he was doing. The ravine walls were steep enough to prevent escape. Broken saplings, burned shrubs and blood-stained leaves lay heaped in piles, complicating the area for horses. He failed to see how anyone managed to survive.

"What made those scoring marks?" he asked after picking out the subtle signs of burns and ash.

Euorn's eyebrow rose quickly. "If I had to guess I'd say Mage fire."

"Mage fire? There haven't been Mages in Malweir in over a hundred years. I don't think one could have survived for so long alone," Faeldrin replied.

"That's what I thought as well, my lord," Euorn agreed. He pointed to a row of ash piles. "Nothing else has that kind of kinetic energy. Not even an alchemist."

Faeldrin looked to where he pointed. *Indeed, only a Mage has such might. But which sort, light or dark?*

"Perhaps we should leave this place," Euorn suggested.

"Do you recall the tales of the dark Mage?" Faeldrin asked. An ominous tone underscored his words.

The scout glanced nervously about. If the dark Mage was responsible for killing the wolves, the Aeldruin were dead as well. Euorn remembered all too well. He'd been there during the final battle of the war. He and Faeldrin fought side by side with men and Dwarves from the southern kingdoms. Averon was the strongest foe to the dark Mages and paid dearly for their defiance. Many of Euorn's friends died that last day.

"More than just the Silver Mage survived," he whispered.

"Aye. And it stands to reason a dark Mage wouldn't kill creatures he or she helped create. The question remains, who did?"

"We should find out sometime tomorrow if we follow the trail," Euorn concluded.

The putrefying stench of decay sickened both land and Elf. Faeldrin returned to the others and ordered, "Let us waste no time. There is a Mage traipsing around the countryside. We must find where his loyalties are."

The Aeldruin rode through the battlefield with astonished looks. Few had seen such nightmarish scenes of slaughter. Gwarmoran packs were usually small, for the larger animals almost always turned on the younger. Seeing so many dead here left the Elves with a growing sense of impending dread. Even the horses felt it. They couldn't break into the clear fast enough.

The air much cleaner, Faeldrin pushed them through the night. They found the campsite shortly after sundown. It was hastily scattered and had little trace of being occupied. Faeldrin found himself starting to like whoever it was they hunted. *Only fools would leave signs of their passing, whereas these people moved quickly and tried to cover their tracks. Unfortunately for them, we are Elves*. The Aeldruin paused only long enough to rest and water the horses. The next day went quickly and they soon found themselves riding into the outskirts of what had once been a village. The sounds of battle shattered the calm morning air. Sword clanged on sword. Men and beasts screamed.

Faeldrin drew his slender rapier without pause and bellowed, "Aeldruin, form up and advance!"

TWENTY-THREE

Battle of Gend

"How many?" Cron hissed. He eagerly drew his sword.

"I don't know. Too many to be caught in the open like this," Grelic said. "Fitch, we need a place to make a stand. Somewhere they can't surround us."

"This way," Fitch said quickly.

They followed him across the center, through Mrs. Winbern's withered gardens and down the main road leading out of Gend. Rounding the corner of what had been the chandlery, he pointed. Grelic looked around the surrounding area. Normally such a position wouldn't be considered but the Goblin vanguard was already on them. Three large piles of rubble, storehouses, Fitch said, formed a loose semi-circle behind the chandlery. Depending on how many Goblins had come it might turn into a death trap. Grelic risked a look back down the street. He stopped counting at forty. *They've brought an entire company.*

"Grelic, I can't risk using my powers," Dakeb said. "If even one of them escapes the enemy will know of my presence and we lose any advantage I may bring."

Grelic let out a crisp guffaw. "I like how you think, Mage. We'll have to see about killing them all, won't we?"

"Unless we convince them to surrender," Dakeb smirked.

"Kialla, I need your bow up here," Grelic called.

She set her quiver down on a pile of burned logs. "I'm not going to get much range in this debris field. Think you can handle a close fight?"

"I'm looking forward to it. Just like old times."

Old times, Kialla recalled, usually had better odds. They turned to watch Cron sprint towards them, thumbing the string of a borrowed bow.

"Best in my class," he said in response to their looks.

Grelic looked closer and noticed it was his own bow. "Shoot as straight as you talk and the first round of ale is on me."

The lead Goblin scouts were one hundred meters away and closing. Time was up.

"Pregen, you and Ibram cover the right. Fitch, I want you to stick close to Dakeb on the left," Grelic ordered.

The thief ran the edge of sword lightly across the back of his wrist. "Where do you plan on being?"

Grelic gave a toothy grin. "Right in the middle. I'm going to see about making new friends."

Pregen watched Grelic stalk forward, silently questioning his own bravado. He glanced at Ibram and asked, "Are you ready for this?"

The former monk didn't reply, but merely drew his sword and loosened his shoulders. The time for talk was over.

"Relax, Ibram, or you're going to get us both killed. Besides, you've already survived the Dwim and dark wolves. A few Goblins are nothing. You probably won't even need to sharpen your sword when this is over. Come on. We need to get into position." He led Ibram to cover behind the furthest pile of rubble.

They didn't have to wait long.

The Goblins had closed to fifty meters when a stiff wind blew through, casually throwing the tiny band's scent at them. Halting, the lead Goblin tipped his head back to sniff the wind with a wide, flat nose. Drool escaped from between twisted and cracked teeth. Humans. More scouts caught the scent and a cry rose up through their ranks. Weapons were raised. Natural pack hunters, Goblins had muddy grey-green skin and stood close to five feet. Most were heavily muscled and overly armored. They weren't exceptional fighters, often relying on strength of numbers. They knew they had the advantage and prepared to attack.

They halted immediately when a huge man emerged from hiding to confront them. He taunted them. Mocking them with his defiance. The Goblin whip master pushed his way to the front ranks. He had one eye and a long, white scar running the length of his face where the other had been.

"What's this?" he snapped.

Grelic placed the tip of his broadsword into the dirt and waited. His feet were spread a comfortable distance apart. His body language suggested he was calm, relaxed. Goblins spit and yelled insults in their foul language. Grelic didn't blink. The whip master cracked his leather and the mob quieted.

"Where there's one, there's more," he snarled. "Move slow, dogs. It's man flesh for supper!"

They started forward under the heavy crack of the whip. Grelic remained still. He was the wall upon which their might would break. The lone obstacle standing between them and a magnificent feast. Goblins strained under the whip. The natural instinct to attack without caution roiled within. It was all the whip master could do to neglect his own primal urges, but this man was dangerous. Otherwise he wouldn't be so foolish as to stand before a Goblin pack alone.

Unseen, Cron feathered his first arrow and drew. His breathing slowed as he sighted in on his target. Taking the wind, distance, and speed of the enemy advance into consideration, Cron pulled the string tighter and loosed. The arrow whistled through the air and struck the smaller Goblin beside the whip master. He fell dead with a gurgled cry.

"Nice shot," Kialla said and fired a matching shot to the opposite side.

Cron was impressed. The Goblins recoiled as a third fell dead. "This makes dying easier."

"What does?"

He fired again. "Being next to a pretty woman."

Kialla blushed and killed another Goblin.

Trapped in the middle of the killing ground, Grelic held his position. Arrows whizzed by without him blinking. Goblins were dying quickly but not enough to force their retreat. Grelic was going to have to get his hands dirty after all. He jerked his sword free and exhaled a slow, deep breath as the Goblins charged. The first scout to reach him fell in two pieces. Hot blood splashed down Grelic's legs. A second heaved a throwing knife. Grelic ducked and swung a heavy body blow that ripped open the Goblin's rib cage. Bones crunched and organs flopped uselessly to the ground. Dark blood frothed on the Goblin's lips before it sank to its knees. Grelic gave his blade a twist and yanked it free.

A third Goblin went down under a crushing blow to the head. Strands of hair clung to Grelic's face and neck as he immersed himself in the killing. His eyes were wild, stern. Goblin warriors lost faith upon seeing their reflections cast back upon them. Grelic was death. The whip master bellowed for the attack. Two more dropped with arrows in their chests. By then it was too late. The Goblin ranks crashed into Grelic.

He met them with sword and fury. His blood boiled with rage. He swung, a short chop hacking off an arm. Grelic kicked another hard in the stomach. A barbed blade caught his right bicep, tearing a small chunk of muscle away. He winced as hot jets of pain lanced through his body. Fists slammed into him. Booted feet kicked. Grelic continued to fight despite the overwhelming numbers. He hacked and slashed. Punched and squeezed. The pile of bodies grew. Finally, the whip master had had enough and sounded the retreat.

Eleven dead Goblins lay at Grelic's feet. He would have smiled if he thought he had enough left to fight off the rest. Truth was, he was exhausted. A week of constantly being on the run and forced into one miserable situation after the next left him with little but his reserves. Grelic cursed himself for getting old when he wasn't paying attention and readied himself for another charge. He figured he had enough left for one good push. After that...

Grelic watched the survivors withdraw, knowing the battle was far from over. Goblins were vengeful creatures. He picked his way through the corpses and went to Kialla and Cron. She flashed an admonishing glare in direct contrast to Cron's open awe.

"They'll come at our flanks next. Maybe behind us," he said.

"What were you thinking, jumping out in front of a full company of Goblin infantry? You could have been killed," Kialla scolded.

"I had everything under control," he replied with a hurt look.

She had her doubts but there wasn't time to argue. The Goblins weren't going to wait long before they attacked again. Kialla checked her quiver and frowned. There were only ten arrows left. Ten shots before she'd have to draw her sword, Lady Killer, and slash her way through the fray. Her heart was racing despite the calm she tried to project. *Get it together. They're just Goblins.*

No matter how hard she tried, she couldn't ignore the feeling of cold dread creeping around her inner thoughts. She felt like they were being pushed in a certain direction. The enemy seemed to drive their every action since leaving the capital. She glanced at Cron, who appeared indifferent to the situation. Frustrated and helpless, she readied for the next attack.

Fitch listened to the sounds of the battle and cringed. Being in one was bad enough, but listening to one rage so close rattled his nerves to the point of breaking completely. The small measure of confidence instilled by Father Seldis at the monastery was waning rapidly. Childishly, he wished Grelic would just kill the Goblins and be done with it. He'd seen enough of warfare and foul magic over the last few days for three lifetimes. He failed to understand why the others seemed so absorbed by it. Violence was not a worthwhile endeavor. Did they want to be killed?

"I don't want to die," he confessed between hyperventilated sobs.

Dakeb touched his forearm reassuringly. "That isn't up to us, Fitch. We are only here for a short time. Some will leave their marks in the annals of history. Others are remembered fondly in the hearts of those they touched. Some are only known for the evil they wrought on Malweir. That, Fitch, is why we are here now. We are the chosen to stand up to evil before it is too late."

He still didn't understand. "I'm no hero, Dakeb."

The old Mage smiled warmly. "What does a hero look like? More often than not the men and women remembered as heroes were simple people with no such aspirations. Don't look down on yourself. Before this quest is finished you shall find your strength. Take heart."

Fitch opened his mouth to reply when Grelic returned. The big man looked like death.

"How many are there?" Dakeb asked quickly.

"At least forty," the giant replied. "We got a little more than a quarter of them."

"They appear to have taken a good piece of you as well," Pregen called from across the open area.

Grelic snorted a laugh. "It will take more than that to do me in, lad." *Not too much more, though. I've spent too much time fighting in bars instead of in the wild.*

"Now what?" Dakeb asked.

Wiping the sweat from his forehead, Grelic answered, "We need to strengthen the flanks. The Goblins won't come at me from the front again. Looks like it's your turn to play, Pregen."

"How long do you figure?"

A black spear struck the ground a few meters away, followed by a blood-curdling yell.

"Now."

A mass of armored Goblins rounded the far corner on Pregen and immediately launched into an assault. They'd learned their lesson from delaying and gave their enemy no time to react. Coming four abreast, the Goblins bellowed ancient war cries. The first one died with a dagger in his neck. The others trampled his body beneath their boots and kept coming. Pregen grinned savagely as he watched them kill one of their own. They were making his job easier, but not enough. Soon enough the Goblins were upon them. Pregen spun and slashed, taking one by the throat and another with a deep cut to the right thigh. Black blood spurted and the Goblin clutched his leg in a fruitless attempt to stop the bleeding.

Ibram breathed jerkily and raised his sword. A small Goblin leapt over a body and flew at Ibram. Blocking the wild thrust with his downward turned blade, Ibram stumbled back. He managed to regain his balance and ripped out the Goblin's stomach. Blood and entrails splashed onto his boots. A second Goblin attacked before the first fell away and drove Ibram to his knees. The ex-monk stabbed upwards and impaled his foe.

Grelic let out a horrible roar and charged into the fight. He barely managed to bring his sword up to bat away a spear aiming for his chest. Then he struck swiftly. The sword sliced diagonally down between the Goblin's neck and shoulder. Two others rushed forward and tackled both to the ground while Grelic's sword was still stuck in the corpse. Hot saliva drooled onto his cheeks. Claws and teeth ripped his face and hands. Grelic managed to curl a hand around one of the Goblin's throats and squeezed. The Goblin sputtered and gasped as life fled. Using the dead Goblin as a shield, Grelic shoved the second off and stabbed him in the heart with his own dagger. The giant rolled to his knees and took a deep breath.

A quick look at the battle left him with improved spirits. Pregen was hacking and slashing his way through the Goblins with the skill and precision of a fencing master. This was the first Grelic had actually witnessed the thief in action and he was suitably impressed. He showed finesse the giant lacked. Grelic preferred to crush through his enemies with brute force. Grace and flare were for men afraid to get their hands dirty. Still, Pregen was holding his own against a foe with no such compunctions.

Ibram managed to get back on his feet. His swings were wild and misdirected. A momentous waste of energy. If Grelic or the others didn't come to his aid soon the man was going to die under a swarm of more aggressive foes. The Goblins sensed it as well and hung just out of his reach. All they needed was a moment's distraction and a spear in his belly.

"Grelic, over here!"

The giant spun in time to see Dakeb plunge a borrowed sword through a leaping Goblin's chest. Kialla and Cron were nowhere in sight, meaning they seriously misjudged the Goblin numbers. A bad feeling entertained him as he tried to decide who to help. One would live, the other would die. Then he saw the Goblin whip master. Larger and more ferocious than the common Goblin foot soldier, whip masters were cruelest of the species. Fitch Iane stood directly in his path. Hope sank.

Uttering foul curses, the whip master backhanded Fitch unconscious and broke their line of defense. Tightening the grip on his sword, Grelic hurried to face him. The whip lashed out and struck his across the ribs. Cold, black eyes stared hungrily back at him. Even in their extreme darkness Grelic found amusement twinkling back. The whip master was taunting him.

Grelic charged. Reaching behind his back, the whip master drew his own blade. They met in a fury of strength and steel. Sparks showered from the force of impact. Grelic recognized that he was outmatched from the beginning. He quickly found himself reeling backwards, parrying blow after blow. Then it happened. He tripped on a small rock and fell. The Goblin howled with delight.

"Scum. It's the knife for you," he spat.

The whip master raised his barbed sword high above his head for the killing blow. Grelic kicked with all of his might, catching the Goblin in the knee and ripping tendons and shattering bone. The whip master bellowed in pain and buckled. His sword fell away, giving Grelic the opportunity to snatch his dagger and land on top of the prone Goblin before he could roll away. He plunged the dagger deep into the whip master's chest, killing him in one stroke.

Nearby Goblins saw their leader fall and lost faith. Others renewed their attack, breaking any hope Grelic had of smashing their spirits. This was going to be a fight to the death. He heard the sudden thunder of many hooves but ignored it, thinking the sound an illusion caused from too much action on the battlefield.

Arrows suddenly filled the sky. Several Goblins dropped after the first salvo. More white-feathered arrows continued to rain down, unerringly striking only Goblins. Grelic thanked whatever god had sent them rescue and ducked low just in case. Cloaked horsemen broke through the defensive line. Halberds and spears slammed into the confused Goblins. The enemy finally broke and fled back towards the opposite side of Gend. War horses trampled them underfoot. Dark blood flew in thick ropes. Bones snapped and broke. Grelic watched a rider spear a Goblin through the back with enough force to propel it through his chest and into the bole of a tree.

The lead rider, his face masked, pointed his sword at the fleeing Goblins and yelled, "Let none escape! Stop them before they can report to their masters!"

Riders thundered through Gend. Grelic kneeled to wipe the blood and gore from his sword and dagger. Exhaustion ate at him. Combined with blood loss, it was all he could do just to stay on his feet.

"Greetings, Grelic of Kressel Tine," the leader said after reigning in beside him. "I am Faeldrin of the Aeldruin."

Grelic smiled weakly and passed out. There wasn't even time to figure out how the Elf knew his name.

TWENTY-FOUR

War Council

Rentor sat in the royal meeting chamber with a dissatisfied glare that he seemed to have more of lately. His red robes of state stood out against the pale backdrop of aged furniture and brass lamps. There'd been no word from Grelic since leaving Kelis Dur and that bothered him more than he was willing to admit to the others. It left his hands bound. He couldn't act until he knew who his enemy was and where to direct his army. His enemy, whoever it may be, had him right where they wanted him. Helpless.

His adopted council sat opposite of him. Father Seldis had quickly turned into one of his staunchest allies, offering wisdom and advice from a completely different perspective. Rentor often found their conversations lasting into the early hours of the morning. A fact not lost on Codel Mres. The king found it refreshing to get another point of view on matters. Too often the politicians wrapped themselves up in their affairs so tightly it was almost impossible to find reality.

He mused that this was where his suddenly strained relations with Codel stemmed from. He loved his boyhood friend like a brother, but there was a disconcerting feeling coming from him. He had grown darker somehow. Rentor passed a fleeting glance at his friend, not liking what he saw. Codel's flesh was particularly pale, giving him a cadaverous appearance. His cheeks were gaunt. His eyes were sunken with heavy, dark bags circling them. He was skinnier than normal and increasingly difficult to talk to. Rentor also noticed how Seldis constantly studied the man.

"They're late," Codel hissed.

Any trace of his original cheer and good humor was gone. He'd turned bitter over the last few months. Rentor wondered whether it was because of the impending war they all knew was coming or something much darker. Evil was at work in Thrae, but where? And through whom? Until Rentor had those answers he was helpless to react.

Seldis passively turned his head towards the minister. "Patience. The army is your greatest asset right now. The generals have much to do in order to ensure Thrae is properly defended. They will be here."

"I have no doubt of that, monk," Codel spat back. "When they're summoned to an audience with the king it would be in their best interests to hasten!"

Both men jumped at the sound of a heavy fist slamming into the polished teak tabletop. "Damnation, Codel! I am the king. Do you hear me whining? They're our first line of defense. Would you alienate the army before the war begins?"

Rebuked, Codel sank back into his red-cushioned chair. "Of course not, sire. Forgive me. Times are particularly stressful of late."

"For all of us. I agree with Father Seldis. Patience is required if we are to discover the truth behind all of this and focus our defense."

"Even with the lives of every man, woman, and child in Thrae at risk?" he asked. There was no mistaking the condescending tone.

Rentor stiffened. "Especially for that reason. I'm unwilling to commit my forces in the wrong direction without careful thought. The enemy knows what we're doing. How or why I do not yet know. Until I can be sure of absolute intelligence, the army stays put."

Codel fell silent. The embroidered dragon on his right breast almost flared to life in the flickering firelight. Rentor eyed him suspiciously. He'd never understood his friend's fascination with dragons or other mythical beasts. Codel had been obsessed with tales and written stories of Goblins and wizards since they were small children. Whereas Rentor was content playing the heroic knight complete with wooden sword, Codel pretended to have magical powers.

The study door opened and General Huor walked in with a blustered look. His cheeks were wind burned and weathered. A steel edge tinted his eyes as he marched up to the king. He bore the look of a man with a foul taste in his mouth. Soldiers often joked when he was out of sight about his lack of humor and severely limited personality. The Iron Legions of Thrae viewed their commanding officer unfavorably, a fact not lost on the king.

"Sire," he said gruffly.

"Huor, please be seated," Rentor replied.

Codel shot the general a disgusted look.

Rentor ignored the barb and began, "I trust matters are progressing according to schedule, such as it is."

"As well as can be expected. Some of our scouts have not returned but the majority have nothing significant to report."

Seldis and Rentor exchanged the same warded glance. The enemy might be inadvertently tipping his hand.

"Which areas haven't reported back?" asked the king.

Huor unrolled a small scroll from his tunic pocket and studied it a moment before answering. "Mostly from the area surrounding Vorshir Lake. There are two still not returned from the plains south of Qail Werd as well."

Qail Werd. The great northern forest separating the Darkwall Mountains from southern Thrae. The forest was older than any of the current kingdoms of men, perhaps other races as well. Many great and horrible secrets were kept beneath the thick, double canopy. Rumors of Elves and a dozen other races dwelling within circulated the academic realm though none could say for certain. Qail Werd spanned the length of the mountains, taking several days to cross. Few dared to enter, mostly due to the proximity to the Deadlands.

"Do we know where Grelic and his people are?" he asked Seldis.

The monk quickly replied, "Somewhere around Gend. I have not been able to sense them for some time. It is almost as if my senses are being blocked, but by what I don't know."

"Are they still alive at least?"

"Yes, from everything I can tell."

The king leaned back and let out a long, deep sigh of relief. "Then we still have hope."

General Huor cleared his throat. "I'm afraid there's more disturbing news, sire."

"Go on."

"Captain Cron is missing. My men have looked everywhere in the city and surrounding area but can't find him. Under the circumstances I find it suspicious at best. Perhaps he is the traitor we're looking for."

Rentor's eyes narrowed dangerously. "I find that highly unlikely, General. Cron is the captain of Kelis Dur, hand chosen by myself for his skills and abilities in battle. Have your men double their search efforts. Treachery may have befallen him."

"That is one possibility, but my men have been searching for a week already. He is not in Kelis Dur," Huor replied coldly. His distaste for Cron bled through his words.

Father Seldis cut in before harsher words were spoken. "Our enemies may already have him. I know Cron. There is no evil or malice in him. He is a true son of Thrae."

"Be that as it may, Father, times are increasingly perilous. We cannot simply dismiss the possibility of his betrayal just because he is a friend," Codel added.

"Very wise words, Minister," Seldis replied.

Codel fumed at the implied redirection.

"A week? Why am I only now finding out about this, Huor? Tell me why no one thought it important enough to warn the king one of his champions has gone missing?"

"Considering his position we thought it wiser to investigate all possible avenues before bringing it to your attention, sire," Huor said flatly.

The apprehension in his voice suggested hesitance and regret. He passed a nervous glance towards Codel, so slight none of the others picked it up. Or so he thought. Father Seldis casually rubbed his chin in thought. He'd seen everything and now studied the general carefully. Confronting Huor here was problematic and would only serve to weaken the already fractured council. Seldis decided to wait to find time alone with Rentor before bringing the subject back up.

"I want him found," Rentor ordered. "My heart tells me some foul deed has claimed him, but if he has turned against us we need to know. Double your scouts, Huor. Keep the army where it is for now, at least until the enemy gives himself away. I will not see this kingdom fail while I still draw breath. If there is nothing else?"

They rose as one and filed towards the doors. Rentor soon stood alone, silently wondering what more he could do to save his people. He'd heard of kings so engrossed with personal power their kingdoms turned to rot and filth. His own father had been such a king. Rentor vowed the day he took the crown to never let that happen again. The fear of becoming like his father kept him grounded.

Father Seldis closed the door behind him and sighed. He'd briefly contemplated going back to speak with Rentor but decided against it. Everything was going according to plan and if he stayed longer than necessary he'd only give himself away. The aging monk slipped down the hall. Huor and Codel were a bit further off, whispering to each other in angry tones. Seldis passed by nonchalantly. Neither noticed the slight hesitation in his gait as he passed. Codel nodded to him coolly while Huor just glared.

An ill feeling reached out to him after he'd gone by. Their private meeting wasn't something he'd been able to foresee. Seldis looked deep into his soul and tried using his powers to discover more. Nothing happened. He closed his eyes and, using his Mage sight, searched out their auras. Foul shadows encircled their souls. Darkness was at work in Thrae and he'd been blind to it from the beginning. He hurried down the stairs and back to the stables. There was much work to be done and no time in which to do it.

TWENTY-FIVE

Aftermath

Grelic winced when Kialla tightened the bandage on his arm. She couldn't help but laugh at the foolishness of it. Old memories resurfaced. She imagined herself running through fields of wildflowers, eager for her father to return. Part of it stemmed from the knowledge that Grelic would be standing right beside him. Always. Constant. Grelic was almost a part of her family and she loved him more than either knew.

"What's so funny?" he scowled.

She tossed her head back and broke out in laughter. The golden song echoed through the ruins of Gend. "You. The big, fearless warrior who's been in more battles than any man alive, wincing from the gentle caress of his field nurse. Really, Grelic, I've seen you take far worse without blinking an eye."

"Wine and ale tend to do that." He grinned, despite his best efforts to remain taciturn. "How are the others?"

"About the same as you, though you managed to take the brunt of the beating. We're getting pretty banged up. The damnedest thing is Fitch came through without a scratch again. I've never been a big believer in luck but he's got to be the luckiest man alive. Two major battles and not a bruise on him."

"It is curious," Grelic agreed. He kept his thoughts private and did his best to ignore his previous vision of her slinking up to him nude and alluring.

Faeldrin and a handful of others had returned from sweeping the village of Goblins. The Elves all wore similar woodland camouflage and were nearly invisible to sight unless looked at directly. Grelic had never seen an Elf before and was surprised to find each bore distinct features separate from the general characteristics of the race. He'd always assumed from tales and hearsay that each Elf was strikingly similar to the next. This was not the case. Elves, he saw, were as different as leaves.

"My apologies for passing out," Grelic said as the apparent leader approached.

Faeldrin gave a curt nod. "Why were the Goblins hunting you?"

The giant was about to snap a comment about being rude when the Mage stepped forward. The Elves bowed.

"Master Dakeb. We did not know you were here," Faeldrin said.

Dakeb waved off the formality. "I had no intention of being here. Matters led me to Thrae and here I must remain."

"We're damned lucky he came too," Pregen pitched in. "He helped save our skins a few nights ago against the dark wolves."

Faeldrin's golden eyes widened. A murmur rose among the Elves. They'd run across the corpses but hadn't known any further information, until now. A sense of appreciation rippled amongst the Aeldruin.

"This is ill news, Dakeb. The dark creatures have not been loose in a century."

"Forces are working against us even as we speak. I have not yet discerned who or what," the Mage said.

"Tell him about the Dwim," Pregen led. He wanted answers more than any of them.

"Twice cursed!" Faeldrin gasped. "Evil is stalking this land. I fear for your safety. Such creatures should not have been allowed to exist."

"King Rentor has hired us to find the source of this threat. We've come this far and it is far too late to turn back now. All Thrae depends on what we discover," Grelic told the Elf. He didn't like how the conversation progressed.

Faeldrin regarded the bigger man. "More than just your precious Thrae is at stake. My instincts whisper all Malweir is in danger."

"Don't you think you're overreacting?" Kialla asked. "Granted, these are grave times, but we've been able to handle what's been thrown at us so far."

"My dear lady, when last these lands knew such peril, the dark Mages nearly destroyed us all. I would not see those days returned. My memories are still too vivid," the Elf said and then fell silent.

Ibram looked up from his sword in shock. He'd heard Elves were long lived, but to have been there during the wars, three hundred years ago, was inconceivable. Many stopped by the monastery during their travels and he'd been fortunate enough to speak with one or two. Faeldrin and his band were hundreds of years old, possibly thousands. Ibram stared up at the Elf's sparkling eyes.

"Yes, we were there. All those long years ago. The Aeldruin stood on the battlefield along with your Iron Legions and the riders of Harlegor. Times were different then. Men understood the meaning of allegiance." Faeldrin looked away, the bemused look he bore fading. "Grelic, I think the tide is against you. If my suspicions are correct, you'll need all the help you can get. The Aeldruin are at your service if you'd have us."

"That is a great honor but you may want to rethink the offer," Grelic replied. He shot Dakeb a guarded look. The Mage nodded back. There wasn't any point in keeping secrets. Besides, Faeldrin was right. They were going to need more help than their tiny band already had. Dakeb's premonition of a dragon left him shaken to the core. Perhaps the Elven mercenaries could help.

"Faeldrin, we have a serious problem. There's a dragon at work, but something far worse as well. I haven't figured it out yet. None of this makes any sense. Thrae is of no military value. There are no great riches to be had. No hidden treasures in the mountains or forests any longer. These are a simple people content with their lives. Yet look around. The burn marks can only be from a wyrm." Dakeb frowned as he fell silent.

"There hasn't been a dragon in this part of Malweir since Kalgor the Wicked attacked the Dwarves of the Bairn Hills," Faeldrin said.

"Nigh on twelve hundred years," Euorn commented. The way he said it suggested he was there as well.

The Elf Lord reached down and picked up a handful of ash. "Yet these signs are unmistakable. Dakeb, it's been a long time since we fought a dragon. Granted, we are mercenaries and our quests have always been noble, but there is only one place large enough for a dragon lair within a thousand leagues of here."

"Aye. Druem," the Mage said.

Another murmur spread through the Aeldruin. The very heart of the Deadlands! No good thing could come of this. Faeldrin bade his Elves to quiet down. "There is more you should know. About a week ago we came upon the ruins of another village. Thim, I believe. Similar to this but on the far edge of the Qail Werd. Evil is moving much quicker than you think."

"Time is running out. I fear our enemy is too far ahead of us. There is some dark game being played in Thrae that I don't yet know."

Faeldrin nodded and asked, "You think it's him, don't you?"

The old man stared at the Elf for a long time. He felt old, used up. He wasn't the same Mage that had ended the wars and kept the dark Mages from ruining the world. He was just an old man tired of fighting. Tired of all of the wars and never-ending nights of cold sweat and haunting failure. Dakeb sighed. It was a breath he'd been holding for years. All of his fears and visions of dark realities were coming true. It was a weight he'd been forced to carry since the fall of Ipn Shal, five hundred years ago.

"Perhaps not," he finally said. "But this smells of his work."

"Whose work?" Cron asked.

"Sidian, the Silver Mage."

They sat around three campfires. The Elves talked and laughed among themselves while waiting for the stag Euorn had brought down to cook. Only Faeldrin and the scout sat with the humans. The sun was beginning to dip over the horizon. Long fingers of shadow and night crept out to reclaim the world. Grelic suggested they abandon the ruins before nightfall, an idea they eagerly followed. Such a place could only attract evil.

Kialla took to herself. She wasn't interested in stories of Elves or Mages. Her body ached from exhaustion. Her hand trembled, slight but uncontrollable. She grimaced. She'd never been afraid in battle. That in itself was a rare gift. Thousands of men wished for the same though most were little more than bones collecting dust.

"Here, you need to eat," Cron said gently.

She quickly dropped her hand and gratefully accepted the wooden bowl of stew and hunk of roast meat. Her stomach growled in anticipation.

"Thank you," she managed between gulps. "I hadn't realized how hungry I was."

Cron flashed her a smile, secretly suspecting there was much more than just being hungry. He'd never fought beside a woman before. Truth be told, he never wanted to. Most fighting men viewed women as liabilities. He'd been no different until he watched Kialla battle the Goblins. She'd held her own and more. Cron had seen men crack and break under less and always passed it off as the unwritten rules of war. But Kialla, she'd stared Lord Death in the eye and made him flinch. Cron was truly impressed and already rethinking his previous opinion. Her being the most attractive woman he'd ever met went a ways in helping as well.

Cron helped himself to a seat and smiled again. He didn't know why, but she had a way of making him more nervous than staring down a hungry bear. "You're welcome. With all you've been through I imagine it's easy to forget the simple things like eating."

Kialla grinned. He made her relax, reminded her of being a little girl again when he came near. "I can't remember much actually. Both battles are somewhat unclear. Personally I think the Mage is putting something in the stew at night. Whatever it is, it's working. I haven't had any bad dreams since he joined us."

She abruptly fell silent, as if he wasn't supposed to know the great and terrible secret.

He took the hint and changed the conversation. "Where did you learn how to shoot like that? Not a single bolt missed."

"My father and Grelic. They taught what they could between campaigns and I practiced by myself when they were away," she replied.

Cron shook his head with disbelief. "And here I thought little girls picked flowers and played in kitchens the whole time."

"I happen to be very good in the kitchen," she said defiantly.

Cron held his hands up in surrender. "I'm sure you are. I wasn't trying to say anything bad."

She finished the last bite of meat. "You have to learn a lot when your father is away all the time."

"Where was your mother?"

"She died when I was still a baby. The fevers took her shortly after I was born. My grandmother came to live with us. She did what she could until it was her time. Then it was just me and my father. Grelic was there, of course. He was like a second father."

Cron decided to back off a little. She obviously held strong feelings for the old warrior and until he discovered what sort, he was going to leave the matter alone.

"What about you?" she asked.

"This is all I've ever known. My father was a soldier, and his father and his father before that. We can trace our military heritage back to the Mage War. Actually, I think most men can. That was the first time in modern history the world needed a grand army."

"I know the histories," she interrupted without trying to hurt his feelings. "I want to know about you."

There's a good sign. "I'm the youngest of three sons. The oldest, Maen, serves along the Thed Mountains. Brith lives with a wife and four children on a farm close to my parents' cottage. I think I was the only one meant for military service. The other two played along with me when I was a child but their hearts were never in it. Like good brothers they let me live out my fantasies. Those were good times. I didn't have a care in the world." He laughed. "We'd chase each other around the fields and woods with wooden swords, really just sticks, and then go swimming in the pond behind the house. When I was old enough I joined the army. I did my job as good as I could and got promoted. Now I'm the garrison captain of Kelis Dur."

"No wife or children for you?" she asked innocently.

"With what time? No wife, though there has been plenty of girlfriends to pass the time." He regretted it the moment he said it.

Kialla stiffened a little. Not much, but enough for him to wince.

"And no children. Well, at least none I am aware of. I spend too much time at work and don't have time for much of a social life."

She asked, "Why do you train so hard? Is the military really worth losing touch with reality? There's more to life than fighting."

He finally brought himself to look up into her soft eyes. Euphoria spread, warming him in cold places. Cron struggled to suppress his growing feelings. "I've given my life to the sword. Now Thrae needs me. She needs my sword and all those I've trained and fought with. The king believes this, so much so that he forbade me from joining you."

Her mind reeled in surprise. "You knew about us all along. This was no chance meeting, was it?"

"No," he confessed. "I'm supposed to be directing the defense of Kelis Dur but I couldn't stay. The ghosts of Reben and Ele haunt me. They died out here, stolen from me under my very nose. I will see them avenged before returning to the capital."

"You'll be branded a traitor."

"General Huor has been chafing to get rid of me since I got promoted. Looks like he finally gets his wish," Cron said dryly.

"How will you be able to go back? They'll arrest you on sight," she said.

"How can I forget about the two brothers I've sworn to protect? My heart tells me this quest is necessary. If, just if, we can succeed here, I know in my soul that Thrae will be saved. I can do no less," he told her.

Kialla reached out and gently took his hand. "You're wrong. It's not just you. We're all in this together, Cron. To whatever end the old gods see fit."

Halfway across the camp, Grelic looked up in time to watch her take his hand and a great weight was suddenly lifted from his shoulders. The nagging despair from his nightmares started to fade.

Dawn came much sooner than any of them wanted, but the long night's rest was both needed and appreciated. Even the Elves, who seldom slept, welcomed the respite from long days of hard marching and hectic battles. The remaining meat was reheated over a fresh fire. Fresh water and a few wild vegetables were brought in and the group ate a hearty breakfast. Men and Elves laughed and shared stories. The overall mood was filled with cheer. Times were coming when the dragon would fill their hearts, but not this morning.

Only Fitch felt out of place. His mind drifted elsewhere. No one noticed him slip away. He had one last thing to do before his demons could rest and it was something he needed to do alone. He walked slowly. His feet suddenly unsure. The Goblin carcasses were beginning to rot, adding to the fetid odor contaminating Gend. Much of his prior sadness was gone. Returning had been both good and bad. He kept walking until he was marching through what had been his life. It was all gone. His home. His beloved wife. At some point he had stopped blaming himself for the disaster, but he'd never forgiven himself for not being there for Shar.

Fitch looked at the ruins, remembering the way Gend had been. Sweet smells drifting up from the bakery. A trader caravan loading and unloading goods at the chandlery. He saw children running down the streets laughing and playing without a care. There was Agnes next to the meeting hall selling her flowers. Fitch felt his heart stutter as he fought back a wave of suppressed emotions. And finally, he was there. The rubble of his home looked nothing like his dreams. Fitch Iane had come home.

He dropped to his knees. His body was wracked with sobs. More than anything he wished he could have said I love you one more time. Guilt from never saying good-bye when he snuck out of the house hours before dawn that final morning. Tears ripped free. The pain was near unbearable. It hurt. It hurt bad, but this was the only way he could be free from the past.

"I'm so sorry," he cried. "I'm so sorry, Shar."

Fitch took the small wildflower he'd picked along the trail from their camp and laid it atop the pile of rubble that had been his home and wept.

Far enough away not to be seen, Dakeb watched the villager make his final amends. As painful as it was to watch, the Mage knew it was absolutely necessary if their mission had any chance of progressing successfully. Through long discussions with Father Seldis, he managed to piece together much of what had happened here. Perhaps the saddest tragedy was that most of the women had been taken as captives, Fitch's wife included. He wondered if he should let Fitch know. It was the same argument he'd had since leaving the monastery a month ago. In the end Dakeb decided against it. Fitch Iane had to learn the truth for himself. Through that revelation laid the path to victory. Sighing softly, Dakeb turned and left Fitch to his lament.

Faeldrin pointed at a spot on their crudely made map. Pine cones, sticks, rocks, and coarsely drawn lines in the dirt comprised borders and features. Though not entirely discernible, with a little orientation he could imagine himself in the middle of it. The others crowded around to hear what was being said. Only the Aeldruin were absent. They were already packing up the camp and preparing to move.

"The rest of my company is camped less than a day's ride east of Vorshir Lake. We'll need every last one of them to take on the wyrm," he said.

"How many are you?" Kialla asked.

Faeldrin offered a dispassionate glance. "The Aeldruin have always been fifty. No more or less. Most of my kind frown upon us, but we serve Malweir diligently when evil arises. This time will be no different."

Grelic stretched out his right shoulder, now stiff from pain. "What's the plan?"

The Elf Lord studied his terrain map. "I'm going to link up with the rest of the company and meet back up with you in a fortnight at Deldin Grim. The Aeldruin could be here much sooner but we need to craft weapons capable of bringing the dragon down. Dakeb, take the easy path. I sense great danger on this journey. A shadow clouds the future. Beware of the old ruins of Malg. Something wicked lies within."

The Mage nodded. "We've long suspected the same. Still, it is the quickest route to the gates of the Deadlands. It's also the only way we can meet you in time. Our path must go through Qail Werd."

"Time is of no consequence," Faeldrin cautioned.

"I know, but I fear. This evil plaguing the lands needs to be stopped. We must hurry before the shroud of darkness falls."

The Elf nodded grimly. "So be it. Until we meet again, my friends."

Faeldrin marched back to his waiting mount and climbed into the saddle. The Aeldruin thundered away, leaving the tiny band only slightly less beleaguered than before.

TWENTY-SIX

Tests

The warm breeze pushing across the open plains felt good. Both Ibram and his horse tilted their heads back. The group moved north at a leisurely pace. Grelic said it was less than ten days to the mountain pass and for that Ibram was exceedingly grateful. Soft living in the monastery left him woefully underprepared for the numerous challenges and hardships of extended travel. He was tired. Tired of it all. They'd been on the run since Eline and been in more battles than he imagined would happen when he first went to Father Seldis. Most of all he was tired of trying to live up to the unrealistic expectations he'd once held. He was starting to believe what the others told him. He wasn't the warrior he dreamed of being.

Worse, Ibram was confused. For so long all he thought of, his very will and dreams, was the quest. He'd heard the tales of men like Grelic since childhood and wanted so badly to be like them. He wanted to live the dream. Only that dream turned into a cold and bitter reality. Death and dying haunted him every time he closed his eyes. Once, he believed he was ready to go out into the world and be a force for justice. The brightness of that vision dimmed the longer this quest went on.

He discovered he had too many questions, not only about himself but life in general. He wasn't entirely convinced this was the sort of life he was intended for. Ibram studied the world around and saw so much life. Birds and animals. Wildflowers bloomed in multicolored blankets across rolling hills and valleys. Trees were vibrant shades of green and full of leaves. He longed to find the inner serenity nature held. To be at peace with the world. Even as he wished it, Ibram knew it was just another dream.

Father Seldis would say that all life was but a series of dreams interconnected through random patterns based on individual choice. At the time it didn't make sense to him. How could things be both interconnected and random? He shook his head, trying to clear some of cobwebs. Strangely, much of the journey was beginning to make sense in ways he couldn't explain. His failure against the Dwim still bothered him, but in light of recent revelations, he didn't feel much heartburn. Ibram had held his own against the dark wolves and then the Goblins. Even Grelic treated him slightly better, though he'd never admit it.

Ibram passed a casual glance over the others. The night with the Elves had done wonders for their morale and well-being. He used to feel sorry for Fitch but the timid villager wore a healthier complexion and was even caught smiling from time to time. That cheered Ibram. Fitch was too young to be burdened by hate and despair. A purple-winged butterfly danced across his field of vision, causing him to smile. Reluctantly, yet starkly and with no regrets, Ibram realized he wasn't meant to be a warrior.

"A nice day," Dakeb commented after noticing the smile.

Grelic agreed. "Enjoy it while you can. I fear there will be too few of them in the coming days."

Ibram frowned, the building good mood dashed like breaking waves on the shore.

Dakeb merely laughed. "Has anyone ever told you that you're the flower of optimism?"

"Many times. Tell me, Dakeb, what do you think of our merry little band?"

Dakeb had been awaiting this question since the day they spoke at the stream. "There's still too much mistrust involved, though I feel it waning. I'd almost say we were starting to bond. No thanks in large part to the number of adventures already suffered."

Grelic shook his head at the term adventures. "Dakeb, my heart tells me one of them is a spy. I can't figure out who though. The situation is muddled. I'm not a great thinker. My skill is in using a blade."

A red songbird landed on a small butterfly bush, catching Dakeb's eye.

"You know something, don't you?" Grelic asked accusingly.

"About the same as you. Not even centuries of Mage work can reveal our traitor. Some mysteries are only solvable through time."

The giant nodded. He didn't completely believe Dakeb. The question was answered too smoothly, too easily for complete deniability.

"Kialla seems happier," Dakeb transitioned abruptly.

Grelic suppressed an angry retort and decided to let his questions rest for the time being. "She deserves it. It's been a long time since she had reason to really smile. Cron's a good man. I've been watching him for many years now. He's a good fighter and a better leader. Thrae is fortunate to have men like him."

"Do you think she's going to fall in love?"

Grelic laughed. "Do any of us? I don't know, Mage. I've never been in true love."

"They say there's someone for everyone, Grelic. It's never too late."

Grelic laughed again, this time tapping the hilt of his sword. "This is my one true love. She's never let me down and doesn't talk back when I want to do something I probably shouldn't."

"Ah, Grelic, smell the freshness of the late spring winds! Ha. I've walked the forests and mountains of Malweir for hundreds of years and the one thing I profess to having no understanding of is humanity. People are frustrating creatures capable of intense love and unfathomable cruelty all in the same breath. Did you know the Mage orders envied man?"

"How so?"

"You have so much to live for. Your lifespan is the shortest of all Malweir's races. It gives you a sense of purpose, a reason for going on. The limit of your days drives you to excel." Dakeb sighed. "Take Faeldrin and his band. High Elven mercenaries! They are a most restless sort. The Elves can live until the dying of the sun and to what end? They've lost their edge, their drive. That's why the Aeldruin have been roaming the lands for two thousand years. Some die, others lose interest and return to their mundane lives. But the result is always the same. You'll always find an Elf ready for a new adventure."

Fitch rode up alongside them unexpectedly. His shoulders were higher, his chest out. Old pride long forgotten had returned after they'd left Gend. The shadows of self-imposed oppression were receding. He viewed the world again for what it was: a place of unending hope and promise. Fitch had already proven himself in both battles and came away without a scratch. Not even Grelic had such luck.

"How are you feeling this afternoon, Fitch?" Dakeb asked.

"About as well as can be expected," he said and smiled back. He was starting to feel like a part of the team.

Golden sunlight washed over the green fields as the clouds parted. "You certainly look much better. In fact, I'd say you almost looked happy."

"I haven't been happy in a long time," he said after a moment. "When better to start again?"

"Very good. What better time indeed. We should always laugh. Life's much too short."

He agreed. Memories of Shar were as strong as ever, and they gave him hope. "I used to ride across these valleys when I was a child. My father had an old dray. He said it would be a shame if we didn't take her out and stretch her legs from time to time. I miss those days."

"Wouldn't it be nice to be so young again?" Dakeb asked, memories of his youth suddenly blooming.

Fitch replied, "Yes. It's a lovely dream."

The landscape gradually changed from light forests and rolling hills to plush valleys of verdant grass. Grelic guided them along a small brook running northeast, hoping to take it all the way to Vorshir Lake. The mighty forest of Qail Werd lay not far beyond it and the Darkwall Mountains after. They were fast approaching the Deadlands. He called a halt just before dusk after finding a suitable place to camp. This far away from Gend, there were no signs of the dragon's desolation. White birch trees filled the forests like shining spears.

Grelic asked Ibram to join him once preparations for the night were made for camp. The former monk did so warily, almost expecting to be berated for yet another reason of minimal importance. He walked half a stride behind the giant. His senses warned caution. Grelic hadn't spoken to him, negatively or positively, since leaving Gend. It was almost as if he'd either conveniently forgotten or didn't want to add insult to injury. They stopped a good distance from the camp, well out of sight and sound.

"We need to talk," Grelic told him.

Here it comes. Ibram braced himself. "Yes?"

Grelic noticed the budding look of defiance and approved. "The easy part of this quest is over. From here on I'm going to need every sword. You have skills and talent, but they are raw. I'm going to change that. Draw your sword."

Ibram instinctively stepped back to avoid the huge broadsword waving menacingly at him.

"What…are you doing?" he stammered.

Grelic edged closer. "I won't say this again. Draw your sword, boy."

Untamed aggression laced his voice. Ibram reluctantly eased his blade free. The giant sprung, not waiting for him to prepare. Taken off guard, Ibram reeled backwards while fending off a series of slashing blows. Grelic was simply too fast and powerful, however. Ibram stumbled backwards and fell. The bigger warrior was upon him instantly, sword pointed at his heart.

"You're dead," Grelic scolded. "So fast and I didn't put effort into it. Get up and try again. Try this time."

Ibram's cheeks flushed. "That wasn't fair! I didn't know what you were going to do."

"Exactly the point. Do you think your enemies are going to give you time to say a prayer before they strike? A good swordsman has to be ready at all times. An easy kill is what we all live for in battle. Now get up and put some effort into this. I'm not going to die because you can't fight properly."

Ibram pulled himself up with a snarl on his face. Grass and dead leaves clung to his clothes and his hair was unkempt. He lunged after Grelic, mimicking the giant's own moves as best as he could. Grelic moved like the wind, much to Ibram's astonishment. Anger took over as every strike met only empty air. His best efforts were met with laughter. Furious, Ibram doubled his efforts. The giant seemed almost complacent fending off the clumsily placed blows. Ibram overcompensated and pushed too much of his weight into an overhand chop. Grelic sidestepped and swatted Ibram with the flat of his sword, sending him sprawling.

"Never let anger control you. Emotion will kill you quicker than clumsiness. You must be dispassionate. Controlled. You must envision the battle in your mind. Picture your opponent's next move before it happens," Grelic said as he got back to his feet. "Luck often settles the fight. We all die when it's our time. Don't be in such a hurry to meet yours. Now, come at me again. This time with a clear mind. Loosen your grip. It'll soften the impact and give you flexibility. You must be limber in mind and body."

He raised his sword in challenge. Ibram took a deep breath. He was very confused. Why did Grelic bring him out here just to humiliate him? He could easily have done that back at the campsite. Nothing made sense to him. Almost reluctantly Ibram returned the gesture. Grelic dropped into a fighting stance. His movements were slow, deliberate. His eyes wary. The battle began anew.

His sword licked out, clinging off Ibram's with a crisp sound. Ibram managed to hold his ground. He recognized the feint, a probe to test his reactions. Grelic nodded approvingly and stepped back. Ibram smiled. Then he realized his mistake as he was immediately hard pressed to defend himself. His blade was slower, almost lethargic compared to the brutal, more experienced swordsman testing him. Bitter realization slapped him across the face. *How ignorant I have been! A test. This is all just a test!*

All of it. The Goblins. The Dwim. Now Grelic. They were all just testing him. Ibram parried a harsh blow that sent sparks of pain up his arms. He adjusted quickly, spinning around and hammering back at Grelic's flank. Grelic dodged, pointing his sword downward to block. Ibram danced his blade up Grelic's, aiming a quick swipe across his midsection. The giant blocked again and retreated. Ibram continued to attack. Harder. Faster. He felt the battle flowing. He used moves practiced a thousand times in the courtyards of the monastery. Their blades clashed together in violent fury, drawing both inches apart. Grelic smiled wickedly.

"Very good," he commended. "That's enough for today. Remember, always fight with patience. You don't necessarily need to be better than your enemy to best him. I don't know about you but this sparring works up a massive appetite for me. Let's go see what's to eat and get some rest."

Ibram walked beside Grelic on the way back.

TWENTY-SEVEN

Repercussions

Fires burned under the weight of mighty Druem. Rivers of molten lava melted the rock walls with unbridled fury. Constant tremors plagued the area. Scourd held a sinking suspicion that the instability was going to become too much sooner than it should. The continuous mining operations weren't helping, perhaps were the cause. Sulfur and brimstone poisoned the air in the caverns and tunnels. He was used to it by now, but there was nothing comparable to the open air of the Deadlands.

The sounds of picks and shovels echoed around the clock. Scourd hated inspecting the work. Slaves gave off a sickening smell he found particularly offensive. Humans were disgusting creatures. The very thought of them turned his stomach. The caverns under Druem were polluted with their stench. Scourd thanked the dark gods for the open skies and the city fortress of Mordrun Bal.

His affinity for the open sky went unshared by the vast majority of his kind. He failed to understand the allure of living underground. The world belonged to them. It was merely by chance they remained shunned. Curses of damnation kept them from enjoying the tender kiss of the sun. Scourd hated man, along with all of the other races of Malweir. His sole aspiration was to wipe them from the face of the world. He hoped his alliance with the dragon would benefit him.

Ramulus and the Hooded Man were searching for something important. He didn't know what or particularly care. Let them plot and dig. Spend more years than a lifetime on an insignificant quest. As far as Scourd was concerned, their conspiracies were merely the opportunity he needed to begin his war. Soon all Malweir would tremble under the boots of the fledgling Goblin empire.

A pair of Gnomes scurried past carrying buckets of water. Scourd resisted the urge to kick them. Gnomes were the most disgusting of all races. Less than a meter tall with unusually large heads, they were known for thievery and spying. A miserable race whose loyalty was won by the depth of a purse. Scourd growled at them, causing them to shuffle away faster. Tepid water sloshed down on the cold, dark stone.

The hammering grew louder the deeper underground he ventured. Once comforting walls of chiseled stone now seemed confining. He wanted more. There was so much more than the pitiful existence grinding out before his eyes. A torch flickered, nearly blowing out. The light was unwelcome, robbing him of his night vision temporarily. He felt the hot breath vanish from the corridor. This wasn't right. He moved faster. A bad feeling grew in the back of his mind.

The tunnel ahead began glowing devilish red. Screams echoed through the corridors only to be abruptly cut off. He was halfway down the corridor when the nightmare erupted. A Minotaur raced around the corner, barreling straight towards him. His giant, seven-foot-frame was on fire. Molten flames ate his flesh. The air smelled of burnt hair. His horns and face were horribly disfigured, almost melting off the bone. The Minotaur fell dead a few feet away.

Temperatures rose sharply. Scourd stopped and looked down at the ruined body of the slave. Loud roaring, rival to that of the dragon, threatened to burst his eardrums. Cold realization hit him. They'd dug too deep! Lava splashed the walls, pouring down the newly constructed tunnel. They'd tapped into an active lava vein. Their incompetence threatened to ruin everything. The ground bucked and trembled. Druem had been inactive for hundreds of years. If it erupted now all would be lost.

The Goblin ran for his life, focused on the twisting stairwell a hundred meters away. Lava poured after him, splashing and hissing wickedly as it devoured everything in its path. The screaming had stopped. Those who hadn't gotten free were gone. He doubted there'd be bones left. Another tremor nearly toppled him to the ground. Sweat poured down his face, dripping into his eyes. He struggled to keep his balance. Death was but a step behind when he gained the first stair.

Scourd started the long climb to freedom. His claws scratched deep marks in the soft rock as he pulled and dragged himself higher. The heat was almost unbearable, threatening to swoon him. His breath came in ragged gasps. The roaring became almost unbearable. Scourd knew he was going to die in the dark gloom of the subterranean world. Delirium taunted him.

He scrambled around the corner and stopped. Terror and fear controlled him, rendering him all but immobile. No coward, the Goblin sat on the stairs and waited for Lord Death to claim him. But death never came. The world stopped shaking. The noises faded to unsettling quiet. Druem went back to sleep. The temperature started to drop. He watched the violent colors fade as the lava stopped flowing.

Confused, he rose. His only thought was that the vein they'd hit wasn't very big. Fortune smiled on him, though through skewed vision. He'd never know how many slaves were lost in the flood as the entirety of the lower caverns was submerged. Years of work had been lost. Frowning at how far behind schedule he now was, Scourd decided to head for Ramulus's cavern. He secretly hoped it would be flooded and his problems dealt with. The hobnails of his boots gave off a crisp report as his legs regained their strength.

Anger filled him. It took every last measure of control to keep from lashing out at the dazed guards and slaves milling about. A flicker of sudden movement caught his eye. Dwim. That familiar sinking feeling played with his stomach. The Dwim laboratories were deep within the lower levels. While he brokered no love for the genetic manipulations, Scourd understood he needed them to spread fear and terror in advance of the coming invasion. Fear, he knew, was the key to every success. He looked up to find himself confronting Ramulus's guards.

"Move, scum," he ordered.

Surprisingly, they obeyed.

"He's expecting you," the larger guard growled.

This unexpected declaration shook Scourd. He'd come expecting a fight. Instead they willingly allowed him entrance. Warnings went off in his head. Yet another thing that wasn't right. It all led to one possible conclusion: Ramulus was unharmed and potentially enraged. Scourd's strategy changed as he stepped into the cavern.

Much to his disappointment, nothing seemed disturbed. The heavy stench of rot and decay choked the air. Scourd momentarily debated which was worse, the stench of dragon or h. He hated both with equal passion. Unlike every other time, he had no difficulty finding Ramulus. The dragon was in plain view, awaiting him.

Potent hatred glared down from the way artificial light reflected off of his pale, almost opaque white-green scales. Vibrant yellow glowed hellishly from his cat-like pupils. Ramulus sat with his leathery wings tucked tightly against his long body. His wingspan was a massive two hundred feet. His tail, the tip bouncing lightly off the ground, ended with twin rows of spikes. Serrated plates lined his massive back. He weighed over sixty tons and had been alive for over a thousand years. He was pure muscle, lethal and dangerous.

"You disappoint yet again, Goblin," Ramulus snarled without delay.

Rage flared in Scourd. "I had nothing to do with this. Your miners dug too deep. The fires…"

"Aren't what concern me. Dragons are impervious to fire."

The caverns trembled from his bell.

Scourd's confusion deepened. What was he being blamed for?

"Your war party has failed, Scourd. Dead to the last."

Impossible. "How?"

"Not your concern for the moment," the dragon said. "The Hooded Man has doubts at your army's ability to defend Druem."

Scourd swallowed hard. No one crossed the Hooded Man. A sudden thought struck him. What was there in the volcano to defend? Did this pair know something he wasn't aware of?

"Are we expecting an attack?" he asked carefully. His real question went unasked. *Who killed my warriors?*

"The Fates have not yet decided. Or so I am told." Ramulus remained civil. "The Hooded Man and I both want security doubled immediately. Reinforce the patrols along the borders. Double the watch at Deldin Grim. I do not want our enemies entering this land unhindered. Stop them, Scourd, else your hide will be hung from these walls."

The Goblin fought for control of his tongue and left his sword sheathed, knowing the dragon would reduce him to cinders in an instant. "My Goblins will stop whatever threat you think is coming. We'll do our job, dragon. Who's attacking?"

He knew he was pushing it but without a proper target any defense he built was useless. Thrae was closest and not a military society. Their Iron Legion were famous across Malweir but Rentor seldom used them. Thrae's geological position made it highly undesirable for potential invaders. Still, should the complacent king uncover the threat and take the war to the Deadlands, it would be most problematic.

Strategically, Scourd knew he was positioned almost perfectly. The majority of Goblins weren't interested in history or their place in the world's view. Scourd was. Since his alliance with the traitor in Kelis Dur, Scourd took genuine interest in hu tactics. He had every intention of bringing the world of men to their knees.

"Your warriors, incompetent as they are, were killed by Elves," Ramulus said passively. Even when relaxed, there was pent-up rage in his massive form.

Scourd recoiled violently at the mention of his mortal enemies. "Elves no longer live in this part of the world. Why are they here? How many?"

"Insignificant questions. The Aeldruin murdered your forces in a single night. The Mage still approaches. I will not have either loose in my kingdom," Ramulus hissed.

"No *Fair Hair* will enter the Deadlands," Scourd bristled, taking offense from the dragon's claim.

He spun and left the wyrm to whatever private ruminations dragons had. Interestingly enough, Ramulus didn't bring up the incident in the tunnels or the loss of so many slaves. Perhaps they'd already found the artifact the Hooded Man sought. Scourd wasn't one for idle speculation but he recognized compounding problems. If what Ramulus said was true, there were enemy advancing on Druem, despite Scourd's own misgivings towards the information.

Too many questions came to life. Elves were troublesome. He hadn't counted on their involvement. He'd heard once that Elves walked in the presence of the gods. Phah! Goblins didn't believe in gods. He stalked back to his quarters with thoughts of murder lighting his eyes. There were too many variables for him to keep up with. His army was ready to launch their invasion south as soon as the Hooded Man announced he had the artifact, but it seemed the enemy was coming to him. He wasn't ready. He decided it was time to get in touch with the traitor again and discover the truth of things.

TWENTY-EIGHT

Bad Memories

The mid-morning haze was finally burning off, giving a shaded view of the surrounding area. Slowly rolling hills steadily gave way to open plains of verdant green. White and blue flowers dotted the landscape, adding beauty to the natural serenity. Ahead, in the distance, lay the great darkness of Qail Werd. Dakeb smiled, if for no other reason than to be in the presence of the mighty forest once more. His last trip this far north left him with pleasant memories. There was something to be said for the therapeutic value of trees.

Kialla looked up into the blue sky and gave a contented sigh. She missed days like this. She and her father used to head out at dawn and spend the day in the wilds. Those days were long gone, but her love for the simplicity remained. She rode up and joined the Mage. Despite the memories, she was left with uncertainty. Perhaps Dakeb could help.

"A beautiful day," Dakeb commented without looking her way. "Reminds me of summers along the shores of Thuil Lake. Even during winter one could look out the massive windows of Ipn Shal and admire the simple perfection. Life should stay so simple I think."

She smiled at the hint of sadness in his voice. "My father took me down into Averon once when I was just a girl. We went to Paedwyn. Kelis Dur is nice but nothing compared to the majesty of Averon. I've never seen equal."

"It is a wondrous place," he agreed. "The ancient kings chose wisely when they made it their capital."

"You make it sound as if everyone worked together and had a singular set of rulers," she questioned.

Dakeb nodded sagely. "Indeed."

"I don't understand."

"This part of the world was wicked and dangerous. When men first arrived they found few friends. Tribes of Goblins, Ogres, and Trolls roamed the lands virtually unchecked. Of all the mysterious races of Malweir, only the Elves bothered befriending the fledgling race of man. Of course there were differences, but none so severe as to ruin the alliance.

"Eventually men came down to the plains and made their claim. Wars plagued Malweir for hundreds of years. Mage-kind didn't exist then, leastwise nothing like later generations. Paedwyn was built after the fighting ended. A council of kings was formed and men spread into different kingdoms. Those of us with the gift were called to Ipn Shal, the center of power on Malweir. The Goblins didn't give much trouble for centuries. Come to think of it, they didn't need to. We provided our own damnation in the form of the crystal of Tol Shere."

"Were you there, at the beginning?" she asked.

"The beginning? No. I came much later though I was there during the Mage War. Once it ended, the kings decided against a singular ruling body. Sovereignty was returned to each kingdom and the order of Mages officially abolished. They even went so far as to hunt down and kill any surviving Mages. Those were foul times."

She felt sorry for him. "I'm glad you're with us. We wouldn't have made it away from the Gwarmoran without you. But tell me, how can you not hate man for what they did to you and your friends?"

He smiled, weak and aged. "I've lost more friends than you can imagine, but it was never man's fault. We betrayed ourselves. I doubt I'd trust a Mage after the amount of devastation we caused."

"Dakeb, how did you survive?"

"Those few of us alive scattered. I went to live among the Elves in the great forest city of Elvanara. Others remained hidden until we were sure no one alive remembered the causes of the war. Gradually some of us reintegrated back into society, but always with a lesser role. As far as the world is concerned, Mage-kind is dead." He stifled a quick yawn. "I intend to keep it that way."

"I'm sorry, Dakeb. Your life must be lonely," she said sympathetically. "Why didn't you just go across the sea to another land? Somewhere no one would ever know your past?"

"How could I? The reason the world was reduced to this madness was by my kind. We should have never made the crystal. Pride and arrogance superseded common sense. Worst of all, the crystal wasn't truly destroyed. The magic needed to do so was lost in the war. As long as the four shards remain I will roam Malweir to prevent the Silver Mage's return."

"Sidian." She wore a grim look.

"Yes. I haven't seen or heard from him in a very long time but my heart tells me he is ever present, lurking in the nether place where light and dark collide. I will not let him destroy the world a second time."

She picked up on the immense sadness in his voice and felt her heart weep for him. "What was it like, before the war?"

"It was a grand age. Perhaps the best in all Malweir's history. Peace ruled the kingdoms. No war, no bitter contests of will. It's hard to believe that man was so civilized back then. Communication, I think, is our greatest weakness. No one takes the time to talk to one another anymore. One of our greatest failings."

Distant thunder rolled across the sky, momentarily distracting him. "Back then the Mages had stations set up in every kingdom from shore to shore. Instant communications were established for the good of the kings. People were generally of the happy sort. There were grand balls and festivals. Commerce and trade flourished, even with the dourest Dwarves. Artists and poets created incredible works. I think I was happy, content at least."

Impossible visions filled Kialla's head. She saw herself wearing golden dresses the color of summer sunlight, escorted on the arms of royal courtiers, and brow the grand libraries through the works of all of the greats.

"I would have enjoyed those days," she admitted, reluctantly letting the visions fade.

"You would have been a queen, my dear," Dakeb told her.

They finally halted around midday, much to the old Mage's delight. He was starving and absolutely fed up with being in the saddle for so long. His talk with Kialla left him melancholic and kept his complaining minimal. Once lunch was prepared, he set after it like a starved animal. Such respite would be sorely missed in the coming days.

The rest of the afternoon crawled by. He and Kialla continued their conversation on and off. Dakeb made sure not to give away too much of himself. There were some things a Mage must keep secret. Especially when they concerned events yet to come. Through it all he kept a watchful eye on Fitch. The villager seemed in better spirits since confronting his demons. He might even be strong enough for what the gods had laid out. And if he couldn't, that's why Dakeb was there. Fitch was a good man, much deserving of a better life. Dakeb wondered why Fate had such a cruel sense of humor.

They camped just before nightfall.

Pregen finished eating and moved off to the side to sharpen his sword. He'd never been much for crowds and this group was already wearing on him. People made him nervous. He'd taken the job because of loyalty to Grelic and the opportunity to line his purse for life off of the king's coffers. He wished now that he hadn't. The offer seemed enticing at first. Go and snoop around a dead village, avoid enemy contact, and report back to the king. Easy money. Or so he'd thought.

Trouble stalked them at every turn. Pregen was convinced there was a mole among the group. Who it was remained a mystery. Each of them garnered specific suspicion. Then again, a man in his profession found guilt easily. Trust was as much an enemy as the man trying to kill him. Who was the spy, though? The problem ate at him, making it hard to concentrate despite him trying to forget it since their attack in Eline.

Common sense said that Ibram wasn't a suspect, seeing as he'd been the initial target. It also meant Ibram could have been planning it from the beginning and had some nefarious purpose in mind. Then there was Fitch. Harmless in every aspect of the word. He'd also been in severe emotional trauma for months, leaving him vulnerable. Who knows what happened in the weeks between Gend's destruction and the qu?

Pregen let out an exhaustive breath. There were too many variables to keep track of. Until he knew for sure, everyone needed to be watched carefully. It was the only way he was going to stay alive long enough to collect his reward in Kelis Dur. The only problem was they weren't going back. Not yet. The Mage was leading them to the Deadlands and what he assumed was certain death. No one returned from that horrid place. No hero, he brokered no intentions about becoming one now. He was an accomplished thief and assassin, but no coward. He'd given his word and meant to keep it, at least to Grelic. Cursing his ill-timed sense of morality, he went back to sharpening his sword.

Across the camp, Fitch curled up and fell asleep not long after finishing his food. Grelic envied him. Decades on the campaign trail and hard living made him impervious to most weather and a host of problems afflicting the common adventurer. It also left him calloused. Fitch wasn't the sort used to long days in the saddle or being hunted by the gods only knew what. His innocence was cause for envy.

Grelic turned his attentions away from Fitch and back to the group. Their conversation bordered on the mundane. They exchanged stories of battles long forgotten and hilarious events that probably never should have happened. *Typical field banter. I've certainly heard and said my share over the years. Makes me wonder just how much longer I have left to do this.*

His gaze fell on Cron and Kialla. They passed longing looks when they thought no one was looking. Grelic smiled. She was almost a daughter and he was a fine man. Grelic just wasn't sure that their pairing was a good idea, not in their professions. Then again, death was as likely an outcome as love.

Inevitably the conversation funneled towards what was to come.

"What can we expect once we enter the forest?" Ibram asked. He'd never been this far north, leaving each day a brand new experience.

Grelic was about to answer when Dakeb cut him off.

"Qail Werd was once the greatest of the old forests. A wonder from the days when man first set foot upon these shores."

"And now?" Kialla asked. Her long conversations with Dakeb earlier left her in no mood to listen to ceaseless banter and elaborate descriptions. She'd grown up with rumors of some dark presence lurking under the branches, deep in the heart of the old forest. No one could confirm it but everyone recognized the quiet menace.

"Now? Who can say? It's been a lifetime since I last walked the trails of the Werd. My certainty of matters is not what it once was. Had Ipn Shal not been ruined, we could have learned of the dragon's coming long before it happened and prepared accordingly. How he's managed to subvert an entire kingdom so quickly is boggling. But I digress."

He cleared his throat and took a sip of spring water. "As to what lies in Qail Werd, the usual I should think. Perhaps that is where our Goblin hunters came from, though I'd guess not. What we really need to be concerned with is the Dwim, perhaps even the Gwarmoran again. Make no mistake, whoever is behind these dark spawn attacks is very powerful, more so than any of you can imagine."

"The sooner we meet up with Faeldrin and his band the better," Grelic said. "We are getting too close to the Deadlands."

"Strength in numbers?" Cron asked.

"Of a sort."

Dakeb agreed. "Thoughts of the dragon aside, I suggest we stay away from the heart of the Werd. There is talk of a tribe of savages living in the deep woods. Hermits mostly, though I have never seen one."

"If they exist. It could just be a clever story to keep people away," Cron speculated.

"The signs are everywhere. Trails with no reason leading off. Partially eaten animal carcasses. Townsfolk are scared to enter."

Ibram's face twisted. "Could the dragon be in the forest?"

"Unlikely," Dakeb answered. "Dragons are mountain dwellers, much like Dwarves and Goblins. Druem is the only peak large enough to house one for hundreds of leagues. No, Ibram. It is the Deadlands we must travel to."

Grelic held up his hand. "First things first. Let's make it to Qail Werd and then worry about the foul land. How long will it take to move through the forest providing we are unhindered?"

The Mage thought for a second. "This time of year? Five days at least. Most of the old road is gone and the sun rarely reaches the ground in late spring."

"What old road?" Ibram asked.

His studies at the monastery were ranged, going back centuries, but he'd never heard mention of the old road. A road was just a road. To think otherwise left him confused. Surely the study of so trivial a thing was not in Harr's best interests.

Dakeb frowned, his concentration broken. "What did they teach you at that monastery? I shall have to talk to Father Seldis when this is finished. The roads, young monk, were created after the great unification wars. The council of kings needed fast and reliable ways to move armies and supplies. Originally they were built in order to combat future uprisings from the Goblins. Engineers from across the world constructed massive roadways of polished stone. They were considered a marvel of the time and were a source of pride for all of the races."

"What happened to them? I've travelled across Thrae and have never seen so much as a trace of one," Cron said.

"A casualty of the Mage War. You see, the engineers infused magic in the stones. Not only did this save countless years and lives but it also reduced the amount of toil and physical labor. No longer did men spend lifetimes cutting into mountains. Mage fire cut out the risk and trouble. We convinced the very ground to transform for our betterment."

He smiled fond remembrance. "Those days are no longer viable. Times are considerably darkened. We face peril from every direction and all will fall should we but stumble. I feel for each of you, for you have never known the beauty the world can provide."

He rose and made abrupt good-nights before ambling off to find a small patch of moss to curl up on. Sleep, however, was long in coming.

Grelic decided it was past time to stretch the horses. Jabbing his heel into his great stallion, he urged the roan into full gallop. The others followed suit. Only Dakeb remained at his casual pace. He was much too old to go galloping across the world with the wind in his hair and no worries. Muttering curses to the impetus of youth, he struggled to keep up for the rest of the day.

The next few days passed quickly. League after league went by at a steady pace. Shadows from Qail Werd gradually loomed across the ever-approaching horizon, dampening the overall mood. Dakeb insisted the forest was safe but no one would listen. The fourth night left them a few hours from the forest borders. At his urging, Grelic allowed a small fire. The Mage placed a ward over the camp and soon the smell of roasting meat settled over them. No one noticed the mixture of herbs Dakeb dropped into the small pot of stew. All they cared was that it filled their bellies and left them satisfied.

Dakeb was the only one to greet the dawn. He let the others sleep, knowing time was fast approaching when there'd be little rest. He looked to the breaking dawn for some dormant sign or portent. Purple and black gradually lightened to grey and then blue but he found nothing useful in the transition. Groaning inwardly, he decided the old gods must have a sardonic sense of humor. Thunderheads broke the horizon, coming down from the Darkwall Mountains. Lightning charged the atmosphere and the land took on an amber hue.

Only once before had he seen such weather at dawn. That day the winds howled and twisted so fiercely he'd never forget the screams or destruction. Whole villages were immolated by the funnel of wind angrily cast down upon them. No one knew exactly how many had died that day. The horrible images still plagued him and it was happening all over again.

He looked frantically around, feeling the sudden charge in the air. The wind stopped blowing, leaving the land encased in deathly silence. Dakeb knew there wasn't much time. He knew from experience that rain and hail was fast coming, followed closely by the funnel. The old Mage quickly roused the others and helped break camp.

Pregen groggily wiped the crud from his eyes. The middle guard shift had been particularly brutal. "What's the hurry? The damned forest will still be there later."

He cringed at the sudden look of anger shot at him and held up his hands in mock defense.

"There is no time!" Dakeb spat. "We must hurry before it's too late."

"He's right," Grelic said after studying the skies. "The weather's changing. A storm is coming."

"More than a storm. There's great danger. We must find shelter right now," Dakeb insisted.

Cron finished saddling his horse. "Where exactly? There's naught but empty plains between here and the Werd."

"We make for Qail Werd and pray."

"We'll never make it in time. It's too far," Kialla added and climbed into the saddle.

Dakeb shook his head. "It's the only chance we've got! Now ride, all of you!"

They left the unessential gear and bolted towards the ever-looming forest. The distance closed rapidly but not enough for Dakeb's liking. He knew they weren't going to make it. Qail Werd was almost unreachable. They'd started too late. Winds were already blowing with the force of a deep winter storm on the open sea. It started to rain, hard and punishing.

Dakeb couldn't help but replay his previous experience with this sort of storm. The air grew hotter. He almost hoped a fire was driving the winds and heat, but that was wishful thinking. They'd be hard pressed to outrun a fire, even on horseback. Nature was almost as dangerous as a Mage in its purest form. Wanton destruction traded out of callous spite. The rain hammered into them now. The stinging pelts were irritating at best, causing their share of groans and complaints. Dakeb had never been a big fan of rain before. This only made his dislike worse. Dark clouds, almost black, rolled across the horizon under a chorus of thunder. He was sure the mountaintops trembled with each clap. Lightning shredded the darkening skies, pushing closer. Time was almost up.

The winds stopped suddenly. Rain turned to hail, coming down in abusive sheets at slanted angles. The sky darkened, turning pitch black in mere moments. One of the horses screamed and bolted. Dakeb laughed at his own short sightedness. *Of course! What a fool I've been. Fear is precisely what we need right now.* He closed his eyes and began whispering an ancient incantation. An invisible blanket of fear spread from his fingertips, surrounding the already beleaguered group.

Dakeb designed the spell to only affect the horses, and it did. They whinnied and screamed in fright before taking after the first horse at speed. The old Mage held on for his life and shouted, "Run! The storm is upon us!"

With no real choice, they charged towards the forest. Nothing could stop their horses now, nothing but the funnel cloud descending less than a league behind. Dakeb hoped his actions weren't in vain. He was convinced he had to succeed. Or no one would be left to stop Sidian. Stop him from what, he still wasn't sure. The end of the world inched a little closer. He shook the dark images loose. There was simply no alternative to success.

A howling scream ripped across the heavens. The strange combination of wind and unabated fury dipped down like a skeletal finger. Grass, rocks, and trees were torn from the ground wherever the funnel moved. Dakeb groaned. It was heading straight for them. His fears developed so rapidly he couldn't focus on anything else. Imminent doom was after them. Shadows closed around them as row after row of massive, overgrown trees slowed their progress. At last, they'd come to Qail Werd. Whether in time or not remained to be seen.

TWENTY-NINE

Lurking Fears

Fitch knelt in the small ditch clutching his ears. He screamed but no one could hear him. The storm drowned out every sound but its own. He wasn't sure if the others were safe or not. His eyes were screwed shut. The protective bubble Dakeb raised was gone, effectively destroyed by the storm's raw power. The cast of fear drained their emotions, leaving him exposed. The last thing he saw before the darkness overwhelmed him was the old Mage passing out. Fitch knew he was going to die.

Heavy winds battered Qail Werd, but the trees were ancient. Their thick roots dug deep and refused to give. They swayed back and forth; branches and leaves ripped away to fill the sky. Small rocks and clumps of hard dirt whipped into the trees like projectiles, tearing gouts of bark. The howling increased at a frenzied pace until Fitch felt his eardrums threatening to burst.

They'd ridden as deep into the Werd as possible before the tornado struck. Grelic's earlier doubts bled away as the full force of nature's wrath lashed out. Dakeb tried his best to protect them with what little strength he had left, but it wasn't enough. The giant clung to a maple tree for all his life as heavy winds smashed rock and rain into him. His body was already covered in bruises and he'd be fortunate to see this through.

When the winds screamed their loudest, Ibram lost his nerve. He screamed back, afraid and angry. The former monk whispered prayers and curses to Harr in the same breath. He begged for salvation but his god remained silent. Ibram briefly considered Harr being angered by him turning his back. Perhaps leaving the Order wasn't wise after all. He wasn't a warrior. That cold reality slapped him in the face. He was just a man trying to live out boyhood fantasies. The stark brutality of the truth mocked him as the storm ravaged the area. Ibram closed his eyes and continued to pray.

Cron sheltered Kialla under his body. His legs were entwined with exposed tree roots for extra leverage. He wasn't sure how much longer he could hang on. His strength failed rapidly. Long years of battle and hardship left him conditioned better than most but even his strength wasn't limitless. A large chunk of rock crushed his spine, hurting him more than he wanted to admit. It tore into his flesh. Serrated edges ripped his tunic and skin. As glad as he was to protect Kialla from the brunt, he wished it wasn't necessary. Another rock like that and he might not make it.

As a leader he made it a habit to always put his men ahead of his own needs and desires. He felt urges and desires with Kialla he hadn't felt since entering military service. Cron felt the urge to protect her; to keep her from harm's way as much as possible despite the fact that she was highly capable of taking care of herself. It was a ridiculous notion that might only succeed in getting both of them killed. Cron recognized his foolishness but didn't want to stop. A woman like that didn't need a man in her life to take care of her. Cron pushed down as hard as he could. There was no way he was going to let her suffer if he could prevent it. Another rock struck his shoulders and he nearly blacked out.

Only Pregen seemed unaffected. The thief dug himself as far into the soft dirt as he could and pulled his heavy riding cloak up over his exposed body. Using a confiscated Goblin shield for additional cover, he tucked his chin to his chest and went to sleep.

The storm died out soon enough, much to their collective relief. Grelic was the first to stretch his sore body and assess the damage. He didn't like what he saw. Darkness was already spreading through the Werd. Smaller trees lay scattered recklessly about. Huge branches, now mostly stripped of leaves, dangled like broken fingers. He smelled smoke from a distant fire. The forest itself was remarkably still. No birds or small animals could be seen or heard. The now familiar bad feeling stayed with him. He set it aside long enough to check on the others.

Cron tried to stand but his back seized up and left him prone. Groaning, he couldn't move. Kialla managed to wiggle out from under him and immediately assessed his injuries.

"Hey, somebody check out the Mage! He doesn't look too good," Pregen called as he stifled a yawn.

Ibram and Grelic rushed to the old man's side. Unconscious, Dakeb's flesh had turned sickeningly pale. His chest rose and fell in shallow breaths. At least he was still alive. Aside from that, he wasn't moving. Ibram wondered if it wouldn't be better if he just gave in and passed away. They checked for injuries but found nothing. Whatever was affecting him went far beyond Grelic's limited battlefield triage.

"Is he all right?" Fitch asked.

Lingering fear slipped back over his face like a protective cover. Grelic wondered how close he was to the breaking point.

"Damned if I know," Grelic said and shook his head. "I've seen a lot of wounds. Seen men die a hundred different ways but never something like this. He doesn't have a scratch."

"Not compared to the rest of us," Cron managed through the pain. Kialla had gotten him up and he let him use her for support as he tried to regain full use of his body.

"Aye."

Kialla glanced down on the Mage. "I say we don't move him until we know for sure what's wrong."

"Look around you, Kialla. We're not in the friendliest of places. They say dark things linger in the Werd. I personally don't want to meet one," Pregen said and threw out his arms in an exasperated gesture.

"I've had enough of your bad attitude," Kialla snapped. "No one wants to hear your bitching anymore."

His hand reflexively lowered to his sword. "Mind your tongue, woman. We all have our opinions. This quest has been cursed since we left Kelis Dur. I say we turn back now before one or more of us get killed."

"Turn and run? That accomplishes nothing!" Ibram fired back. "All we'd do is let them know they won. Are you ready to throw away the lives of everyone in Thrae because you're afraid?"

"Careful, boy, you speak words you don't understand. This isn't our job," he said, turning to the group. "We're not here to fight a war. Let the army do that."

Cron cleared his throat. "The army isn't even preparing for war. Our forces are frozen in the middle of a feud between the top commanders. If the enemy strikes now he will crush us. Grelic, I think there's conspiracy at work in the city. Too many front line units have been reassigned to the outlying border posts and quiet villages out of the way."

"What are you saying? That your very generals want us to fail?" Pregen asked. Much of the anger had burned out, leaving him deflated.

"I'm saying that there are traitors in the city. Traitors with the king's ear. Rentor is a strong man and a good leader, but even a king may be beguiled during perilous times. Treachery roams the halls of the castle."

"It makes sense," Kialla agreed.

"You would say that."

She shot Pregen a withering glare.

"She's right," Grelic said. "We all know that our every move has been tracked from the beginning. As secretive as Rentor was, only a handful were told. All were among his closest advisors. There must be a traitor."

Pregen remained steadfast. "That still doesn't prove anything."

"Either we're being followed or one of us is the traitor," Fitch piped in.

They stopped their bickering and turned to stare at him. Each face ranged in emotion, from fear to amusement. Grelic had a wild flicker in his eyes.

"He's right, and I for one would like to believe we're being followed," Ibram said. "Pregen, look at me. I'm no hero. I was a monk a few months ago and a poor one at best. I've never had to steal for my next meal or kill to stay alive. That doesn't make me any less of a man. I'm no braver or better in battle than any of you, but I refuse to let my kingdom get destroyed when I had a real chance of saving it."

Kialla smiled fondly at him. This was the first time she'd been impressed with the boy. True to himself and the selfish ways he'd chosen years ago, Pregen clapped softly.

"Bravo," the assassin soothed. "Touching words that don't solve what's our best course of action. What do we do with the Mage?"

"We let him rest. If his injuries are internal, moving him could be the worst thing for him. If his condition doesn't change by morning we head to the rendezvous point with the Aeldruin," Grelic told them.

"It could kill him," Kialla countered.

Grelic nodded. "A chance we have to take."

"What about tonight? As much as I hate to admit it, the thief is right," Cron said. "We're too exposed here and who knows where the horses have gotten to."

Shadows were quickly spreading across the moss-covered ground. The tiny band could barely see twenty meters in front of them and hadn't the slightest clue as to where they were. Only Dakeb had ever walked under these boughs and he was in no condition to help. Grelic felt lost.

"It's too dangerous to move him right now. We still don't know what's wrong with him," Kialla repeated.

"Staying here could kill us," Pregen retorted.

"Enough of this!" the giant bellowed. "Kialla, you and Ibram scout the immediate area for a suitable campsite and try to find our missing horses. As much as I hate to admit it, I agree with Pregen. We're too exposed in this position and I don't trust the forest."

"What am I supposed to do?" asked the thief.

"Help the rest of us make a litter."

An hour later the weary adventurers managed to move Dakeb's inert form to a shallow cut in the forest. They painstakingly dragged the litter, careful not to jostle him too badly. The Mage hadn't moved a muscle on his own. That worried Grelic as he studied their camp. Large boulders and a thick stand of pines provided enough cover to satisfy him. Anyone coming at them in the middle of the night would be forced to do so head on.

The giant finally sat down and rested when he was sure he'd done all he could. He chewed on a chunk of dried rabbit. Too many thoughts troubled his mind. Dragons, Mages, Goblins, and creatures that shouldn't exist. He didn't know what tied them together. Couldn't figure out why they were intent on besieging Thrae. Something far more sinister was at work than a mere invasion.

Goblins and dragons didn't want lands or power. They stayed in their caves and mountain fortresses. They didn't collect riches or treasures. They killed for pleasure and lust, burning villages and spilling as much blood as they could before being forced back to their haunts. Infighting killed as many

Goblins as wars with the other races. So what could be the motivation behind this insurrection? It didn't make sense to him. Grelic had a sinking suspicion Dakeb knew more than he was letting on. As long as the Mage remained unconscious, possibly dying, the quest was in severe jeopardy.

Cron half dragged-half crawled over in the middle of the night. He couldn't sleep either. "All quiet?"

"For the most part. Something very big walked by not too long ago. I don't know what, and right now I don't want to know. We're fine as long as it keeps moving away."

Cron drew his sword out of habit and laid it across his lap. "I never imagined doing something like this. I should be leading companies into battle, not sneaking through forbidden forests and running from fell creatures."

Grelic agreed. "We're in bad shape if you get that bad. I'm over twice as old and about at the end of my time. I'm going to need your sword before this is finished."

"Go get some rest, old man," Cron chided. "I have the watch."

The giant offered a weak smile. Exhaustion gripped him. Cron reminded him of his own youth, thirty or forty summers ago. Thrae had been much simpler then. War was war. Any political positioning among royals and ministers stayed hidden. The people rallied under the banner of the king. Those days were long gone. Grelic surmised the same sort of behavior was taking place across Malweir, all leading towards some apocalyptic nightmare none of them could fathom. His suspicions led him to believe his tiny band of mismatched heroes were all that stood in the way.

He was walking off when Cron whispered, "Don't worry. I'll make sure Pregen doesn't go anywhere."

Grelic chuckled softly and found a dry place to sleep.

"Did anyone else hear that horrible howl in the middle of the night?" Fitch asked.

Kialla rubbed the crud from her eyes and went to check on Dakeb.

"How is he?" Grelic asked, ambling back into the camp after relieving himself.

She shook her head. "No change. He didn't hear it, that's for sure, Fitch."

"Lucky man," Pregen vented weakly. He hadn't slept a wink.

"If you say so."

Ibram dropped his head to his hands. "Can we not start this again? We're all tired, cold, and hungry. I say we fill our bellies and find a way out of this accursed place."

An agonizing groan rose from the deep wood. It was as if the very earth wept beneath them.

"I don't think the forest likes being mocked," Cron said nervously. "Perhaps a more friendly tone is required."

Pregen groaned softly. He was starting to think he'd never understand these people. "Nonsense. How can a forest have a conscience? What you're suggesting is pure superstition. You're making it sound like the trees are sentient beings. They're just trees."

The ground shook again, swaying them angrily. Fitch's knees buckled from the tortured sounds emanating from the heart of Qail Werd. He'd never been the superstitious sort, never gave much thought to ghosts or ghouls until Gend was ruined. Everything he'd experienced since then only confirmed his deepest fears. The forest was against them. If not against, it was certainly warning them. Something sinister lurked in the green depths.

"I don't think we should talk anymore," Grelic cautioned. "One way or the other, this place is alive. I don't care to find out the truth either. We need to get out of here."

"What about Dakeb?" Ibram asked.

The longer they spent together the more Ibram was coming to look on the old man as a father figure. He couldn't stand to see the man suffer, for it reminded him too much of Father Seldis. He wished there was something he could do to help. He hated feeling helpless.

"We need to try and move him."

Cron folded his arms across his chest. His back felt better but it was still unimaginably sore. "Are you sure he can handle it?"

"No, but I'm not sure we can afford to stay here, either," Grelic answered. "Faeldrin should already be on his way to the pass. We can't afford any delay."

"I agree. Let's hope Dakeb's condition doesn't worsen along the way. I don't relish the thought of facing a dragon without his magic."

Grelic glanced around. The forest was lightening, finally showing him the true extent of the damage. Nothing but devastation in every direction for as far as he could see. Grelic had a feeling the mayhem spanned the breadth of the forest. *No wonder the Werd seems angry. It's been hurt.* The giant looked skyward but the sun was hidden behind the rise of the ground. A thin mist clung to their ankles as if afraid to let go.

"We'll need rope to secure him to the horse. The sooner we start the better. I want to be moving within the hour," Grelic said.

They crept through Qail Werd as unobtrusively as possible. The only sound they made was the constant scraping of the makeshift litter against the leather saddle. At first they cringed from the noise, certain it was going to attract unwanted attention. Memories of the beasts and creatures moving through the distant darkness mocked them and soon they were all absently searching for monster-sized tracks.

The mood among the group remained dour. No one bothered speaking, fearful any comment would only cause consternation. Grelic led them northward as best as he could. The going proved extremely difficult, however. With no sun to guide them, he was forced to guess. Having never travelled these roads before, Grelic had no idea how far off they'd drifted. He only hoped it wasn't too far. No big believer in monsters, the giant had little doubts that whoever had sent the Dwim and Gwarmoran wasn't going to stop at the forest edge. His face knotted with grim determination, Grelic led them on, heedless of the scattered pairs of glowing amber eyes watching them from the safety of the trees.

Codel Mres slumped unconscious. His great stores of energy and health were depleted. Every ounce of strength had left his body. Wrinkles claimed his pale flesh, as if decades had come and ravished him with a passing flurry of time and anger. Sweat covered him. His robes hung loosely from the withered mass of his body. His eyes were rolled back into his head. If not for the constant twitching in his fingers and toes, he might have been dead. Unused to magic, Codel's body and spirit couldn't handle the pressure of the weather spell he'd just performed.

Across the room, wreathed in shadows, stood another man. The Hooded Man. His stature was minute, yet impressive. There was no misunderstanding in him. He was the very definition of dangerous. Whoever saw him turned away, hoping to forget they'd ever met. His pale gaze stared ominously from beneath the hood he always wore.

The Hooded Man stalked across the room, hovering over Codel's inert form. He looked down upon the traitor with disdain. If it weren't necessary for his overall plans, the Hooded Man would have already had Codel killed. He despised traitors in every form. Unfortunately, he wasn't in a position to do so. Plans were still being developed. Wheels were turning too slowly. Operations under Druem were behind schedule. The Hooded Man scowled at the relative failure stymieing him. Perhaps it was time to unleash the dragon. He was going to have to return to the Deadlands and take control personally. Too much was at stake and every delay was costing him dearly.

The Hooded Man held his hand over Codel's face, sprinkling a soft brown powder on him. "Awake."

Codel coughed once and choked. His eyes bulged, suddenly nauseous and out of breath. He gasped before his calculating eyes fell on the murderous figure standing over him. "Ma…master."

"The storm was unsuccessful. My powers were blocked," the Hooded Man said. "They have a Mage among them."

"What do we do?"

"I shall deal with this relic myself. I have a feeling he is an old friend. Prepare Thrae for conquest. In one month's time my armies will begin their invasion. I don't expect to find any difficulties in this campaign," he said the instant before he simply vanished.

Codel sat in his chair, noticing the frostbite on his fingers and lips.

THIRTY

Captured

The forest had a musky smell. Vibrant green moss clung to many of the trees and rocks, providing a tender blanket and adding vitality to the ancient lands. Time held no meaning under the storied branches of Qail Werd. Shafts of golden sunlight broke through the canopy at various intervals, lending an almost angelic beauty. Deer and small animals moved around again, though careful to stay away from the group.

Cron's stomach grumbled at the thought of freshly roasted venison. Days of dried meat and stale bread were taking their toll on him, on them all. He almost wished Grelic would stop them long enough to bring down one of the stags so they could have a proper meal. Almost. Discipline, training, and the hard life of a soldier kept him focused and squashed any complaints his stomach had.

They'd been traveling at an agonizingly slow pace for almost two days. Dakeb's condition hadn't changed and they were growing more concerned by the hour. If something wasn't done soon, Kialla worried he might die. They finally halted at midday for a quick meal and to check on their fallen companion.

"How is he?" Grelic asked solemnly.

Kialla brushed a strand of crimson hair from her face. "No change. I don't understand. He's not wounded. There's no visible sign of injury. It's almost as if his soul has been taken."

Grelic turned and walked away. Her answer was disturbing, displeasing at best. He needed time alone to think. So much was happening and they'd lost all control of the situation. It was almost as if their enemy was mocking them from his volcanic wasteland. Grelic forced the thought of how good strangling his opponent with his bare hands was going to feel.

Cron slipped in behind him and the two spoke softly. Something Grelic didn't want the others to hear.

"I'm starting to have doubts," he told the soldier. "We need the Mage."

Cron's eyebrow rose. "You didn't start out with him."

"That was before we understood the dangers awaiting us."

"As much as I don't like to admit it, Pregen may have been right. We can always turn back. Get more help. I can have a legion ready in under ten days."

"We don't have that long. Something tells me time is running out," he replied. "How can you be sure of their loyalty? For all we know, the throne has been usurped and we're the traitors now."

Cron shrugged, not wanting to think heavily on it. "True, the generals have their networks in place to ensure obedience throughout the kingdom, but a man in my position understands the potential threats better than most. I know whom I can turn to and whom to avoid. Most of the rank and file are loyal to Rentor."

"We may have need of them before too long."

"What are you thinking?" Cron asked.

"Someone's going to have to try and sneak back to Kelis Dur and warn the king."

"Who?"

Grelic grimaced. "That's the problem. I still don't trust half of these people. The only thing I can think of is one of the Elves."

"They won't be easy to slip in, even should Faeldrin agree to it. Security was already tightening when I left and Elves don't exactly blend well with hum. This could be more dangerous than we thought."

"No more so than tackling a dragon with a bad temper," Grelic laughed. "I hope that old man recovers."

They both stopped to pass worried looks back at Dakeb.

Ibram swallowed the last of his canteen and closed his eyes. He hadn't realized just how tired he was. It seemed every moment of the day was taken in some fashion or another. Grelic constantly drilled him on the sword, while Cron explained the finer points of strategy and tactics. He thought less like a monk and more like a warrior. Some of his earlier doubts and self-incriminations faded. The desire to take up the sword and defend those less fortunate, once repressed by his dismal failures, resurfaced and grew strong.

His confidence, still badly shaken, rose. He wasn't afraid to look Grelic or the others in the eye anymore. Wasn't afraid to voice his opinion before the group. He was at last a man and it was past time he started acting like one. Ibram glanced over the rest of the group. For the first time he realized he was just like them. All possessed individual strengths and weaknesses. More importantly, all needed each other. That in itself was more comforting than a warm blanket on a cold winter night. Ibram smiled.

Then he stared down at Dakeb. The Mage hadn't moved since the storm and Ibram was starting to think it was all too convenient to be raw nature. He cursed his lack of discipline back at the monastery, knowing he should have taken his studies more seriously. Surely Father Seldis would know what do in this situation. But Ibram's mind was always elsewhere. Lost in an odd malaise none of his brothers understood.

Ibram knew what it was. It was the irrepressible desire to know something forbidden. Something better than the pale existence of the Brotherhood. Though raised by monks, Ibram never felt at peacee within the simple walls of the monastery. The robes and endless hours of study seemed so mundane and lackluster. Not that he knew any other way. All he had were dreams until Fitch came along and presented the perfect opportunity to strike out and make his mark on the world.

He reached down and sympathetically touched a hand to Dakeb's shoulder. Ibram recoiled from shock at the immediate feeling of raw power flowing through Dakeb and into him. *This shouldn't be!* Ibram quickly withdrew his hand and looked around to see if anyone was watching. Then the impossible happened. Dakeb stirred. Not enough to raise his hopes, but just enough to ease that nagging feeling of dread.

Ibram wasn't sure if he should tell the others or not. The last any of them needed right now was false hope. He reluctantly decided to stay quiet and wait for the tired Mage to awaken on his own. They needed him to come back. He had to.

"All right," Grelic announced. "Time to move."

They carefully rolled Dakeb onto his litter and hooked it back into the saddle. Their nerves were more frayed this close to the heart of the Werd. The heaviness of the forest slowly gnawed at their resistance. Moods darkened. Worst of all, Grelic knew whatever stalked them was getting closer. Watching their every move. Studying how they carried themselves, the readiness to do battle should the need arise. Whatever it was, the giant didn't think they were going to last much longer before meeting. Grelic wanted out of the forest and into the comparative safety of the Elven mercenaries as soon as possible, Dakeb or not.

He gave his horse, his most trusted friend through the years, a soft pat on the side of the neck and gently stroked the bridge of his nose. The horse snorted affectionately. Grelic knew the beast was as anxious to leave as the others. One thing he'd learned as a young man was to listen to the animals, for they often had a better understanding of the natural world than hum.

"I know, old friend," he soothed. "I don't like this either, but what choice do we have? A few more weeks and we'll be home. Just stay with me that long."

It's only going to get worse before it gets better.

"Grelic, we're ready," Cron called.

Right. Time to go.

Unseen through the thick underbrush, five monstrous forms moved swiftly nearby. They ran parallel to the group, constantly pausing to sniff the air. Their sharp, curved horns tore stray vines and clumps of moss hanging from lower branches. They snorted, communicating in soft grunts. Their menacing eyes darted through the forest: searching, hunting. Each bore a rusted tulwar smeared with blood and gore stains. There was no question as to their intent. They were hunting.

Darkness blanketed Qail Werd in silent ceremony. Shadows and wicked visions came alive, removing any trace of friendliness the ancient forest held during the day. They rode on until they couldn't see and stopped for the night. Once halted, they set about the tasks and chores that had become second nature. Dakeb remained their number one priority. Until he was back on his feet, they remained in trouble.

"This is getting irritating," Kialla snarled after walking away from the Mage. "His heart is beating. His pulse is fine. Damnation if his eyes even adjust to the light when I lift the lids. I can't find anything wrong. Why doesn't he wake up?"

Frustrated, she spit in disgust and sat down with her head in her dirty hands. It took every ounce of self-control to keep from crying.

Grelic stopped Cron from going to her. "She's a strong woman, Cron. Right now she's feeling what the rest of us have been. She's tired, exhausted, and feeling helpless. Give her a little time alone."

"We don't have time," he replied.

His eyes burned hotly through the darkness. The giant merely nodded. "Sometime tonight."

"Do you think it's time we told the others?" Cron asked.

"We should. Especially if it comes to a fight."

The soldier wiped away some of the fatigue from his face. "I'll go gather them together. We need to do this quietly, just in case our *friends* are within earshot."

Moments later a host of anxious faces stared up at Grelic. He sighed at the weight of responsibility driving him down. He wasn't a leader. In fact, he much preferred fighting alone. Now he had no choice. He was the over-aged leader of a ragged band of would-be heroes. He wondered what he did to deserve this burden.

"What's going on now?" Pregen asked sourly.

Grelic fought back the urge to backhand the man. "We're being hunted and have been since the storm blew over. I don't know by what, but they're big and there are a lot of them. No one unsaddles the horses or packs. I have a sinking suspicion we're about to get attacked."

"What makes you think that?" Ibram asked.

"Watch the forest," Cron said. "We haven't seen a deer or anything else for almost two days. This evening even the birds are absent. We're getting attacked tonight."

Pregen felt his courage sink. This new threat was almost too much. "We need to mount up and get out here. Grelic, I've heard those things moving in the night as well and this area can't be defended. We need to leave."

At least he said we. Grelic frowned.

"That's what they're waiting for, to see if we break and run. We stay. We wait."

Fitch was surprised. "Wait for what? If these things are coming, we should leave. I'm with Pregen on this one."

"It's not that simple," Cron added. "These things can see in the dark and this is their territory. Don't you think they know every ravine and every stream from one edge of the forest to the other? If we run, they will wipe us out before we get far."

"What if it's the Dwim? Or the Gwarmoran? They can't know the forest any better than we do," Kialla theorized.

"The tracks are different. They're bigger and go on two legs. The space of the prints indicates massive strides. Whatever they are, they're big and clever enough not to be seen."

Pregen maintained his form and sarcastically asked, "So we're staying here why?"

"To draw them in. Once they're completely focused on us we'll be able to slip away in the confusion," Grelic said.

"They'll neglect the outer perimeter!" Ibram exclaimed. "What do we do until then?"

"Nothing," Cron told them. "We go about our routine the same as usual. Any change will only let them know we're on to them. Get some sleep if you can and keep your hands on your swords."

They drifted back to their tasks. An underlying chord of fear strained them. None were able to focus, instead casting furtive glances into the trees. Sleep was an illusion. Only Grelic managed to start snoring within a few minutes. Kialla was amazed. She failed to understand how he could remain so casual in the face of imminent danger. Secretly she wished for that same confidence and experience.

Grelic awoke to Cron's hand gently rocking him. Neither warrior spoke. The giant calmly picked up his already drawn sword and rolled up into a crouch. Time was up. He heard them first. Heavy feet crunching dried leaves and branches despite attempts at being stealthy. *At least the leaves he had Fitch and Ibram gather and lay down around the camp worked.* Grelic almost smiled. The beasts might be cunning but they were far from stealthy. Once his eyes adjusted to the gloom he caught a glimpse of Cron drawing an arrow. A quick look around the camp showed him the others in different states of preparedness. For some odd reason, Grelic imagined he was the only one who had gotten any sleep.

His thoughts were shattered the moment the first hulking shape barreled into the tiny clearing. Cron's bow thrummed twice in quick succession and the attacker fell. Any thought of victory was short lived as another four took his place. Grelic came up swinging. His broadsword ripped into an opponent's stomach, tearing entrails and bone loose. He ducked under a crushing blow from the spiked tulwar aimed at his head. Bark and moss flew from the tree behind Grelic. The giant stabbed into the ribcage and twisted his blade. His foe was dead before it hit the ground.

Another beast fell under a pair of arrows lancing his throat. Grelic almost had hope for victory until he noticed the night was teeming with violent red eyes and quickly moving figures. Hope quickly turned to despair. Across the embattled campsite, Fitch was clubbed to the ground. He fell over Dakeb's body and was still. Grelic parried a slash from a crudely made sword and kicked. His boot heel broke bones.

Ibram and Pregen fell almost at the same time. The assassin clutched his shoulder in pain and collapsed. Ibram was punched in the jaw, mercifully knocked out. Grelic couldn't see Kialla, but he couldn't stop to worry either. Cron's bow fell silent and Grelic was alone against a horde of snarling, panting monsters. He bellowed and swung his sword.

The shadow in front of him ducked and Grelic's sword lodged in a tree. A hoofed foot kicked him down before he could jerk the sword free. The giant fell but bounced back to his knees. He could see his enemy more clearly now. Their horns. Their prolonged snouts. Rows of large, gleaming teeth. Bodies covered with soft brown fur. Grelic was reminded of cows.

A large one, the leader, he guessed, pushed his way through the throng to confront Grelic. Drool hung from his teeth and anger flitted dangerously in his eyes. Grelic tried to rise but too many hands held him down. The leader snatched his hair and leered at him.

"Go ahead, you big bastard. Do it," Grelic said and spit in his face.

The others took great amusement from the petty act of defiance and laughed. The last thing Grelic remembered was a heavy crack on the back of his skull and the horrible laughter as he fell into darkness.

THIRTY-ONE

Dragon Hunters

Faeldrin and his patrol arrived at their base on the eastern reaches of Vorshir Lake three days after leaving Gend. Cheers and applause rose in greeting from the rest of the Aeldruin. They'd been without their leader for far too long. The Elf Lord watched the faces of his troop and frowned at the subtle apprehension in their eyes.

"Hail Faeldrin!" cried a slender, light redheaded Elf.

Faeldrin slid from the saddle and hugged his brother. "What news, Mearlis? Why is the camp in such a foul mood?"

"Evil creatures stalk the night. We lost Tai in a raid two nights ago. The Goblins know we're here, but we can't figure out how."

The Elf Lord laughed. It was a bitter, hollow sound. "If only Goblins were the extent of our problems. We've been signed for a much larger task and, unless I miss my guess, it goes to the root of our Goblin troubles."

"Tell me why I have a sour feeling in the pit of my stomach," Mearlis said.

He'd been the first to join Faeldrin all those years ago. They'd shed blood and drank till the wee hours of the morning. He'd even been there for the birth of Faeldrin's only son. If anyone knew how the Elf Lord thought, it was his brother.

Faeldrin smiled. "We're going hunting, my brother."

Mearlis patiently waited. He was used to the little games.

"There's a dragon loose in Thrae."

"A dragon!" Mearlis exclaimed. "We can't fight a dragon or have you forgotten we can't fly? I don't like this, Faeldrin. It's too ambitious, even for you. How in the name of Phaelor can we expect to take down a wyrm?"

Faeldrin clasped his brother's shoulder and said, "Have faith. The enemy is strong and even hope stands against us."

"And you honestly think we can kill a dragon? Your ambitions might get us all killed." He fell silent, spending long moments in deep thought. The decision was already made, however, and Mearlis was honor bound to stand beside his brother. The fear of facing one of the greatest powers in Malweir with just fifty Elves all but overpowered him. It was one of those rare moments Mearlis wished he'd gone back to his old life.

"We're with you. You know that," he finally said. "I don't know what you have in mind to fight the wyrm, but we're all with you."

Faeldrin's eyes twinkled. "Dakeb is with us. He and a small envoy from Kelis Dur are going to meet us at Deldin Grim in eleven days. Until then we have much to do. We'll need hundreds of arrows fletched and I think around five ballistae to do the job."

"We're to haul all of that across northern Thrae? Why not build it when we get close enough to the dragon?"

"Because nothing grows in the Deadlands."

Mearlis paled.

"There's only one place large enough for a dragon to hide this far north. Druem. Cheer up, Mearlis, we've a Mage on our side!"

"I heard you, though your words offer no comfort. You've been on a long journey. Rest and recover your strength. I will talk to the others. Food will be prepared shortly."

Faeldrin finally let his shoulders sag. He was no stranger to the hunt, but Mearlis was right. Fighting a dragon far surpassed any expectations he'd had when forming the Aeldruin. Perhaps he was being arrogant, though he intended to look upon it as being overly confident. Headstrong and determined, Faeldrin virtually forced him out of the communal living in Elvanara. The vast majority of Elven-kind wanted nothing to do with adventure, having done so much when they'd first arrived on these shores. Faeldrin suspected they might have gone home if their complacency didn't lead to the forgetting of boats and the ways of the sea.

He remembered the journey across the waters with fondness. Thousands of years ago the Elves undertook their greatest adventure. None of their years on Malweir compared to the breathtaking scope of their journey. Images of their homeland faded, blurred around the edges. Faeldrin finally found a challenge rival of that journey. A dragon! Despite the dangers, he found himself already growing apprehensive. He walked back to his tent, whistling nervously.

Dusk overtook them by the time he finished freshening up, changing his clothes and eating. The remainder of his company, including those who had made the patrol across Thrae, stood arrayed in a half moon before him. Mearlis and Euorn took the center. Faeldrin cast his gaze over each Elf. Their crystalline eyes sparkled with determination, giving him his answer.

"Welcome, brothers," he began.

They bowed as one in ordered discipline that only decades of working together accomplished. Faeldrin returned their bow as a king in review of his finest troops.

"I'm not going to mislead you with long speeches or fancy words. The fact of the matter is dangerous times have befallen us. Thrae is just the first to feel the sting of this new threat. You know of which I speak. The great enemy has returned. I followed a band of Goblin marauders across northern Thrae. They were attacking a small group of men when we finally caught up and destroyed them."

He went on to tell of his meeting with Dakeb and of the hero Grelic, legendary among men and Dwarves. Lastly he spoke of the dragon and the mission into the Deadlands. The Aeldruin visibly balked at the prospect of entering such a wasteland, but none voiced their dislike.

"I don't need to remind any of you what happened the last time the dark Mages rose from the shadows. Malweir was almost torn apart, yet we stood strong in the night and beat back the tide. Dakeb is an Elf-friend and a personal friend to many of us. He believes, as do I, that the Silver Mage is at work in the Deadlands."

Euorn stepped forward. "Faeldrin, every last one of us is with you, but I bid caution. We had magic on our side in great numbers during the war and there were no dragons to contend with. Dakeb is my friend, aye, but even he isn't so powerful as to defeat both wyrm and dark Mage."

"Let Dakeb worry about the dark traitor. Magic for magic," another seconded.

Faeldrin grew impatient. Any debate now would only prove senseless. "We have two weeks before meeting up at the pass of Deldin Grim. There's plenty of time to figure out who gets to fight what."

Nervous laughter, the sort only a soldier on the battlefield had, rippled through them.

"Mearlis has our instructions. Work hard and diligently. Let's show these Goblin scum the pride of Elven engineering. There's a dragon in need of slaying."

They cheered, momentarily forgetting the troubles of the future. Tonight was one of mirth and song. The quarter master broke out a barrel of stout rum imported from the Bay of Cuerlon, far to the south. A roaring fire blazed in the center of the camp and a pair of Elves hauled a wild boar on a spit for the feast. Yet, behind it all, the sound of saw and hammer echoed throughout the night.

The Elf Lord made his way among his brothers, stopping to speak with each of them. They laughed and shared tales and fond memories. Through it all he kept his brooding private. He fletched arrows, sharpened his sword, and helped cut down trees for the machines. After working up a sweat and feeling out the mood of most of his people, Faeldrin retired to his tent.

He wasn't tired. Elves seldom slept. Rather, he had the nagging feeling many of his friends, his brothers, weren't going to be coming back from Druem. Mearlis found him hours later, standing before a small pine table studying old maps of the Deadlands. A dagger stuck in the point of Mordrun Bal. Mearlis handed his brother a tin cup half filled with rum.

"It's no fun drinking alone," he said.

Faeldrin considered refusing but took the cup and let the spiced liquor warm his throat and stomach.

"What's troubling you?" Mearlis asked.

"Time," Faeldrin replied. "There is no time."

"We'll make it to the pass on schedule. They've already collected enough wood for two ballistae."

Faeldrin shook his head. "I'm not worried about that. Deldin Grim is one of the worst mountain passes in Malweir and I'm willing to bet it's heavily guarded. The Goblins need numbers in order to win. This feels different. We're going into the middle of their homeland. Deldin Grim is the only way in for a hundred leagues in either direction. That is my dilemma. If we had time we could skirt around the Darkwall Mountains and cross the Deadlands to attack. What happens if the dragon strikes while we're in the mountain pass?"

"That's what Dakeb is for, right?"

"Let's hope so," Faeldrin answered.

Mearlis absentmindedly studied the map. "Exactly how do we kill a dragon? Goblins are easy, but a wyrm! Do you realize that only two have ever been killed since the Elves first came here?"

"Nonsense. Dragons are like everything else. I'm sure that number is skewed."

"That isn't reassuring. I doubt we have time to send an envoy to the dragon realm and ask for one who happens to dislike the one in the Druem," Mearlis said sarcastically.

"Relax," Faeldrin said. "It's not that bad. I'm sure their hides can be pierced, perhaps not as easily as ours. That's why I have you and those wonderful ballistae. Make sure the engineers use green wood. Dragon hide is much tougher than armor. This is going to be an incredible adventure, don't you think?"

"How do you remain so confident? This is a suicide run."

Faeldrin balked. "Such words hold little meaning for a race that lives forever."

"We're not immortal, Faeldrin. Elves die too."

"This isn't a personal quest. Malweir is in danger and needs our help once more. Think what will happen if everyone with a good heart stayed home to wait for the end. What nobler cause could there possibly be?"

He laid a hand on his brother's shoulder. "We have a chance to do good for the world, Mearlis. The dragon can be killed and we're going to do it."

The Elves toiled for another five days, working around the clock. Each ballista was carefully crafted for durability and maneuverability. Twenty shafts per weapon were cut and crafted. Each was as thick as a torso. Smiths infused a coating of steel on the tips, adding to their lethality. Archers spent the days on the practice range, firing until their arms stung and felt heavy. The echoes of mock combat ranged across the dew-covered fields. The Aeldruin were going to war.

Faeldrin summoned his captains on the fifth night for a final council. "The time is now upon us. We have seven days to reach Deldin Grim. How prepared are we?"

Euorn spoke first. "Blades are sharp and we've enough arrows to take down a small army."

"The ballistae are finished and packed for transport. Some of our finest work," Aele declared. The chief engineer beamed with pride. "The added steel tips can pierce stone. This little dragon shouldn't pose a problem."

"What about the crews?" Faeldrin asked.

"Ready as they can get in our limited time. They need to practice drills but I've worked in training time along our route."

The Elf Lord nodded appreciatively. "You are the finest captains in Malweir. What we undertake isn't comparable to anything in recent history. Not since the Mage War has there been a threat so grave. Should we fail, the world as we know it will be forever lost. Take heart, for the powers of darkness are not the only ones at work. Dakeb has come out of his seclusion to lead us. We have never known defeat and I have no reason to believe we will this time. Go and prepare your teams. We march at dawn."

They saluted and filed out of his tent.

"Mearlis, a moment," he said and stopped his brother and waited until the tent flap closed. "I want you to send your fastest rider back to Elvanara and warn them. Should anything happen to us."

Mearlis had been awaiting such a command. "Buin left this morning."

"I should have known better. Thank you, brother. Now go and get some rest. It's going to be a long ride."

Faeldrin stood alone for a long time. He wasn't in the mood for questions or pre-battle banter. Tonight was for solitary prayers and reflection.

THIRTY-TWO

Awakening

Grelic's head felt like angry Giants were trying to crush stones on it. He tried sitting up and was stopped by shooting lances of pain from his eyes to the back of his head. Closing his eyes in a fruitless attempt at relieving the pain, he lay back down and let out a soft moan.

"Nice to see you're still in the land of the living," Cron whispered from across the primitive cell.

A single torch glowed from the far corner. Grelic finally managed to open his eyes without it hurting too much and looked around. Much of the cell was mired in gloom. The floor was sticky, almost wet from slush and waste. Moss grew on the walls. The ceiling was low, or so he thought.

"Where are we?" he asked.

Grelic tasted blood. *Probably bit my tongue when they hammered my skull.* He reached up and discovered the back of his head was swollen and throbbing. His throat was dry and scratchy. A sure sign he'd been without water for some time.

Cron edged closer. "Not sure. Somewhere underground is all we've been able to figure out. Our hosts haven't exactly been generous."

Grelic rubbed his temple softly to ease the building pressure.

Cron continued. "I got two of them before they got me. The next thing I remember is being hauled into a cavern by some sort of creature I've never seen before. They're huge, Grelic. Bred for war and mostly animal."

"You said we. Who else is still alive?"

Cron scratched at the stubble growing on his chin. "Just about all of us near as I can tell. No one's seen Dakeb or Ibram yet. Whatever these things are, they clearly had orders to take us alive. The gods only know why."

"Sacrifice or a hearty meal no doubt," Grelic said in a vain attempt at humor. "Is there anything to eat or drink?"

"Scraps of some sort of meat still on the bone. There's a pool of brackish water to your right. We did save you a half loaf of stale bread. Anything is better than nothing, right?"

Grelic greedily consumed the offered bread. There was no telling how long they'd been down here or how much longer they would be. Already his thoughts turned to strangling one of their mysterious captors and making an escape. The problems with that plan considerably outweighed the advantages. His eyes gradually adjusted to the subterranean darkness. Lichen ran the ceiling in patches. Water dripped constantly down some of the outcroppings and juts in the walls.

The mystery deepened. He'd been underground before, though never enjoyed it. Not even Goblins made their homes in such filth and disarray. What were these beings that had so easily overpowered them? Grelic tried thinking of all of the creatures and races he'd encountered in his long years of war and adventure. None matched their captors. Not even the foul Dwim.

Suddenly ashamed for getting so distracted, he resumed the conversation. "How do Kialla and Pregen fare?"

"Better than you. She has a nasty bruise on her left shoulder and Pregen's missing a few teeth." Cron laughed at that thought.

Even Grelic smiled. "That ought to dampen his charisma."

"And sour his attitude even more. All in all, we're in good shape. No weapons, of course. And none of us remember being violated."

Grelic frowned. None of this made any sense. "Why capture us? Have they demanded anything?"

"Not a word," Cron replied. "They come in, growl barely decipherable words warning us to back away, and drop off a platter of slop. They're not very talkative or hospitable, and there's more. Not one has raised a hand against us since we arrived. I don't know about you, but I find that damned peculiar. Oh, you can see it in their eyes. All they need is an excuse, or permission, and they'd be more than happy to tear us apart. Watch them when they come in. They take it as a challenge when you stare back. Whatever you do, don't back down. I think they respect strength and courage."

"The only thing on my mind right now is where the latrine is," Grelic groaned.

Cron gestured all around. "You're living in it."

Ibram didn't know how long he'd been drifting in and out of sleep. He also didn't know what had happened to the others. He swore Fitch and Pregen were dead; murdered by the monsters that had come in the night. Despite himself, Ibram fought hard to maintain some semblance of composure. Perhaps he was becoming a warrior after all. Grelic's training definitely helped. He was stronger, moved better in a fight, and held a more developed understanding of how to react to his opponents. None of that had mattered the night the monsters came. They tore through the small band with extreme prejudice and ruthlessness. Even after losing several of their own, the monsters pressed the attack.

He was placed in a separate cell with only Dakeb for company. The Mage remained unconscious. An earlier examination showed no additional injuries. Ibram wished the stricken Mage would rouse and help make the world right again. He felt lost and alone. And then, through the tightening hold of misery, Ibram remembered something. Watching Dakeb's shallow breathing reminded him of the night he'd touched the old man and what had happened after. Ibram was scared at first, but then curiosity took over.

He crawled over and sat beside Dakeb. Ibram looked through the gloom for any sign of their captors. He didn't know if the others were alive or dead but owed it to them to escape this place and warn King Rentor. The thought of being killed by the monsters appalled him. Ibram took a nervous breath. Dark thoughts scurried around the caverns of his mind. *Do I have the power to awaken Dakeb?*

His fears went to the Mage. Thoughts of accidentally killing him tormented the former monk. He'd sign his own death warrant. Perhaps more disturbing was the fact that if he did indeed possess the necessary magical qualities, why had he no previous knowledge of them? Was magic a latent thing until moments of great distress? That thought scared him more than dying. A potentially dangerous force, he had no idea how to control what he had done.

"I hope you're more ready for this than I am," he whispered to Dakeb with a shaky voice.

Ibram breathed deep and raised a hand. Too many visions and possibilities flooded his mind. Too many defeats and brutal possibilities. It took everything he had to keep from pulling his hand away. Time slowed. Every heartbeat was a frozen second in the nothingness of time. Sweated beaded across his brow. His mouth went dry, almost making him gag. He immediately recognized the sensations he was feeling. It was fear. Dark. Loathing. The visceral scream before blinding darkness. Ibram wasn't sure he was ready. In fact, he knew he wasn't.

"I'm no hero," he said softly. "I am exactly what they said. A would-be warrior with a wooden sword. I'm not ready. This isn't what I wanted."

He could hear Grelic snarling at him now. Cursing him up one side and down the other. Even Fitch would frown upon him. He really needed a friend right now, more than anything. Growing up in the Order's monastery was stringent at best. Every second of their day was filled with one regimen or another. Independent thought was neatly discouraged through political and theological manipulation. Ibram fondly recalled the many times he'd snuck off to play at being the omniscient swordsman trying to save the world.

None of that mattered now. He was alone. Alone and going to die unless he managed to save Dakeb. Ibram took another slow, steady breath. It was a technique Father Seldis himself taught. He closed his eyes and offered a silent prayer to Harr, hoping the old god would listen. He held his breath and lightly touched the palm of his hand to Dakeb's chest.

Thunder exploded in his head. His eardrums vibrated, threatening to burst under intense pressure. Pain became intimate. His familiar demon tempting him with wicked devices. Bolts of light shredded his vision. Madness rushed up from the depths of despair to claim him. The muscles on his neck strained to the point of tearing. Ibram struggled to keep from screaming. Warm urine ran down his leg. He started shaking. A rat scurried away. Not even the vermin wanted to be nearby at this fell moment. Ibram's teeth started chattering uncontrollably. His eyes rolled back into his head. Then the impossible happened.

A soft lavender glow spread from Ibram's hand. It quickly enveloped both Dakeb and the warrior-monk. Pebbles trembled around them. Wonderful humming stretched from corner to corner of the cell. Ibram blinked in and out of consciousness. The light flashed to dark purple, almost indigo, and darkness took him. Ibram collapsed beside Dakeb.

The old Mage gasped suddenly. His eyes shot open.

Grelic stared angrily at the hulking monstrosity standing in the doorway. Devilish eyes glared back, wordlessly accepting the challenge. Muscles tightened, rippling beneath his brown, fur-covered skin. Grelic knew he wanted to swing and start the fight. The desire for revenge had to be there. Surely this monster had been among the group responsible for capturing Grelic. Many of those monsters died that night. As much as Grelic wanted to get into a fight, his memories of his previous beating were too vivid.

The rusted iron gate swung inward. Three of the beasts slid inside. Heavy tulwars hung in their hands. Behind them walked a smaller, more intelligent one of their kind. He had antlers instead of horns and carried a long staff. He was old, his face wizened from many long decades. Some sort of spell caster or mystic, Grelic assumed. He leaned closer for a better look.

"Back!" warned the largest beast. The tulwar raised, inviting pain.

The shaman snarled something in their own language and the guard returned to his previous stance.

With crystalline eyes of remarkably sharp clarity, the shaman stared at the prisoners. "Forgive them. We often tend to fight first and think after. Agree?"

"Yes, I agree. All part of the business," Grelic replied. *Impressive. A primitive creature with a working knowledge of courtesy and the common tongue.*

Sadness lingered in the shaman's eyes. "You will come now. The lord wishes to speak with you."

Cron reached over to help Grelic up before returning to Kialla's side. The guards snarled and shoved, herding them with little restraint out of the small cave and into a large tunnel. Clawed fingers maliciously dug into Grelic's shoulders. It was meant as a reminder of what might happen if the shaman gave the word. Grelic didn't fight it.

The shaman led them down winding corridors of polished stone. Slime trails ran down the walls at various places, giving the place an unclean feel. More of the strange lichen grew, lighting their way. Rocks protruded like teeth from the ceiling and floor. Grelic found it odd that there were no loose rocks or dirt. It felt as if some great fire washed the place clean and smoothed it over.

Deeper down the shaman led them. He was disinclined to talk much the further they went. The differences between species made him uncomfortable and could only serve as a distraction should the prisoners try to escape. Grelic tried asking questions but only felt the claws go deeper. He winced but refused to cry out. Tiny rivers of blood trickled from the wounds.

"This way," the shaman urged when they arrived at an intersection with two guards standing watch over the tunnel to the right.

The shaman led them past the guards and into a torch-lit tunnel. Guards lined the path at intervals. Their faces were impassive, as if they'd witnessed this same event hundreds of times. Torchlight flickered off of their black vests. None bothered to glance at the prisoners or the shaman.

Kialla reached out and instinctively gripped Cron's hand for support. Neither said anything. They didn't need to. A silent understanding passed between their looks. One of the guards knocked their hands apart and snarled menacingly. The shaman turned back at the sound and glared threateningly. The guard backed off. Grelic noted the display with increased interest. Whatever else the shaman was, he was feared and respected. Grelic stored the knowledge and found himself looking up at a pair of massive iron gates.

"It's about time you woke up. I was starting to get worried," a familiar voice called from the dimness of unconsciousness.

Ibram rolled over as best as he could. His eyes flew wide from sudden shock. Dakeb was awake! He couldn't believe it. "How…what happened?"

Dakeb stroked his chin thoughtfully. "I should be asking you that question. You brought me back. All I did was lay there."

"What did I do?"

The Mage smiled. "You finally unlocked your latent ability and can now pursue your true destiny. My dear Ibram, you have the gift. You were born to be a Mage."

Ibram's heart almost stopped. He refused to believe what his heart knew to be true. An unexplainable feeling resonated deep within his soul. It silently whispered agreement to the Mage. Ibram was about to reply when a handful of their captors arrived.

"Speak no more of this for now," Dakeb cautioned.

A wizened being with faded antlers eased into the chamber. He bowed slowly, never taking his eyes off of them. "Honored Mage, Lord Thorsus wishes an audience."

Dakeb returned the gesture. "We shall be honored to attend."

Ibram stared in disbelief as his captors turned into escorts and they began the journey through the underground kingdom.

THIRTY-THREE

The Minotaur King

Grelic, Pregen, Cron, and Kialla were paraded into the massive throne room and told to behave before the shaman left them. The nearest guard offered a knowing look. Grelic fired his own baleful stare and clenched his fists.

"Now isn't the time to be a hero, Grelic," Kialla warned quickly.

"Don't want to be one. I just want a little payback for the beating he gave me."

The guard barked a laugh. Saliva and bits of partially chewed meat flew into Grelic's face.

"Not now," Kialla urged. Her voice carried a deadlier tone.

She was the only one still armed. Lady Killer stayed tucked in her right boot, carefully hidden from the clumsy inspection upon capture. Though it was created by the Elves, she harbored no illusions about being able to overpower the entire tribe and make good their escape. She guessed she might be able to kill one before having her brains dashed against the floor.

The giant scowled at her. Not because he was angry, but because she was right. He didn't want to die underground unless there was no other way around it. "You're lucky I like you."

The guards mocked him when they noticed the tension leave his heavy shoulders. Kialla flashed him the same loving smile she'd given him since she was knee high.

"Thank you," she whispered.

They were herded into a line in front of a massive throne of aged bones. Cron swallowed back the fear rising in his throat. He couldn't imagine what creature was forced to surrender its bones to construct this horrible throne. Two more of the wizened shamans emerged from behind the throne where velvet tapestries of the darkest purple hung. It was the only part of the cavern where Grelic found signs of habitation. Curious, he let his gaze wander.

The chamber floor was made entirely of emerald marble run through with veins of gold with a dozen pillars evenly spaced around in a huge circle. Intricate sculptures and designs covered each from floor to ceiling. A stone pedestal sat to the right of the throne. They couldn't see into it but the sound of trickling water echoed from within. More carvings covered smooth portions of the walls. They were of dragons and more of the huge, horned, bull-like captors. Finely woven tapestries, clearly of foreign origin, hung at odd intervals. Each was a vibrant color of the rainbow and bore heraldic emblems. Torches added an eerie mixture of light and shadow.

Whatever else they may be, Grelic recognized a warrior society. Their entire culture seemed to revolve around battle and warfare. Their dedication and devotion was praiseworthy. So much so that Grelic found himself carrying growing respect.

A heavy stone door groaned open from the far side of the chamber. A third shaman entered, this one hobbling on his staff. Behind him walked Ibram and Dakeb. Mouths dropped open as they looked upon the impossible.

"You didn't think I was dead, did you?" Dakeb asked in response to their disbelief. "Young Ibram brought me back, but now is not the time for explanation. I believe their king is about to enter."

"Dakeb, it does my heart good to have you back at our side, but what manner of beasts are these?" Grelic asked softly.

The shamans touched each other's hands and began to hum.

"We are guests of the Minotaurs, my friend. I'd quite forgotten about them in all of our excitement."

Cron asked, "Are they friend or foe?"

"We shall see."

As if on cue, a smaller Minotaur stepped in front of the huge golden gong and rang it loudly. Echoes danced in their ears, inspiring a range of emotions from startled to fright to awe. Twin lines of large bull warriors dropped to one knee and lowered their horned heads as another pair opened the heavy curtains behind the throne. Kialla gasped and clutched Cron's forearm as the Minotaur king entered his throne room. The soldier winced in pain.

The Minotaur king had to bend slightly to pass his immense frame through the doorway. Even Grelic balked at his size and power. He stood over nine feet tall and was extraordinarily muscled. Thickly corded shoulders and neck carried the weight of his massive bull's head. His right horn was broken in half from a battle long ago. He kept the scar as a reminder of the cost of victory. Mottled grey fur spotted his face and chest, betraying his age. The muscles of his arms were easily as thick as Grelic's legs. A bone necklace hung proudly on his chest. He had a thick mane growing down his back and an even thicker mat on his chest. The very ground trembled as a pair of shamans escorted him to the throne.

Once seated, the Minotaur king looked at each of them with a penetrating glare. He found nothing remarkable about any of them. Not even the big man who had supposedly killed four of his warriors. He snorted upon seeing the female and cursed the cruel twist of fate that made man the dominant species on Malweir. *If I only had their numbers. The world would tremble beneath my hooves.* His eyes fell on Dakeb and he bowed his impressive head. The ring in his nose dangled seductively. "Mage, you honor us with your presence. It has been long since one of your kind visited Malg."

His voice was deep and rumbling. Grelic was reminded of water crashing onto rocks at the bottom of a fall.

The old Mage bowed slightly as a smile warmed his wrinkled face. "Sad times have befallen both of our races, Thorsus." He smiled again at the

Minotaur king's surprise. "Oh yes, I remember you quite well. Your contributions at the battle of Shadom Gein will never be forgotten. It is thanks to your armies that we were finally able to besiege Ipn Shal and end the war."

"I am honored you remember me, though I was but a captain then. This is not why you are here. Tell me, Master Mage, why did you come into the Werd with such evil?"

The question was bold and direct. Thorsus learned long ago not to trust the devices of men. His respect for Dakeb didn't immediately transfer to the others.

"I don't understand. We bring no evil, though we've been confronted by it since starting our quest."

Thorsus leaned forward, clutching the skull locked in perpetual scream on the armrest. "The storm you rode was conceived by ill purpose. My shamans have yet to determine your innocence."

"The storm was not of our doing. True, it followed us, hunted is more like it, but we surely intended no harm to any of your kind."

The Minotaur king seemed to consider this for a moment. "Be that as it may, you brought much destruction into Qail Werd. This has been a haven for us for a long time. We have had no wars since the dark times. We want nothing to do with the troubles of man. The old alliances are no more. Today the Minotaur tribes stand alone."

Dakeb lowered his head ever so slightly in defeat. He was unsure what to say. What could possibly change their minds? How much could he keep secret before the very mission became endangered? Too many questions with little or no answers. He started to feel the weight of his years. He didn't know what Thorsus was thinking but knew well enough not to pressure him. He'd learned centuries ago that the mythic race was proud, stoic, and meticulous in their actions. Added pressure would only grate on the king.

"Mage Dakeb," he said and finally broke the silence. "I would speak with you in private council. You may bring the fledgling Mage. Your kind has earned my respect and I do not forget."

The others balked at the mention of a young Mage. Surely he didn't mean Ibram. Seeing both of them alive again was too much in itself, but to hear the massive bull proclaim Brother Ibram a Mage was staggering. A leering glare from Grelic eased some of the building tension. As much as he wanted to speak, Grelic knew this was the one time to remain silent. He watched the scene develop with unsurpassed interest. This was a first for him, despite all of his adventures and travels.

Dakeb bowed again. "What of the others? My friends are all in this together, Lord Thorsus. What happens to one shall happen to the other."

"They will remain in their cell and be given a proper meal. No harm shall befall them unless I determine you have come to do harm." His tone suggested no room for argument.

Dakeb sighed. "Then I request I receive the same treatment. I don't deserve better than my friends."

The Minotaur king raised a thick, questioning eyebrow. "You are a Mage. That alone grants you special privilege."

"If only such were still true. The time of the Mages is long past. My kind, what few of us still exist, are unwelcome in most kingdoms."

"What you and your kind did for my people will be long remembered fondly. For that I am personally in your debt. Mages will be given their place in my halls according to their rank."

"What of the others?" Ibram boldly asked.

Even the shamans looked on the youth with new light in their eyes.

Thorsus laughed, deep and resonating. The throne room echoed his sudden mirth. "The young Mage is bold. Impetuous. Perhaps there is hope for all of us. Your friends will go to their cell and be well cared for. You have my word. Both of you shall come to my chambers for further discussion. As you say, dark times are falling and I have need of your council. My word is final."

Thorsus nodded and the servant banged on the golden gong again, ending the audience. The ranks of warriors marched out in regimented precision. Grelic moved off on his own, trusting to the secret negotiations between Minotaur and Mage. Regardless of the outcome, it was the only real chance they had at getting out of Malg. He motioned towards the door to Kialla and she fell in line behind him. It took a more menacing look to make Pregen follow, but soon they were being led through the winding corridors.

The Mage watched them go with the slightest hint of apprehension. Their reunion had not been what he'd hoped for. Knowing they still lived was small comfort. Naturally Dakeb had known about the Minotaur kingdom under Qail Werd. He was one of the ones who'd helped them relocate after the dark times. Dakeb could only trust in their intentions. Normally war-like and aggressive, Minotaurs preferred a fight to sneaking around. Yet the general feeling he took from Thorsus and the shamans was one of hiding. It hurt him to see Malweir's proudest warriors reduced to a cowering mass of hollow strength.

Waiting until they were alone with one of the shamans, Dakeb asked, "Tell me, why is the mood here so dark? Thorsus spoke of us bringing evil to the Werd. My instinct warns me something else lurks under the great forest."

The shaman eyed him cautiously, contemplating how much to say. "It is as you say. Dark times are returning to stalk us. We are to pay for the crimes of forgetting." He smiled thinly. "No more can I speak. It is not my place. Lord Thorsus will tell you all you must know, Mage."

Momentarily defeated, the old Mage whistled softly. There was too much for him to think on to be content with half riddles and mystic answers. Answers he more often than not intended to give. Clearly the shaman had been instructed on what to say.

"How long have you lived down here?" Ibram asked, just to break the somber atmosphere.

The shaman was more than happy to change the subject. "Our home has been here for three hundred years. Before that we were a nomadic people. Then the dark Mages stole our lands, enslaving whole tribes to be used as slave labor and worse. Many horrible experiments were done to our kin.

"We rallied to the side of the loyal Mages during the great war. Many times did our might sweep the battlefields, turning defeat into victory. Those were glorious times! Sadly, the wars left our kind too decimated to maintain our open kingdoms on the central plains. Fenis, sire of Lord Thorsus, led us here to the boughs of the great Werd. It has been home and friend to us since."

"Were you there? During the war?" Ibram asked.

The shaman gave him a sad look and kept walking.

Schooled and trained as a monk of Harr from a young age, Ibram was taught to believe in every man or beast's free will and inert goodness at the core of their soul. He'd vaguely heard of Minotaurs in one of his readings but never imagined meeting one in person. Father Seldis never spoke of such things. Especially not about the dark times. Was Seldis a Mage?

His suspicions regarding Seldis seemed based on fact now. Dakeb awakened latent powers Seldis had been grooming for years. Suddenly his entire life took on new meaning. Natural doubt assailed his ego. He wasn't a Mage. He couldn't be. Yet Dakeb and the shamans assumed such and more. It bothered him to think everyone else knew more than he was being told. So intent on self-thought, Ibram failed to notice the immaculate perfection of his surroundings. The passage was arched, etched with alabaster carvings of Minotaur history. Beautiful statuettes sat on marble pillars every twenty meters, each illuminated by curious pale light that almost made them look alive.

"What is this place?" Ibram asked.

The shaman rapped the iron tip of his staff on the marble tile every time his left foot hit the ground. The sadness was gone from his features, replaced by strong pride. "The heart of the Minotaur kingdom."

A gilded door swung outward in invitation. They had come to the king's private chambers.

THIRTY-FOUR

Thorsus

Thorsus leisurely sat on a comfortable-looking chair filled with down pillows and silk coverings. He was just as tense as in the throne chamber, despite the casualness of the present setting. The walls were covered with animal skins and various skulls, trophies of past hunts, and glorious campaigns. Enormous rugs and blankets made of exquisite animal hides lay scattered across the floor. A small pool in the far corner of the chamber contained various ornamental fish. A lone tree grew on the island in the center. It was the only piece of greenery they'd seen in the underground kingdom.

The Minotaur king beamed upon seeing his guests enter. "Ah, Master Mage, welcome to my inner sanctum. This is the one place in all our lands I feel comfortable."

"Truly a place for kings and lords," Dakeb replied with a grin.

"Yet not up to the standards of the Mage order?"

Dakeb laughed. "Hardly! I wish I had something so grand awaiting me upon the end of this task."

Thorsus rubbed his thumb and forefinger together. "Ever sly with your words. I have missed speaking with your kind. Dark have been our days of late and you mention your task without waiting. More is at work here than I know."

Both men took their proffered seats, relaxing on the softness of the blankets and pillows. Though small in nature, it was the first luxury either had had since leaving Eline. Ibram immediately became too relaxed and sleep crept upon him. Neither Dakeb nor Thorsus were inclined to keep him awake.

"Youth," Thorsus said. "If only we were so young again. How much easier would life be? Don't you agree?"

Dakeb briefly remembered events from three centuries ago. "Yes, perhaps too much. We have entered the winter of our days, Thorsus." He leaned closer and said, "There is a dark Mage on the loose. We did not kill them all during the war. Now one has come back to rebuild the crystal of Tol Shere and open the gates to release the dark gods."

"You know who it is, don't you?" asked Thorsus.

Dakeb dropped his head. "I do."

"Hmmph. It is not an easy thing, having to face a friend like that again. I shall ask no further," the Minotaur king confided.

"Don't mind me. I'm just an old man with few friends and even less to do with my last few years. Thank you though. Now, I suspect you have a tale of your own for the telling."

"Ever wise. Our last few years have been fraught with danger. It started two winters ago when a strange darkness settled over Qail Werd. At first just a few of our foragers and hunters went missing. No more than one or two as the weeks passed. That shadow crept into our hearts. More came up missing. We sent a great war party to the north. To the Darkwall Mountains. Less than half returned. Many of those were no longer of sound mind. The shamans said it was like they'd been broken in two. I decided to make a stand in the forest. No more raid or war parties. That did not stop the enemy from coming after us."

He shifted his great weight. Fur stood on end on the back of his neck. "Goblins and Trolls, followed by other dark creatures my people have no names for, came cutting and hacking. We fought as bravely as our ancestors, but it was not enough. Our people continued disappearing. No one knows why or where they go for their bodies are never recovered. They simply disappear. I believe they are taken to the foul lands."

Thorsus fell silent. His face was twisted and mottled with rage. Knots of anger protruded from his forehead. The tale was hard to tell, even to one of the trusted Mages. Despite their trust and loyalty to the now extinct order, the business was for the Minotaurs. His fist balled in frustration and he slapped the arm of his chair.

"I'm afraid it gets worse," Dakeb added softly.

Pregen threw the rock as hard as he could. It shattered upon impact, sending a small cascade of dust and pebbles to the floor. His face was swollen and hurt from losing so many teeth. And he was angry. "What qualifies him for special treatment while the rest of us suffer?"

Cron swallowed the last bite of roast fowl and wiped his mouth. "This isn't what I call suffering. Sit down and relax. We have no idea what's happening with him."

"So we just sit here and wait to see whether we live or die? Like sheep heading to the slaughter," Pregen fumed.

"Will you sit down and shut up for once? I'm tired of listening to you complain about everything!" Kialla snapped.

She'd finally had enough of his childishness. The temptation to draw Lady Killer rose and faded just as fast. Killing him wasn't going to solve their problems and she wasn't that type of person. Granted, she'd enjoy it, but the pleasure would instantly turn to regret and self-loathing. Men like Pregen always got theirs went it came down to the end. Part of her hoped it didn't. The rest of her wanted to be nowhere around when it happened.

Grelic rubbed his forehead against the building headache. He leveled a stern gaze on the assassin and said no more. The conversation ended without another word. Mired in misery, the giant felt things beginning to fall apart. They'd been fed better than a king's banquet and shown at least a measure of respect from their hosts after initially being imprisoned. He'd been in worse, but with better company.

"What is our next move?" Cron asked once Pregen stormed off to the far corner of the cell.

Grelic rubbed one of his sore eyes. He was beyond exhausted and nearly at the point of burning out. "I honestly don't know. We don't seem to be too bad off at the moment. The food helped. I was growing tired of travel rations and cold campsites. I say we try to rest and forget our troubles until Dakeb returns. Regain our strength while we can."

Cron raised an eyebrow. "If they decide not to play nice?"

Grelic laughed.

"I'll admit one thing: this goes far beyond the adventure I was expecting when I left Kelis Dur. I wonder what the future has in store for us," Cron told him.

"How unlike the Captain Cron I know. Always has his head in the moment and never thinks too deeply on the future. You're tired," Grelic said.

"Aye. Tired of a great many things. I want this over so I can go home and fix things in the capital. If it's even possible."

"One impossibility at a time," Grelic cautioned. "One at a time."

Ibram awoke to the sweet smell of roasting rabbit. Drops of fat sizzled and sputtered as they hit the flames. A pitcher of almost black liquid sat on the small table next to him. His mouth watered and his stomach growled mightily. Until now he hadn't realized how famished he was.

"Eat, young Mage," Thorsus growled between drinks from the stone mug in his hand. "You're wasting away! Hardly fit for a Mage."

Both Dakeb and the Minotaur shared a laugh.

"He's still much too young for the kind of experience needed to know about such things, as I was saying before he woke up," Dakeb said.

"Too young for what?" Ibram asked.

Thorsus laughed again. "To know when to stop and eat, boy. Now drink! It's the finest ale we brew. Guaranteed to make you a bull!"

Ibram took a tentative sip before diving in to the murky liquid. The ale was thick, too heavy for his liking, and burned going down his throat. His stomach churned immediately. Thorsus watched him intently and burst into a fit of laughter as Ibram's face took on a green tinge. Even Dakeb found it difficult to control himself.

"Stay with us and you'll soon be a man," Thorsus snorted.

Ibram wiped some of the sweat building on his brow. "If I stay with you I might not live long enough for that."

"Eat…eat. Let the hare take your mind from the ale." Thorsus turned to Dakeb. "Long has it been since such mirth filled my halls. I am in your debt, Master Mage. Perhaps we may be able to help one another."

Dakeb felt a great weight slide from his shoulders. "Given the circumstances I say we both need all of the allies we can get. Let us renew the bonds of alliance so that Malweir may be at peace again."

"I'd almost forgotten the sound of such words. Troublesome is the darkness hiding my heart, Dakeb. Too many of my people have disappeared beyond the mountains. I fear for the future. Much of our strength is lost. I can't help but wonder how long before the curtain of doom falls."

It hurt his heart to hear defeat coming from the Minotaur's mouth, but Dakeb knew that similar pain was being felt across the world. Dakeb cursed the day they decided to create the crystal of Tol Shere. He never came to understand how so much evil stemmed from the overwhelming desire to do good.

"Evil is thriving again. It is for all races to band together to stop the return of the dark Mage. Only through such unity can we hope to defeat him."

Thorsus flinched at the mention of the dark Mages. "What help could we give? We are not as strong as we were during the dark times. We cannot fight a war."

"I intend to stop this before it comes to war. Thrae is being torn apart from the inside as well as out. The dark Mage needs confusion if his plans are to succeed. It is an old trick of his. The only way to stop him is to get into the Deadlands and the Goblin stronghold of Mordrun Bal. That is where all of the answers lie."

Thorsus cocked his massive head. "What else do you know? Why does the Mage want my people?"

Dakeb paused. Until now he only moved on assumptions and idle thoughts of treachery. If the enemy behind all of the nefarious acts being conducted truly was the Silver Mage, he wasn't going to be able to keep secrets from his allies. Then there was Ibram to consider. His world had just come undone. All the truths he once believed turned to subtle deceptions, keeping him ignorant. This was a dangerous time to learn he was of the blood of Mages. Finally, Dakeb looked back to Thorsus.

"I believe Sidian searches for the shard I once hid under the mighty volcano long ago," he said flatly. The admission struck deep.

Ibram nearly choked on the piece of meat in his mouth. "You hid it there? But why?"

"To prevent the past from repeating," Dakeb replied stiffly. "Those few of us who remained didn't have the lore or ability to destroy the crystal. One night we held council and it was decided that I would take the four shards and hide them across Malweir. Even then we had a foreboding that the war was not wholly finished. The rest of my kind went into hiding. They protected the lords and ladies of the kingdoms, often without them ever finding out. Rumors of a shadow stalking the land spread after a time. Some of us set out to learn the truth and only one returned."

"Do you believe this really is the work of the dark Mage?" Ibram asked.

"I don't want to, but it makes sense. The shard is under Druem. So long as it remains hidden we have a chance at victory," Dakeb replied.

"What help can the Minotaurs provide?" Thorsus asked.

Dakeb smiled. "We need supplies and a guide through Qail Werd."

"And after the Werd? The pass of Deldin Grim is guarded by more than just Goblins and Trolls. Dark creatures lurk in the hidden crevices. My people can show you the secret ways."

"It won't be that easy. We're expected to rendezvous with the Aeldruin at the base of the pass in four days," Dakeb told him.

Thorsus reeled in surprise. "Elves! I thought they did not exist anymore. We haven't heard of their exploits since the war. Does Faeldrin still command?"

"I doubt they'd listen to anyone else," Dakeb said and laughed.

Thorsus nodded his appreciation. "It is good to have friends like that in bad times. I am glad the Elves have allied with you, Dakeb. Seeing Faeldrin again would ease my spirits. It has been too long since the Elves graced these woods."

"Perhaps a meeting can be arranged once our task is done."

"I would like that. But come, I've kept you long enough. Time is of the essence, as you say. Guides shall be awaiting your party at our gates. Your friends will be set free and taken to the stores to fill their packs. Take what you need. The Deadlands are not a friendly place to travelers. I shall send Krek with you. He knows the mountain pass better than any other. If the enemy awaits, as I suspect, he will know what to do."

Dakeb bowed. "Thank you, Thorsus. I wish there was some way I could repay you."

"You already have. Hope is renewed. Whether victory or despair awaits us, there is hope. Rid the Werd of the dark Mage and we can take care of the rest."

"You forgot the dragon," Ibram added.

Both stared at him in surprise.

"Dragon!" Thorsus exclaimed. "One of the sky riders has not been seen in this part of the world for centuries. Are you certain?"

"Very. We found dragon marks in a village some days south of here," Dakeb replied while glowering at Ibram. "Worry not, old friend. This is a task made for a Mage and we are fully prepared to deal with the wyrm."

"This changes matters."

Ibram couldn't have agreed more. Old doubts resurfaced. He wasn't sure if going into the Deadlands was their best choice.

Dakeb said, "Nonsense! I've just cure for dragons."

The Minotaur king waited for an explanation.

"A surly old Mage who's seen enough of war to last a lifetime."

The hall trembled under Thorsus's laughter. "Very well. Let us see to your friends before the wyrm comes looking for the man bold enough to topple mountains."

THIRTY-FIVE

Lament

"You understand what I'm asking of you?" King Rentor asked the grizzled, old sergeant standing before him in dress uniform.

Sergeant Notam gave a sharp nod. "Yes, sire."

"Whatever you do will be unofficial. I cannot risk open war with my own men before the enemy strikes. You're certain you can accomplish this?"

Another nod.

Notam was already growing irritated. He hated being questioned, by anyone. Give him a job and it got done to standard. He'd made a career out of breaking young officers and stubborn farm boys pretending to be soldiers. His tenacity and unorthodox training methods were renowned throughout Thrae. He was the thing of troopers' legends and tall tales. Many a new recruit quailed at the thought of having Sergeant Notam as their instructor.

Rentor leveled his gaze and asked in a very serious tone, "How much can you trust this man?"

"Sire, I'd put your life in his hands without question," Notam replied. His stark white uniform was belted at the waist and had black buttons. Rows of ribbons and medals protruded from his chest, matched only by the green cord wrapped around his left shoulder. His polished boots reflected the sunlight. *And with good reason. It's his brother, after all.*

Satisfied, Rentor sighed. "I have a sinking feeling men like this might be all that stand between life and death. You may go now. I urge caution. The enemy has spies everywhere, even in my throne room." He emphasized *my* with disgust.

"Sire, you don't live long in my profession without being cautious." Notam saluted briskly and marched away.

King Rentor stood alone for many long minutes. Events were finally starting to unfold. He'd done everything he could think of to prevent total disaster but still had a nagging doubt about the future. He simply was unsure of too many things.

Rain drizzled from gutters and rooftops. The air was sweet despite being trapped in between the closely built homes and shops. Tumultuous grey clouds hung low to the ground. The tender crack of lightning played harmony to the rumbling thunder. Father Seldis stood on his balcony with his head tilted back. Cool rain splashed his face. It felt good. Satisfied by the freshness of it, he wiped his face, pulled up his hood and kept walking.

He'd never enjoyed Kelis Dur's crowded streets and occasional squalid living conditions. Like many of his kind, Seldis needed the open air and wide plains to roam. City life was akin to captivity. The monastery was a godsend compared to what these people were forced to endure. Seldis passed several homeless along his route. Seeing children like this always broke his heart. Being powerless to change it hurt worse. The monastery's coffers weren't filled with much more than enough to sustain its own meager needs. Yearly donations continued to trickle into Thrae's orphanages and halfway homes, though not enough to ease Seldis' concerns.

The steel cap on the bottom of his walking staff clicked softly on the faded red cobblestones. He avoided small puddles and tiny streams running down the sides of the streets. This wasn't the sort of night he enjoyed being outside in but the hour was late and time of the essence. No one paid another old man swathed in robes much heed, figuring him for a beggar.

He finally reached his destination and rapped on the aging back door. A gruff-looking man opened the door, staring down on him with menace. A thick moustache concealed his upper lip and, added with shoulder-length hair and thick, bushy eyebrows, gave him a wild quality.

"What do you want?" he snarled. His voice was slurred, as if his tongue was too large for his mouth.

Seldis grinned. "Must we go through this every time? I would like a drink if you please, Kernak. Now, are you going to let me in or do you plan on keeping this old man out in the rain?" Rain pooled in his cupped hand.

Kernak snorted annoyance. "Sometimes it's worth it just to see your reaction." The door swung open with an agonized squeal. "He's awaiting you."

Seldis passed on saying thank you and brushed by. He was careful to drip as much water on Kernak as possible in the process. The soldier scowled deeper but held his tongue. This was neither the time nor the place. A few torches were scattered carelessly about the room. The smell of smoke clung to the air. Seldis coughed. He hated coming here and made it known every time he was summoned. His eyes settled on the imposing figure seated before a cackling fireplace. Plucking up his robes, he took the opposite chair. Seldis was no fool. He knew a half dozen more men hid in the shadows waiting to fill him with arrows should something go wrong. *Every time.*

"Must we go through this charade?" he asked with casualness few others would.

Rentor looked away from the hypnotic dance of the flames. Sadness hung in his gaze. "You know as well as I that these precautions are necessary. Or so my wife insists. There are times when I feel like a prisoner in my own kingdom."

They both chuckled.

"Wine?"

Seldis smiled and reached for the pitcher. He took a long drink, exhaling a most satisfied breath. "There's nothing like it on a night like this. As pleasant as this is, there must be a reason for our clandestine meeting."

Rentor wiped a drop of the red wine from the corner of his mouth. "Aye. I believe the hour is finally upon us."

Ah, where has all the time gone? "How much longer do you think we have?"

Rentor shrugged. "It's hard to say. My instincts tell me Codel and his followers are ready to move. But it doesn't feel right. He's not that sort of man, Seldis. I've known him all my life. He's always stood at my side."

"And in your shadow. Corruption has a way of stealing the strongest of us," Seldis answered.

"Could it be the generals are behind his subversion? A part of me refuses to believe my lifelong friend has turned rogue so easily. Someone is guiding him. He's never been one for plots or political intrigue." Rentor forced a laugh. "Even tactics seemed foreign to him. Such a simple concept."

"You're right, of course," Seldis agreed. "Someone else is guiding him. They've twisted his mind. Codel Mres is no longer himself, Rentor."

He left out his mounting suspicions. Seldis hadn't spoken to Dakeb since the night the king came to the monastery to check on Fitch Iane. Neither of them really knew the driving force behind the insurrection, though all evidence pointed towards the Silver Mage. He remained the only dark Mage unaccounted for after the battle of Ipn Shal. No one else in Malweir was as devious or hateful.

"Whom exactly do you have in mind? General Huor seems to have his ear."

"Possibly," Seldis replied. He wasn't ready to raise the cry against the dark Mages or Huor without definite proof. The backlash across Thrae would be severe and spread quickly. Many innocent people would be taken and killed in a massive witch hunt. Seldis had no doubt on this. It always worked that way. He'd lost track of the number of men and women brutally murdered in the suspicion of heresy because some damned fool sparked a scare. Thrae would be no exception. If such an accusation broke out, the kingdom would die in flames.

All of this was happening so fast. Seldis hadn't had much time to think, much less formulate how to stop his foes. The Silver Mage was moving remarkably swift, however. It wasn't very surprising. He'd had hundreds of years to plan his revenge while the few remaining Mages weren't even sure of his existence. Seldis and Dakeb were always a step behind their former friend.

"I know little of your armies and the men who fill the ranks. Your own spies are the ones who can inform you better than I."

Rentor presented a diplomatic smiled. "There's something you're not telling me, Father. But no worries. My spies are indeed working hard to discover the truth. I fear what they may find. Father Seldis, I'll not be the last king of Thrae. Too many before me sacrificed for us to live free. Watching it all end now would be a disgrace to everything they stood for."

Seldis had always enjoyed their conversations, though of late they'd taken on dark undertones. He wished it wasn't so, and that he might be able to enjoy the autumn of his life wandering the lands with Dakeb once more. Oh the freedom of it all. Part of him often thought of days long past when Mages openly traveled the world without fear of persecution.

Thoughts like that often led back to poor Fitch Iane and Brother Ibram. There'd been a hundred times he'd wanted to tell Ibram the truth and begin his training. Dakeb argued against it from the beginning. The time was never right for it. Whenever Seldis asked when, he was dismissed with an idle wave. No one knew when, and that became a major issue. There were no Mages left to scour the lands in search of those trainable in the arts. There was no temple, castle, or academy to train the youth. Seldis was afraid the title of Mage was going to die not long after they did. He spent many lonely nights cursing their misfortune. The days had once been glorious and filled with such promise. Now only the prospect of darkness remained. His one hope lay in Fitch and Ibram being strong enough to see the task through. Sidian had timed his offensive well. Mage-kind was in its darkest hour.

"Fear not, priest of Harr. I shall not ask your secrets," Rentor said and leaned a little closer so that his words didn't carry. "I think when this sad affair is done there are a great many things we should discuss, you and I."

Seldis immediately picked out the mischievous twinkle in the king's eyes. "I should enjoy that, provided we stem the tide of darkness and you bring enough mulled wine to last the night."

Rentor's chuckle was hollow. "All pleasantries aside, what can you tell me of the days to come? The Order of Harr is said to harbor prophets and mind readers. What do you see for the future of Thrae?"

Seldis rubbed his bottom lip. "People talk too much. It doesn't take a mind reader to know what's going on in another's. All one must do is pay attention and understand the complications facing modern man. A beggar can become a prophet on a good day. It's mostly guess work. I've never been much good at it myself. Once, long ago, I knew some with the talent. They were gifted men and women but that was another time, another land."

"That was not the comforting answer I was looking for," Rentor scolded.

"Should it be? These are uncomfortable times. You don't know the horrors coming, Rentor. The Silver Mage is the physical manifestation of a nightmare untamed. It will be all any of us can do to stand against the tide. Strength and courage are our best allies now," Seldis snapped back.

Rentor snorted. "Those I have plenty of. How can I fight a war when I'm not even sure of the loyalties of half my army?"

"I don't have an answer. We must play out the hand given us."

Finishing his wine, Rentor poured another glass. "How goes life at the monastery? Any more willing recruits come to join the flock?"

Seldis gladly obliged the change of conversation. Every little escape was appreciated. For now at least, they were two old friends speaking of simple matters. "Few men willingly come to join the ranks. The old gods no longer hold sway over Malweir. Youth is too impetuous. These children today are anxious to go out into the world and make a name."

Laughing, Rentor said, "It is no different from when I was a child. I can still remember going hunting with my father. How I wished he'd let me go out on my own. Do you have any idea how much I wanted to bring home a great horned stag just to see the looks on my family's face?"

"The dreams of youth are so innocent," Seldis agreed.

"Let us hope our children live to have such."

They sat in silence, listening to the gentle crackling of burning wood and sipping mulled wine.

THIRTY-SIX

Partings

Thorsus led the guards personally. Their cloven feet rumbled through the winding corridors and halls of Malg with unsurpassed authority. The Minotaur kingdom was alive again. Rage and pent-up emotions reverberated through the limestone walls. Warriors gathered in great numbers, waving their weapons and snarling battle cries. Thorsus felt their hunger. He desperately wanted to be back in the heat of battle. To feel the sting of combat as warriors fell around him. He let loose a throaty roar that spread among the guards.

At last the procession arrived at the dungeons. Thorsus was mildly surprised to find his guests standing in a group behind the door. The larger of the humans was in the front, clearly their leader. The Minotaur king knew him by reputation. Respect was metered accordingly. He wanted to test the giant in combat or perhaps join him in fighting their common foe. What tales would be sung! Entire kingdoms would kneel to their might.

Stepping before the door, Thorsus carefully eyed each of them again. The slender one missing teeth had the feel of treachery about him. The Minotaur's instincts warned to keep this one caged for he was surely no good for the mission. Careful not to voice his outspoken opinion, Thorsus bowed slightly to them.

"My apologies for keeping you here so long, but times are not what they once were. We need caution, even in Qail Werd. Speaking with Master Dakeb, I have come to know the importance of your quest and would see you on your way."

His heavy, black eyes fell on Fitch, who meekly stared back. Again the Minotaur king laughed. "You wonder how it is I can speak your tongue so well when others cannot? That is a tale long in the telling and there is no time. Perhaps when you return for the victory feast I shall indulge you."

He motioned for a guard to unlock the door and made a sweeping gesture with his arm.

Grelic grinned fiercely. "Let it never be said the hospitality of the Minotaurs is lacking."

"Many would argue otherwise."

"Goblins and Trolls are a filth in need of cleansing. Perhaps you and I should strike up the sword and go to war ourselves." Grelic enjoyed the thought.

Both knew it would never happen. The Minotaurs ruthlessly attacked in the forest and Grelic responded in kind. Desperate times made them unsteady allies but the killing of so many of Thorsus's warriors demanded repayment. He'd wait until after the dragon was dead to see how far he'd go in trusting the massive bull.

There was a momentary flicker of misgiving in the Minotaur's dark eyes. The loss of so many warriors to the humans was still too near to let go. It faded quickly as he remembered his promise to Dakeb. "Indeed."

He spoke to the guards in their language, sounding like no more than grunts and snorts to Grelic's band. They passed disapproving glances among each other and Grelic noticed Thorsus's rising anger. His nostrils flared, vibrating the thick, iron ring. Any debate ended immediately.

Thorsus faced his guests. "My warriors will escort you to the arms room. There you will find all of your weapons and perhaps a few others that may better suit your quest. I leave you in their capable hands. Much is still needed to be said with the Mages. I take my leave of you now."

He bowed stiffly, as if unaccustomed to the act.

"Thank you," Cron replied when he noticed the giant's sudden reluctance. He reminded himself to ask Grelic about it the next time they were alone.

"This way. Come now," snarled the smaller of the two remaining Minotaurs.

Friendly enough in his own hostile mannerisms, the Minotaur was focused on performing his king's orders. Cron had come to understand them, slightly, and almost admired the young bull leading them. He respected the militaristic culture and wished he had a battalion to throw into his own battle lines. Still, he found it disturbing that the Minotaur kingdom thrived under Qail Werd without the king of Thrae knowing. Considering how large the human population had grown and expanded, Cron feared for his kingdom should Thorsus ever decide he'd had enough.

They came to the end of the tunnel and Cron's eyes widened in amazement. He'd been around weapons and smiths all of his life but had never seen anything comparable to the Minotaur armory. An enormous cavern stretched out before them. Coal fires bathed the cavern with a hellish glaze. Smiths and apprentices hammered freshly poured steel. Great racks of swords, tulwars, shields, and heavy war bars lined the beginning of the bottleneck cavern. Spears and axes sat piled in large numbers. So much weaponry led Cron to imagining this fearsome army rampaging across Thrae. Impressive was an understatement.

An aged male standing behind the small counter of stone in the near corner eyed them sharply. Minotaurs didn't trust strangers, much less a pack of humans, so deep inside the secret places of Malg. Much like his fellow warriors, the aging arms master had spent a lifetime dedicated to the arts of warfare and peace. Where humans fought because it was their nature, Minotaurs fought to attain peace.

"Ah, the humans," he growled.

Turning his back, the arms master went about collecting their weapons. He hefted Grelic's broadsword with the ease of a child, much to his amusement.

Even Pregen couldn't keep from grinning despite the profound sense of negativity he felt. The steady *ca-ting ca-ting* of hammers striking cold anvils haunted him. Soon they were strapping their weapons in place and refitting for the continued journey. Grelic and Cron perused the Minotaur-made weapons, collecting what looked useful.

"Thank you," Kialla told the arms master with a genuine smile.

The Minotaur snorted, about as close to acknowledgement as he was willing to give. Like Thorsus, he had marched with the Mages at the siege of Ipn Shal. Friends and fellow warriors he'd known for decades fell that bloody day. An arrow had pierced one of his lungs as they stormed the wall. Many good souls, too many, fell from the blind hatreds of a handful. The arms master blamed humans for the ills of the world. That the group before him hadn't even been thought of at the time meant nothing.

Their guard led them back into the puzzling warren. No one bothered talking. There was a growing excitement. The time had come to return to the quest and move forward. They followed the Minotaur down long and winding corridors. Unsure why, Grelic suddenly realized that they hadn't seen any females during their internment. He wondered if that had been deliberate or if the females of the species were just incredibly rare. Either way, it could mean nothing good for the dwindling population.

The other issue vexing him was the complex variety of mastery of the basic language. Lower-ranking warriors spoke it brokenly and in choppy sentences whereas Thorsus and many of the shamans sound like they'd been educated in one of Averon's academies. The disparity was fascinating and any answers he could discover would help him differentiate between their importance. Right now it was an added complication he didn't need.

They finally came to a halt in the reception hall. Their guard held up his hand and said, "Lord Thorsus awaits."

Legs burning from the steady uphill climb and a decided lack of use over the last few days, Grelic knew they were close to the surface. His face held a tight grimace. *No doubt anxious to be rid of us. Good. I need to feel the open air on my face again.* They found the Minotaur king standing in front of the remarkably small door leading out of Malg. A massive double-headed battle axe was strapped to his back. Grelic spied the skill and craftsmanship the blades were made with and recognized the handiwork of the Dwarves.

"The time has come for you to return to your quest. I have spoken at great length with your Mages and though I tried, they will not be swayed from this fool's errand. Should you return alive, you are more than welcome in the great halls of Malg."

"We would be honored," Grelic replied.

Dakeb and Ibram slipped out from Thorsus's shadow, along with a youthful-looking bull. Old hunting instincts in Grelic recognized a trap. Why else would one of the Minotaur warriors be accompanying them? A sinking feeling gnawed at the pit of his stomach. *What games are they playing?*

"Good, we are all here. Time to go already," Dakeb said with a sense of finality. He turned to Thorsus. "I would have liked for our stay to be longer, but there is much to be done. Perhaps we shall meet again, Minotaur king. It has already been far too long since we talked as brothers."

"Journey safely, Master Mage," replied Thorsus with the authority of a king. He wasn't pleased by the sudden change of events, but knew full well that this may be their only chance at ridding the lands of a horrible evil. "Krek will guide you to Deldin Grim. He is young by our standards, but a tested warrior with more than ten kills. He shall do you good, Dakeb."

The scout nodded sharply, clearly unimpressed with the pitiful hum but more than willing to prove his worth in his king's eyes. Dakeb smiled respectfully. He'd noticed the conflict the moment they met and decided it would prove interesting on the journey, if nothing else. The Mage then looked to each of his companions. A mixture of emotions confused them. He wasn't sure which was the biggest threat. Of course, he knew who the spy was. That bit was fairly obvious to his heightened senses, but a spy and a threat were vastly different entities. This quest was already dangerous enough without matters suddenly compounding.

He silently wondered how long it would be until the first of them snapped.

Sunlight beamed down on them, forcing them to shield their eyes from the suddenly hostile glare. The heat warmed them soothingly and did wonders to erase the cold and damp impressed upon them by Malg. Thorsus remained in the cooler shadows, amused by their reactions to the sun. Part of his unusual enjoyment stemmed from the knowledge that each had been certain they were going to die lost underground.

"This is as far as I go. Krek will take you the rest of the way. You can rest assured that your arrival has delivered newfound hope and meaning to my people. War bands are already forming to cleanse the Goblin filth from Qail Werd. Go with the peace and giving of the Minotaurs. My handlers will bring your horses out. You shall be pleased to find your packs filled and ready for a long journey. Fare thee well, humans, for the fate of Malweir rests in your hands and hearts," Thorsus told them.

A flock of pure white egrets erupted from a stand of nearby trees. They circled the clearing once before trailing off to the east. The old Mage took the display as an obvious good omen. *Now if only the rest of the path was so mild.* Cool wind blew through, sending refreshing chills through each. Surprisingly, many of Dakeb's new companions found themselves invigorated. They were going to need it. It had been many years since he'd last entered the Deadlands and the memories remained foul.

The Deadlands were exactly that. No sentient being would purposefully live there. The air was hot and humid year round. Every breath felt like the air was trying to kill you. Foul winds scorched the forever plains, blanching everything sickly yellow and brown. Fields of thorn bushes seemed to be the only thing that thrived there. *And now the Goblins have rebuilt their strength and invited a dragon, no doubt under the control of the Silver Mage.* Between those two, which were extraordinarily powerful, and the multitudes of Goblins, Dakeb was not looking forward to his return.

His private memories were interrupted by a handful of approaching Minotaurs leading their horses out from a small game trail leading back to Malg. Dakeb had always liked horses and their finicky temperaments. He much preferred the feel of fresh spring grass bouncing under his feet, but the exhilaration of riding instantly made him smile.

Grelic and the others wasted no time in mounting up. It was a toss-up as to who was more anxious to get away from the hospitality of the Minotaur king. The old Mage followed suit and took his own reins in hand.

"I don't know if we shall ever meet again, Thorsus. It was a blessing to cross your paths and now that we are leaving I find myself wishing to have your army at my side," he admitted quietly.

"The days of old are long gone, my friend," Thorsus replied. He carried undeniable regret in his voice. "I am forced to look after my own people now. Should the day of despair come crashing down on this land, we will meet it with all of our might. The old alliances are forgotten by most, yet the people of Malg shall return to fight beside men should the dark Mage rise again."

He looked to the others. "Farewell to you all. You have earned my respect and curiosity. Never let it be said that my hospitality was denied to you. Now go and may you meet an end worthy of song and tale."

The handful of warriors and shamans raised their fists into the air and bellowed ancient battle cries. Krek, most of all, seemed excited. Pride beamed in his features and his roar went louder than even Thorsus's. Dakeb supposed he couldn't blame him. This was a momentous occasion, if not fatal. The deeds of this obscure handful of people held the balance of good and evil in their hands. Most would have shied away if they knew the implications associated with their future actions.

Thorsus gently pat Dakeb's horse on the neck. He leaned close to the Mage and whispered, "I say this for your ears only. Look not to trust for victory. One of your band will betray you before the end. Do not let his deeds foul your quest."

Dakeb nodded solemnly but said nothing. Thorsus nodded back, so slight it was almost imperceptible. He stood and watched as the band of would-be heroes rode off to certain doom.

THIRTY-SEVEN

The Road to Deldin Grim

Qail Werd was much less ominous now that they fully understood the source of the myths and legends. While there were no demons or manifestations of the netherworld roaming beneath the trees, Grelic and the others certainly maintained wary respect for the Minotaur kingdom. Thorsus and his folk had earned the giant's trust and confidence. No doubt that was why Krek had been sent along. The Mage could have easily led them out of the Werd and to the pass of Deldin Grim.

They set up camp when dusk came much sooner than they anticipated. Soon a roaring fire warmed them and the smell of roasting meat filled the air. Krek chewed so loudly he almost drowned out the subtle crackling of the fire. Only Pregen paid it any attention. He scowled with disgust as he watched pieces of partially chewed meat fly from Krek's mouth. Ragged strips of almost raw meat dangled between the Minotaur's entirely too large teeth. Pregen turned away before he threw up.

It was almost laughable. Pregen knew the bull was never going to get invited to a formal ball in any civilized kingdom. Surprisingly enough, Pregen missed the glitz and glamour of royal banquets and fetes. He'd spend the majority of those nights chasing and seducing young maidens to the bedroom for his own satisfaction and the chance of fattening his purse. Royalty seemed the best for that. Besides, most were rich beyond measure and wouldn't miss a few gems and baubles here and there.

The one thing Pregen found no satisfaction in was bedding common folk. He'd been born to a poor family with the typical sad drama of poverty. His mother drank herself to death while his father was a simple street thug who preyed on young men and women for money and various degrees of carnal pleasures. Fortunately he died while Pregen and his sister Reinna were still young.

Pregen accepted the burden of responsibility of raising his sister without having a clue how to do it. He learned how to work the streets early out of sheer necessity. He made a fairly good time of being a pickpocket and two-bit hustler. Reinna plied her meager household skills as a maid and assistant in different kitchens. Neither of them made enough to get by. Pregen was fairly confident life couldn't get any worse when he came home after an unsuccessful day of petty thievery to find Reinna gone.

He searched frantically but found nothing. The house was in ruins, if theirs could be considered a house. It was more akin to a rundown shack than living quarters. Pregen ran out into the streets shouting her name at the top of his lungs. Cold winter rain stung him. The mournful wail of street dogs echoed his plea. For the first time in his life, Pregen Chur was alone. Though he never stopped looking for her, he never learned so much as a clue. It wasn't until years later when she walked back into his life.

He hardly recognized her. Reinna was dressed prim and proper, so unlike the poor, parentless waif she'd been. The reunion was tearful. She cautiously explained how she'd been kidnapped and sold to a minor nobleman who treated her decently, even allowing her to sleep in a real bed. The story broke Pregen's heart, not because her life took an upswing, but because she had no intention of returning home. She was moving south to Averon and would not be coming back. Reinna kissed his cheek and held him lovingly one final time. Then she was gone.

Pregen gave up trying to make a semi-honest living after that. He devoted himself to learning how to become a proper gentlemen. That's when he learned where the real money was. Jewels were easy picking and, as he later discovered, the women enjoyed his heady street-like quality. For a time, life was good. Then word reached him some years later that Reinna was dead. She'd been killed by her aristocrat husband during a drunken rage. Pregen flew into his own rage. He cursed everyone from himself to his worthless parents and even the gods. Long nights he delved into sorry and self-inflicted misery. His hatred steamed, threatening to consume him. Then he stumbled upon a plan. Seeking out the cheapest smith, Pregen contracted a handful of weapons and struck out in search of Reinna's murderer.

It took a while and the road was fraught with inescapable peril, but Pregen finally tracked the beast to his lair. Consumed in a cloak of violence, Pregen had the good sense to wait his victim out. He watched everything. Who came, who went. How many guards the men had. Which servants were loyal and which were decidedly less scrupulous. Through it all, his hatred kept him going and when the time was right, he entered the manor.

Looking back, he probably shouldn't have killed the guards. They seemed decent enough but Pregen was fairly confident they had a part in getting rid of Reinna's body. He watched as they gurgled their last breaths in a mouthful of blood. When at last he reached the main chamber, he noticed the strangest thing. His heart began to beat too hard. His palms were dry and his mouth still wet. It was almost as if killing was the most natural thing.

Delighted and repulsed by this newfound freedom, Pregen stole into the chambers with death in his heart. He found the man in bed with a beautiful blonde. Rage whispered and Pregen struck. He fell on both with unsuppressed fury. The man died almost instantly from a slice across the throat but the woman's pain was long and drawn out. Pregen saw in her the love and stolen grace from Reinna. For that, she paid dearly. Her death was pure revenge.

Pregen stumbled away from the carnage covered in blood. Too many thoughts and sensations assaulted him at once. Darkness claimed him. When he awoke, Pregen knew what his calling in life was. He went on to become one of the premier assassins in northern Malweir. Visions of that fateful night haunted him to this day. He gave Krek one last look before shuddering and going to sleep.

Fitch found it difficult to take his eyes away from the young bull. He guessed they were about the same age, or at least comparable, given the long lives of that race. The Minotaur strode through the forest with uncanny ease and an almost haughty attitude. His gait was swift and confident, as if it were the most natural thing in the world. Fitch was immediately impressed and started to like the bull. He doubted he'd be able to leave his own people so easily to travel off into untold dangers, perhaps even death, with a handful of complete strangers.

"Why you stare?" Krek snarled from across the fire.

Fitch recoiled, embarrassed at getting caught. "I'm sorry. I didn't mean to, it's just that until the other day I'd never heard of a Minotaur."

Krek snorted and tossed another log on the fire.

Fitch pressed, "How long have you been a warrior?"

Now it was the Minotaur's turn to blush. He stared intently at the flames, at the way heat burned down the wood and turned almost white. "No questions."

Fitch refused to back down. "I'm not even a warrior, if that helps. Up until a few months ago I'd never seen a battle."

This grabbed Krek's attention. "Why you here?"

Lowering his gaze, Fitch struggled to keep the old sorrow from resurfacing. Then an idea struck. Maybe he needed to talk about it. Seldis and Dakeb both told him so repeatedly in the past. He'd hurt too much to understand at the time. But now, with Krek sitting across from him and just about everyone else asleep, he felt the need to get it all out. "My village was destroyed. That's what started this whole mess."

He went on to explain in detail the events of that day and what he knew of events leading up to their capture by the Minotaurs. Krek listened intently. He refused to admit it, but the bull warmed slightly to the young human. He wasn't sure why, because humans were generally pathetic genetic specimens. They had thin hides and were ill equipped for long periods of hardship. They were weak compared to the older, more rugged races on Malweir. Krek had been ingrained with the belief of their inferiority. Why then, he often questioned, were there so many of them? One of the shamans once explained the reason as being they needed numbers to make up for their lack of durability. At the time it made sense. Looking at the small human across from him, Krek wasn't entirely sure.

He spat at the fire. "Garg! Bah! Filth needs cleansing."

Fitch winced at the Minotaur's word for Goblins but couldn't agree more.

"Sleep now. I guard," Krek told him.

Fitch found sleep easily that night. Something he hadn't done since leaving the Order of Harr's monastery.

The first signs of Goblins came at midday. Krek halted them as soon as he caught the scent. Scowling, the Minotaur readied his tulwar. Grelic and the others immediately prepared for battle. They'd been hoping to exit the Werd and link up with the Aeldruin before having to fight again. That dream tumbled around them in a heap of disappointment. Swords drawn and arrows nocked, they formed a loose half circle.

Krek knelt down and touched a Goblin footprint. The ground was still soft. He scanned the area around him. His scowl deepened. Signs of their passing were all about. Broken branches. Piles of waste. The foul Garg were despoilers of the land and made no such constraints in the once mighty Qail Werd.

"Many Garg," he growled in hushed tones.

Grelic used his own experience to examine the signs. "Many is right. Close to a full company I'd guess. Heading east. They look to be moving in a hurry."

A bird cawed from the unseen distance.

"How long ago?" Cron asked.

"Less than a day," Grelic cautioned. "They are heavily armed."

"A war party," Cron said.

"Aye. But heading where?"

Eyes fell to Krek. To his credit, he stared back unflinchingly. "Malg."

There was a faraway look in his eyes, as if he longed to return to his underground kingdom to stand beside his brothers when the attack came. A low growl escaped his lips. Because of these wayward hum he would not be there to share in the victory.

Cron looked back at the trail they'd been following. "There's nothing for it. A hundred Goblins won't make it very far."

"Let's hope the dragon isn't with them," Kialla said.

She regretted it the moment the words left her lips. She wasn't the sort to believe in luck or other such nonsense, but she also didn't want to be the one responsible for bringing down the wrath of the gods. She may not believe in luck, but Kialla was very superstitious.

"Ever the optimist," Pregen said, rolling his eyes. He braced for the wrath of a sharp tongue. Or two.

Instead all he got was a silencing glare from Grelic.

The early summer heat was stifling, especially under the thick canopy. The day was still young and sweat already trickled down Grelic's arms and back. His sharp eyes scanned the forest fervently. Krek sensed his unease and was already searching for prey. Qail Werd had become hostile territory. A stag elk crossed the trail ahead of them and froze. His soft brown eyes locked with Grelic and for a moment knew courage. So many others meant nothing but certain demise. Unable to suppress the overwhelming urge for self-preservation, the stag bolted back into the safety of the trees. Cron almost laughed. The Minotaur shook his head at their strange ways and pushed on. The sooner he guided them to Deldin Grim, the sooner he could return to the battle at Malg. Grelic and the others fell in line behind.

Night fell on them quickly. They hadn't seen any further signs of Goblins during the rest of the day, but Grelic remained cautious. If the enemy was moving unopposed this deep in the Werd, they could easily spring a trap at any given moment. Any delays now would surely make them miss the rendezvous with Faeldrin. They'd barely managed to recover from the first half of their journey and had need of strength and energy before reaching the Deadlands.

They dined on what remained of the elk and a pot full of wild vegetables and mushrooms found nearby. No one had any idea how much longer the quest was going to last and Grelic insisted on living off of the land for as long as possible. Krek stalked off shortly after eating. He gave no reasons and none were asked. Grelic knew what he was mad about and quietly let him go. It never hurt to have an extra set of eyes watching the night. Cron took the opportunity to pull Grelic aside.

"What was that between you and Thorsus? I had the feeling we were about to meet an untimely demise."

Anger flashed behind Grelic's eyes, then he smiled tightly. "Two old bulls used to being in charge. That's what happens when two people like that lock horns. So to speak."

"You should calm down," Cron advised. "We could have been killed."

"I have news for you: we would have been killed long before that if we didn't have Dakeb. That crazy old Mage is the only thing keeping us alive."

"That bothers you, doesn't it?" Cron asked.

"Worries me is more like it. What happens if he gets killed? That doesn't bode well for the rest of us," Grelic said. "Thorsus could have killed us at will, but didn't because of Dakeb. The dark wolves almost had us, but again Dakeb stepped in. Ibram's misadventure with the Dwim in Eline. Need I go on?"

"No, but what of poor Ibram? Imagine the nightmare he's gone through since he was told he's a Mage. I wouldn't wish that on anyone."

They looked across the small campsite to where Ibram and Dakeb sat in hushed conversation.

"I still don't understand," Ibram told him. "How was I chosen for this? I never wanted to be a Mage. Magic doesn't interest me."

Dakeb rubbed his hands together thoughtfully. "It's not so simple as picking and choosing. You see, magic is very powerful and has a mind of its own. Those of us gifted never asked for it. Not even during our strongest hour could we determine why this is so. But we did learn how to recognize the signs. It usually begins during late childhood. The temple at Ipn Shal had trained teams scouring Malweir in search of gifted boys and girls of every race with the potential to make the world a better place."

Ibram remembered reading in the monastery's libraries about the Mage orders. Once proud and distinguished, they soon fell into decay and ruin. Great scholars theorized they'd believed too much of their own mythology and succumbed to the vastness of their power. Perhaps that's what propagated the rise of the dark Mages and the near destruction of Malweir. No one knew for certain, but Ibram clearly recalled one specific fact: the Mages had been considered child stealers and were resented by a large portion of the populace.

"If times were different, you would have been identified much sooner and taken to Ipn Shal," Dakeb said. A tear formed in his eye at the mention of his beloved home. Magnificent beyond compare, only ruins remained.

"That doesn't mean I want to become a Mage," Ibram protested.

Dakeb sighed. "Sadly, it is not up to us to choose. Go and get some rest. We'll speak more on this in the morning."

The would-be warrior stumbled off to sleep, discovering he was more tired than he thought. Dakeb did the same. He smiled, truly smiled, for the first time in centuries. Malweir had hope once again. He only prayed there was enough time to follow through.

THIRTY-EIGHT

Rendezvous

The forest began to thin out. Massive trunks were replaced by saplings and shrubs. Golden streams of sunlight filtered through the slender canopy. Moss brightened the area, adding calmness and serenity. Dakeb breathed the fresh air and let out a long sigh.

"I've always loved the feel of the forest," he said, to no one in particular. "Not so much the ancient hearts of the great Werds. No. They've been alive much too long and tend to be bitter and full of contempt. There's nothing like a mean-spirited tree that can't go anywhere."

Despite the lightheartedness in his laugh, Fitch found himself sneaking looks at the surrounding trees. Where he once considered fanciful imagination he now pictured angry beings uprooting themselves and falling upon them in a fit of blind rage.

"Why should they be angry?" he asked timidly.

Dakeb eyed him mischievously. "Imagine if you had to stand in one place and see the same sights for hundreds of years. What kind of mood would you be in?"

Laughter rippled through the group. It did little to ease Fitch's apprehensions. He felt as if one of the mighty oaks was going to reach down and snatch him up. *Just one more thing to worry about. Dwim, dark wolves, Goblins, dragons, dark Mages, and now trees. What did I do so wrong in my life to arrive here?* Fitch wondered if there was any safe place left in the world. Such thoughts reawakened memories of his wife. He missed Shar. Every night he fell asleep thinking of her face. The image faded ever so slightly with time. Blurring around the edges. When she was gone he feared he was too.

The old Mage sensed his internal suffering. The pain bothered both of them, though Fitch had no way of knowing. As a Mage, Dakeb was forced to keep much to himself. Withholding certain information was necessary when so many forces worked in opposition. He'd lost track of the secrets kept and never spoken. Every last one stayed with him, haunting his waking thoughts and corrupting his dreams. Dakeb wasn't sure what the extent of Fitch's role in this adventure was, but he had a sinking suspicion it wasn't going to be good. For reasons he still wasn't sure of, Dakeb kept seeing the face of Fitch's beloved Shar.

"Do you think Faeldrin will be there?" Cron asked Grelic, unconcerned about Fitch or Dakeb's trees.

They rode side by side without once looking at each other. Both kept their eyes on the forest. Krek may have been steering them towards the mountains, but the enemy seemed to be everywhere these days. Neither particularly wanted to have another go with the minions of the Silver Mage before linking up with the Elves.

The giant grunted. "No reason for him not to be. The Aeldruin are famous for their punctuality. If he said they'll be there, they will be." He leaned closer. "It's just a matter of figuring out where *there* is, compared to the terrain."

"What do you mean?"

Grelic made a sweeping gesture. "Qail Werd runs for hundreds of leagues along the spine of the Darkwall Mountains. Sure, we know where Deldin Grim is, but it's a large pass and Faeldrin will be able to find a suitable place for his mercenaries to hide should the dragon pop up. How much time are we going to lose trying to find them?"

"I'd like to think he is smart enough to set pickets and look for us," Cron said.

"Providing he gets to us first. What if we arrive before they do?"

He left it at that. It was in the late hours of the morning when Krek stalked out of the thickening undergrowth. The faintest trickle of sweat dripped from his brow. Grelic frowned his apprehension. The furrowing scowl etched on Krek's face sorted out his thoughts. Only one thing was capable of riling up the young bull more than Goblins. Elves. Grelic almost smiled.

Krek fixed him with a withering glare. "Horse tracks. Hours old."

"The Elves?" Kialla asked.

"Possibly," Grelic replied, not wanting to assume anything.

An overwhelming sense that their hunters were close on their trail lingered. He'd done his best to ignore the feeling since leaving Malg, but it resurfaced again. One step behind and lurking wickedly in the shadows, he could almost feel them. Hope made him answer quickly. Hope and the sudden need for companionship. Not for the first time did he feel the strong desire to retire. *Just a little more, you old fool. Just a little more and you can find out how normal people live.* The only problem was he wasn't sure if that was the sort of mundane life he actually wanted.

"Krek, how much further to the forest edge?" he asked.

The Minotaur thought for a moment. "Close. Reach valley soon."

"Do we stay here and wait or press on?" Cron asked.

Looking around, Grelic replied, "I'd just as soon be caught in the open if we have to fight. At least that way we'll see them coming."

"Don't you think about anything besides battles?" Pregen snipped.

He'd been growing more impatient since leaving Malg. Dakeb had taken notice and immediately grew worried. For reasons he still wasn't sure of, Dakeb kept silent. Whispers in the dark warned him the time was not yet right. There was still travelling to be done before Pregen Chur would come to meet his gods.

Grelic snarled. "It may be the only thing keeping us alive. Mind your tongue or I'll knock a few more teeth out."

The assassin shot him a vicious glare but kept his mouth shut. He knew when he was outmatched. "Krek, take us into the open. The sooner we get there the sooner we're done with the mess."

The comment instantly drew Kialla's attention. Something clearly bothered Grelic and she was probably the only one he trusted enough to confide in. He was the rock holding this quest together. She feared what would happen if he broke down.

They rode on.

Cron took the opportunity to drop back and speak with Dakeb. Questions were bothering him and he needed answers.

"Beautiful day for a trip through the woods, don't you think?" the Mage asked with a healthy grin. "Always made me feel good. There's nothing like the soft grass underfoot."

"That's a fancy thought indeed," Cron nodded. "I'm curious though, how is it our young Krek here speaks in broken sentences while Thorsus and his shamans act as if they were educated in Kelis Dur?"

"I was wondering when one of you was going to get to that. Make no mistake, captain of Thrae, Krek and the warrior class understand everything we say. Don't dumb them down by assuming otherwise. Men have a tendency to underestimate the other races. It is an old failing."

"They are the first other race I've ever actually met, other than Goblins," Cron admitted. "Truth be told, I hold no expectations, at least none that I'm aware of."

"A good field commander should always know his potential enemies. Not that I am saying the Minotaurs are capable of mounting a campaign to reclaim the northern kingdoms. Quite the opposite. They are a most peaceful people so long as you don't get on their bad side."

Cron bristled at being told how to do his job and found the comments off the mark. "Dakeb, the Minotaurs."

The Mage wore a stunned look. "Of course. Long ago, when the elder races first came to these shores and men were nonexistent, no two races spoke the same language. Those were terrible times. First came peace and the urge to cooperate for the good of the land. Peace, however, is not the way of life. There has always been conflict in one form or another. Not all is for the worst. New technologies rise from war. New philosophies and customs. Perhaps more importantly, new understandings."

"New hatreds and enemies as well," Cron added.

"Indeed. All that changed when man came. Vast and vicious wars were fought. One hundred years came and went in constant struggle. Wild magic developed in all of the races but it wasn't until the sons of Gaimos fled to Ipn Shal and constructed their home. The magic called to them. Called them away from land and lords. Meetings were secretly held in dark corners. Envoys were sent to those found to have the gift. Those were the very first Mages. Finally, after years of plotting and fleeing, representatives from each race meet in that most sacred place."

"The ruins of Ipn Shal."

Dakeb smiled fondly. "Aye. Though it was naught but an empty spot beside Thuil Lake at the time. The wars ended and peace settled. The magnificent complex of Ipn Shal rose and people from all walks of life came to learn and study. Some came to work, some to join our private guard. Kings and leaders sent their heirs and announced successors to learn and develop so that they could return and be equals. So, you see, every royal house learned what became the common tongue. Of course some needed a little magical influence to move their tongues this way or that," he chuckled. "Just about every race can speak the common tongue."

Cron stifled a soft yawn, Dakeb's answer being too long to keep his total attention. "I understand Thorsus better and it stands to reason the shamans are the custodians of their people, but what of the rank and file? How is Krek's speech so primitive?"

"Have you tried living in a dank cavern for hundreds of years? The answer is remarkably simple. Cut off from the rest of the world after the Mage War, the Minotaurs simply had no use for common speech. They're forgetting."

"Considering how little we know of these smaller races it makes sense," Cron said. "I don't think Rentor knows they live in his kingdom."

"Some things are best kept quiet. If Rentor doesn't know, chances are his enemies don't either. Think of the potential damage the dark Mage can do should he learn of the secret kingdom of Malg."

"I'm thinking more along the lines of how much the strength of the Minotaurs can help us. The Goblins wouldn't stand a chance," Cron admitted. "Of course there is still the dragon to deal with but that's why you're here."

Don't put too much faith in me. I still don't know the extent of my strength. There are still areas I have yet to be tested. "Thorsus and his kind wouldn't be welcomed or accepted in Kelis Dur."

"Do you think it would come to that?" Cron asked.

He'd been wrestling with thoughts of anarchy and chaos running rampant across Thrae as the war edged closer. Those visions seemed ever closer the further they plowed into the mystery of the Deadlands. Life used to be simple. He never thought to spend long hours wondering over what might or might not happen should the kingdom be invaded. Everything changed that fateful day in Gend. Cron found himself in a world he didn't understand. Political intrigue and positioning were as alien as the Minotaurs. He didn't have the stomach for games on any level. This thinly disguised disdain put him in contempt of his superiors. He almost decided to return to the city and lead the defenses. The part that bothered him the most was the prospect of having to fight his friends.

"The future holds too many variables. Even I can't discern it," Dakeb said. "Always fluid and difficult to grasp. Men often suffer from the fallacy of thinking fate and destiny are within their ability to control. If only they knew the truth."

"The truth? Surely men have some measure of control. You can't expect me to believe that all we do is for nothing. Our actions shape the future," Cron argued.

Dakeb fought to keep his grin from spreading. It had been decades since he and Seldis had a thought-provoking conversation like this. "Only to a minor extent. Do you think what we do today is going to have impact on whether it rains tomorrow?"

"That's the weather, Dakeb. We don't control that."

"Why not?"

"It is too vast. We don't decide if it's going to rain any more than when the wind blows or the ground trembles."

Dakeb nodded. "So the Dwarves mining in the deep earth have nothing to do with provoking a quake?"

"Of course not. How can a pick and hammer shake the world?" Cron replied.

"How can what we do today shape the world in the grand schemes of time? If you kill a man today, tomorrow you know you'll be a fugitive. That much is easily rectifiable. Don't kill anyone. But the scheme of things is another matter altogether. Who in Thrae remembers what it was like one thousand years ago?"

"You contradict yourself, old man," Cron smiled. "One moment you say we can't do that and the next you give an example of how much we have affected our destiny."

"Therein lies the dilemma. Think how easily it would be for men to make their own future in a preordained path! What troubles or life-shaping experiences could there possibly be without some measure of freedom? The old gods would be usurped from their heavens and wicked men might reign." Seeing the confusion building in Cron's eyes, the old Mage let out an exaggerated sigh. "I don't pretend to fully understand myself. Perhaps if the gods wanted us to understand we'd be gods ourselves. Imagine how bad off we'd be!"

Cron chuckled. "All Malweir would be on its head. I believe I'm more confused now than when we first started this conversation."

"You definitely have the makings of a future Mage if so," Dakeb replied.

They looked up because of an unexpected snarl from Krek. Finally, the edges of Qail Werd lay before them.

"Many tracks," the scout announced, pointing left and right.

Grelic rubbed the stubble on his chin. "Too damned confusing to follow."

"That's a lot of tracks," Kialla added. "It'll be almost impossible to figure out which ones are the ones we need to follow."

"That's why they did this. Our Elves know their business. Goblins aren't very smart to begin with. This will just make it harder for them to figure out our intent."

Cron stared at the hoof prints, hoping to make some sense of it all. Even his keen eyes and natural instincts proved useless. The Elves were indeed good. "What do we do now? There's no point trying to look for them. Do we sit and wait?"

A crisp breeze tousled Grelic's hair. After days in the musty confines of the once great Werd, the fresh air felt invigorating. He longed to ride his stallion over the open fields again. The thought grew so strong he nearly forgot his current situation. "I don't think waiting for them is going to be much of a problem."

"What makes you say that?" Pregen asked suspiciously. The surrounding area was calm, almost supernaturally still.

The giant's gaze focused on a copse of ash trees.

"Because we've been waiting for you for quite some time, Master Chur," Euorn's voice called out from behind them.

The Aeldruin had been true to their word.

THIRTY-NINE

Betrayal

Three men stood in the empty storage room in one of Kelis Dur's garrison barracks. Each bore somber expressions foretelling of the horrible chain of events they were about to initiate. Yet for all of their desire and inert malevolence, none could bring it upon themselves to gaze upon their fellow conspirators. Only one, hidden behind the shadows of his hood, bothered regarding the others. And, though they couldn't see his eyes, each felt the intense hatred burning.

"Is everything in order?" the Hooded Man asked in a gravelly voice.

Codel Mres flinched despite his bravest attempt not to. "Yes, m'lord. King Rentor has no idea what is about to happen. I have taken care of everything, just like you ordered."

The oppressive hood shifted to the overweight general standing to his right. Evil managed to manifest itself in so simple a thing as the turn of his head. The lone torch attached to the far wall flickered without any wind. The room was cold, almost freezing. "General, how long before your forces can secure the city?"

Huor bobbed his head nervously. "They are. I have units positioned strategically across this part of Thrae to push in and seize control of the major cities as soon as the current government is removed. All we need is the word to begin."

"You're sure Rentor suspects nothing? There can be no room for failure. Operations under Druem are proceeding well. Soon the crystal shall be mine."

Codel managed a brief look at his master. "What of Thrae? You promised me this kingdom."

Shadows gathered menacingly around the Hooded Man, making him look larger, more menacing. "You dare question me? Remember who makes this fanciful dream of yours reality. You mean nothing to me, Codel Mres, traitor-son. I've seen hundreds of leaders and would-be kings come and go like so many passing seasons. For all of your scheming and selfish thoughts, history won't even recall your name. The one goal of this endeavor is the shard. Nothing else matters. Speak to me again and I shall crush the air from your lungs."

"Yes, m'lord," Codel whimpered.

The Hooded Man turned back to Huor. "The hour is almost upon us. As soon as I take control of the king, send your army into the city and enforce martial law. Kill any that get in your way."

Huor bowed meekly. "But m'lord, how do you plan on removing Rentor? The might of the military is easily subverted but his palace guards are loyal to the death."

"Then we will give them what they want. Let me worry about Rentor. My minions are already at work. Be ready by dawn."

Not giving them room for further conversation, the Hooded Man gathered his robes and disappeared in the shadows. General Huor and Codel stood staring at the empty corner where he'd been.

"I don't like this," Codel whined. "Too much can still go wrong and I think he's going to replace me the moment this coup is ended."

Huor scowled. Thoughts of replacing the sniveling bureaucrat before it got that far delighted him. "Pull yourself together, Minister, or I'll run you through myself. We have a job to do and you falling apart like a child is not conducive to our success. You started this mess, now buck up and see it through."

Part of him strongly desired to see Rentor dragged before his people and beheaded like a common criminal. The only thing missing would be the complete and utter humiliation of Cron. The one man in all of Thrae who successfully managed to inadvertently thwart all of his plans time and again. Every single instance where his people were in position to make a bid for power ended with Cron countering. Huor hated the man more than anything and desperately wanted him dead.

Codel stared back at him as if he'd just been stabbed.

"Go back to your gilded halls and prance about until we're given the go-ahead," Huor ordered.

"Where are you going?" Codel asked.

"To the encampment just north of the city." Huor stormed off, leaving the once best friend to the king standing alone with naught but suspicions and doubts. He wondered how much longer it was going to be until Lord Death came to claim him. Codel started to sweat. His skin, once crisp brown from the sun, had taken on a pale, waxy sheen. Fear kept him from sleeping. He barely ate and hadn't enjoyed a woman in months. Codel Mres felt as if he was slowly slipping away.

Surely Rentor had to doubt him. Everything he'd done, right down to the way he behaved, was embarrassing and telltale. Rentor had to know. He had to. Deeply engaged in his compounding misery, he never noticed the tiny shadow of a bat spread its wings and flutter away through a slender crack in the ceiling.

Drifting over the tiled rooftops of Kelis Dur, partially hidden behind thin wisps of clouds and the ever-darkening landscape, flew the little bat. Normally such a night was filled with snatching bugs from the sky. But not this night. This night the bat was tasked with much too important of a job. Large predators soared through the night. Unhindered, the bat spiraled down towards an open window with the warm glow of candlelight filling the frame.

Father Seldis sat beside a gentle fire drinking from a decanter of mulled wine. His eyes were sore and bloodshot. The nerves in his right hand twitched the way they always did when he'd strained too much. His eyes drifted closed. Seldis hadn't realized just how exhausted he was. The last few days had put a terrible strain on him. *Not much longer now and I can finally rest.*

He could almost see his friends through the haze of distant memories. All of them were smiling, but seemed sad. Seldis frowned. That shouldn't be. His memories were from before the breaking. Long before the darkness of that terrible war. Occasionally he spent time thinking of what he could have done differently to change things for the better. It was pointless and never ceased to further his depression and guilt.

Seldis suffered from two agonizing secrets. The first he'd managed to conceal for over three hundred years. Though he was fairly certain Rentor had guessed, and that being only recently, less than a handful knew he was a Mage. Or perhaps it was proper to think of himself as a former Mage. Seldis had turned his back on the order when the idea of creating the crystal of Tol Shere was approved. Years later, he continued to regret his decision to leave. As a result, he suffered from massive depression. That was his second and most damaging secret. One he'd been battling for so long, he almost looked forward to the coming struggle.

The bat drifted through the window, circled the fire once to ease away some of the midnight chill, and settled on Seldis' outstretched palm. The Mage smiled softly and brought the creature close to his face. He listened intently to the confusion of chirps and squawks as the bat told what it had seen. It was a tale he didn't want to hear but no less than he expected. Mixed emotions collided as he thanked the bat and bid it on its way. The hour was growing late and there was still much to do before he could rest.

The halls of the royal palace of Kelis Dur appeared more like a morgue to the king. Rentor paced down the faded marble floors like a predator through the jungle. His massive frame stalked slowly, each step deliberate and calculated. Hands clasped behind his back, he watched the moonlight streak through the ten-foot-high windows lining both sides of the main hall. The atmosphere was haunting, surreal. He wasn't a superstitious man, but dark dreams scarred his nights of late.

Ghosts walked in his nightmare landscapes. His father and grandfather scolded him from the grave. There was shame in what was happening around him and they made no efforts to hide his displeasure. Condemning and accusing, the admonishment of his forefathers stung. Rentor slowly felt his world being ripped away. He'd lost any notion he once had of ruling with a firm yet gentle hand. Current situations weren't going to allow for it. Too much had already been lost because he'd been blind to the dealings of his own court. Now, decades after they became the closest of friends, Codel Mres was coming to kill him.

Laughter suddenly filled the hall, deep and troubling. *No, Codel doesn't have the nerve for killing. He's a snake.* He recalled how his one-time friend retched half the night after a gruesome skirmish with Dwarven axe throwers. Rentor had lost that fight but had earned the respect of his opponents. Dwarves were notorious for their love of ale and deep sense of honor. That honor kept the growing bonds of friendship between their two kingdoms since the war ended.

Codel Mres, however, was a man without honor. He didn't dare do his own dirty work. Not here in the king's own lair. No. If it was coming soon, and Rentor was certain of it, it would be assassins. Rentor slowly thanked Grelic for taking Pregen Chur on his crusade. Thoughts of the assassin chilled him. Death stalked the shadows whenever that man came near. The thought of the drunken giant brought him mixed emotions as well. There was no great love lost between them, but deep down Rentor knew Grelic was a good man. He wondered if they would ever have become friends if they'd been allowed more time. Surely the quest was dead by now. He hadn't heard word of their progress in over a month and Rentor seriously doubted he had much time left.

Determination gripped him. It was time to prepare. He'd already sent the queen away, off to visit one of her cousins in Averon. Naturally she'd fought and protested the entire way. He expected nothing less. Still, much of his heart was ripped away when her carriage finally disappeared across the horizon. He had come to rely on her strength and dispatched wisdom more than he wanted to admit. He could deal with dying in the name of his kingdom but would never be able to live if anything ever happened to her.

Rentor strode into his dressing room with newfound clarity. It felt good to strap on his sword again. He didn't enjoy killing, though he had no qualms when the situation warranted it. He debated putting on his armor. An assassin would expect such and find other ways to kill him. Realistically, a good assassin could kill him without ever being seen. If he was going to die he wanted everyone to know that he was the king of Thrae.

"Sire, you have a visitor waiting in your private study," a royal guardsman said as soon as Rentor emerged from his chambers.

That's the trouble with being king. Everyone wants all of your time. He wished he had time to take the queen on a proper vacation. *Somewhere nice and arguably perfect.* Matters were too severe to allow the dream a chance to grow. The only way he was going to get a vacation was by surviving the next couple of nights and crushing the coming coup. He sighed. An idea of his guest was slowly forming.

"What does he want?" he asked.

The guard swallowed. "He wouldn't say, sire. He kept calling me a damned fool for wasting his time and to go and get you before it was too late."

Rentor bit back a snort, his suspicions confirmed. "Tell me, Nilas, how did you feel being dressed down by an ancient?"

Nilas flushed slightly before answering. "Can't say as that I particularly enjoyed it much, sire. I'd a mind to knock some manners into him though. Probably would have if he wasn't a senior and asking to speak directly to you."

One of the first things Rentor did when hiring his guardsmen was find out as much as he could about their lives. Nilas was a good man who'd scraped his way out of a meager existence in a farming community with no name. He grew to be a solid soldier and a friend to the aging king. The second thing Rentor did, made easier by accomplishing the first, was encourage his guards to speak their minds. Albeit with a certain modicum of respect, especially in public. That special bond of trust proved extraordinarily successful. So much so that lesser nobles adopted the same policy.

Rentor slapped Nilas on the shoulder. "That sounds about right. Be careful with the senior comments, though. In case you hadn't noticed, my hair is just as grey."

He gestured for Nilas to continue down the hall. Chuckling softly, the royal guardsman obeyed. Rentor immediately resumed his apprehensive posture. He scanned the passage as if it were a gauntlet into an enemy stronghold. Even the shadows were his enemy now. Men like Pregen Chur were uncommon, but enough to get the job done when it came down to it. Thrae wasn't a large kingdom, making it next impossible to go into hiding. A man could lose himself for a lifetime in Harlegor or Antheneon.

"Begging your pardon, sire, but why are you wearing all that armor for? Some of the boys might start thinking you don't trust us to protect you right."

Nilas also scanned the shadows.

"Suppose something happens to you. I'd never be able to live with myself if I didn't do what I can to help. Besides, I'm not going to let the likes of you rogues have all of the fun."

"Fun as it may be, that's our job," Nilas said matter-of-fact.

"What job is that?"

Nilas looked up at him. "To get hurt in your place. Seems to me that's the whole reason for a royal guard. Every last one of us knows we might need to die for you, sire. And every last one of us is willing to do so. You go and have your meeting, sire. Me and the boys will be just fine."

"There are times when I envy you," Rentor said with a heavy heart.

Nilas looked shocked. "Why would you say that, sire? You're the ruler of a whole kingdom and can get anything you want. Why would you want to trade with a mere guard?"

"I'm not so sure I can explain. Let's just say you have infinite more freedoms than a king will ever know. I'm trapped, Nilas. Trapped by politicians and simpering bureaucrats with no ideations other than their own success. There are times I can't even use the privy without being accosted. My entire day is dedicated to others."

The guardsman nodded understandingly. "Just like us, sire. Least you get to tell people what to do. We just do it. Here we are. He's inside."

Nilas stepped aside and bowed. They'd all been told a hundred times over that when alone with the king there was no need to stand on protocol. Still, most of the guards respected Rentor enough to continue doing it.

"Thank you, Nilas. I'll remember to scold him for you."

"No need for that, sire. I'll be right out here just in case."

Rentor smiled and opened the aged wooden door. A small fire took away the late night chill. Flickering lights illuminated rows of books and the lone man resting comfortably in Rentor's personal chair. The king eased into the chamber and closed the door behind him. This was the one room in the palace he felt totally at ease in. As if nothing bad could touch him. He was about to greet Seldis when the door suddenly burst apart. Splinters and shrapnel sprayed into the room, Nilas's head rolling in with them.

Rentor drew his sword and bellowed, "Seldis, get down!"

Then the demons came.

FORTY

Sacrifice

Rentor recoiled as a pair of undead creatures burst into the study. Both secreted rage. Their laughter was the hissing of snakes. The king knew he wasn't leaving this room alive as he stared into the blackness of their eyes and saw only pain. They'd been hu once, long ago, but had been twisted and broken until only a ruined waste of flesh remained. Almost wooden skin and long, rakish nails silently threatened him. Nilas' dead eyes gazed up in horror, forever etched. The guard never stood a chance. Rentor decided he didn't have much of one either.

Blue fire exploded from behind him, quickly engulfing the study with ungodly brightness. The Dwim hesitated. They sensed death approaching. A low chant accompanied the flames. It was a language they'd heard too many times during the transformation process from woman to undead. The tongue of the Mages. The Dwim attacked.

Rentor brought up his sword. He'd never seen the likes of these demons and had no knowledge of how to fight them. It didn't take much to imagine being ripped apart by their claws. He let out a bellow from the pit of his stomach and charged. The Dwim laughed mockingly. Rentor was in mid-swing when Seldis slipped in front of him. The old man's eyes had rolled up white and his palms were upturned. Sounds so alien Rentor doubted they were words escaped Seldis' lips. The king struggled with the instinct to push the crazy old man to safety even as he recognized the coming assault. Rentor dropped back.

The Dwim were frozen. Their muscles strained for freedom. Their claws, once so vicious, hung limply at their sides. They let out a bloodcurdling wail. Rentor heard the pain in their cries and watched as ice formed over their bodies. The blue light burned brighter, forcing him to look away. The Dwim were not so fortunate.

Accustomed to darkness, the Dwim had sensitive eyes. The light burned away the protective film, eating through the corneas and deep into the nerve stems. Slowly the light dimmed. When Rentor was able to look on the scene, he was both shocked and more than a little terrified. Seldis had stopped chanting and stood limply. The room was silent. The Dwim had been turned to ice, frozen solid.

"How did you do that?" Rentor asked in disbelief.

Seldis ignored him. "Quickly, Rentor, strike before the spell wears off."

Rentor raised his sword and stood before his would-be assassins, studying them carefully. They were abominations. Twisted perversions of life still watching him through ruined eyes. Enraged that they should attack him in the sanctity of his own castle, Rentor took two powerful strokes to shatter the

Dwim into thousands of pieces. He was still breathing hard when he turned back to Seldis.

"Are you all right?" he asked.

Seldis tried to nod but sharp pain lancing through his forehead stopped him. "I'll be fine. I'm just not as young as I used to be."

Rentor helped him to his feet and over to the cushioned chair. He then poured two glasses of water from the slightly chilled pitcher on the table against the far wall and offered one to his friend. Seldis accepted it and drained it in one swallow. With nothing more he could do for his friend, Rentor hesitantly collected Nilas' head and closed his eyes.

"You were a damned good man," he whispered to the mangled body in the doorway. "For what it's worth, I'd still trade places with you. Be at peace, my friend. I shall miss you."

The moonlight cascading through the much smaller windows had a haunting feel. Rentor couldn't place his finger on it but knew that all was not right.

"There's not much time," Seldis called.

Leaving his murdered guardsman, Rentor went back to the study. He finished his own water and eyed Seldis carefully. The old man looked fragile and weak. "Seldis, what is going on here? I've been expecting Codel to turn on me but not even he has command of such foul creatures."

Seldis, patriarch of the Order of Harr, opened his tired eyes. "This is not the doing of Codel Mres. This goes much deeper and infinitely more devious than anything his limited mind is capable of. Rentor, your childhood friend has thrown in with the last of the dark Mages."

"That's impossible. Everyone knows the Mages were destroyed centuries ago," Rentor protested.

Seldis' eyes opened wide. "Do they? That's what people were led to believe. We thought it was safer that way. Mages were extremely unpopular after the war and the few of us left alive decided to go into hiding. Some of us took up honorable positions across the land. Others became wanderers, doing good deeds whenever they were needed. It was our darkest hour, yet we managed to make the most of it. Now all of that seems to be coming undone."

"You keep saying we," Rentor said slowly. His mind raced towards improbable outcomes.

Seldis frowned. *Out of everything I said, you pick out that. Interesting.* "Yes I did. I am one of the last Mages in Malweir, though I haven't used that title in a long time."

"I don't understand any of this."

"I quit the order due to certain disagreements and decided it was best that I made a quaint existence in a forgotten kingdom. Little did I know it would come to this."

Rentor's eyebrows pinched together. His head hurt. "Seldis, I'm confused about a great many things. How do you still know magic if you haven't used it in so long?"

"It is a gift. We are born with it and were close to discovering the origins of magic when the war began. What else bothers you?"

"If there is a dark Mage on the loose, why would you want to keep it a secret? Shouldn't the people be warned in case of another war? I don't like the idea of what might happen because no one was warned."

"Do you really believe telling people accomplishes anything? I've seen what happens when public knowledge overtakes a kingdom. Panic. Mass hysteria will sweep the land. It'll start slowly enough, in one village or the next. Let news of the dark Mage spread and his reputation alone will kill hundreds. Bad men and wicked beings will be drawn to him and soon he'd have an army to begin his war anew. I'll not see such days revisited. The dark Mage is pure evil and must be stopped. Quietly," he said, stressing the last part.

"My people are already being killed, Seldis. How many more need to die before word of this gets out?" Rage was building. He suddenly felt like he was being used.

"As many as necessary," Seldis said agonizingly. "You have no idea what it was like the first time. The very breaking of the world was upon us. The dark Mage isn't concerned with Thrae. He's after a much greater prize."

Rentor kicked at a piece of melting ice next to his foot. "The presence of these demons suggests otherwise."

"The Dwim. I'd thought that dark art was lost forever. Only a handful knew the spells necessary to create such. We'd thought they were all killed. Confronting the Dwim here in Kelis Dur means our enemy is stronger than Dakeb or I thought."

"How many more are there?" Rentor asked.

Seldis shook his head. "I don't know. The dark Mage and Codel Mres aren't stupid. He knows Mres isn't strong enough to get the job done by himself. The more Dwim he sends, the easier it will be to subjugate Thrae after the insurrection."

"You said he didn't want my kingdom," Rentor countered.

"I said he's not concerned with it. Make no mistake, he's a madman intent on the ruination of the world. Thrae is but the beginning. You've heard the rumors of him moving in the east, deep in the land of Gren. If he succeeds here he'll use Mres as a puppet government loyal only to him. Rentor, we have to keep him from stealing the throne. This isn't his main effort but the dangers are twofold. General Huor is ready to march against the throne. All he awaits is the news of your death to place Kelis Dur under martial law."

"Staying alive seems to be more problematic of late. What will it take to stop the Dwim?" he asked.

"Your sword is going to have to suffice. I don't have the strength left for much more. You must brief your guards," Seldis said.

"Nilas was supposed to go and rouse the others." He looked at the Mage smugly. "I suppose we'll have to do that now."

"Then let us hope we don't encounter many more along the way," Seldis grimly said while staring at the melting pieces across the floor.

"That's the plan. Are you well enough to move?"

Seldis nodded. "Better now than later."

With Rentor in the lead, the unlikely pair eased through the shattered doorway and down the hall. The blood had stopped flowing, leaving thick pools on the marble floor. They gingerly stepped around the pools. Seldis clutched his turquoise robes and lifted them off the ground so as not to get them dirty. Thin clouds rolled in, concealing the soft moonlight.

"I don't like this," Seldis whispered.

What he really wanted to say was they were moving too slowly. Opportunities for the enemy to strike grew with each passing moment and there were no places to hide if need be. On the other hand, there were no places for assassins to hide, either. Aside from the Dwim, the odds were fairly even. That didn't prevent him from having a nagging suspicion.

He decided to speak to ease his own nerves. "The Dwim have no love of light. Some theorize even moonlight hurts them."

"What do you think?"

"No one has seen one since the war. I'm not sure what to think. How much further to the guardroom?"

Slowly poking his head around the corner to make sure it was safe, Rentor said, "Down the hall and to the right. There's about twenty of my best on duty at all times."

I certainly hope they're your best. You'll need them before this night is done. "We'd best hurry before more come."

Rentor could have laughed if the situation weren't so dire. They shuffled down the hall with the Mage leaning on him for support. A waxy sheen covered the old man's flesh. His breathing had grown shallow. Rentor was fairly certain the old man was going to die from heart failure long before they met the Dwim again. He went as easy as he could, considering everything that stood against them. The relative security of the guardroom was still a hundred meters away.

His boots echoed with authority down the halls in stark comparison to the slippers Seldis wore. Rentor was reminded of a fawn traipsing through the forest. Suddenly he heard running. A faint hiss in the night. His heart froze. It was already too late. The enemy was almost on their heels. Seldis shrugged free and turned to meet them. His strength was fading quickly and Rentor needed all the time he could get if there was any hope for the future. The Dwim hissed their pleasure and slowed to a crawl. Four of the creatures spread out and crawled closer.

Rentor ground to a halt as soon as he felt Seldis' weight leave. Eyes wide in shock and horror, he turned to watch his old friend amble towards instant death. *What are you doing? The guards are so close!* Seldis offered him a final glance. He was sorry for a great many things. Close to three hundred years old, the Mage was tired and ready to move on. *How refreshing it will feel to enter the next life. This world has grown very old to me.* His sacrifice planned, there was no better time. He only hoped he had enough strength left to fight off the Dwim long enough for Rentor to escape.

"Go," he told the king.

Rentor gave a curt nod and raced towards the guardroom. His calls for aid echoed down the hall. Guardsmen poured from their ready room with weapons in hand.

Colorless lightning danced from Seldis' fingertips. His wicked gaze fixed on the Dwim, Seldis forced them to hesitate. There wasn't supposed to be such a dangerous foe in Thrae. Created for the sole purpose of murder, the Dwim were cold and decidedly calculating. They were smart enough to realize the presence of a magic user meant the consequences outweighed the projected results.

"Come on then," Seldis said. "Let us see who walks away from this night."

The lead Dwim lunged. His attack was low, aiming to take out the Mage's knees. Seldis lashed out simultaneously. Bolts of blue lightning burst from his fingers to strike the Dwim in the face and chest. There was a brief moment of resistance before the monster's leathery skin caught fire. It fell screaming. Smoke poured from its mouth and its fingers and toes burned like torches. An ungodly cry filled the hall.

For a moment only Seldis thought he caught the faint tones of a woman's cries. The genetic manipulation died before he was able to decide for sure. He knew the Dwim were once human. Killing them was the smallest kindness. The other three paused, reconsidering their attack. Seldis took a step forward, intending on continuing his assault, but his body had had enough. He sank to his knees, breathing hard. The Dwim attacked with renewed vigor.

They forgot the king or his family. Bloodlust stirred in their hollow hearts. They snorted and raged. Hungry for the taste of warm flesh, the Dwim advanced rapidly. Claws and fangs shredded his robes, tearing burning gaps in his flesh. Seldis saved his screams. The pain was almost unbearable and he so desperately wished to escape it. But it was too soon. If he gave in now, Rentor wouldn't stand a chance. The Dwim would tear through him and his meager defenses in a matter of moments. Sidian would surely be victorious if that happened.

Seldis had one hope. As long as the Silver Mage's focus was here in Kelis Dur, he'd be oblivious to Dakeb and the others moving closer to Druem. All success hinged on Dakeb now. Claws went deep, hooking his ribs. Seldis cried out and inspired the Dwim into greater frenzy. All three dug and bit. The Mage felt his life slowly escaping. *Not much longer and I'll be with my friends again.*

He saw their faces as darkness crept around the corners of his vision. They smiled and beckoned for him to take their hands. They offered salvation. Liberation. Seldis reached out. One of the Dwim punched the side of his head, nearly rendering him unconscious. Enraged, the dying Mage gathered what remained of his power and lashed out. The Dwim were caught unaware as they continued their furious assault. Seldis pitched back and threw his arms wide. Madness swarmed into the minds of the Dwim. None of them could move. Their internal organs were squeezed and crushed with massive amounts of pressure. Their bodies broke and died. All three Dwim dropped in lifeless heaps. So too did Father Seldis the Mage.

Rentor led the charge into the fight, already knowing it was too late. They wheeled around the corner and ground to a halt. Tears welled and broke free. It was with a heavy heart that he sheathed his sword and went to the bodies. He took a small measure of solace from the smile on Seldis' face.

"Well done, old friend," was all he could manage before grief consumed him.

FORTY-ONE

The Last Night

The Aeldruin encampment was alive with rumors and talk of Mages, Minotaurs, and a giant of a man who wore a perpetual scowl. Strange days had indeed befallen them. Krek drew the most attention. Old hatreds ran deep between their races though few could recall the origins. There'd been virtually no contact between Minotaur and Elf since the fall of Ipn Shal.

Guards escorted the small yet steadily growing group through the neatly ordered rows of camouflaged tents. Cook fires made Dakeb's mouth water, even though he'd eaten but a few hours earlier. He detested travel rations of any sort. Thoughts of a freshly cooked meal entertaining him, he arrived at Faeldrin's command tent. Their escort bowed before returning to his duties. Faeldrin greeted them with open arms and a warm smile. The Elf Lord looked refreshed and surprisingly young considering how long and difficult their trek to the mountains had been.

"Ah, my friends. It is good to see you again. You're late though. We were beginning to get worried. This close to the Deadlands the dangers become extreme," he said.

Dakeb replied, "We were in safe hands as it turned out. There were a few bumps and bruises along the way but all worked out for the best."

The Elf's jewel-like eyes fell on Krek. He decided not to remark. This was no time to bring up old dogma. "Come inside. Surely you must be hungry after so long a ride."

He took amusement from Krek's initial hesitancy.

"I've never been one to turn down a free meal," the old Mage said, patting his stomach for emphasis.

"We just ate," Kialla reminded him.

Dakeb flashed that slick smile of his. "Different cultures, different foods my dear. Besides, it would be downright rude of me to refuse. You don't want to insult our host's hospitality so soon, do you?"

"I see you've lost none of your golden tongue through these long years," Faeldrin laughed.

"I can only sacrifice so much, you know."

They settled around a table filled with roasted rabbit and vegetables. The Elf Lord proved a most generous host. A rich, dark red wine was brought out for them to enjoy. Grelic passed on the offer.

Faeldrin finally addressed Krek. "My scouts tell me you guided these people to us. For that I am in your debt. I am Faeldrin and the Elves around you are the Aeldruin. We are mercenaries for all intents and purposes, but with good intentions."

Thumping a meaty fist to his chest, Krek replied, "Krek."

"Welcome to my camp. You are our guest and friend so long as you remain in our company. No harm will come to you. You have my word," Faeldrin said.

He didn't know what the young bull was thinking or the other way around. Krek did struggle to keep from laughing at the thought of being protected by the scrawny Elves. Satisfied with making the necessary efforts of diplomacy, Faeldrin turned his attention back to the Mage.

"You have a tale for the telling, Dakeb. I'm curious to know how you came to be in the company of our friend Krek here."

"Indeed there is a tale. Fortune was with us."

Dakeb gave the young Minotaur much credit for not dropping his food and attacking Faeldrin. While there was peace, it was fragile and not going to last. Keeping the situation from blowing up was going to be tricky. Dakeb fought back a sigh. There wasn't time to sort this out properly. He went into great depth over what happened in the time the Elves parted company with them in Gend. Even Faeldrin balked at the mention of the horrible storm that drove them into Qail Werd. He was particularly interested in learning more of the hidden kingdom of Malg. By the time the tale ended, Faeldrin had a better understanding of their plight and a curiously growing respect for Krek.

"An interesting tale," he said as Dakeb eased his parched throat with a glass of wine. "It makes our endeavors seem almost trivial."

Faeldrin went on to explain the making of the ballistae and the relatively uneventful trek along the mountain road. Cron breathed a sigh of relief at the mention of an Elf scout being dispatched to Kelis Dur. The Aeldruin seemed to have taken care of everything.

Grelic set down his apple core on the table and wiped the residue from his mouth with a sleeve. "Now that the pleasantries are out of the way, we need to get down to business. How difficult will it be getting through the mountains?"

Faeldrin showed them the map covering the table. The corners were frayed and yellowed from time. "We're less than a day's ride from Deldin Grim. I've already sent out scouts to the east and west with specific instructions to only recon, not engage. There are far too many Goblin patrols roaming for my liking."

"We came across tracks for a war party in the forest," Kialla told him. She blushed after catching Cron's smile.

"It appears our enemy is ready to make his move. Time is running out, I'm afraid," Dakeb added.

"Hmm, if that is so, how difficult will it be for us to make it past Deldin Grim? Fifty riders dragging giant bows aren't going to go unnoticed. Is there another way?" Grelic asked.

Faeldrin shook his head. "Not for hundreds of leagues. We'd have to skirt the entire Darkwall range and then ride back. The pass is the only way into the Deadlands."

"We'll never make it if they discover us. They can keep us bottled in the pass long enough to bring the full weight of their army down. That's not a chance I'm willing to take, considering we have no idea how large a force awaits at Mordrun Bal."

"Or the dragon," Fitch piped in.

Faeldrin flashed a smile. "We'll take care of the dragon, Master Iane. He'll either fall dead from the sky or flee back to his roost in shame."

"But you've never fought a dragon before," Ibram added.

The Elf Lord squared on the former monk. "And you've never taken a life before this quest. Don't lecture me on what my people have done. One way or the other, I'll have your dragon."

"The pass it is," Dakeb cut in. He saw no point in arguing over what might or might not happen. "I can attempt to conceal our presence but without promises. These are dangerous times and our enemy will be able to sense any use of my magic."

Pregen made no effort to stifle his yawn. He always found talk like this tedious at best and mundane on every level. The desire to abandon his companions and return home continued to strengthen, stymied slightly by talk of rebellion and war in Thrae. Leaving one battlefield to enter another wasn't a wise business decision. The longer he stayed with these people, the more he regretted accepting Grelic's proposal. Suppressing a groan, he downed the rest of his wine.

"I've had enough doom and gloom for one day. If it's all the same to you, I'd like to find a place to sleep a little and contemplate tomorrow," he interrupted.

Frowning at Pregen's rudeness, Faeldrin managed, "Of course. I don't wish to keep any of you too late. The way ahead is dangerous, but largely known to us. Aleor is waiting outside to take you to your tents."

Only Grelic and Dakeb chose to stay behind. Both felt there was still much to discuss before they struck out on the final leg of the adventure.

Aleor greeted the others with a widening smile. He was the friendliest Elf in the camp and the perfect choice for the task. Kialla appreciated the gesture as she and Cron walked side by side in the fading daylight. They were close enough to touch. For his part, Cron enjoyed that closeness. He'd had strong attractions to her from the very first time they'd met but was unsure what to do about it. Neither of them needed any romantic entanglements now.

He cursed his sudden weakness. He was a soldier. A defender of his kingdom and that had to come first. There wasn't time for women or serious relationships. Still, he couldn't help but notice how attractive she was. Her high cheek bones and smoothly angled face hinted at hidden tenderness. She was toned and lightly tanned, adding a certain exotic feel to compliment her dark, auburn hair. Her personality was sparkling even in the worst situations. If he didn't know better, he'd say he was falling in love.

There'd been women in the past. At fifteen he even thought he was in love with Lien Tal. They'd practically grown up together. She gave him his very first kiss and, together, they enjoyed the pleasures of each other's bodies under the new moon. Then he left and joined the army. Trips home became rare and often short. Before he knew it, Lien was married off to a baker's son and had a brand new baby girl to care for. Cron was happy for her but suffered many nights with the loss.

That's when he stopped thinking about tomorrow, stopped worrying over what he didn't control. His job became his sole focus. There were certain houses he visited when the loneliness grew too much. Not quite a relationship, but an acceptable release of tension for an army officer. Duty and Thrae always came first. Until he met Kialla. He'd spent more time than he wanted thinking about her. Their discussions ranged from her father and upbringing to what the future might hold.

Her laughter brought him back to the present. Cron was shocked to discover their hands were woven together. He looked around quickly, hoping no one was paying attention. Fortunately, the others were focused on their own affairs. Satisfied his secret was safe, he breathed a quick sigh of relief. He also made no effort to disengage.

Kialla passed him a seductive glance, dazzling him with her smile while laughing at one of Aleor's jokes. Cron felt like pushing his head into a bucket of cold water and keeping it there. He'd never been so glad to reach his tent as he was right then. Flap closed behind him, he enjoyed the Spartan accommodations, which were more than adequate for a night or two. He sat down on the small cot and ran his hand through his hair, trying to push away thoughts of Kialla. The harder he did, the more prominent she became. Then an idea struck. He needed to exercise. An hour or so of calisthenics would be enough to take his mind off of her.

Stripping down to an undershirt and trousers, the captain of Kelis Dur started stretching. Most of the Elves were gathered around the campfires or off out of sight. Warmed up, Cron pushed himself to the limits of his endurance. Sweat streamed down his face and soaked his shirt. His muscles burned, screaming for relief. He swung his sword until his sore hands couldn't grip it anymore. Only then did he stop.

Satisfied his urges were evicted, Cron dropped his sword and found that bucket of water. He stripped off his sweat-soaked shirt and poured the lukewarm water over his head. It was refreshing, making him shiver. The soldier set the bucket back down and snatched up his belongings before stalking back to his tent. He meant to snatch a quick bite to eat and then fall asleep.

She knew she shouldn't, but Kialla couldn't help watching Cron through her slightly parted tent flap. She'd already made up her mind. Tonight was the night. Her only fear came from not knowing what his reaction would be. That uncertainty terrified her more than she cared to admit. She'd never been in love before so the term held no meaning for her. What she did know was her heart fluttered when she was around him and it was often difficult to think straight.

Kialla gasped as he eased out of his shirt. There were a handful of scars on his back, reminders of the hard life of a professional soldier. His body was extremely toned with just the right amount of muscle to make her heart beat faster. He was lean and hungry, just the kind of man she enjoyed.

Water rushed over him and he went back to his tent. Kialla waited until he was out of sight before stalking her way to him. She moved lithely, like a hunting lion. Her mind was made up. Every step had confidence and grace. She knew what she wanted and was determined to get it. She slipped into his tent without him knowing.

He stood with his back to her. Kialla watched him, an almost animalistic desire running through her body. Arms folded across her chest, she watched him push his trousers down over his hips. Standing in just a pair of undergarments, he was the vision of perfection. Kialla cleared her throat. Cron spun around.

"Kialla! Wh…what are you doing here?" he stammered.

She gave him her most seductive smile and started unlacing her bodice. The garment was on the ground before either of them spoke.

"We shouldn't be doing this," he protested weakly.

She closed the gap between them and covered his mouth with hers. Her kiss was hard, urgent. For a moment he was too stunned to react. Her tongue slipped into his mouth, swirling around his while her hands caressed his back. Finally, his hands broke free and he gave in to desire. She shuddered from the feel of being touched. Her skin flushed. Her knees weakened, threatening to buckle. She kissed him harder.

Cron let himself go. Primitive urges long suppressed burst free. He pulled away from her devouring kiss and left her gasping for breath. Lust burned in her eyes. Without waiting, he curled his fingers inside the band of her trousers and jerked them down. Kialla eagerly stepped out of them. He watched her tanned body in the flickering lamp light. Watched the way her soft breasts rose and fell with each breath. Her nipples hardened under his gaze. The curve of her flat stomach and patch of auburn hair between her gorgeously shaped legs beckoned him. Unable to control himself, he rushed back into her embrace.

She lay draped over him, kissing his chest. Kialla enjoyed the sound of his heartbeat. It was so calm, so gentle. Everything was perfect. She knew that on the other side of that tent flap the very world was falling apart but in here, right now, all was the way it was meant to be. She felt like a child again. Safe in his arms, Kialla closed her eyes and drifted to sleep. It was the first time in years she'd been able to know tranquility.

When she awoke sometime in the middle of the night, she ran her hand over his thighs. Or rather, where he should have been. Her fingers brushed empty sheets. Kialla's first thought was that he'd walked out on her, having taken what he wanted. Her eyes flared open in uncharacteristic panic only to find Cron staring back at her from the field chair across the tent.

"I woke up a little while ago and didn't want to disturb you," he told her once he noticed the distress in her eyes.

"You should come back to bed."

He grinned. "I will. I just wanted to watch you sleep."

She propped herself up on one elbow. Auburn locks dangled in her face and the blanket slid down past her breasts. "Like what you see?"

"That's not fair."

She returned his grin. "No, it's not. Now come back to bed and make love to me."

Kialla lifted the blanket and rolled on top of him once he slid back into the bed.

"I love you," she whispered as she lowered herself onto him.

The camp was broken down before the morning dew evaporated. Scouts returned in the night with positive results. The mouth of Deldin Grim was open and unprotected. When Faeldrin questioned them on this the scouts replied that they'd ridden close to a league into the threatening pass and found no signs of the enemy. The Elves took this as a great omen and excitedly started taking down the tents. Faeldrin walked among them, taking the time to speak with many. He shook hands, slapped a few on the back, and helped with the work. There was an unbreakable camaraderie involved, forged by hardships unimagined. Every last one of them respected and trusted the other with their lives. The majority of civilians would never know such.

By the time the last vestiges of night were gone, the Aeldruin were ready to move. They smiled and joked with each other in ways only soldiers understood. Suddenly heedless of their proximity to almost certain doom, the Aeldruin broke out an ancient battle hymn. Spirits lifted. The morning sun edged across the sky and grew bright. The vast, open sky stretched forever in crystalline blue. A slow breeze cooled the sweat on each of them.

Faeldrin said, "The gods are with us. Today is going to be a good day."

"It'll be a better one when my sword drinks Goblin blood," Grelic replied.

"Patience, Grelic. You'll get the chance very soon. I expect we'll have to cleave our way through the Deadlands, one Goblin neck at a time. What say you, Master Mage?"

Dakeb knew better than to speak the truth. No one really wanted to know what he thought. "Danger is aplenty in the coming days. We should enjoy the tranquility of this moment while it lasts."

Alarms were going off in his mind but he refrained from speaking further. Dark thoughts of what lay ahead nipped at him. He was afraid they were going to find out all too soon the hidden meaning behind his warning. This was the moment he had long dreaded and, now that it was upon him, wanted to avoid.

Faeldrin spurred the column forward. The Elves were going to the Deadlands and to war.

FORTY-TWO

Deldin Grim

The Aeldruin column seemed insignificant compared to the looming heights of the Darkwall Mountains. The mirth from the morning was gone. No trace of happiness was to be found. Weapons were drawn. Hands twitched with anticipation of the ambush each of them imagined. Long, threatening shadows reached down from unseen peaks. Temperatures dropped considerably in the mountain shadows. An unmistakable pall clung to the air.

"I don't like this," Cron whispered.

Supernatural mist clung to the feet of the great mountains. The Aeldruin continued pushing deeper into the murk. When asked, the scouts replied that the way had been clear the day prior. The Elf Lord sensed a trap.

Grelic scanned the terrain for clues. "It rained here recently. This morning, but how? It wasn't wet anywhere else."

The ground had that soft texture immediately following a shower. Cron attributed the dampness to dew and mist but the closer he looked the more he noticed pools of fresh water. "Perfect spot for an ambush."

"Speaking of such will only bring ill down upon us," Faeldrin replied. He shivered despite the warmth of his cloak. "We should go no further until morning. Too much can go wrong in the darkness and I don't trust the mist."

"We should send scouts back into the pass," Grelic suggested. "I'll go. I want a look at what we're dealing with."

"I'll join you," Faeldrin said.

Once it was decided, the rest of the Elves moved off to the side of the road and found a relatively suitable campsite. They'd been on the road for three days and now found themselves at the foot of the mountains. Faeldrin forbade any fires and they passed on erecting any tents. A double guard was established. They weren't willing to take any unnecessary chances. Dakeb stalked off into the growling darkness to emplace a series of invisible alarm wards should the enemy attempt an assault. The Elves broke out dried travel rations and ate in the gloom.

"Dakeb," Faeldrin said between bites of a rather hard biscuit. "I'd like to know more about the pass. Surely you've some hidden knowledge or fading memory of this dreadful place."

"I do, though I'd just as soon forget them all. The armies of the dark Mages used Deldin Grim to rush down and take Prince Belian and the knights of Averon from behind, slaughtering them to the man. Trolls and worse burned the bodies and ate the horses. They sent the heads back to Paedwyn."

Faeldrin was about to retract his request. This was not as inspiring as he'd hoped.

"Deldin Grim is perhaps two and a half leagues long and wide enough for three wagons to pass side by side. The way is relatively smooth from centuries of heavy use. Occasional landslides block the way and the sun never touches the ground. Winter is nigh impassible and spring rains turn the pass into grey sludge. Now, however, is the perfect time to push through. What I fear is time. The little we have left is fleeting at best. I fear the dark Mage is nearly finished."

Grelic stared at the Mage. The bad feeling he awoke with strengthened. It was as if all he'd done had been manipulated in the favor of the dark Mage. For a while events happened without issue. They'd lost the sense of being tracked after the Minotaurs captured them. Now, so close to the end, Grelic felt eyes watching their every move again. There seemed little doubt they were being set up. It was just a matter of time before the hammer fell. He didn't like sitting idle.

"How soon can you be ready to leave? I'd just as soon get into that pass while the mist remains," he asked Faeldrin.

"Give me one quarter of an hour and I'll be ready. I'm taking two others along should we encounter any unforeseen difficulties."

"You'd best hurry. I've emplaced wards to keep us safe but men fight better when their captains are present," Dakeb cautioned.

Aleor nodded silent agreement.

Faeldrin looked around the group of assembled faces. They were just as determined as he. A good sign. "Very well. Rest as much as possible. We march at dawn."

Fifteen minutes later three Elves and Grelic were riding up into Deldin Grim.

There was no moonlight. Not this deep in the heart of the pass. Deldin Grim was ominous in every aspect. Neither sun nor moon penetrated this deep into the pass. They rode slowly. The horses grew more skittish the deeper they went. They'd been bred for the open plain, not the unfamiliar darkness of the mountains. No amount of reassuring pats or whispered encouragement eased their apprehension.

Grelic led the way. Despite the rising sense of gloom and potential disaster, he remained comfortable. He'd done some time in large armies, fought the battles much bigger than any of the others. People said he was a natural warrior. Which was true. He'd been swinging a blade for more years than he could remember. He much preferred working alone or in small groups. The full strength of the Aeldruin was almost too much to bear. If not for the dragon lurking under Druem, he might have already struck out on his own.

He sighed. Current events went well beyond his limited measures of control. Grelic didn't necessarily enjoy killing. He'd been one to figure that men of all races deserved to live according to their own choosing. If some decided to rise up and start trouble he had no problem sending them down to the grave. Rentor once asked him how many men he'd killed. Grelic only shrugged. A man who killed in battle shouldn't burden himself with the pain of knowing how good he was. The king laughed in response. Struggling through the battle of Kressel Tine made him see the light. In battle, Grelic became the perfect killing machine.

The night lost some of its edge. A thick cloud cover hung low in the sky. Small, shadowy objects darted over their heads. Bats. Grelic started to have misgivings about his eagerness to scout the pass. Common sense told him the Goblins had more than enough defenses to hold off a pack of Elves without suffering great casualties. That's if the dragon didn't swoop in and fry them first.

A sudden noise ahead disrupted his thoughts. His hand instinctively dropped to his sword as the noise grew louder. It had a familiar sound to it. Something he'd heard many times before. It reminded him of a child crushing dried leaves. He and Faeldrin edged closer to investigate. Grelic caught the faint yet distinct sound of water splashing over stone. He let out the breath he'd been holding. The demons his fear propagated turned out to be naught but an ordinary waterfall. They kept riding.

His eyes adjusted to the gloom but he almost wished they hadn't. Total darkness served his frame of mind better. At least that way when they got attacked all he had to do was react. The semi-dark gloom left him with too much to think on. Grelic cursed his luck for bringing him here. Goblins were notorious for slinking about in the dark places of the world, preferring to move at night where their deeds would go unseen.

A soft hiss stopped the group.

Faeldrin pulled his horse as close to Grelic as possible. "We've reached the far end of the pass."

"How much further?"

"Just around this bend. No more than a few hundred meters," the Elf replied. Unlike Grelic, they saw perfectly in the night.

They slid from their horses, handing the reins to Aleor. Elf and man crept on foot the rest of the way, hoping to make less noise. The mouth of Deldin Grim slowly widened until they couldn't make out the walls. Haunting torchlight suddenly reflected off of the pass, robbing Grelic's night vision. Thoughts of sneaking into the Deadlands slowly died. The sound of rough voices grinding in a foul language mocked them.

"Trolls," Faeldrin whispered.

It only gets worse. Grelic's hope faded. Two monstrous towers of black stone were carved from the mountainsides. Goblins and other dark creatures patrolled the crenellated levels. He counted fifty before they became too much to keep track of.

"They won't need a dragon to finish us," Grelic replied. "This is a death trap."

"Agreed. There's no way we can fight our way through an entire garrison. It appears our Mage isn't up-to-date on the fledgling empire here."

Grelic absentmindedly scratched his chin. "What should we do?"

"Hard to say. If time is running out as Dakeb says, we'll never make it all the way back around the mountains. There's no point in trying to fight our way through this. We should get back before they spot us. I don't like the looks of those battle Trolls. Perhaps Dakeb will have a better way to deal with them."

Grelic's heart warned that Mages weren't infallible. Keeping his tongue to himself, he followed Faeldrin back to the horses. Harsh laughter trailed after.

The journey back through Deldin Grim was eerier than the trip in. Appearances were the same for the most part though they immediately picked up on the building tension. Despite Grelic's concerns, they arrived back at the main body without incident and proceeded to summon a hasty council. Faeldrin wasn't sure whether to remain calm or give in to his apprehensions. The camp had an unusual feel he couldn't quite place. His Elves were quieter than usual and it didn't take long for him to discover why.

Three figures stood beside Dakeb. They barely came up to his shoulders. Each had similar features. Black, matted hair hung down unevenly to their shoulders. Their faces were flat with no distinguishable characteristics. Lean muscles and large brown eyes stared up at the Elves.

"I wasn't aware we had guests," he said with a suspicious smile. "I would have dressed more appropriately."

"As well you should have," Dakeb seconded. "These are the Pell Darga. They live in the Darkwall, seldom coming down from their haunts. Their language is broken but understandable. I believe they are one of the old tribes, long forgotten by the rest of the world. They might prove useful."

Grelic eyed the diminutive men cautiously. "What brings them down now?"

Their leader glanced to Dakeb before addressing them. "We wish to help. I am Cpur, patriarch of my clan. Goblins hunt my people for sport. Hundreds have died for this reason. We will help destroy Goblins."

"Hundreds?" Grelic asked incredulously while thinking about the boost a hidden army this deep in enemy territory could give.

Faeldrin nodded approvingly. "How do you know we're here to kill Goblins?"

"We have watched you for days. We'll help."

Grelic couldn't help but laugh. "Brave little bastards!"

"I killed six already," Cpur claimed boldly. The look in his eyes dared anyone to question his statement.

"The Aeldruin accept your offer, Cpur. We are glad to fight alongside the Pell Darga," the Elf Lord replied.

"I didn't think we'd come here to fight a war. We're after the dragon, right?" Pregen asked with idle boredom. "This is really starting to grind on me, Grelic. I wish we'd make up our minds and be done with it."

Kialla scowled and drew back to strike him. He threw up his hands in disgust and stalked off.

"A rather depressing man," Faeldrin said. "Is he always like that?"

"More often than not," Grelic admitted. "I'm starting to regret bringing him. He does have a point. We came here to stop the dragon. If what Dakeb claims is true, we need to be quick about it."

"Quick is in the interpretation. It's a three-day ride across mostly open terrain. The only constant is Druem. Up close or far away, it dominates the landscape," Dakeb told them.

"We'll never get the chance to find that out if we can't get past the garrison at the far end of the pass. Goblins, Trolls, and more bar the way. I fear this quest may be finished," Faeldrin said.

"There is secret way through mountains," Cpur told them. "Big enough for your machines. Guardians should not see us if we come out at dusk."

Faeldrin clapped once. "This could be the break we're looking for! If we can circle the garrison and get into the Deadlands undetected, the Aeldruin will return to help you cleanse the mountains of Goblins."

"Agreed."

The mood brightened immeasurably and the call went out. The Aeldruin wordlessly mounted up and prepared to ride.

FORTY-THREE

Secret Ways

The Pell Darga moved with confidence rival to the Elves. Grelic discovered his growing respect for the stout people and hoped they were equally fierce in battle. Their short spears were sharp and blackened against moon or torchlight. They crawled over rocks and practically disappeared unless viewed directly. Dozens more had joined them after entering the mouth of Deldin Grim. The Aeldruin column set out as the sun broke the horizon. Many said their morning prayers and bade the light good-bye. It would be long before any of them were kissed by golden rays again.

Cpur led them unerringly into the pass as soon as night lifted. Deldin Grim proved to be a drab nightmare. The rock walls were sickening shades of grey and brown. Unusual stenches permeated the air, as if a thousand trees had died and were decomposing in a watery distillery. Evidence from the rains was gone. Most of the sludge had dried in thick, chalk-like dust that coated everything. It lent the Pell a spectral appearance. Kialla thought the only things missing were chains and blood-red eyes.

No wind blew this deep in the pass. The air was old, stagnant. They were reminded of a cemetery on a cold winter night. Shadows clung to everything. Despite the assurances of the Pell Darga, the Elves constantly searched for Goblin scouts. Even Dakeb argued against the futility of it. The Goblins were secure in their mountain fortress. Based on what Faeldrin and Grelic reported, they were arrogant and certain of their dominance. Surely they weren't expecting a head-on assault.

Grelic agreed with the old Mage. It wouldn't take much to beat back the Aeldruin as they were. Cavalry was no good against fortified defensive positions, especially with the strength of those two towers.

"How much further before we branch off? I don't want to take the chance of running into a patrol," Faeldrin voiced his concerns.

Cpur gestured. "Not much. My people already wait for us. They keep the way hidden from Goblins."

A rider came flying up behind them, kicking dust and rock. His face bore a dire look.

"What is it?" Faeldrin demanded.

"A Goblin raiding part returns. They'll be in the pass within the hour," the scout reported grimly.

Cron paled. "There's no way we can get this caravan to the secret path in time."

"Nor can we fight. The sound will rouse the garrison and have them pouring down our throats," Grelic added.

Faeldrin scowled at their lack of luck. "Our choices are limited. What are their numbers?"

"Close to one hundred."

Faeldrin punched his fist into the palm of his other hand. "Damnation. We couldn't even kill them quickly if we had to. I say we attack and hope the other lot doesn't join in. It's the only chance we have."

"Perhaps there is one other way," Dakeb interjected. He looked to Cpur. "Are your people ready?"

Cpur nodded, his back stiffening with pride. "We will handle Goblins. They never trouble anyone again. We keep moving."

With no other course of action available, Faeldrin gestured for the Pell to continue.

Cpur guided them through another opposing stretch of Deldin Grim. Places looked as if drab cliffs were leaning down on them, threatening to crush them out of blind hatred. He stopped at one point where the shadows were particularly deep. The leader of the Pell Darga chirped and a dozen of the smaller warriors crawled down from the rock face. He barked orders in his native language and his warriors quickly pulled aside the elaborate camouflage concealing their secret pass.

Grelic was impressed. The Pell Darga worked without sound and moved the heavy stones aside with relative ease. It wasn't until the Aeldruin rode into the cave that he saw why they were so easy to move. The boulders were nothing more than heavy screens stretched and manipulated over a lattice of branches and rope. From the outside they looked completely natural. Grelic suddenly felt much better about leaving the Pell behind to handle the Goblin raiding party.

"How far does this tunnel run?" Faeldrin asked Cpur.

"A few hundred meters before it becomes a small pass. We come out almost a league from Deldin Grim."

Faeldrin nodded. "Today may just work in our favor. Aleor, lead them out of the cave. I'm staying to ensure the rest of the convoy moves into cover without incident."

"I'll stay as well," Grelic seconded. "Maybe a few Goblins will make it this far. It's been too long since I had a reason to swing my sword."

Cron smiled wanly. "Me too."

Kialla elbowed him swiftly, her message clear. She wasn't going anywhere without him. Grelic watched their little exchange and realization dawned. He didn't know how he'd missed the signs, despite their casual closeness from the beginning. Too many new thoughts competed for his attention. He thought how happy her father would be. The horrors of his earlier nightmare were finally laid to rest. Grelic knew peace at last. Now all he needed to do was keep her alive long enough for her to enjoy her choices.

Lord Death was out there, drawing closer.

The Elf Lord turned and gave Aleor the go-ahead. Elf and Pell took off into the short tunnel and the Deadlands beyond. All too soon all that remained were the three obstinate humans and the Elf. The Pell had returned to their haunts while the rest of the Aeldruin rode through. Once done, they'd climb back down and secure their passage.

"Can you hear anything?" Cron asked.

Grelic shook his head. "The battle might be too far away or already finished. I've half a mind to ride back and know for certain."

"What are we waiting for? Let's go see if our little friends are as fearsome as they claim. I don't relish the thought of having a Goblin war party on my tail," Faeldrin said.

"Is that such a good idea?" Kialla asked. "They might have been beaten and the Goblins are already marching towards us. If we ride into them there's no way we can escape. They'll find the secret path and we'll be finished."

A shadow moved, barely noticeable. Only Grelic noticed it.

"I don't think we need to worry about Goblins discovering the Pell Darga paths. Even if we get killed, these mountain people seem more than capable of defending themselves. Come, we're wasting too much time," he told them.

Drawing his sword, Grelic headed back towards the beginning of the pass. They'd only made it a few hundred meters before a nauseating smell permeated the air. Kialla gagged. With no wind, the air was stiflingly thick. Rot and decay wafted up to assault their senses. Cold dread spread over the group. Grelic had seen many obscene things in his time, but this was an act he hadn't witnessed in years.

Dark shapes could be seen moving just ahead. The light mist had returned, blanketing the unwinding stretch of Deldin Grim. Something fluttered past one of his ears. He watched unfamiliar birds drift off into the mist. *At least we don't have to sneak around worrying about running into a fight anymore. They know we're here.*

Grelic rode point while the others fanned out in an arrowhead pattern behind. Weapons were drawn. Hearts beat faster. Despite the ghostly feeling suffocating them, they took comfort in knowing an honest fight lay just ahead. Weeks of running, hiding, and imprisonment wore their nerves thin. Crows chattered. The stench strengthened. Grelic idly wondered how much death it took to poison the air in such a short amount of time. Something stirred in the mist. It grew larger, heading straight for them. Cron set an arrow to his bow and drew a bead.

The barrel-bodied Goblin burst from the mists. He bled from a dozen cuts. His black uniform was in shreds. Normally black eyes, cold and calculating, were wide and terrified. He had no weapons. He took them by surprise so quickly they failed to notice the handful of Pell warriors chasing the

Goblin. Short spears zipped through the air and took the Goblin in the back. He pitched forward with a gurgled cry and died. The Pell Darga slowed and retrieved their spears without a word.

"Damnation," Grelic uttered.

The Pell disappeared back into the mist. Doubts of the Goblins winning through evaporated. Faeldrin entertained ideas about what he could do with an army of the squat mountain people at his side. His promise came back to him. Taking the Goblin fortifications at the inner mouth of Deldin Grim suddenly appeared much easier. A nod from Grelic and they rode on, morbid curiosity pulled them deeper into the carnage. Corpses littered the pass amidst pools of cooling blood. All were Goblins. Flies buzzed everywhere.

"This certainly ends doubt," Faeldrin said and sheathed his sword.

Cron stuffed his arrow back in the quiver and looked down into the agonized face of a dead Goblin. "We should leave this place. Nothing good can come from this."

Grelic turned and decided to let his horse stretch its legs. The others followed suit. They'd seen enough. Soon all four were galloping back towards the secret path.

Kialla desperately wanted to be away from this awful place and on the open plain. Tormenting visions attacked her every time she blinked. This was not the way she planned on going to war. Come to think of it, the more time she spent dwelling on the vast array of possibilities, the more she came to understand that this wasn't the life she wanted to live at all. It was fine for men like her father, like Grelic. Everything she had seen lately convinced her it wasn't for her.

The change began in Gend when they decided to go to the Deadlands. She'd never had an issue when it came to killing but she never looked forward to it either. Growing up in the home of a legendary warrior left her with a hard shell. No one had ever gotten to her heart before, no one until Cron. Around him she felt complete, like nothing bad could ever touch her. She didn't know love before him.

There were certain degrees of anguish associated with the unexpected revelation. Cron was a strong man filled with passion for his job and loyalty to kingdom. It was enduring and she loved him more for it. Right now though she really wanted to go home and abandon the possibility of dying, forgotten in a hostile land. This was the first time in her life she felt like there was the chance at making something substantial out of life. A brief glimmer of hope into a world she knew nothing about. Until this task was complete, her dreams of the future were going to wait. She looked up in time to see the entrance to the secret path. The imminent danger had passed.

"I rather like these people," Faeldrin said about the Pell Darga, his song-like voice danced above the *clip-clop* of hooves.

"They come in handy in a fight," Cron agreed. "I'd never want to get them mad at me, that's for sure."

"True enough, but I believe they are just what we need to turn this campaign back into our favor," the Elf Lord said.

Grelic's eyebrow arched. "What do you have in mind?"

"Think about it. These stalwart fellows just wiped out a full company of heavily armed Goblins in a matter of minutes. If we can convince Cpur to bring his full force to bear we might be able to draw attention away from the main mission and clear the pass."

"Use them to fight for us? We can't do that," Kialla protested.

Faeldrin emphatically shook his head. "Not for us, but with us. We marshal our forces and assault the Goblin towers at the mouth of the pass. Draw out the enemy. With the Goblins marching to counter this new threat you'll be able to make your way across the plains and into Druem almost unnoticed."

"Sounds like you're not planning on coming with us," Grelic stated.

"I'm not. My Aeldruin would be useless under the mountain. With any luck we'll put up enough of a fight to draw out the dragon and kill him here. That gives you all the time you need to stop the dark Mage."

Cron suddenly felt uneasy. "What if the Pell Darga say no? You can't fight an army with a handful of Elves. It's suicide."

The Elf Lord gave a haphazard shrug. "Then we make a new plan."

Sunlight kissed the far darkness. They were coming to the end of the tunnel.

Faeldrin stopped. "It's the only real chance we have. I'll provide the diversion. You take Dakeb and stop the Mage."

"If the dragon catches you in the open..." Grelic left the thought unfinished.

"Then we sacrifice ourselves for the greater good. I'm no hero, Grelic. I'm just a simple Elf trying to do the right thing. The Pell Darga need help. I can't sit by and watch, knowing what these Goblin scum are doing. They deserve the same chances as the rest of us. My Aeldruin can fight this dragon, maybe even win, but we need to be in the open. Make him come to us and we have the advantage." The Elf Lord seemed particularly pleased with his rationale. He watched the doubt in their eyes flicker and crack. *One more push and they'll see it my way.*

"We can do this. The dragon isn't our primary concern anymore. It's the largest threat, but the dark Mage must come first. We have to stop him from finding the shard of the crystal. Grelic, I remember the last war and I do not want to see those days renewed. Perhaps this time evil will be stamped out for good."

Grelic wasn't overly excited with the thought, but he wasn't the one with the final decision-making authority. If anything, they needed to come to a consensus. "The risk is great, and many could die. Let us see what Dakeb has to say first."

Faeldrin didn't like the answer but accepted it. They'd obey Dakeb's wisdom, just like in the past. He was highly confident his plan would succeed. Wheels started turning and he made his plans for war.

The Aeldruin were drawn up in a defensive semi-circle. Ballistae were loaded and angled down every avenue of approach. There was no way the enemy could get close enough to mount a serious attack without suffering extreme losses. The Deadlands stretched out ahead of the Elves. Scrub trees and dying brush, all withered shades of brown, filled the plains. A single road to the left ran from Mordrun Bal to Druem.

Thick, black smoke billowed up from the volcano. It choked the air with ash and plague. The wind bore an acidic bite. Dust clouds shifted over the desiccated soil. All life had died here in a single day. The sun remained behind a perpetual veil of heavy clouds. It felt like the gods had forgotten this part of the world and let it wither.

Cron let out a low whistle. He'd never imagined anything so desolate.

Dakeb spied them first. "Ah, welcome back! I trust all is well in Deldin Grim?"

Grelic laughed. "Something tells me you already know that answer. The way behind is secure. The Pell Darga surpass my opinions."

Cpur beamed with pride. "Fighting is our life."

"At least until the Goblin threat is removed," Faeldrin added. Both Cpur and Dakeb looked up to the Elf Lord. Faeldrin smiled. They'd taken the bait. He slid from his horse and clapped. "Let me tell you what I have worked out so far."

FORTY-FOUR

The Shard

Scourd listened to the grim rumblings in the earth far beneath Druem and was reminded of looming disaster. The Hooded Man was forcing them to dig too deep. Already the Goblin had lost a large part of his slave labor force and over a dozen guards during the last accident when Minotaur workers ruptured an active lava vein. Scourd couldn't afford to lose any more if he expected to maintain schedule. Rumors of the enemy moving against them heightened his nerves. Several patrols were missing and his soldiers grumbled about the future. All of his carefully laid plans for dominion were slipping away.

Sitting alone in his private chambers, Scourd closed his eyes and tried to think of a way to salvage victory. The task proved more difficult than he anticipated. He couldn't fight an enemy he couldn't see or know. One of his scouts mentioned the Aeldruin, but that seemed unlikely. The Elven mercenaries were whispers of imagination told to young warriors to keep them from becoming too arrogant. Still, their very name struck fear among his people. Doubt rippled through his ranks and he didn't know how to stop it.

A foul mood hovered around him. Scourd clutched his sword and went out into the main halls. Perhaps killing one slave wasn't too much to hamper their efforts. He smiled savagely at the thought of beating one of the men of Thrae to death. Strong muscles flexed in anticipation. There was nothing so satisfying as seeing warm blood escape a beaten enemy. He'd hardly made it down the main corridor to the barracks and kitchens when a thin, black-green Goblin hobbled up to him. Scourd's mood darkened.

"Make this good or I'll have your hide," he snapped.

The Goblin cringed backwards and hissed. "They found it!"

Scourd stared for a moment, unbelieving. Operations had been ongoing for over two years. It hardly seemed possible the end had come. A dark place in his mind saw armies of Goblins ravaging Malweir. *End? No. This is but the beginning. Soon I'll be able to lay waste to the world, shaking the yoke of the Mage and his impetuous dragon.* There'd never been a Goblin empire. Scourd believed that time was now.

"Where?"

"The lower levels, near the dragon's lair," the imp snarled.

Scourd stormed past the smaller Goblin, shoving him forcibly into the jagged rock face. He wanted to run but deemed it undignified. Powerful legs drove him through the labyrinthine maze of tunnels and course halls. His heartbeat quickened. Ages seemed to pass. Too many frustrations clouded his thoughts. He fought hard to resist the urge to kill whoever held the stone and keep it from going to the Hooded Man. Mage or not, he was just a man and Scourd's sworn enemy.

A crowd of slave masters and warriors surrounded the slave holding the crystal. The culmination of months of brutal labor and anxious wait boiled down to a seemingly insignificant piece of crystal. None of the Goblins knew what to do with it. The purple crystal, barely larger than a fist, wasn't a weapon. There were no magical powers emanating from it. For all purposes it held little value.

"Out of the way, scum!" Scourd ordered.

He barreled his way to the center of the throng. The slave stood there, shaking. His clothes were ripped to tatters and he was haggard and starving. His muscles were worn away until his skeleton showed in disgusting poses. His head was lowered, as if afraid to stare up at his overlords.

Scourd viewed the slave with disgust. Lacking the hesitations of his warriors, the Goblin Lord ripped the shard from the slave's hand and raised it to his eye for inspection. Even with his brooding plans, Scourd found little significance in a thing so small. He snarled and curled his diseased fingers over the shard. The slave whimpered again, drawing Scourd's ire. He moved so fast his actions blurred. A blade shined in the flickering shadows. The slave grunted and collapsed. Blood trickled down the dagger and over Scourd's hand.

"Move the rest to their pens," he ordered.

Whips cracked. The crowd immediately dispersed. A taller Goblin leaned over to Scourd. "Why keep them?"

"Use them to keep making weapons and armor. Then we kill them all."

Scourd headed back to his chambers.

Nauseous green light glowed off of Ramulus's horns. Mage fire turned the expansive cavern into a haunted, pale world. The dragon cooled himself in the small lake nestled in the far corner. He didn't move and hardly breathed. Powerful arms folded across his broad chest. The horn jutting from his chin stuck out menacingly, the tip barely touching the water surface. His pale, ice-colored eyes were drawn to a fine slit, watching.

Flies danced around his eyes and nose. Ramulus didn't blink. Druem rumbled again. Small boulders dropped from the ceiling, breaking on the hard lava ground. Still the dragon remained still. Falling rocks didn't concern him. It would take the entire mountain collapsing to harm him. There was but one thing he truly feared: the Silver Mage.

Ramulus felt sharp tremors of fear whenever the Mage was near. His visits to the Deadlands were few, often weeks passing without word, but Ramulus knew better than to hope the Mage had forgotten him. Stories travelled on the winds of a new, dark kingdom rising in the east. The Silver Mage had conquered Gren a human lifetime ago and had been transforming it into a living nightmare ever since. The once flourishing city of Aingaard had become the symbol of pain and doom.

Always the Mage hungered for the lost pieces of the crystal. His very lust was driven by it. Ramulus knew of the terrible destruction brought about by the crystal and how it could be used to allow the dark gods back into the world. A dragon cared nothing for such things. He and his kind had watched from afar as Malweir fell to ruin during the Mage War. Dragons had no part in the war; after all, what business did the great wyrms have in the sad affairs of man?

He wasn't sure when he fell under Sidian's cunning spell. Ramulus hated the Mage and wanted to destroy him as much as the urge to return to his broken mountain home west of the Jebel Desert. Until now he doubted the crystal shard was here. There were thousands of inconspicuous places across Malweir the shards could have been hidden. Why the heart of the Deadlands? It made little sense to the dragon. So Ramulus, close to one thousand years old, sat in his cavern and waited to see how events unfolded.

FORTY-FIVE

Insurrection

Light drizzle blanketed central Thrae. Not hard, just enough to thoroughly wet everything and make life miserable for those unfortunate to be caught outside. Such was the late night of the renegade armies poised to sack Kelis Dur. Dull campfires eased the torment, slightly. Summer was passing on and fall drew ever closer. None of the men cared much for the upcoming festivals and holidays. One thought drew their focus: at dawn they marched on the capital and began the rebellion.

General Huor pulled his bearskin cloak tighter around his shoulders. Troubled dreams kept him awake lately. Dark creatures haunted his nightmares. He felt his soul slowly being torn from him. Huor shook his head to clear away the demons lurking on the edges of his vision. Tonight was too important to suffer from the complexities of sheer paranoia.

His gaze swept over his army. Most of the camp was asleep in row after row of campaign tents. Few of these soldiers were experienced. Only a handful of veterans from the Dwarf war remained and those were getting long in the tooth. The rest were relative rookies. He knew it ensured none of them held strong ties of loyalty to Rentor. That would come in handy when the fighting started. Huor held no misunderstandings about the coming battle. The fighting would be fierce. No doubt the king's loyalists would fight to the last man. Many of the men sleeping around him would not live to see the following night.

Huor drew a deep breath and moved out among the camp. Cooks were already up and preparing a modest breakfast for the battalions. Guards and pickets patrolled the perimeter. Huor seriously doubted anything bad was going to happen and there certainly wasn't going to be time for his foe to mount a counterattack. If all went well, Rentor was already dead and Codel Mres was solidifying his position as the new regent. He expected a rider any moment carrying instructions to begin the offensive.

"Morning, General," a burly guard said and nodded from the shadows of a thorn tree. His travel cloak hid the man completely in the near pitch black. "Damned day for a battle, eh?"

Huor nodded back. "It makes it easier to wash the blood off, trooper."

"That it does, sir."

"Any movement since you've been on duty?"

The guard shook his head. "No sir. Not expecting any either."

Huor knew better than anyone that overconfidence was a fine line bordering arrogance. Too much stood in the balance to afford any weakness right now. He also knew that to reprimand the man for his strong opinions was a dent in morale. That was the one thing capable of ending a campaign before it started. Experience told him his army needed to enter the battle on a high. His endeavors in brutality were no different.

There was a mood building in the camp. The men were ready for a fight. He felt the electric undercurrents rippling from tent to tent. The urge to kill, to swing their swords. The ability to kill was the true empowerment of man. The power to take a life was akin to godliness. Huor never felt more comfortable than in the throes of a fever-pitched battle. It had been years, and several pounds, since he last felt the sting of war. The sounds. The smell. Even the adrenaline rush of fear right before the lines clashed. He took another deep breath. The calm before the storm. This was what it meant to be alive.

He clapped the guard on his shoulder. "There won't be. We have them by surprise."

The guard smiled as Huor stalked off to find the warmth of a cook fire.

The scout returned to the command tent. He was covered with sweat and rain and breathing hard. His mission had been long and grueling but the information he'd gained was invaluable. Guards let him through the lines, offering a drink from their canteens and a quick bite. Once inside the tent he saluted and made his report.

"Sir, the enemy army is camped right where the old man said they'd be. They have a double line of security with roving guards moving in opposite directions. They're not very alert though. The main body of troops is still asleep."

The young blonde major looked skeptically to his field commander. "What do you think?"

Commander Whorl was a bear of a man with iron-grey hair and a perpetual scowl. He'd lost his right eye at the battle of Kressel Tine and refused to disgrace himself with an eye patch. ""How many troops are we facing?"

"Between two and three thousand, sir."

Whorl actually laugh. It was a deep and bitter sound. "Use archers to fire the camp and then a cavalry charge while they're still asleep. Follow with infantry battalions. Use the horse to capture Huor and his renegade commanders and the fight is over."

The major nodded thoughtfully and turned to the grizzled sergeant sitting in the corner. "How about you, Notam?"

Notam rubbed his chin. "It's what your brother would have done."

Major Maen was speechless. He'd grown up playing soldier with his brother, Cron. At that age they were inseparable. In fact, Cron was the reason he'd joined the army. Now Cron was the reason he'd agreed to Seldis' scheme to stop Huor's insurrection.

"Cron was a good man and knew his way around the battlefield. You served with him for many years and I value your opinion." He shot Whorl a look. "Both of you. Get the men up and ready to move. We're outnumbered so this won't be easy. Speed is the key. The archers will fire five volleys. Time the cavalry charge with the last round. The confusion of five hundred horse will disrupt them enough to let our infantry sweep in and cordon off the center of their camp. I want Huor alive. His fate is in the king's hands. Good luck to you all. We move out in one hour."

His officers saluted and broke council.

"Notam, hold fast please," Maen asked.

"Sir?"

"I have a special task for you and your men."

The insistent whistle of two hundred arrows flaming through the waking dawn went largely unheard. The second and third volleys were in flight before the first managed to set fire to a handful of tents. Guards, those that hadn't been killed by sappers before the attack began, tried to sound the alarm. By then it was too late. Hooves pounded the ground in a thunderous roar. A horse whinnied as the front ranks crashed into the enemy camp.

Men fell bloodied and screaming. The sick crunch of steel cutting naked flesh and breaking bone sang a horrible song. Soon bodies began piling up. The cavalry formed a loose wedge and drove straight for the center, Whorl rode at the tip. His broadsword cleaved enemy attackers without mercy. Once he would have considered these men friends. Thanks to their treachery, they weren't even countrymen. They were the enemy. His horse trampled a confused soldier to death. Whorl grinned savagely and pointed his sword towards the central cluster of tents.

"Push on! Take the traitor!"

Hundreds of infantry pushed in behind the enormous gap torn in the enemy lines.

General Huor dropped his mug of soup at the sound of thunder. Fires flared to life everywhere he looked. The glow cast a chilling pall over the myriad of cavalry emerging from the waning shadows. Men raised the call to arms but Huor knew it would not be enough. Even if they managed to awaken in time and put up a fight, the enemy was already inside the perimeter. His worst nightmares were coming true.

Huor cursed Codel Mres and the damned Hooded Man. Most importantly, he cursed himself for allowing this travesty to happen. He had the numbers, the element of surprise. He had the backing of the politicians and secret benefactors wanting change. How could things have gone this wrong before he even started? He rushed to his tent to arm himself. Rentor may still live, and the carefully planned insurrection crashing down around him, but Huor was determined to die well. He owed himself that much.

Notam and thirty men left the main camp as soon as Maen finished with him. Each of his crew was handpicked and covered only in light clothing. Soot was smeared across their faces and hands. None of them carried more than a dagger. Any unnecessary noise would give away their presence and end their mission abruptly. They moved like wraiths. Tiny shadows through the greater darkness. A lone picket stepped in front of Notam. The sergeant ran his blade across the guard's throat and kept moving.

Picket lines were the more dangerous of the two lines of defense Huor had established. Stationary and hidden, attackers often couldn't see them until it was too late. Fortune smiled on Notam this night. Had they been a little off to the left or right and they would have been spotted. Notam exhaled a breath of relief as the body struck the soft grass. *So far so good.*

He halted at the edge of the tree line and motioned for Essen, the lead scout. "Where are the corrals?"

Essen pointed. "Skirt the tree line west for a few hundred meters. The area is lightly guarded and at the rear of their trains."

The grizzled sergeant gloated silently. Huor's own arrogance was going to be his downfall. Notam's men raced towards the corrals where hundreds of enemy horses were about to be set loose.

The point of the wedge was already at the heart of the enemy camp. A wake of bodies trailed behind them. Infantrymen marched into the gaps and formed solid squares ringed with shields and pikes. General Huor's conquering army was crumbling at a rapid pace. Men lost heart at the unexpected ferocity of the combined assault. Front ranks turned to flee only to become trapped in the press of bodies surging towards the fight. Panic gripped them. Dozens were crushed to death in the growing confusion. Hundreds more threw down their arms and surrendered to the infantry.

The insurrection was finished.

Huor ran for his life, gathering men along the way. He felt the opportunity to counterattack was still there if he could gather enough soldiers and reach the horses in time. The illusion of victory dwindled. He watched helplessly as too many of his men ran off into the night. There was no way he could even think about taking Kelis Dur now. The death toll was rising and already in the hundreds. Fires spread, burning those unfortunate enough to be caught inside. Huor's heart dropped as his meager band finally gained the corrals. Several men already lay dead and the pens and fences burned. Of the horses, there was no sign. He had lost.

Turning to his men with his bravest face, Huor said, "Fight or flee, the choice is yours. I command you no longer. Go now and find whatever end befits you."

No one moved at first. They stood staring at their leader in disbelief. How could he suggest failure? Then one man sheathed his sword and walked off into the night. Another pair followed. Only four turned to go back to the battle. Soon, General Huor was alone. Honor demanded he surrender and accept his punishment. At the very least he'd be banished from Thrae, his lands and holdings taken in the name of the king. Death lay at the opposite end of the spectrum. Either way his life was finished. His one hope lay in revenge. If could only find Codel and the Hooded Man he might be able to avenge himself and the hundreds of dead men stretched out around him. That would certainly ease the pain of death.

The beaten general sheathed his own blade and stalked off into the night in search of a mount. He never made it past the corral. A handful of men emerged from the night to surround him with poised daggers. He reeled in shock, for they appeared as demons to him. Faces painted black and echoing the shine of flames, they sought his death.

"Don't move, General," said a voice from behind.

Huor recognized the demon's voice.

Field Commander Whorl dismounted and looked around for the first time since charging into the fight. Dawn had claimed the world. Fingers of blue stretched across what little darkness remained. Pieces of flaming cloth blew in the wind. Smoke and ash choked him. He picked out several vultures already circling. The dead weren't even cold yet. Bodies lay strewn for as far as he could see. Most belonged to the enemy. Whorl almost felt sorry for them. The attack had been so swift it was impossible to mount a defense. They folded quickly and their leaders had abandoned them. Whorl wouldn't be satisfied until General Huor was in custody and on his way back to stand trial for his crimes. Until then this was a hollow victory. He walked over to Huor's tent, took the lone standard still blowing in the wind, and snapped the staff over his knee.

"Segregate the prisoners by rank. Officers and enlisted. Search every corpse. I want Huor found. Take all of the documents from his tent back to Major Maen and have the surgeons start taking care of the wounded." His anger ebbed towards the end. There hadn't been official word of friendly casualties but he didn't imagine them to be overly high. Still, he feared the worst until he knew for sure.

"What about the rest of the camp, sir?" asked a slightly wounded captain with blood drying on his sleeve.

Whorl looked around. His one eye was cruel and suddenly vindictive. "Burn it all."

The captain saluted and set about his task.

Notam walked into what remained of the enemy encampment with a profound sense of relief. He'd accomplished his mission without losing anyone, though one man took a nasty cut across the top of his thigh. He'd also captured the leader of the insurrection and helped restore Cron's name and honor. Not too bad for a night's work. He was surprised at the amount of carnage and destruction done in such a short time. The battle lasted less than an hour before the enemy capitulated. Confiscated wagons were already being loaded with wounded, from both sides, and taking them off to the makeshift field hospital set up at the edge of the camp. Too many sons of Thrae lay dead. Notam knew they would be buried in separate graves. At least those still loyal to King Rentor. Traitors would be burned and forgotten in disgrace.

"Are you satisfied, General? Your greed sent these men to their deaths," Notam growled in Huor's ear.

Before he could respond he was shoved forcibly and led to Field Commander Whorl. At last the one-eyed veteran smiled.

Maen leaned back in his field chair and exhaled the breath he'd been holding since the strike force left. He thanked the scout for news of the victory and finally allowed his nerves to calm. He'd managed to prevent civil war but something unspoken still nagged at him. He just wasn't sure what. Maen rose and went outside to watch the dawn. Somewhere out there, lost in the world, was his brother. He didn't know where or how to find him, but he vowed to never stop until they came home together.

Kelis Dur slept peacefully. Stray dogs dug through trash and drunks lay where they'd passed out. Nothing seemed out of place except for Codel Mres running for his life. The Dwim had failed to kill Rentor. His trust in General Huor's abilities were marginal at best and the Hooded Man all but told him he was useless to the main objective. Codel barely had time to collect a cloak before royal guards burst through the front door of his luxurious home.

He'd made it to the sewers, where he thought he'd be safe. Such was not the case. It wasn't long before the baying of hounds in the tunnels behind him forced him to run again. Heart pounding, he ran harder. The only sounds were his ragged breath intermingling with the splash of his slippered feet as he ran through the scum and waste of the city. Fear propelled him yet also made him hesitate. He suddenly realized he had nowhere to go. Even if he managed to make it to Huor's camp, what would he do? The appearance of so many guards led him to believe the rebel general had been defeated. Else the city would already be under siege.

Misery entered Codel. All of his plans evaporated. He once aspired to become king but Fate betrayed him. Codel hardly noticed as the surrounding blackness took on a bluish tinge. That haunting feeling turned to pale mist. Time froze. He instantly recognized where he was. Codel dropped to his knees to pray. The giant man in armor strode from the ghostly light. Moisture glistened from his bald scalp. He looked down on the quivering man and hefted his massive battle axe. Lord Death had come to claim his prize.

"It is time, Codel Mres," he said in a booming voice.
Darkness followed the swinging axe blade.

FORTY-SIX

The Deadlands

The air was very dry. Malweir's sun burned down hotly through the thick cloud cover, bathing the tiny band sneaking across the expanse of the Deadlands in sweat. Ancient Druem loomed ahead, but Dakeb assured them it would be at least another day before they gained the foothills. Pregen insisted the old man wasn't reassuring and all but begged to stay with the Elves. He much rather wanted the option of escape back into the mountains. Here awaited only death.

"What a miserable place," he complained. "How could a land be so desolate?"

Dakeb looked back over his shoulder. "War and corruption turned this land from green to brown, Pregen. They are the bane of civilization but it is the way of the world. All societies rise from obscurity, become more than what they were meant to be and fall into ruin. You didn't think that right was reserved for the Mages did you? Even Thrae will fall as Fate deems fit."

"What are we fighting for then?" Kialla asked. Her interest suddenly sparked.

"We fight to keep evil at bay. There are many plains of existence. Ours is but a strand in the great cosmic web. There are forces out there wishing to destroy all that is good and pure. World enders. If they succeed, our way of life is finished. The dark gods will devour all souls and leave Malweir a husk of decay. We fight, dear Kialla, because if evil is allowed to grow unchecked, we are all doomed. Empires rise and fall, but it is in our hearts to rebuild anew."

Grelic wiped the crust from the corners of his mouth. "You paint a bleak future, Mage. Is our future in such doubt?"

"The future is fickle. It flows and ebbs without regards to our wishes. What you do or don't do can affect any number of possible tomorrows. One never knows how matters will play out. But it is all we can do to protect what little we have and keep the great darkness at bay."

"My skin would crawl were I a lesser man," the giant admitted with a broken laugh. "Perhaps we should save talk of doom for when we stop this dark Mage of yours. A cold mug of ale would go good with such conversation."

"I agree," Cron added. "Besides, chances are the enemy has patrols roving the countryside. We're not here to fight a war. They'd overrun us with no effort at all. We need to enforce tactical discipline if we're to reach Druem undetected."

The conversation slowed but continued on into speculation of what might happen. Much of it was lost on Ibram and Fitch. They hung at the back of the group with Krek. Fitch impossibly believed they were safer in the back, at least until Pregen told him they were surrounded by Goblins and it didn't matter where they rode.

"What are you going to do when this is over?" Ibram asked, trying to shake the feeling of being hunted.

He wasn't sure what made him ask the question. Maybe it was the overpowering heat. His tongue was thick and his mouth felt clammy. It wasn't just the heat. A thick odor reminding him of death clung to everything. Their clothes reeked of it. Their skin was tainted with an unhealthy pallor. Ibram knew the others felt it. He also knew they were wise enough to keep silent.

"A bath would be nice," Fitch replied with a wry grin.

Truth be told, the villager hadn't thought of it. His old life was dead, right along with Shar and all of his friends in Gend. Retribution had consumed this new life. His sole purpose was to help these few people on their quest to prevent a war. What would happen when the dark Mage was defeated and they returned to Thrae didn't worry him.

"I don't know," he said with a sad head shake. "Everything has changed so drastically this past winter, I feel lost. All of my dreams were taken from me. I shouldn't have survived, Ibram. I know I shouldn't have."

They rode on in silence. Ibram knew nothing he said would ease the burden of shame Fitch felt.

Fitch eased some of the tension. "Maybe I'll head south towards the sea. I've always wanted to see the great sailing ships. You could come with me."

Ibram sighed. "I wish I could. I'm afraid Dakeb won't let me now that the Minotaurs helped expose my powers. I don't care to be a Mage but can't see a way around it. Do you ever wonder what it was like? The age of Mages? Malweir must have been a most wondrous place. What if we could bring it back?"

"I don't know, Ibram. That age fell, just like Dakeb said," Fitch replied.

"That's the beauty of history. We can learn from mistakes and ensure they don't repeat themselves. Think about it! Technology and science bringing man-kind to levels never before reached. Imagine stone roads and grand libraries where all of the folk in the world can come to study and learn. No more wars. Just peace and prosperity."

Fitch felt his eyes water. "I'm afraid you're living in a dream. Everything I've seen on this adventure tells me we are made to war with each other. Peace is a lie."

"Wouldn't you like to see the end of violence?"

"More than anything," he quietly replied.

Krek halted suddenly. His nostrils flared. Muscles tensed. The Minotaur, after taking the lead scout position, turned his gaze skyward. Hunter instincts took over and he crouched under the branches of a broken tree. He snorted once and raised his tulwar.

"Everyone down," Grelic hissed and hurried to the young bull. "What do you smell?"

"Wyrm," he said in a low growl.

Grelic cursed. Mordrun Bal was still a day away. If the dragon spotted them now it was all over. There was nowhere to run. They'd be incinerated, even with Dakeb along. Thrae and the rest of Malweir would stand open to invasion. The Aeldruin would die for nothing and wouldn't have knowledge of the others' demise.

The giant shuffled back to Dakeb as quietly as possible. "Krek smelled the dragon."

"If he discovers us…" Cron started.

Grelic held up a hand. "I know. Dakeb, can you do anything?"

The old Mage took the time to search the skies for the dragon. "No. If I used magic now, the Silver Mage would be alerted. We're still too far from Druem to risk it."

"What can we do?" Cron asked. His fingers curled reflexively around the hilt of his sword. He knew it was useless but the gesture was comforting.

"Do? Nothing. We sit and wait until the dragon passes. It should be safe to carry on after that."

"Didn't we come here to kill the beast?" Pregen asked.

Dakeb frowned slightly. "We did, but matters are much more complicated since leaving Eline. Let Faeldrin and his Elves worry about the dragon. We must stop the Silver Mage from getting the shard. If he succeeds in re-forging the four pieces of the crystal he will cover the world in horrible darkness. Everything you know will be corrupted by his filth. There are very few Mages left to oppose him."

"You stopped him before," Grelic suggested.

"At great cost. It took ten of us to destroy the crystal. Of those ten only two survived. If we don't stop him now, before he has the shards, we will never have a second chance. This is it."

The air suddenly grew warmer and then unbearably hot.

"Be silent. The dragon is near."

Dakeb's warning didn't need to be said. Dull fear began throbbing, gaining strength the closer the wyrm came. Their greatest nightmares echoed in their minds. Air pressure doubled as the great wyrm sailed overhead. His massive bulk blocked out what sunlight filtered through the clouds. His wings made a vile rushing sound. His bellow trembled the very ground. They clasped their hands over their ears in a vain attempt at keeping his voice from gripping their souls. Tears streamed down their cheeks and madness seeped into their imaginations. Then he was gone, heading east in search of a meal and seemingly unaware of the invaders in his kingdom. Grelic slowly rose to his full height in defiance to the dragon's raw power. He stared long at the sky.

Faeldrin watched as Cpur and a handful of Pell Darga began making their way towards the Goblin outpost blocking the mouth of Deldin Grim. Dusk turned the sky into a hazy morass of grime. Torchlight already flickered from the ramparts and crenellations of the twin gates flanking the pass. The Elf Lord wished he knew how many Goblins awaited them. Despite having the Pell, he had an uneasy feeling with this operation. The Aeldruin were cavalrymen. While there'd been occasions in the past of sieges and dismounted warfare, the Elves were more comfortable on horseback.

He paused to look behind. The ballistae were camouflaged in the scrub trees along the mountainsides. Only a blundering patrol or possibly the dragon would be able to spot them. The Aeldruin waited in the shadows, eating a final meal of travel rations. None of them were talking. The air was still and thick. Tension electrified them. Pre-battle jitters spread from Elf to Elf. Even after hundreds of years the Aeldruin succumbed to the same frailties as normal men.

"This should prove interesting," Aleor commented as the last of the Pell Darga disappeared into the shadows.

"To say the least," Faeldrin replied.

The younger Elf watched the blackening sky. "Do you think they know about the Trolls guarding the pass?"

"I don't think they care. Trust me, Aleor, Trolls are the least of my worries."

"The most being?"

He ran a fingertip over one eyebrow, smoothing the slender hairs back in place. "Well, providing we capture the pass with limited casualties, we have to hold both sides of the keep. Then there's the actual Goblin army out there. How many thousands do you think are waiting for the signal to invade the lower kingdoms? Let's not forget about the dragon. We must plan on being attacked from the air and ground simultaneously. This will be unlike any battle we've ever fought."

"But we are the Aeldruin. We've never lost a battle. That has to count for something," Aleor countered.

"Perhaps," Faeldrin conceded. "But one thing is certain. We'll be heading back to Elvanara for volunteers to replenish the ranks when this is finished."

Cpur returned alone at the break of dawn. Dark blood stained his clothes and weathered brown skin. He bore no expression though Faeldrin sensed he was filled with satisfaction. He gestured for the Elf to follow.

"Give me ten men and we'll be back shortly," Faeldrin told Aleor. "Have the company ready to move. We attack as soon as I return."

They clasped forearms and Faeldrin took off. The trip was short, only three hundred meters and made in silence. Cpur traversed the rocks with the ease of one who'd grown up in this harsh terrain. His movements were fleet and nimble; so much so that the Elf often found it difficult to keep up. Daylight showered the jagged spires of the Goblin fortress. Faeldrin was repulsed.

The black, rock walls emanated a foul presence, but there was more. Faeldrin looked closer at the dark shapes littering the field in front of the ominous structures. The spires jutted into the sky like broken teeth defiling the sanctity of the heavens. Decay blanketed the area, hazing the image of the fortress.

Faeldrin was surprised to discover the shapes he thought were boulders were in fact bodies. Most were half dressed with barely a sword in their hands. All bore varied degrees of pain on their dead faces. A pair of Trolls slumped against the open doors at the base of the towers. Both had several short spears sticking out of them and their throats were cut. The Elf Lord's mouth dropped open.

Hundreds of Pell warriors could be seen scurrying over the ramparts. Most of them were carrying or dragging dead Goblins down to the edge of the scrub forest. Although he disagreed with what they were doing, Faeldrin appreciated the psychological effect of seeing so many of their dead when the reinforcements arrived from Mordrun Bal. Pools of dark blood dried in the warming sun. Faeldrin's skepticism turned to wonder and awe.

"How in the world did they manage this?" one of his Elves asked.

Faeldrin could only shake his head. "Don't question it. I expected to lose many lives taking this fortress. The Pell Darga are an addition I didn't foresee. Go back and bring the others forward. I want to hurry up and start preparing our defenses."

The Elf nodded and rode off. They were still a long way from thinking about victory, but Faeldrin found himself smiling anyway. He figured he had roughly two days before the Goblin army learned of the defeat and managed to deploy a counter strike. Two days of doubt and fear. Once the battle started and he got a feel for it, everything would be fine. It was the build-up that bothered him. Hundreds of years and Faeldrin still found waiting the hardest part.

Soon enough and the dying will begin. He still wasn't sure if they'd be able to kill the dragon.

FORTY-SEVEN

The Calm Before the Storm

Grelic lay among the dead branches and scrub brush. His eyes shifted over the ruinous buildings and hovels three hundred meters away. Mordrun Bal was desolate at best, nightmarish at worst. The perfect place for Goblins and other foul creatures to breed in the dark. Every instinct Grelic had warned him to turn and head back to Thrae. Hundreds of Goblins could be seen shuffling through the twisting streets, moving in and out of the buildings. He couldn't see any way they'd be able to sneak past so many. The situation seemed hopeless.

He lay there for most of the day. It felt good not moving, though he knew he was going to be sore when he finally did get up. Two days of forced marching through the Deadlands and a night of disturbed dozing had left them all weary. Grelic wanted one good night's sleep before tackling Druem. He and Dakeb agreed to recover some of their strength during the day and sneak in under the cover of darkness. The only problem with that was the vast amount of Goblins between them and the volcano.

Grelic's eyes drooped. The afternoon sun was scorching, promising to worsen before dusk. Sleep enticed him like some nameless woman from his dark past. He fought the urge with all his might yet his eyes continued to betray him. He wasn't sure how long he spent struggling through the netherworld of waking dreams. The crisp sound of a whip striking flesh snapped him out of it. Formations of Goblins were marching out of Mordrun Bal amidst the snarl and curse of the whip masters. Grelic tensed, fearing they'd been discovered. Then common sense took over. There was no call for so many to be deployed just to capture a handful. No. These forces were already moving out. Something had stirred them up. Grelic dared to rise up and get a better look.

They were marching towards Deldin Grim. Faeldrin had done it!

"Good news," Grelic said in a confident whisper. He waited for the others to come closer. "Most of the Goblin army is marching south. By dawn they'll be too far away to make a difference. We shouldn't have much trouble getting inside the volcano now."

"Faeldrin was more successful than we hoped," Kialla said.

Cron wasn't convinced, though he didn't want to ignore the importance of the development. "They must have left a garrison. Goblins are vicious beasts, keen in the arts of killing. If the dark Mage is half as quick, he'll have left a garrison big enough to beat us."

"What about those things that attacked us in Eline?" Pregen asked. He hated to admit it, and never would aloud, but the thought of facing the evil creatures again terrified him.

Dakeb laid a reassuring hand on Pregen's wrist. "Leave them to me. Creatures born of magic die of magic easily. They won't pose a problem."

"The advantage is ours," Grelic said and wiped his forehead of sweat. "Though we still have the small issues of the dragon and Mage."

"Let the Elves worry about the wyrm," Dakeb said. "I have a feeling the battle in the pass is going to be more than enough to draw the dragon's attention away. Plan on getting inside the catacombs and focus on finding the shard while I face the Silver Mage. He is the worst threat." His voice tapered off with the sorrowful tone reserved for battlefield commanders anticipating great losses.

"What happens if he already has the crystal?" Fitch piped in. He was no military man by any means, but even he understood the dangers of what they were getting into. Nightmares of Gend haunted him relentlessly the closer he got to Druem. All of Father Seldis' work was unraveling. Fitch wasn't sure if he'd be able to overcome his resurging fears.

The old Mage's smile surprised Grelic most of all. "In that case, we happen to have a thief in our company."

Pregen froze. "No. If you think I'm going anywhere near another Mage you're insane."

"You are a thief," Kialla said.

"Yeah, and a damned good one. I break into women's homes, aristocrats. A good thief tends not to be caught robbing people when they are home. I appreciate my head attached to my neck. Find someone else to do it."

Dakeb's voice remained steady. "Relax, Pregen. Do not concern yourself with the what-ifs of the situation. When the time comes we will all know what to do."

Pregen shot Fitch a foul look but said no more.

Up until now, the young Minotaur sat quietly listening to the men complain to one another. He had no taste for talk. Minotaurs were warriors by nature and wasted little time in pointless discussion. Wars and battles were won by sword and axe, not fancy words. He yawned and stretched.

"All right then, we rest up until dark and strike when the moon rises," Grelic told them all. "We move light and fast. Since none of us are familiar with Mordrun Bal, it's going to take time to find the entrance into the volcano. Kill only the Goblins that are in our way. We can't afford to fight the entire garrison. In and out. I want to be riding away by dawn. Who's taking first watch?"

"I got it," Cron volunteered.

"Everyone else get some rest. It's going to be a busy night."

Krek smiled impatiently. Finally, they were getting somewhere.

"You should be sleeping," Cron whispered when he heard Kialla creeping towards his position.

She pulled even with him and watched the dwindling activity in the Goblin town. "How can I possibly sleep?"

"A soldier learns to take sleep where he can get it. There's no point worrying over what may or may not happen. You do what you can with the circumstances you're given."

Kialla whispered, "You're not scared?"

"What would be the point? We live and we die. Some of us are fortunate enough to choose the manner of our demise. I chose to come on this journey. I may not be looking forward to dying here, but if I must, what choice have I?"

She took hold of his hand and squeezed. "Please don't get killed."

"I'll try not to, love."

Kialla let out a slow breath and watched with him.

Fitch couldn't sleep either. He tossed and turned in the arid environment. More than anything he wanted to escape. To run away and never look back. It wasn't hard. He'd abandoned people before. The shame of that moment weighed heavily on his soul. He wasn't sure what would happen when the sun went down, but Fitch spent the rest of the day trying to find the measure of his courage.

Krek, Grelic, and Dakeb were fast asleep. The young bull snored lightly. Pregen lay on his back staring up blankly. Ibram meditated off to the side. All of his doubts and deepest desires clashed together in a bitter struggle for domination. He secretly wondered which man was going to show up tonight. He'd been found wanting before and was more than determined not to let that happen again. Ibram wasn't a monk, nor was he a warrior or a shade of a Mage. He was confused and afraid. So much had happened since Father Seldis took him to the king's gardens and had him join the quest. Grelic showed him how to fight. He'd killed. Dakeb taught him the beginnings of magic yet he remained untested. The enemy facing them was filled with battle-hardened murderers who wouldn't give a thought to killing him. Ibram searched the depths of his inner conscience for peace.

"Don't worry yourself, young Ibram," Dakeb soothed once Ibram opened his eyes.

Ibram stared off into the withered stalks of brown-yellow grass. "That's easy for you to say. You've been using your magic for hundreds of years. I didn't even know I was like you until a few weeks ago."

"You're very glum for one so young. I suppose I might have been so when I was your age, but times were definitely better. If only you had seen the world then, Ibram. Still, be happy for what you have. Rejoice in the gift of magic, for it is a thing so few of us have."

Ibram shot the prone Mage a mistrusting look. "More like a curse."

"Why do you say that?"

"Look at what the world has become since the war," Ibram answered, instantly regretting the venom in his voice. "I…I didn't mean…"

Dakeb ignored the comment, knowing Ibram was merely venting frustration. "This is true, but think on this. Magic was largely responsible for the creation of the crystal. Men were responsible for corruption and greed that went into it. How much better have the rulers in Malweir tried making this world? War. Famine. Plague. Alliances shift as easily as the winds in this age. The Mage War may have started it, but we have been in decline ever since."

"If you could, would you return the world to the golden age?" Ibram asked.

"With degrees of modification. Those were glorious days when all races felt at ease with each other. You could travel from one coast to the next and not suffer assault. We, as a civilization, have digressed into a near barbaric state. I would see Malweir regain its lost prosperity, if only for a while."

Ibram shook his head in doubt. "I don't understand. What assurance is there that any new order won't recreate the same horrible mistakes? The crystal is the root of evil, Dakeb. What can a new order of Mages accomplish in the face of that?"

"There you are wrong, my young friend. The crystal in itself is far from evil, but it is the manifestation of the malice and cruelty in the hearts of men. We cannot change who we fundamentally are or what lies within us."

"You make it sound as if there is no hope in either direction we seek," he replied sadly.

"Hope is often what we make of it. Imagine what I have gone through, all of the grief and misery of losing my friends. My world. Seeing everything I knew dissolve down the paths of war. All I cherished is naught but fading memory and has been for centuries. Look into my soul and learn the definition of what it means to truly be alone."

Ibram thought on that for a moment. The sun was just past late afternoon and starting to set. "Is there any hope?"

Dakeb smiled warmly. "There is always hope. No matter how dark the night gets, there is always hope."

Faeldrin stood atop the highest tower looking down over the ruined expanse of the Deadlands. He'd never seen such a waste and secretly hoped he never had to again. Elves and the Pell Darga were busy turning the Goblin fortress into a defensive bastion from the coming assault. He already noticed vast improvement. That was good, because time was running out. The cloud of dust first spied by scouts near midday drew steadily onward. The Goblins would be here soon.

The sun was already setting and would soon be hidden behind the twisted Darkwall Mountains. Faeldrin enjoyed what little warmth remained. He had no illusions as to what the dawn offered, supposing the Goblin host continued to march throughout the night. His thoughts turned towards Grelic and the ragtag group of men pushing deeper into this nightmare. It suddenly occurred to him that he taken the better end of the spear.

FORTY-EIGHT

Regret and Tribulation

The moon rose orange, haunting the rooftops of Kelis Dur. Dusty clouds turned the sky into a vision of despair. Those with faint hearts locked their doors and bolted the shutters. Many prayed for the night to pass. It was the day after the assassination attempt on the king and rumors ran wild. Guards and soldiers patrolled the streets, but even they held fear in their eyes.

Inns closed early for fear of dark assassins regrouping to finish their task. People whispered of a renegade army camped outside the walls. These were ill days if men tried to murder kings. A few of the seedier taverns remained open. Their doors seldom closed and rarely had patrons of quality. There was healthy profit to be made under the blanket of gripping fear. People needed an outlet. Rich and poor alike crowded the taverns on what many referred to as the Demon's Night.

King Rentor lacked the desire to drink. He watched the darkness of his city from the balcony to his private chambers. Sorrow crossed his features. His eyes were red, puffy. His beard still smelled of dried blood and bile. Worried creases aged his face far more than his sixty odd years. He'd never felt so alone but took a measure of comfort with his wife being far away to the south. What he needed was advisors. The loss of Father Seldis had been severe and left him with a hollow place in his psyche. So much ill had been done he feared it would never be undone.

It was a ridiculous notion. He had little control of tomorrow; much less the present, no matter how well developed he schemed. Even a king still fell prey to the vagaries of Fate. Surviving the assassination was bittersweet. He'd beaten Codel's plans but now lacked a true confidant capable of steering him in the proper direction. Worse, he now lacked insight into the enemy's camp. To make matters worse, Codel had disappeared. He closed his eyes and recalled the last conversation he'd had with his wife before sending her south.

"We can't control what happens to us. All we have is our lives to lead as well as possible. Evil will always be around, waiting for a misstep. Good is in our hearts, love. For that we need to be grateful. So long as purity beats within us there will always be a chance," Melena said as she ran her hand gently down his back.

He sniffed back on the mucus clogging his nose. "Your words would lend me courage were it not for the horrors reaching my ears. Never before have such nightmares walked our kingdom."

She offered her husband a hand towel to blow his nose and kissed his cheek. "Those things we can't control. I would do anything to help you get through this, Rentor, but you must remain strong. For all of us. Gossip chokes our people. The maids whisper of leaving for the south and people speak of ill creatures stalking the land."

"Aye dearest. The vilest creatures one could conceive. I should have listened to Father Seldis more closely. Perhaps we wouldn't be mired in such a mess."

Rentor closed his eyes, trying to recall a time before the hardship. He saw only bad things barreling towards him. The world seemed full of promise when he was a boy, leading him to wonder what went wrong. His father was well liked and as good a monarch as lean times permitted. Rentor all but emulated the man. Yearly festivals in his honor brightened the population. A statue of the late king riding a horse decorated the central fountain square. It had cost a small fortune and no bit of convincing to get the Dwarven craftsmen to come up from their mountain haunts to build it.

All of that was behind him now. If anything, Rentor ruled a shadow kingdom. Devoid of mirth, Thrae had fallen under evil's sway. He felt desperate to stop the rot from spreading further. All was not lost. Somewhere in the wild were two groups of his most trusted people. Grelic and his small band of heroes moved closer to the heart of darkness. Rentor could hardly believe it when the Elven mercenary rode into his city and told their strange tale of Mages, dragons, and Elves. Word came at last that Cron still lived and was about to battle alongside Grelic. The king couldn't believe his good fortune. His best captain lived, but until the insurrection ended Rentor couldn't let anyone know. Could the tale grow any stranger? Rentor wished them the best and offered prayers to Harr, there being little else he could do.

His heavy brow furrowed at the conflicting thoughts playing havoc in his mind. The notion of an army of traitors awaiting on the edge of the surrounding forest irritated him to great ends. Codel Mres, once his staunchest friend, had turned rogue and now disappeared. Thousands of soldiers were with General Huor. The portly general had never been an overly brave man, making his actions irrational. Rentor spent hours trying to discern some purpose behind this insurrection. Neither man seemed the rebellious sort. Someone or something was fueling their aggressions. But who? He had no answers.

Not wanting to spent useless hours trying to grasp his dilemma, Rentor went to bed. Sleep was long in coming and did not last long. He was awoken shortly after dawn by hurried pounding on the door. Groaning, he opened one eye. The bright light seemed unnatural, as if it held personal vendetta. He wondered if this was an omen. There was an almost unknown quality of warmth in the air. Surely doom would not come upon them on such a glorious morning? The pounding grew more insistent. Rentor reluctantly swung from the comforts of his bed and stalked to the door. The look on his face was one of his meanest.

"This had best be good, Sergeant," he growled.

Swallowing the lump in his throat, the sergeant replied, "Sire, a rider approaches the main gates. He carries the white flag of surrender."

"Report," Maen said. It was all he could do to keep the apprehension from his voice. This was the most dangerous time. He'd bested the rebellion and taken the rogue General Huor into custody. There was no way the king or any of his advisors could know that yet. Maen was faced with a most dangerous proposition. If Rentor suspected a trap, any messenger sent to Kelis Dur would be run down without a word spoken. The same would be true if he rode back in force. He hated waiting and such decisions were often above him. For the thousandth time he wished his brother was here. Cron would know exactly what to do.

Notam fought back a ragged smile born from a decided lack of sleep. "The gates are open. King Rentor will come meet you outside the portcullis. Once he's satisfied that we are who we say he'll order his archers to stand down."

"I don't like this. We're taking a horrible risk. Too much can go wrong," Maen replied dejectedly.

"Like it or not, we're at war. This may be the only opportunity we have to save Thrae," Notam said. He'd been through too much to worry over discrepancies of conviction. What troubled him was Cron's disappearance. He had an ill feeling about his friend.

Field Commander Whorl watched the camp for a moment, casually scratching his scar. "Notam speaks the truth. We cannot fault the king for any misgivings towards the enemy. This is the only way."

Maen slammed a fist on the frail wooden table. "Damnation. He sent us on this quest. Why should he not trust us now? I wish Father Seldis were around."

"Rentor can't afford to trust us for the same reasons he needed to doubt Huor or the minister. Face it, this is the only way," Notam urged with a scowl.

Maen was much like his brother but lacked the same decisiveness Cron bore.

"Fine. This is what we'll do. Have Huor bound and thrown on a horse. He rides right behind the command group. Bring one hundred men along as escorts. When the way is clear we'll send a message back to the others to bring in the prisoners. It is for the king to decide what to do with them. Tie them tightly and make sure they feel the full effect of their shame."

"Do you really think this will work?" he asked in a more subtle voice.

Notam snorted. "We'll soon find out."

Maen nodded. That would have to do. "Ready the men. We leave in one hour."

The midday sun over Kelis Dur was bright and hot. Citizens emerged from the relative security of their homes to stare in amazement. Weeks of heavy clouds full of disease were suddenly washed away. Archers and king's guards rushed to the walls and took up firing positions. Despite being warned away by constables, the people thronged to the gates and walls to catch a glimpse of the traitor general. Rentor didn't bother suppressing rumors from sweeping the city. The people needed something to feel good about. The blanket of oppression was too heavy, pushing many to the breaking point.

He took his place at the front of a small column and waited. Rentor had trouble believing it was actually Notam who'd delivered the message. After losing one of his dearest friends and higher ranking officers, he was uneasy trusting anyone. The sword dangling from his hip was comforting. It reminded him of days gone by when he was strong. Ruefully, he marched with final purpose.

"Sire, the delegation is formed up and waiting outside of the city," the Sergeant of the Watch reported with a crisp salute.

Rentor nodded. "How far do they stand?"

"Still within arrow range."

"Open the gates," Rentor ordered.

"Aye, sire. Open the gates! Come on lads, put your backs into it."

The iron portcullis ground open. Crafted centuries before to protect the people from the ravaging bands of marauders, the gates were a proud representation of what men could achieve when times grew dire. Rentor never dreamed they would someday protect them from his own army. He signaled the party forward with a nod.

Banners shuffled in the light breeze, funneling tensions across the open plain. Six riders calmly sat atop their horses waiting for the king's party. Rentor halted a handful of paces and forced his gaze away from the bound and gagged figure of Huor. Every instinct he had wanted to run the man through with as many swords as he could grab. Instead he focused on Maen and Notam.

The young Major saluted and made his formal report. "Sire, the enemy army has been neutralized. Thrae is free to return to normal affairs. All of Huor's senior leadership is either dead or captured and we present Huor to you."

"Major, you have done your kingdom a great service," Rentor said tersely. The measure of mistrust hardly tainted his voice. He turned to Huor. "You will be tried and executed publicly, Huor. Should the judge deem you guilty, of course. Sergeant, take this filth to the dungeons."

Huor glared menacingly and struggled against his bonds. Maen went on to describe the battle and Field Commander Whorl brought forth maps and troop dispositions for the both armies. None of it made sense to the beleaguered king. Whatever foul designs Codel and his underlings had in mind for Thrae seemed effectively dealt with. Now all rested on Grelic and a handful of the oddest assortment of companions he could imagine.

By nightfall Huor swung from the gibbet. It wasn't long before the crows came.

FORTY-NINE

Mordrun Bal

They moved in single file under the cover of darkness. Grelic took the lead. His hulking shadow seemed darker in the foul night. The others moved like wraiths behind him. Cron and Kialla followed next, then the Mage. A much disappointed Krek trailed. Fitch, Ibram, and Pregen filled the middle. The peril was too great to entrust the rear position to any of them.

Despite growing danger, Grelic reveled in his element. He missed the sense of purpose and fulfillment of being on a battlefield. All of his previous skirmishes led him to this final task. His eyes darted back and forth, searching for signs of a rear guard left behind. His mighty broadsword danced with every step. Grelic pushed past row after row of dilapidated hovels. The stench gagged him. Waste and rotting carcasses filled the shadows and shallow pits carelessly dug between the buildings. He felt a nasty sensation in the pit of his stomach and choked back his rising bile. The Goblins could easily turn Thrae into such squalid ruin. Anger boiled within him.

The distraction proved costly. A sentry emerged from the alley behind him. The surprised Goblin balked at the sight of so many alien figures creeping through Mordrun Bal and drew his sword. He managed to blink once before a shining silver dagger plunged through his grizzled throat. Cron rushed forward and caught the body before it hit the ground.

The giant spun around, releasing his white-knuckle grip on his sword and let out a long breath. Kialla jerked Lady Killer from the corpse and wiped the blood off. She reassuringly touched Grelic's arm and passed a look of relief. He shrugged and kept moving. None of them knew exactly where they were going and time was against them. Still, they needed to be more wary.

They gained the main boulevard and halted. Torchlight flickered wickedly from random intervals. Roving patrols marched up and down the streets. Grelic cursed silently. He should have figured security would be stepped up with the army deployed. Goblins were crude beyond barbaric, but when it came to fighting, they were professionals. Making matters worse, their commander seemed to know his business.

Dakeb eased next to the crouching giant and scanned the streets. He leaned as close as possible and said, "If they have this much security out, the entrance will be well protected."

Grelic grunted softly. "Our task has become more difficult."

"It also makes it easier to find the way inside," the old Mage said and grinned.

"I like how you think," Grelic said, instantly picking up on his meaning. "The only problem is making it to the entrance unnoticed. There's too many here to do that quietly."

"Leave that to me. Ready the others to move on my signal." Dakeb closed his eyes. "Grelic, they must remain together. Whoever gets lost will not survive."

Casting a final, concerned look, Grelic left the Mage about his business. He'd always contended that there were some things best left unknown. He passed the message to each of them without truly understanding what was happening. The small band huddled down and waited. They didn't wait long.

Dakeb sat in the dirt and held his palms up towards the sky. Searching back through centuries of memories, he recalled the words of incantation. Thick, choking fog began to pulse from his fingertips. Then from his pores. Temperatures dropped to near freezing throughout the Goblin town. Goblins stopped what they were doing and shifted nervously. Superstitions ran high among them. Several snarled and cursed in their dark tongue. Whip masters shouted to no response.

The fog was waist high. Entire sections of Mordrun Bal were already blanketed. Fear rode the swirling mists. Goblins balked, leaving their posts in abject fear. They fled to the imaginary security of their barracks. Not even the lash of a whip stayed their fear. Soon the fog grew so thick they couldn't make out shadows a foot in front of them. Mordrun Bal was enthralled with terror.

Dakeb rose to his feet, unsteady after such exertion. The lines on his face were deeper. "Now Grelic, strike north and fear not. My eyes can pierce the fog. We must move quickly for it will not last long."

"Will we be affected as well?" he asked.

"No. Only evil must fear tonight. Hurry! When the moon rises the spell shall fail."

The giant nodded sharply and ensured the others hurried behind. The next few minutes were going to go by fast. Grelic sprinted. Only Krek appeared enthused with the prospect of facing near impossible odds. Any true Minotaur relished the thought of battle.

They raced past scores of milling Goblins. The urge to strike down the enemy was great, but Dakeb warned them against it. There wasn't time. The trek was more traumatic for Fitch. Each Goblin devolved into shadow-driven shapes of demons. He smelled smoke and saw his home burning. Dark shapes became the broken corpses of his friends, his family. They cried out in agony. They cried out for the damnation of their murdered souls and it grew too much to bear. His own mind screamed in agony. Fitch started to snap. Madness crept up from the reflection of his soul and struggled for control. Hatred and innocence battled in a silent war. Fitch Iane felt himself slowly slipping into the iron grips of dementia.

They ran on, oblivious to the internal conflict of their villager companion. Only Dakeb understood what was happening. He understood and was powerless to help Fitch. He knew the depths of the young man's despair. Seldis told him everything in the days after monks had found him frozen and near death in the mountains. Dakeb wanted to cry for the boy. Much of the future depended on the actions of one man. His life was almost a waste.

Grelic cut down a pair of quivering warriors standing in their path. Hot blood splashed on his cheeks and forearms as the bodies toppled. He smiled. The fog ahead shifted. He could make out several Goblins massed just ahead. They were guarding the entrance to the tunnels under Druem. Grelic readied his sword and charged only to find himself standing in the open. Swirls of fog drifted apart. He frowned. The moon was rising.

Goblins slowly shrugged off their paralysis. They stared back at Grelic and the others in shock. The giant was among them while most were still trying to draw their swords. He struck down the closest with a mighty overhead swing and then dropped down to slice open the stomach of another. Cron, Kialla, and Krek rushed into the fight with recklessness that made even the battle-hardened Mage balk.

Grelic fought without thought of the others. He felt he should be back in Deldin Grim with Faeldrin, not here in the midst of the Goblin kingdom. But Dakeb had insisted and Faeldrin agreed. Rage, pent-up and demanding, finally boiled over. The score of Goblins barring his way felt the full effect of that rage. Bodies piled around him. Pools of blood grew deep. Gore and ichor dripped thickly from his sword. Grelic succumbed to the berserker frenzy. Goblins pushed and shoved to flee but it was far too late. The giant didn't stop until no foe stood.

The others were less fortunate. Goblins correctly picked them for softer targets and focused their attacks on the Minotaur. Kialla slashed her dagger across an exposed throat and suddenly cried out as burning pain lanced through her shoulder. She dropped to her knees with the foul blade plunged in to the hilt. Cron roared and ran her attacker through. Blood frothed from the dying Goblin's mouth.

Krek fought hard enough for all of them. His people had longstanding animosity towards the Goblins. This night was one of revenge. The heavy war bar crushed skulls and snapped bones. Krek snorted and let out a terrifying bellow that trembled the ground. The Goblin counterattack waivered. It proved a costly mistake. Grelic charged in from behind and they fell in a throng of cries.

The battle raged ahead of them and Pregen had no intentions of charging into the middle of it. That momentary hesitation reduced him to being a babysitter. Pregen glanced around and found the Mage, the would-be Mage, and sniveling villager crowded about him. While he harbored no illusions about Dakeb's worth, the other two mired him in uselessness.

"What's happening out there? Do you think they need our help?" Ibram asked, straining to look over the assassin's shoulder.

Pregen readily stepped aside. "Go and find out if you're so eager to die."

He snorted his distaste when the former monk didn't move. *Coward.* Pregen silently wished all of them would rush into the fight. That would make it easier for him to sneak away unobserved. He was left indecisive, however. The road back to the mountains was long and dangerous. There were little, if any, clean water sources and virtually no protection from the grueling sun. The trip was tantamount to suicide. His only other choice wasn't much better. Pregen had an eerie suspicion that he wasn't going to be coming back from Druem. The assassin did his best to shake off the feeling but the premonition had already taken hold. He jumped when someone grabbed his arm. It was only Dakeb.

"The path is clear. Quickly. We must get inside," the Mage urged.

Pregen didn't like the sound of that. The tone of Dakeb's voice compelled him against his better judgment. It made him *want* to go under the volcano.

"What about the others?"

Dakeb shook his head. "There is no time. They must go down a different path if we have any hope of succeeding."

"We shouldn't split up. We need them," Pregen argued.

The Mage looked up with pleading eyes. "So long as they're fighting, the Goblins will attack. The enemy won't notice us moving among them until it's too late. If ever you have known courage, let it be now, Pregen Chur."

Pregen sighed. Control of his own life slipped away and he was forced to follow the Mage. He didn't bother looking back to see if Grelic or the others noticed. Didn't even look to see Fitch and Ibram close behind him. Instead he followed Dakeb under mighty Druem blindly, trusting a half-cracked old man and a handful of misfits.

FIFTY

The Battle of Deldin Grim

"Come on then!" Mearlis shouted from behind the black rock of the captured Goblin keep. Crenellations stuck up like hideous teeth hungry for the taste of raw flesh. "What do you suppose they're waiting for?"

Faeldrin stared off into what had become a roiling mass of enemy soldiers. Dawn broke across the far horizon. The sun was red as blood, an ill omen. Rank after rank of infantry marched to a halt just beyond arrow range. They were packed tightly, displaying none of the fear the Elf Lord had hoped for after seeing so many of their comrades strewn casually across the surrounding area. He could see the front ranks carrying cruel-looking barbed pikes. Silver standards blew in the stiff breeze.

He watched grimly as even more soldiers pressed forward. The concentrated sounds of their footsteps and clanging armor was as thunder on a hot summer night. Loose rock broke free from the ragged mountainsides. Flocks of vultures, already gathered for the veritable feast littering the plain, circled high above. Faeldrin felt their presence more than noticed it. The smell of death was already ripe in the air. He had little doubt it would get worse.

A company of war Trolls pushed their way towards the front of the army. Each carried mighty double-headed battle axes and were armored in plain leather jerkins. They were monstrous creatures, each standing close to ten feet tall and so heavily muscled they often appeared sluggish. Their mottled grey-brown skin blended perfectly with their surroundings. Dimwitted at best, their prominent brows and narrow, beady eyes displayed none of the intelligence the Goblins possessed. They were bred for heavy labor and for killing. Faeldrin grimaced in the knowledge that no arrow or sword would be of use against their near impenetrable hides. Trolls feared no weapons but fire. The Elf Lord smiled secretly, for he had a surprise for them.

The rear rank of the army carried long-scaling ladders and something else Faeldrin couldn't make out. He had no idea how many had come to lay siege. A guess took him between two and three thousand. He whistled appreciatively. Odds were decidedly against him. Even with Cpur and his mountain folk, the Elves were sorely outnumbered. They'd be hard pressed just to hold the walls. The Elf Lord paused to check the stone and wood barricade hastily constructed across the mouth of Deldin Grim. Suddenly his carefully laid defenses appeared meager. All it would take was the Trolls to smash it asunder. He didn't even want to consider the dragon.

"I believe they are waiting for a sign," he replied.

"A sign? What could they possibly need?"

Faeldrin gave his brother a confident smile. "Why wait to find out? Let's give them an invitation."

He reached down and picked up the ash long bow that had seen him through numerous tough times. Faeldrin took his time, drawing the arrow from over his shoulder and setting it to string. A slight wind funneled through the pass to kiss his cheek and playfully tussle his hair. The bow creaked under the strain of being drawn. He took careful aim and loosed.

Humming on the under currents, the missile sped fast and true. Goblins were too immersed in the throes of a building rage to notice one small arrow streaking towards them. Believing themselves safe, they didn't think the Elven weapons would be a threat. Whip masters lashed out to get the army into assault ranks. The arrow struck a dead tree a few meters ahead of the front rank and both exploded in flames. Three Goblins fell, heavily burned. The Trolls mewled, fright in their eyes. Their ancient fear forced them away. Chaos gripped the front of the enemy host.

Faeldrin nodded.

"That worked nicely," Mearlis commented. "They should be quite incensed now."

"That's the idea."

"How did you know that little plan was going to work?"

He was beaming now. "The Pell Darga are crafty people. Cpur used his best engineers to ensure distance was correct. A subtle demonstration. I also had them coat the nearest trees with their flammable gel. We have close to a hundred explosive arrowheads ready. The paste is highly combustible, similar to corrosive tree sap. They'll be more hesitant in coming at us."

"Until the dragon arrives."

"Worry about that when it happens. That, we are prepared for," Faeldrin said. *At least I hope so.*

"Let us hope your other tricks have the same effects. I'm going down to ensure the defenses are ready. Those Trolls are going to be murderous when they get their act together." Mearlis shrugged and walked away.

"You have such a way with words," Faeldrin said to his back.

"You're the positive one here," Mearlis laughed and disappeared around the corner.

The Elf Lord remained, watching as panic spread through the enemy ranks. It was slight and relatively ineffective once they figured out what had happened. Faeldrin hoped their confusion lasted awhile longer. He needed every moment he could get.

A horn sounded just past midday. The sound was twisted and ugly, reminding the Elves of bad times. They rushed from the shade to their battle positions and beheld their foe. The Goblins wasted no time trying to organize back into ranks. Ladders and strange harpoon-like devices with long coils of rope resting on platforms were being moved up behind the front ranks. Archers followed, then the main body.

Faeldrin counted their strength and found the faintest flicker of hope. The Goblin archers were practically useless, though effective enough to keep the Elves' heads down while the front ranks charged. The first assault was designed to fail. It was costly. It was also designed to capture the defenders' full attention. Faeldrin almost smiled at the predictability of the move. He would have if not for the host of Trolls itching to attack. If it weren't for the massive, armored creatures, the Goblin ranks would smash upon the black rock in broken tides. Trolls had a way of changing everything.

Again the horn bleated a baleful tune. The Trolls responded first. They clashed their heavy weapons together. The sound had a wicked metallic shred that grated the skin. Loosing their first volley, Goblin archers reloaded and took aim again.

Safe behind the ancient stone, the Elven defenders patiently avoided the poisoned barbs whistling by. The dead wood shafts clicked across the rock face, falling harmlessly. Faeldrin dared enough of a glance to confirm his suspicions. A third horn blast sent the massed ranks towards the keep. He prayed his Aeldruin held their fire until the proper moment. If not, the siege might already be lost.

All around him Elves readied for battle. A current of excitement, fear, and uncanny calm shrouded them. They'd been through such horrible times before. While many of their ranks had fallen in battle, the Aeldruin never left the field to the enemy. They were going to need divine intervention to do so today. Faeldrin might have felt better if he knew how many of the Pell Darga warriors waited in the shadows or where they'd disappeared to. He hadn't seen Cpur since the morning after they sacked the keep. Close to one hundred of the brown-skinned warriors stood ready to fight the oncoming army, but there was no sign of their leader.

The Goblin war machine attacked. Hundreds of squat, muscular warriors howled in bloodlust and sprinted towards the barricade. Faeldrin waited until they were well past the rows of prepared trees before giving the command to fire.

"Archers! Fire!" he bellowed.

Dozens of shafts sizzled through the air, bringing death to many Goblins. The charge was too strong, though. Follow-on warriors clamored over the corpses of their brethren. The Elves continued firing. True to thought, the Trolls carved a path through the center of the ranks to attack the barricade. Faeldrin's eyes were drawn to the mighty wedge of Trolls. Even from this height he saw the malicious intent burning in their eyes. Only two possible outcomes remained. They would either die in the process or drive the Trolls back. Either way, that barricade was coming down. He only prayed Aleor and his crews were ready. If not, there wouldn't be any need to worry about the dragon. Trolls brushed aside the lesser Goblins and advanced. Another volley of arrows sped towards the walls.

Faeldrin gripped the stone wall. *Come on. Just a little further, you nasty bastards.* The line drew even with the front ranks. Goblins hurriedly moved aside lest they were trampled beneath the lumbering monsters. They drew even with the trees. The Elf Lord fired his explosive tip arrow. His shaft sped true, striking the dead tree in the center of the line. Fire erupted in wicked explosions. A Troll fell, bathed in flames. Two others dropped their weapons and ran off.

Two rapid flights of arrows struck various tree boles and detonated. Flames blazed, sending plumes of rich, black smoke curling high into the sky. Bodies, Trolls and Goblins alike, were flung through the air in ragged lumps of destroyed flesh. Charred skin permeated the air. The advance halted. Panic gripped the Trolls and many more followed the first pair. Those few that had escaped the inferno bellowed their rage and ran towards the barricade faster.

"Damn," Faeldrin muttered and sprinted to his alternate firing position.

Elven defenders on the ground focused their energy and readied to meet the horrors of the Troll assault. Trolls only had two weak spots: their eyes and their armpits. Anything else was a wasted shot. There were tales of Dwarven war bands spending hours trying to kill a single Troll. In every case the casualties were high. Faeldrin pushed those thoughts aside and dropped into position.

Consumed by unnatural rage, the Trolls blindly sped towards the fragile defense. The first of them reached the shallow ditch spanning the pass and leapt over without second thought. He was dead before his feet touched the ground. Frenzied with bloodlust, none of them noticed the single arrow until it struck the gelled substance filling the ditch. The explosion thundered throughout Deldin Grim. It was the sound of a god dying. Elves and Goblins recoiled to cover their ears. Tremendous pain pounded them, drowning out the screams of the dying.

The Troll advance was finished. Only a handful remained, and those were bloodied and broken. Whip masters lashed out at the retreating creatures only to be crushed underfoot or thrown aside. Having lost momentum, the Goblins retreated out of arrow range to regroup. Dusk was already approaching.

Faeldrin finished gnawing on a piece of stale, dark bread, washing it down with a swig from his canteen. He rubbed at the soreness bothering his neck and shoulders. If anything, it made the sensation worse. Hours had passed since the first attack with nothing happening. The sounds of construction could be heard from the Goblin camp but the night hampered any chance of seeing what was being built.

Never in his wildest dreams did he imagine to find himself holed up in such a foreboding place while waiting for an enemy army to break through and slaughter them. Death clung to everything. The catastrophic scene was most disturbing. Every so often the flutter of wings announced another flight of vultures swooping in for a quick bite. The Elf Lord didn't mind so much, but seriously doubted the Goblin commander was inclined to call a truce in order to reclaim the bodies. Without meaning to, Faeldrin fell asleep.

He was awakened a short time later. Euorn stood over him, an intense look blazing in his eyes.

"What?" Faeldrin asked.

"The enemy readies to attack. Mearlis sent me to rouse you."

Faeldrin grinned sheepishly. He hadn't even realized he'd fallen asleep. Damned funny thing war was. Once the initial surge of emotions settled and the battle took on a more protracted pace, fatigue set in. Apprehensions tended to run high during sieges. It was all his warriors could do to keep their emotions from running wild. Faeldrin recognized this as the most dangerous time. The part when an attack might come at any given moment, or not.

"Is everyone in place?"

Euorn nodded briskly. "We've seen to it."

"What of the Pell Darga?"

"No news, my lord. We still have those hundred that stayed behind but there has been no sign of the others. I fear they might have abandoned us," the Elf replied.

Faeldrin wasn't so sure. "I don't think so. They are a most hardy folk from what little I understand of them. Cpur is not the one to cut and run, given his hatred of the Goblins. Worrying about them doesn't help. Let's see to the attack. Where is Mearlis?"

Euorn helped him to his feet and headed for the stairwell when a shrill voice cried out in the night.

"Incoming!"

Both Elves spun about. Balls of fire rocketed towards them. Faeldrin grabbed Euorn and threw him down as one of the missiles exploded against the crenellation. Black rock and flame washed down to the ground.

""They've got catapults!" Faeldrin shouted over the roar of more incoming rounds.

Flaming boulders continued to pulverize sections of the keep, each one tearing away some part of the defense. The vibrations went deep, reverberating up his legs. The Goblins weren't going to waste much more time attempting a frontal assault. They aimed to bring the fortress down on the defenders' heads. The Elves ran towards the command group, stopping to dodge two additional rounds. They found Mearlis standing over a kneeling healer and the broken body of a warrior spitting blood. Three other bodies had been lined against the near wall, arms folded over their chests. The attack was not going well.

"We count ten catapults. The Goblins built them well. They are out of our range," Mearlis reported with frustration.

Faeldrin looked his brother over. He was covered in grime and dust. A few bloodstains peppered his sleeves. A tiny trickle of blood ran down the right side of his face from his tousled brown hair. Faeldrin then took in the dead. All three he'd known for a mortal lifetime. The butcher's bill was going to be much higher before this affair concluded.

"We sure pick interesting fights," he said halfheartedly.

Mearlis grunted.

Another salvo bombarded them, this time striking the barricade.

"A few more like that and we'll be forced to retreat," Mearlis said, brushing off a new coat of dust.

A pair of Elves ran by, carrying a litter.

"We've got to do something now. A few more salvos and there'll be no need to retreat. We'll be crushed," Faeldrin replied. "Riding out is out of the question. They'd kill us before we could penetrate their ranks enough to reach the machines. If we retreat, the Goblins retake Deldin Grim and we lose any chance of hunting that dragon."

"It would also cut off the strike force in Mordrun Bal. Dark decisions need to be made," Mearlis added.

One of the ramps on the far tower collapsed after taking a direct hit. Unexpectedly, one of the Pell warriors emerged from the shadows wearing a lopsided grin. The Elves stared down on him, wondering what he knew and they didn't. The rest of the night passed without further incident. There wasn't an infantry assault. The Trolls were gone. Slowly, the Elves reclaimed their dead and offered rituals of passage to the next life. Faeldrin went to each of his warriors and made small attempts to raise their spirits. They were remarkably high considering what they'd endured thus far. Some complained about the pounding in their ears. Others laughed over the Goblins' inadequacies. The false bravado was a necessary thing. Each wondered how much worse the next attack was going to be.

Sentries reported large fires springing up from the rear of the Goblin camp. Columns of smoke choked the darkness. Dawn let the Elves see how bad the damage to the twin keeps was. Holes large enough to pour entire battalions through were scattered up and down the walls. The center barricade was crumbling. Some sections continued to topple throughout the night. Faeldrin knew they couldn't sustain another assault.

"What do you suppose those fires were for?" he asked Aleor from high atop one of the observation towers.

The scout shook his head. "Hard to tell. My eyes don't spy any of those damned catapults though."

Faeldrin peered harder. Something about the scene didn't feel right. Just what, he couldn't place his finger on. "What are all of those black shapes flanking the rear of their main camp?"

Aleor drew his collapsible spy glass. "Bodies. They look like Goblin bodies."

How? Who? Questions leapt into his mind. The Elf Lord had a guess but wasn't sure until a runner found him and announced that the Pell Darga had returned.

"They didn't run after all," he said and smiled.

Any thoughts of victory were short lived as the horrid sounds of the Goblin war horn blew on the winds.

FIFTY-ONE

Desperate Measures

Dark blood and gore dripped from Grelic's sword. The weight of his muscles trembled from exertion. He wasn't as young as he liked to think. Even his legendary strength was nothing compared to the destructive forces of time. His breath came in haggard gasps as his heart struggled to slow down. A host of corpses lay at his feet. Sensing no living foe, the giant allowed himself to relax. That's when he noticed half of his group was missing.

"Where's the Mage?" he asked sharply.

The others stopped what they were doing. Kialla winced as the bandage Cron wrapped around her wounded should was too tight. She passed Grelic an I'm fine look and noticed the horror in his eyes. A quick sweep of the area confirmed her suspicions. More than just Dakeb was missing.

"None of them are here," Cron snapped as he raced to search the nearest hovels. "Do you think Pregen forced them away?"

Grelic shook his head. "Unlikely. Dakeb could have turned him to stone for trying anything so foolish."

"Then what?" Kialla asked.

Krek dropped to a knee and sniffed deeply. The reek of the Goblin village was overpowering yet he managed to pick out Dakeb's scent. His coal black eyes narrowed. Muscles on his back and shoulders bunched. Without a word he pointed in the direction the Mage had gone.

Grelic cursed. "Right under the mountain! Damnable Mage. We were supposed to stick together. This is not good."

Stabbing his sword into the ground, Cron looked around in despair. "Now what? None of us know what that crazy old man was planning. There's no way we can expect to go up against the dark Mage with swords and brawn. We can't win like this, Grelic."

"Are you suggesting we leave our friends to whatever torment lies under that mountain? I am many things, Cron, a coward is not one of them. I'm going down into Druem to find the Mage. Come or stay, it's your choice," Grelic said with a menacing glare.

"Damn it, Grelic. We're all in this together. You know I'm with you, but we need a plan. We can't just go in there unorganized."

The giant relented. "We have one. Go inside and kill them all."

Grelic hefted his broadsword and headed towards the tunnel entrance. Darkness gaped hungrily at him, yet it held no sway. His mind was decided and no amount of petty terror was going to keep him from seeing this task through. Then came a great clamor from behind. The Goblins had regrouped and were marching on them. The four warriors spun to face the new threat, knowing they'd never make it into the tunnels in time. Grelic suddenly envisioned them trapped between this new group and the one pouring out from under Druem. The hammer and the anvil.

Krek bellowed and snorted the ancient cry of his people. The wild look in his eyes when he turned to face Grelic left little doubt in any of their minds as to his intentions. "Go! I fight. Go!"

Grelic struggled with indecision for the briefest of moments before saluting the young bull with his sword. The Minotaur was brave, seeking to embrace the honor of his people. Chances were they were all going to die this night anyway, why not meet the end of his choosing? Grelic thought he saw the young bull smile before he turned and charged into the approaching mass of Goblins. Grelic snatched Kialla and Cron by their arms and jerked them towards the tunnel before they could follow the Minotaur.

Scourd stood in Ramulus' cavern for the second time in a week. Both he and the dragon were before the Hooded Man. This was a most dangerous time and the Mage had arrived the night prior. The crystal shard sat in a Dwarven crafted strongbox locked away in Scourd's chambers. So close to success, not even the dark Mage was willing to take unnecessary risks.

Sidian, the Hooded Man and last of the dark Mages, watched his minions from the sanctuary of his hood with guarded interest. Disgust etched his face. There was a time when both creatures would have been held in utter, blind contempt. He'd owned the ears of kings. The fates of entire peoples. Then came the war and the beginning of the dark times. Greed and corruption took hold of him, subsuming the man he had once been as the will of the dark gods became his own. Foul desires twisted his soul until nothing but hatred remained. He took that hatred and perverted it to serve his will.

Goblin and dragon. Both were unwilling allies in a game they didn't understand. Both also had secret agendas they thought he knew nothing of. Sidian would have to remove both before they had the opportunity to enact their plans. But not now. Too much was happening for him to lose these valuable assets. A deliciously wicked thought awakened. Sidian looked first at the fat Goblin warlord and frowned. Of all of the creatures in Malweir, he found Goblins the most perverse. Oh how he longed for the old days when a Mage was respected above all else. When Goblins hid in their caves and didn't meddle in the affairs of man. The return to those days would have to wait. Foul deeds were afoot and his plans at stake.

"Your army in the pass is floundering, Scourd," he criticized.

"How can you know this?" the Goblin snapped back, instantly suspicious of Sidian's motives.

Sidian leaned threateningly close. "I have witnessed it. The Elves put up a worthy fight and are aided by the Pell Darga."

Scourd spat. "The mountain monkeys? Bah. We can swat them aside as we have always done. They are of no concern."

"Not this time. The Elves bring a secret weapon capable of destroying your entire army. We've come too far to lose now. Ramulus, you must go to their aid. Only a dragon's breath can defeat this ancient weapon. Leave quickly and finish them before dusk. It is the only way."

"What of the shard?"

Sidian folded his arms across his robed chest. "It remains here until you return. We shall go to Gren together, as agreed."

The dragon accepted the answer and reared up on his hind legs. Membranes lacing his wings, thick cords of power and strength, strained in irrepressible fury. Mage light electrified his already luminous green body. The horn protruding from his chin throbbed with hunger. His cold, ice-colored eyes stared thoughtfully at the Mage. "Very well, Mage. I shall go, but do not seek to betray me."

The force from his powerful wings sent Scourd tumbling. Water and debris clogged the stale cavern air. The ground trembled under the sheer power of the dragon. Ramulus beat his leathery wings a handful of times, glad to be stretching, and vaulted towards the opening in the high ceiling. Scourd picked himself up and watched the great wyrm disappear. He silently wished the dragon a violent demise.

"And for me?" he asked once the atmosphere calmed. He swore he caught the gleam of teeth through the near impenetrable darkness of the hood.

"Our enemies are coming for us. Send the slaves back down into the tunnels where they struck the lava vein. Make them dig. Flood the caverns until lava pours back into the Deadlands. Make this place burn."

Scourd tensed. Mordrun Bal would be destroyed. *What are you up to, Mage?*

"Bring the shard to me and give the order to evacuate Mordrun Bal. We march on Thrae at dawn."

Sidian faded in a flash of shadow, as if it were the most natural thing in the world.

Every shadow concealed demons. Each new turn offered nightmares. The walls were polished to unnatural smoothness. Torches were spaced out, more for the slaves than their captors. Goblins had exceptional night vision and often required little to no light to see by. Sulfur laced the air, bordering on noxious gas. The caverns of Druem were poison to the very soul.

Pregen Chur nervously followed the Mage deeper into the heart of the mountain. Every instinct told him to get out while he still could. He turned and watched the huddled figures of Ibram and Fitch fall in behind. They were pathetic in every regard. A would-be warrior and the frightened villager. Pregen cursed his ill fortune and resigned to follow the Mage deeper.

"Where exactly are you leading us?" he hissed at Dakeb's back.

The brown cloak seemed to pick up speed. "We must find the shard before Sidian does. Hurry, now."

Pregen froze in place. "Dakeb, this dark Mage of yours isn't even here."

At that Dakeb stopped and turned. "He is much closer than you think. Prepare yourselves, my friends. The Silver Mage awaits."

Heavy silence forced his words to soak in. Fitch clutched Ibram's arm, struggling to keep his feet lest his knees gave out. "I don't want to be here. Let's get out."

Panic threatened to consume him.

"We've no choice," Ibram replied gently. His own courage was but a thread of false bravado. "Dakeb knows what he's doing."

They pushed further into the tunnels. The sound of boots marching threatened them with discovery or worse. Dakeb huddled them together in the pitch of shadows clinging to the walls. Four Goblins marched past. They reeked of filth and ale. Each bore a cruel, barbed sword and had whips coiled at their belts. Even drunk they appeared malevolent. One of the wooden-skinned Dwim marched at their front.

Ibram shuddered as too many powerful memories rushed back. The Dwim strode with unnatural stiffness. Each footstep whispered death. The way they moved, the poise with which they carried themselves. Ibram had hoped to never see another, but his luck was ill. The Dwim slowly turned and looked down the tunnel where they were hiding. Ibram stared back into those cold, dead eyes and understood the true meaning of fear.

He felt the Dwim stare directly into his soul. Every secret, every scrap of life he'd ever clung to was laid bare in that brief moment. The Dwim's mouth twisted into a smile. Tortured mouth the vision of misery, it turned and marched on. A sudden grip on his arm jerked Ibram out of his stupor. Dakeb's warm eyes calmed him.

"Take heart, young Ibram. Much is left to be done this night and I will have need of you before the end," the Mage whispered. "My strength alone cannot defeat the Silver Mage. Only together can we succeed."

Ibram managed a nod. The surprise of Dakeb's confession disturbed him. What could one of the most powerful Mages in history possibly need in him? He suddenly grew afraid of the answers.

Dakeb poked his head around the corner and ensured the hall was clear. What he discovered proved disheartening. The tunnels seemingly stretched on endlessly in each direction. He didn't know which way to turn. Either way presented great danger but only one was the correct path. Dakeb knew what he had to do, though he was loath to do so.

"What's the hold up?" Pregen asked. His knuckles turned white from the strength of fear in his grip on his sword.

"We must separate. Take Fitch and head to the right. Ibram and I will go left. Find the shard and double back to the surface, and find Grelic. This is the only way. I have no recollection of this place. We are lost," he answered.

Pregen shook his head vehemently. "That's not a good idea. What happens if we get ambushed? This whole hair-brained scheme of yours is bound to fail."

"There is no other way," Dakeb insisted.

"You're playing at something," Pregen accused.

The old Mage smiled. "Finding the Silver Mage and renewing an old acquaintance is my priority. You grab the shard, thief."

Pregen watched Dakeb disappear into the darkness ahead and suppressed a groan. This was not what he wanted. The only reason for agreeing to Grelic's proposition in the first place was the promise of an easy job and handsome compensation. Nothing seemed to have gone right upon leaving the lush pickings of Kelis Dur. The entire adventure devolved into a series of deteriorating nightmares. He was no prophet but even a blind man could see the way out was narrowing ever so slowly.

Making matters worse, he now had to babysit Fitch. Dakeb strongly argued that the man was useful and still had some mysterious part to shaping the future but he was damned if he could figure it. The only comfort Fitch provided was another warm body in the tepid atmosphere beneath Druem. If not for that Pregen would have already killed him and slipped away.

"Search for the damned crystal," he muttered. "How are we supposed to do that if we don't know where we're going? This is an impossible warren filled with everything nasty. We'll never find it."

"You're the thief. Haven't you done this before?" Fitch asked timidly.

Pregen whirled about, nearly snapping. Further thought made him realize Fitch was actually right. He was a thief. And a damned good one at that. If anyone had a chance of finding the missing shard it was him. Pregen forgot, for the moment, that this entire quest was bordering well beyond the impossible and remembered the old ways. *Where would I keep the crystal? In the most secure location naturally. But where is that?*

He absently scratched the tip of his dagger against a cheek. *Think, man. Where?* A twinkle brightened his eyes. "I've got it! Fitch, we need to find the main quarters. If they found the crystal it will be with whoever is in charge. We should be going up, not down."

Fitch wasn't so sure, but anywhere was better than standing in the middle of the Goblin kingdom.

"Are you sure we should have split up?" Ibram asked. "I don't feel half as comfortable without the other two."

Dakeb kept marching, as if following some unknown aroma. Part of him knew exactly where Sidian was waiting. Part of him wanted to find his old friend, if only to avenge so many of his friends. Yet another part of him wanted to turn and flee. Even his courage knew limits. He hadn't seen Sidian since the very last night during the battle of Ipn Shal. While Dakeb often spent time thinking about the past, he always felt dread at the prospect of meeting Sidian again.

"They would only be in our way," he replied. "You must believe me, Ibram. Had Fitch and Pregen come along we would have wasted valuable energy protecting them. Neither of us have that to spare. If we are to be successful it's going to take every ounce of effort and concentration. Sidian is a powerful Mage and not easily beatable."

Ibram hung his head. "I understand, but still. I'm afraid, Dakeb."

"As well you should be. Fear does many things. It heightens our senses, makes us more aware. It also reminds us of our own mortality. I would much rather be afraid than arrogant."

Dakeb pushed on. Corner after corner sped by until Ibram finally gave up trying to remember which way they'd come. He was impossibly lost. Druem was bizarre and more complicated than any placed he'd ever ventured. He suddenly wondered how much easier his life would be if he'd just stayed put in the monastery. But the monk life wasn't for him. He'd known that from the beginning. Stringent rules and an exceedingly drab lifestyle led to complacency. That's when his mind began to wander. Eventually it led him here, traipsing under a dead volcano in search of one of the most hated villains in Malweir's history. Ibram drew a breath and followed on.

When at last they rounded the final, wide corner, Dakeb and Ibram came face to face with a solitary figure waiting for them in the middle of a vast chamber. Sidian smiled.

FIFTY-TWO

Into Druem

The noise was tremendous, unlike anything he'd ever heard. Goblins were everywhere. They opened all of the cells and began herding the slaves out. Whips cracked across naked backs. Strings of blood flew through the air. People screamed. Someone sobbed in the unseen distance. Alfen Bew knew he was next. *This is the end. I'm finally going to die.* He'd lost track of how many he'd seen die or be transformed into those hideous monsters. Memories of seeing the woman Shar after she'd been turned into a demon haunted his dreams. She had been warm and caring. The only one who bothered looking after him in the deep darkness. Now she was the ruinous definition of evil. Alfen prayed for her while knowing it was already too late.

A Goblin stalked towards his cell. Alfen cradled himself in the corner, his body trembled with fright. The prospect of death didn't bother him anymore, but he was deathly afraid of sharing a fate like Shar. She deserved better. So did he. But the gods were cruel, uncaring monsters incapable of understanding life. He questioned how any god who truly cared for his disciples allowed them to be mistreated so. The Goblin walked right by without a glance. Alfen Bew sighed but refused to relax.

"This is madness," Kialla growled. "How are we supposed to track anyone in all of this? There's no signs, no footprints, not even a damned bloodstain. I've never seen a place so sterile."

Cron rubbed her shoulder. "Relax, love. We'll find them."

"Before or after we run into the dragon?" she countered.

He refused to answer. Grelic stopped them at a large intersection. He shared her frustrations but had nothing useful to contribute to the situation. He'd spent a lifetime of fighting and tracking but never in the confines of underground. The labyrinthine maze of tunnels and passages led them down every direction save the one they needed to go. After a while he found himself admitting they were lost and had next to no chance at finding their companions.

Grelic returned to Kialla and Cron. He wanted to feel relieved that they were just as confused as he was, but that served no purpose. Somewhere in the twisting complex his friends were in grave danger. All three knew there was a chance Dakeb and the others might already be dead.

"How's your shoulder?" he asked, unsuccessfully trying to stall for time.

Kialla winced as she gently rolled it. A fresh bloodstain seeped through the bandage. "Well enough until we get out of here. Now what?"

Grelic didn't have any answers. "Let's go look for a fight. Hopefully we'll bump into Dakeb along the way."

Cron nodded and took the lead. He had no love for confined spaces but knew the only way to find anyone in here was to keep moving. He didn't need to worry much. Something found him, and in a bad way.

A squad of Goblins emerged from a concealed tunnel once he passed the entrance. It was a toss-up as to who was more surprised. The only difference stemmed from the fact Cron was looking for a fight, the Goblins weren't. Shaking off his initial shock, he plunged his sword into the nearest Goblin and charged into the other five. Kialla's dagger sped past his head in a silver flicker. Near black blood spurted from the Goblin's neck.

Cron ducked under a wild slash and ripped a deep cut across his opponent's inner thigh. The Goblin screamed and buckled. Cron pushed harder and stabbed downward between the neck and shoulder. A sharp elbow cracked his ribs, driving the breath out. Jagged teeth sank into the meat of his right shoulder. He grimaced and fought against crying out. The remaining Goblins swarmed him, driving him to his knees.

Cron knew he wasn't getting any help from his friends. The path was too narrow for Grelic or Kialla to force their way in. Feeling control slipping, he stabbed up into the exposed belly of the nearest Goblin and let go of his sword in favor of the small dagger tucked into his belt. A sword was too long and clumsy for this kind of dirty work. He'd be torn to shreds long before killing them all if he continued with the suddenly cumbersome weapon. Dagger in hand, Cron began to jab and swipe while fending off kicks.

His first lunge took a Goblin in the groin and carried up into his stomach. Someone clubbed down on his back and he dropped further. He stabbed hard into a sandaled foot until he heard the clink of steel striking stone. The Goblin yowled and limped away. The ground ran slick with blood. Impossibly, Cron managed to fight his way back to his feet. He climbed over the press of bodies and drove the only unwounded Goblin back against the wall. Fighting and thrashing for his life, the Goblin spit blood when Cron's dagger sliced up through his jaw and into the brain. At the end of his strength, Cron struggled to catch his breath. The Goblin he'd wounded in the foot was trying to limp away for help.

"Get down!" Kialla barked.

He fell forward just as the arrow whistled through where his head had been. The feathered shaft caught the escaping Goblin in the neck. The pure force of the strike propelled the body to the ground with a sickening crunch. This fight was over. Shouldering her bow, Kialla rushed to his side with a concerned look. He gave her a lopsided grin and a stole a quick peck on her cheek.

"I'm fine. Most of the blood's not mine," he tried to assure her. Pain all but crippled him, forcing him to wonder if he was ever going to be right again. He'd been part of too many nightmares. The soldier met Grelic's stern gaze.

"Good work," Grelic said approvingly.

Cron exhaled slowly. He didn't have much fight left. "They had to have come from somewhere. I say we follow that tunnel."

Grelic didn't see many alternatives. "One way is as good as another. I'll take point. We can't let you have all the fun."

Cron hurt too much to laugh.

The tunnel stretched forever. Sloping downward and unlighted, Grelic and the others had but a single torch to keep the shadows at bay. They'd been fortunate not to run into any more Goblins, though Grelic wasn't prone to trusting blind luck. He pushed as hard as their condition allowed, often having to stoop to avoid cracking his head on the low ceiling. Finally, the tunnel ran into a dead end.

Suddenly trapped, he forced his nerves down and searched for the way out. Like Cron suggested, the Goblins had to have come from somewhere. All they had to do was find the locking mechanism controlling the hidden door. Grelic wedged the dying torch into a crevice and started looking. An axe might have delivered better results. The smoothed walls all looked the same. He growled, low and menacing. Not even Dwarf tunnels in Kressel Tine were so smoothly bored.

A tiny whisper in the back of his mind cautioned him to turn around and head back to the main corridor rather than waste more time down here. More Goblins could have entered behind them and were already heading down. Grelic didn't particularly enjoy the thought of dying in the cold dark.

"This is impossible," Cron gasped as his eyes covered every inch of the walls. "There's no way the switch is on this side."

Grelic wasn't convinced. "It must be. How else did that squad get out? We're missing the obvious."

Holding his hands out futilely, Cron asked, "Missing what? This is a dead end, Grelic. I say we double back before it's too late."

All three knew it might already be too late. A passing patrol would surely have noticed the carnage left without any trouble.

"No. It's forward or nothing," Grelic said. "For all we know the entire mountain is alerted to us. Now help me look. There has to be a trigger, a latch, something, damn it."

Kialla plucked the torch from the wall and waved it over the stone. She grimaced. Soon they'd be trapped in pure darkness. Any hope of finding the trigger would be lost. The dull sensation burning deeply in her shoulder was spreading. The bleeding had stopped but unless they had time to sew up the wound she was at risk of infection or worse. She closed her tired eyes and leaned against the wall.

It felt good to catch her breath. Kialla once again debated whether this was the life meant for her. The notion of abandoning this life of war pressured her already conflicted mind. She awkwardly thought of having children, a wild idea never once entering her mind. She shook her head to clear away temptations. Thinking like that was only going to get them all killed.

Pushing off the wall to steady herself, Kialla noticed the most peculiar thing. The wall closest to her hand was convex and coarse. Curious, she ran her fingers over the stone, feeling the roughness hidden in the stone. The patch was no bigger than her fist. Kialla fought back her smile. Every instinct wanted her to push the button shaped area. She gave in. The hidden tunnel door slid open noisily. She'd done it! The way was open.

Grelic leaned over and kissed her forehead. "Little sister, I don't know what you did but you just saved us. Come on."

They stepped out of the tunnel and into a nightmare none of them comprehended.

Krek resisted the urge to barrel head on into the rushing mass of enemy warriors. There was much honor to be claimed for such a deed, but he would pay the ultimate price. Traveling and fighting with the humans taught him much about the difference between honor and arrogance. The only chance he had for survival lay in speed and stealth.

He finished arranging the bodies in front of the entrance to the tunnels and dashed behind a row of squat buildings. Krek sniffed the wind for approaching Goblins. Thin clouds hid the moon, bathing the lands in an unnatural combination of pale light and darkness. The Minotaur grinned. It was a perfect night for killing. The surrounding area clear, he climbed atop the nearest building and slithered to the edge.

Lying prone, he looked down on his foe. Close to forty of the barrel-bodied enemy surged down the street he'd just left. Most were fully garbed in boiled leather armor and armed to the teeth. Others hardly had time to snatch up a sword when the first battle started. Their eyes mirrored looks of caution, of unfiltered hatred. Krek felt positive many of them would rather be killing Elves than hunting ghosts in Mordrun Bal.

The thought of Faeldrin and his spindly Elves made Krek momentarily long for their long bows. The Elves could easily strike down so many opponents without losing a single warrior. He snorted quietly. There was no honor in killing from a distance. After tonight, Krek was finally going to be a fully fledged warrior. His deeds would be sung in legends centuries from now. The young bull continued to watch.

Goblins noticed the piled bodies of their brothers and skidded to a halt. Fear rose in their throats. Several of the bodies were hacked apart or clubbed savagely, as if a vengeful demon had come upon them. The front ranks approached more cautiously. A great enemy was loose in their city. One capable of tearing them to pieces.

"Forward, scum!" snarled the ogre-like whip master as he jostled his way through the ranks. "Move or it's the lash!"

They snarled and hissed back. Some reflexively clutched their weapons to strike. The smell of blood eased their initial fright. Slowly the mass surged ahead. They eyed the ominous entrance to Druem warily, for the darkness held many things. When the whip master burst to the front rank, even he took pause.

"What's this?" he asked no one in particular.

The eyes of the dead stared back at him mockingly.

Krek struck that moment. He leapt from the roof, tulwar poised overhead. The weight of his fall drove a handful of Goblins to the ground. Krek kicked, punched, and bit his way back to his feet among the confused enemy. He attacked with unrepressed fury. Each blow of the tulwar made a sickening crunch as bone and flesh were crushed. Chaos broke out among the Goblins. The demon had come for them!

FIFTY-THREE

The Butcher's Bill

No one noticed the near invisible speck circling high above the ragged peaks of the Darkwall Mountains. Dawn was breaking but the world remained in the grip of the eerie semi-darkness. Ramulus circled lazily, for the great wyrm was in no rush. His crystalline eyes watched and saw everything. The Elves patrolling the ramparts of the twin fortresses. He watched the Goblin camp, restless and preparing for the next assault. He saw the strange brown people who lived in the mountains as they ranged the open plains in search of stray Goblins.

He found it all very amusing. Dragons suffered none of the foolishness mortals seemed to revel in. They lived in their caves and roosts with little concern for the rest of the world. The last thought brought a scowl to his elongated face. He hadn't been free since the dark Mage came unto the dragon lands in search of the first shard. Ramulus lost his freedom on that cold winter day. Now the foolish mortals below were all going to pay. But not yet. Ramulus decided to wait and watch awhile longer. After all, what was time to a dragon?

Mearlis watched the Goblin camp with growing disinterest. They'd been besieged for the better part of two and a half days and the Goblins hadn't come any nearer to breaking through. The sickly sweet smell from the last attack remained pungent, acrid even on the humid morning air. He shuddered from the memory of watching so many Goblins die screaming as they burned. The Elves had poured large cauldrons of their explosives down on the enemy as they tried to climb their assault ladders. Several corpses still clung to the ruined ladders.

The worst part was that complacency was already setting in. He'd already caught fragments of whispers over the poorly coordinated Goblin attacks or how the enemy had no chance to break through. Some of the Aeldruin laughed and assumed their duties halfheartedly. Mearlis recognized the danger but didn't know how to combat it. He hoped Faeldrin had the answer.

"What news this morning?" asked the Elf Lord as he yawned and stretched away the last traces of slumber.

Mearlis pointed down. "They're preparing for another assault."

Faeldrin walked to the edge and looked down. The smell of roasted meat tempted him. He wondered where they'd gotten the meat from. Perhaps the rumors of cannibalism were true. Either way, he didn't wish to find out. He glanced at his brother. "You have that look in your eyes. What is it?"

Mearlis absently rolled his eyes. "We're becoming complacent, Faeldrin. I have a bad feeling, something I can't explain, nagging at the back of my mind. This is too easy. It makes no sense to waste an army like this. They're being slaughtered just as fast as we can kill them and none of their commanders seem willing to retire. That bodes ill."

Faeldrin let out a repressed sigh. He'd felt the same since they beaten back the Trolls. A dozen scenarios played out in his mind's eye. Something was indeed amiss, though what he couldn't tell. The Goblin war horn played a sorrowful dirge.

"Time again," he grimaced. "How is that lonely note supposed to inspire their soldiers? It makes me sad."

He grew tired of hiding behind the devilish black rock of the castles, longing to ride forth into the enemy army. He wasn't alone. Every last one of the Aeldruin felt the same. They were cavalrymen, not infantry or skirmishers. Hiding behind stone walls was insulting, bordering on cowardice. Even so, the mercenaries reaped fine glory onto their already storied name.

Elves rose from their resting positions and took their places on the walls and barricade. Only three had been killed and a dozen wounded thus far. Faeldrin kept the numbers running through his mind. Casualties were minimal but they wouldn't be able to sustain that pace for long before the Aeldruin became combat ineffective.

"Arrows! Incoming!"

He ducked just as hundreds of black shafts filled the sky. A handful of screams from those too slow to react accompanied the *clank* and *tink* of arrows striking. Faeldrin immediately understood what was happening. This attack was a diversion. Another volley landed, and another.

"They didn't have this many archers the last time they tried this!" Mearlis yelled.

Indeed they hadn't. Faeldrin risked a glance through one of the crudely made bolt holes. The sun was cresting the far horizon, bathing the plains in brilliant yellow. He dropped his eyes on the advancing infantry and drifted to rank upon rank of archers. It didn't look good. Satisfied, he ducked back behind cover.

"They were resupplied during the night," he said.

Mearlis shook his head. An arrow struck the wall near his head and skipped off in a shower of sparks. "I really wish they'd get this over with so we can focus on that damned dragon."

Faeldrin grinned fiercely. "I didn't tell you the best part. Their infantry is massed under a canopy of heavy shields. The wedge is pushing for the barricade. They're going to batter it down while the archers keep us pinned down."

Mearlis looked down and saw the iron wedge draw closer. Worse, he saw their plan had a chance of succeeding. With such a sustained rate of fire, the Elves wouldn't be able to redirect their own fire down on the advancing infantry without serious risk.

"What do we do?" he asked.

Faeldrin drew his sword. "Let's go fight some infantry."

Together they crawled to the staircase and hurried down to join the defense.

"They seek to break us!" Aleor told the Elves on the barricade. He pointed, "See, look there. They're bringing battering rams. Heavy infantry is forming up in column behind for the final thrust into our perimeter. I don't think we can hold."

Faeldrin spied his enemy. Hidden beneath a ring of iron shield came the heavy rams. The heads were carved in the likeness of fire-breathing demons. He had the idea that they'd seen war before and, no doubt, success. Behind the initial engineer assault came close to a thousand infantry bearing axe, sword, and war bars. Too few Elven arrows bounced off the thick shields.

"Not good," he finally said.

He didn't bother to explain what they all knew. If the infantry managed to break through, the sheer weight in numbers would swarm over the Elves. All stood to be won or lost on this assault. Faeldrin retracted his earlier thoughts that Goblins were unorganized. A new dark thought entered his mind. The Aeldruin had been set up!

The Silver Mage knew exactly what he was doing. Pride and the jubilation of easy victory quickly changed to arrogance. He angrily punched the rock. That arrogance led the Elves to where they now stood. Archers were virtually useless and the main body was outnumbered better than ten to one. *That's a lot of killing. There's no possible way we can win this. I have damned us all.*

A sudden thought sparked. He rounded on his war leaders. "Bring up the ballistae. Archers may be of no use to us now but we've still got a fight to win. Quickly now! Detail two squads to bring them up."

Aleor and Mearlis overcame their initial confusion and dashed off shouting orders. Neither knew exactly what Faeldrin was planning, though both had a good idea. If this last minute scheme worked it would break the Goblins for good. If not, their quest was doomed. Elves ran through the field of fire to gain the secreted weapons. The sun was already starting to warm up. Shadows receded into the crags and deep mountain ravines. Arrows struck all around. A handful of Elves pushed and pulled the heavy weapons forward. Faeldrin cursed. They were moving too slowly. The Goblins were within two hundred meters.

Finally, he shouted, "Help them! Everyone!"

The rest of the Elves manning the barricade exposed themselves to fire in order to finish the task. Three fell. Both ballistae were rolled into position and ready to fire moments later. The Aeldruin had trained extensively in the time since joining with Dakeb. Elves emplaced both weapon systems and loaded. Gunners sighted in on the enemy wedge and the defenders hurried back to the barricade to take up sword and shield.

Faeldrin stayed with the gunners. "Put both shots right down their throats. Once that wedge shatters I want you to keep up your fire into the infantry."

"Yes sir!" both gunners replied and adjusted their aim.

Cocking arms cranked back, rounds loaded, the ballistae were ready. The Elf Lord whispered a silent prayer. He'd never been the one to kill for pleasure, but at this moment he wanted every last one of the Goblins dead. He slowly raised his right hand.

"Fire!" he roared and dropped his hand sharply.

Both weapons thrummed as the heavy projectiles rocketed forward. The Goblin wedge advanced, grunting cadences and slamming their heavy shields. The effect was meant to inspire fear, having proved successful numerous times. A handful of Elves were brave enough to risk getting shot just to watch the enemy attack. Those who did saw the heavy timber projectiles slice into the wedge with unparalleled fury.

Body parts flung in every direction. Shields dropped amidst a shower of dark blood. The mighty rams hit the ground with bone-crunching sickness. Few had time to scream. The bolts ripped through the shielded wedge and into the front ranks of the follow-on infantry. Massed so tightly together, they never stood a chance.

Rear ranks continued to advance, unaware of the horrors they were forcing onto their comrades. The Elves wasted no time watching the effects of their gunnery. Firing levers were already cocking to fire again. The ballistae let loose again and dozens more died. The offensive broke after the third salvo. Goblin archers drew back, staying long enough to cover what was left of the infantry.

Despite the severity of the present situation, none of the Elves bothered to return fire. Some stood in simple disbelief. Others felt elation. All stared at the nightmare scene in various shades of shock. Close to five hundred bodies littered the battlefield. Blood pooled so thickly the air was drowning in the smell of iron. A few of the Aeldruin dropped to their knees and vomited. It was a scene none of them ever wanted to see again and wished to have never seen in the first place.

Faeldrin wiped the bile from his lips and watched the disorganized regiment of Goblins flounder about. A deep sense of loss rattled them. They realized they couldn't win. Too many lives had been lost. This single, costly siege laid to waste their dreams of conquest. An eerie silence drifted over the slaughter. For his part, the Elf Lord knew his Elves would never be the same again.

"I believe we have won for the day," he said dryly.

Mearlis found difficulty forming the right words. "Shouldn't we ride out and end this now?"

Faeldrin shook his head. "There's been enough killing. Let them retire and think about what happened. Fear will keep them from attacking any time soon."

"What if the dark Mage comes? Or the dragon?" Aleor asked.

Faeldrin half smiled. "The dragon we are ready for. At least as much as we can be. Let's hope Dakeb has a handle on Sidian. Or the Goblins may still win the field."

Lazily circling Deldin Grim, the great dragon Ramulus rode the air currents and watched the battle develop. He'd suddenly grown bored, and hungry. The dragon roared and dove. His time had come.

FIFTY-FOUR

Dark Reunion

"Back!"

Dakeb shoved Ibram aside and raised a shield of shimmering, colorless magic before a blast of vermillion magic crashed into them. The old Mage buckled under the impact. Hissing laughter followed the attack. Dakeb let out a slow breath and thanked his reflexes for not failing. A figure sidled out from the shadows.

"Dakeb! How good it is to see you again," Sidian taunted.

"If you say so. I, for one, had hoped to never see you alive again."

Sidian glowered. "These chance meetings are becoming quite boring. It doesn't need to be like this. The others are dead. Their lives and dreams no more than faded memories for you and I. Seldis was the last. My creations killed him in Kelis Dur some nights ago."

If he was expecting a reaction from Dakeb, he was disappointed. Dakeb already knew what fate had befallen his friend. Only Ibram seemed stunned by the news.

"What's this? A new pet?" Sidian asked upon seeing the young monk. "Can't let the old ways go, can you? I recall the arrogance of that age. Scouring the lands in search of those with the gift. The forgotten children of ancient Gaimos. Taking children from grieving mothers against their will. You would return Malweir to such a state?"

Dakeb leveled his gaze contemptuously. "We were all taken by the dream. Do not hold the nature of your being against the order, Sidian. You were chosen by the gods to serve higher purpose. Many parents grieved at first."

Lightning bristled over his cloak. "You know nothing of my grief! I was torn from her arms by knights of the order before I knew how to speak. Her hair was in my hands even when they brought me to Ipn Shal. She died of a broken heart not long after. I visited her grave on my very first trip away from the temple. Then I learned what twisted fate befell my father. He turned to drinking and fell in with whores and thieves. A petty criminal cut his throat in a dark alley in Paedwyn for a mere handful of copper coins. Don't lecture me on grief for I know it well."

"Your grief is of your own choosing. We were all victims of the same deed. You and your dark brothers turned and used that against the orders. I cannot help you with your loss. Nor will I allow you to continue this quest," Dakeb replied evenly.

"Allow?" Sidian bellowed in rage. "You overestimate your worth to this world. There is nothing you can prevent me from doing. How long have we played our little game? Two centuries? Three? You can't possibly think you have enough strength to best me after all this time." A demonic gleam lit his eyes. "The age of Mage-kind is finished, Dakeb. Our arrogance saw to that. The crystal of Tol Shere was a harbinger of doom to us all. Every ounce of malice, corruption, and hatred was pulled forth into the lands. The fault lays in all of us, *brother*. You, me, the hundreds of dead and thousands of civilians who paid the price."

"Those people died because of your greed," Dakeb accused. "Your kind has always lusted for power. That is why I took the shards and hid them across Malweir. The cracked crystal must not be remade."

Sidian spat venom. "What can you do to stop me? You took the four shards to the corners of the world and I have already found all but one. One left before the return of the dark gods."

"This shard does not yet belong to you, else you'd have run back to your dark master in Gren. Oh yes, I know of your dreams of empire."

"This conversation is over." The Silver Mage stepped back into the shadows. "You should not have come here. The cracked crystal shall be remade and the rise of the dark Mages will cover all Malweir. You are too late. With the last of the great order of Mages dead, I shall finally fulfill the prophecy. Good-bye, old friend."

Sidian lashed out with violent green hellfire that washed over them both.

"I've never seen such a place," Cron gasped, trying to comprehend what he saw.

Even Grelic nodded in agreement. Dozens of bodies, if they could still be called such, were hung from rusted shackles at various points along the walls. All were wasted away until their bones clearly showed beneath the fabric of their flesh. The stench was worse than anything they'd ever encountered. Piles of bones cluttered the shadow-laced corners. Row upon row of cages and cells stretched the length of the dim chamber. The giant edged closer and gently poked his broadsword into the yellowed skin of what used to be a man. Sickly puss leaked from the wound. Grelic gagged.

"They look to have been dead for some time," he managed.

"Who could have done this?" Kialla asked, dismayed. Suddenly she was more frightened than at any other point in her life. "How?"

"My guess is this is the work of Dakeb's dark Mage. I'd say the majority of them were failed experiments."

Cron asked, "And the others?"

Grelic shook his head. "Savage entertainment? Look at the bite and claw marks. Evil was at work here."

He stalked off to continue searching. The ground was soft, almost musty with the pulp of a hundred victims. Everywhere he looked there were instruments of torture. Madness. Grelic wasn't a god-fearing man, but what his eyes saw made him question the foundations of theology. How could any god allow such filth?

"It's a torture cell," Cron uttered.

Holding the torch over a long metal table, Grelic wasn't so sure. "No. It's a laboratory."

"I don't like this," Cron admitted. "Grelic, we need to leave. I don't want to get caught in this death trap when the madman returns."

"Agreed. Search the cells for survivors, then we make for the tunnel," Grelic ordered, and the three separated.

Kialla wanted to voice her disapproval but a bare whisper kept her quiet. She knew deep inside that she'd never be able to look at herself again if she were responsible for leaving anyone behind in this madness. Dutifully, Kialla carefully covered her nose and mouth and went looking.

The chamber was a long ellipse. Cells and cages were burrowed into the rock and sealed with near unbreakable iron bars. Grelic had no doubt they were infused with magic to better contain the prisoners. Most of them held assorted remains in various states of decomposition. Rats and mice crawled across the corpses, tearing chunks of flesh away with their needle-like teeth. Kialla wanted to stab them but knew there was no point. They were only doing what they were designed for.

A number of cells were conspicuously empty despite looking very lived in. Kialla shook her head. This didn't make sense. Why would there be so many living cages in a slaughterhouse? Her best guess was that they were used to hold the results of whatever hideous experiments happened down here. She was just about to give up when the faintest flicker of movement caught her eye. Kialla drew her sword. Someone, or something, was still alive.

Emerging from the fourth chamber, Pregen disgustedly punched the wall. Not finding the shard was getting irksome. He'd searched everywhere. All of the usual hiding spots or favorite places. Nothing. None of his tricks or intuitions seemed to work. He cursed quietly in case there were any Goblins lurking about and idly chewed the inside of his cheek. *Think, damn it. It must be here. There's no other place to look.*

For his part, Fitch stood quietly until frustration and anxiety got the better of him. He eyed the thief with new found uncertainty. "Where could it be? This isn't safe."

Pregen whirled on him. "Don't you think I know that, village boy? If I knew where it was we'd already be on our way out. I don't even know what it looks like!"

Fitch blushed. "What can I do to help?"

"Stand there and shut up. I can't think with you making this racket. Keep an eye out for Goblins or worse."

He wasn't sure what made him say that last part. Perhaps it was from having had too many encounters with worse on this quest. Or it could have just been fate. Either way, his words were about to turn prophetic. He left Fitch on guard and entered the last room on the level. If this didn't produce the shard, he hadn't a clue where to go next.

The barrel-bodied Goblin storming out of the room bowled him over. Pregen saw his enemy's eyes widen with shock. He also noticed something else. This Goblin was extraordinarily nervous. Pregen rolled to his feet with dagger in hand and stared after the Goblin. Not only was he an officer, it looked as if he was in charge. He slammed Fitch against the wall and disappeared around the corner.

"That's it!" Pregen shouted.

Fitch pulled himself off the wall, dazed, and asked, "What? What are you talking about?"

"He's got the stone. We need to catch him before he takes it back to the Mage!"

Pregen was shouting now. All thoughts of secrecy were gone as he was within grasp of the shard. He forgot the petty cowardice holding him back. All of the latent inadequacies marking him a lesser man. This one deed, if performed correctly, had the potential to save Malweir and redeem his family name. Pregen raced ahead without consideration for anything else. He had to get to the stone before it was too late.

He ran so fast Fitch couldn't keep up. Still stumbling from the force of the blow, he barely managed to worm his way through the twisting passages. Soon he didn't even hear footsteps. Fitch was impossibly lost. Worse, he knew it. Despair crept into the hollow corners of his soul. Whispers urged him to break down and cry, and he would have if not for the shame of having done that exact same act when Goblins destroyed his village months ago.

Shame scarred him, forcing Fitch to buck up and face reality. Pregen might already be in need of help. While he was no accomplished warrior, Fitch believed in friendship and his own skill set. Hunting and tracking consumed his previous life. Both Pregen and the Goblin had bolted so quickly they were bound to leave tracks. All he had to do was pick them up.

Doubling back the way he'd came, Fitch ran headlong into one of the Dwim. The nightmare creation reeled back and crouched to attack before Fitch blinked. The frightened villager eased back and fumbled for his dagger. He managed to take a long look at the creature for the first time. It was nothing like Ibram had described. It was much worse. Still, Fitch found something familiar about it. Like he'd known it for years.

The Dwim inched closer and Fitch felt his world suddenly collapse. The body was horribly disfigured and almost wooden. The face was withered but still bore an uncanny resemblance to a human being. Months of nightmares and torturous visions came crashing to a head. Recognition robbed his strength.

Fitch stared into the eyes of his beloved Shar. She'd been twisted and broken into one of the Dwim.

Blood soaked almost every part of his body. Fatigue assailed his powerful frame but still Krek battled on. He bled from a dozen wounds and was near the limits of exhaustion. A host of Goblins already lay piled around him. Goblin warriors stalked warily just out of reach. None of them seemed interested in fighting the bull Minotaur. If Krek didn't know any better he'd say they were waiting for some sort of sign to save their lives.

A horn sounded from the dismal village and those Goblins still able took flight. The fight was over and the enemy warriors were abandoning their posts. Krek slumped down to his knees and howled. Great honor had been heaped upon his name. At last he was a warrior.

FIFTY-FIVE

Dragon Attack

Faeldrin noticed it first. A fast moving shadow growing larger and barreling straight for them. His heart dropped. "Dragon!"

A great cheer arose from the Goblin army. The tide of battle had turned. Elves scrambled as the first blast of flame struck the highest tower on the eastern keep. Stone and flesh melted in one organizing groan. Ramulus soared overhead, exposing the luminous green belly plates. He bore no fear of the skinny Elves.

Faeldrin snatched a stunned Aleor by the collar. "Get them into firing positions before we're all slagged. Snap out of it! This is what we came for."

The Elf warrior eased out of his daze and stared back at his lord. "I…I'm sorry."

"Save it for when we return to Elvanara. You can buy the first ale."

Aleor grinned tightly and hustled back to the ballistae.

Mearlis watched the dragon loop around to prepare for another assault. "You're optimistic."

"Ha. It's not going to be too much longer before he burns this entire area. We might as well dream of drinking ale when we die." Faeldrin forced a grin. "Cover!"

Streams of fire washed across the barricade, turning hundreds of Goblin corpses to ash. Portions of the wall crumbled away. Faeldrin edged back from the keep and watched the dragon. As impressive as the wyrm was, he must have an exploitable weakness. For a brief instant Faeldrin considered appealing to the dragon's sense of infallibility. He somehow doubted that was going to work, though the idea of engaging a dragon in a verbal duel proved fairly amusing. Then it dawned on him. The dragon exposed himself right before and immediately after attacking.

"What did you see?" Mearlis asked.

Faeldrin replied, "His stomach is covered with diamond-shaped, thick scales. I'd wonder if our ballistae can penetrate. Each time he finishes spitting fire he flaps his wings and arches his chest." He took off.

"Where are you going?"

"To direct the gunners. We have a shot at this, Mearlis. We can win."

Faeldrin left his second in command and brother thinking the exact opposite. At least the Goblins seemed content with letting the dragon do all their work. The Elf Lord ran past the wreckage of both weapons used to break the Goblin charge. Several of the logs were still burning, as were a pair of corpses. He ran on, as much as it pained him to leave his friends aflame. Faeldrin swore to avenge them and if not, he'd be seeing them very soon.

Aleor and Euorn emerged from behind a screen of boulders when they saw him coming. Both wore a grim look bordering on defeat.

"Status?" Faeldrin asked without delay.

Euorn sighed. "Cypr and Tly are dead. Both weapons are destroyed. We were going to try and fire off a shot on that last pass but he was too quick. We weren't able to load them before he struck."

Faeldrin winced. "It's a good thing you hadn't or this little plan of ours might already have failed."

"How do you mean?"

"The dragon would have flamed the entire pass if you'd have hit him. This way we still have the element of surprise. He doesn't know we want to kill him. Are the other weapons in position and ready to fire?"

"Yes. Euorn is commanding the battery on the right and I've got the one on the left. Each piece remains hidden behind a screen made by the Pell Darga. All we need is a way to convince him to fly directly towards us."

"You make it sound difficult," Faeldrin said. "At times you are too pessimistic."

The taller Elf shrugged. "One of us needs to be. What's your plan?"

"He needs bait. I'm it."

An eyebrow arched. "How exactly?"

The Elf Lord smiled, charming and brilliant in the pale light. "By giving him something worth coming after. Is my horse saddled?"

"Yes, though I'm fairly certain he's not overly enthused about riding out like this. You honestly intend to just sit there in the open and wait for the dragon to attack?"

"Unless you have a better way."

"My better way involves us turning around and heading for home. This is madness, Faeldrin."

He laughed. "I know. That's why it will work."

"He's coming back around!" came a shout from one of the keeps.

Faeldrin felt his heart race. "Keep them under cover until you see my signal. Don't move until I give the command."

"How will I know your sign?" Aleor shouted to the already leaving Elf.

"Because it looks like I'll be ready to become a snack!" Faeldrin shouted back over his shoulder.

Ramulus rocketed towards the Elven positions. Unnatural mist wreathed his enormous body. The effect made him glow. Fire spit and dripped from his nostrils and mouth. Hatred poured from his very spirit. Faeldrin suspected it was a forced hatred. Dragons seldom got involved in mortal affairs. The Elf Lord held his breath. The air had gone dry. All of the moisture evaporated after the first attack. He reached down to stroke his horse's neck. The gesture was meant to bolster his own confidence.

He watched the ground come alive with flames as the dragon roared by. Faeldrin knew this was the only chance he was going to get. He donned his silver helmet and rode out into the fury of the battle. His gold-trimmed cape of dark crimson matched the destructive fires reflected off his polished armor. He drew his sword.

Ramulus had already grown weary of the games the Elves seemed intent on playing. A respectable foe would already have had the grace to die. But these Elves insisted on hiding and avoiding the death he spit. Anger consumed him and the great dragon gave in to his passions. He wheeled about for another pass. If this proved as unsuccessful as the others he had every intention of landing in the middle of the pass and setting everything aflame until the very heart of the mountains burst.

He needn't have worried. A glint of sunlight announced his foes' champion come to challenge. Garishly decked out in resplendent armor, the Elf warrior waited in the middle of the pass with his sword raised high in challenge. Ramulus drew back his lips. A sword was next to useless against his natural armor, and for a brief instant he considered letting the Elf live out of respect. That moment died quickly.

Snorting displeasure, the dragon tucked back his wings and dove. Wind whistled off his luminous green hide. Lines of vapor trailed after him. Faeldrin felt certain he was going to be crushed. His horse bucked, rearing back on frightened legs. As much as he wanted to, the Elf Lord couldn't abandon his plan now. Doing so would condemn his warriors, his friends, deep in the heart of the Deadlands and quite possibly the world.

If ever he needed things to go right, it was now. Faeldrin tried taking a deep breath to relax but the air was too hot. He'd never been more afraid in the many long centuries of his existence. This single deed went far beyond any task ever done in the storied history of the Aeldruin. Dakeb owed him greatly.

The Elven gunners tracked the great wyrm from their concealed positions. None of them had ever seen a dragon. Euorn and Aleor vaguely recalled a brief encounter with a lesser dragon some three hundred years ago, but it was nothing comparable to the monster they faced here. Remarkably, many of the Elves eyed the upcoming fight with as much as excitement as apprehension. Dead or alive, they were about to become famous.

None of them had training in siege warfare. Few of them believed in the ballistae until seeing them in action against the Goblins. Bolstered by this, they couldn't imagine failure. Each of them shared Faeldrin's vow to kill the dragon or die in the process. That singular notion inspired the Aeldruin more than any blustering speech. They'd come to accept the fact of their deaths, making them more dangerous than any foe the dark Mage could conjure. Now they watched and waited as the dragon screamed downwards towards their leader.

The Elf Lord watched the mighty wyrm come and felt his heart tighten. *What am I doing? I can still escape. Escape? Pah. It's already far too late for that.* The dragon was upon him. Faeldrin dug into his saddlebag and pulled out a long cylinder with a pointed tip. He waited until the last possible moment, when Ramulus opened his great maw. Fumes mingled with trickles of fire. Faeldrin didn't flinch. He struck the bottom of the cylinder with the heel of his free hand.

Bright yellow light exploded upwards in a shower of smoke and sparkles. The horse reared again, tossing Faeldrin to the ground before running off. The flare did its job as it streaked into the sky. Ramulus spread his leathery wings and pulled up as hard as he could to avoid the flare. He also exposed his entire chest and stomach to the Elven gunners. Ballista bolts thrummed into the air.

The first bolt slashed past the stunned dragon's head. Ramulus narrowed his eyes with the unfamiliar feeling of fear. The second bolt punched through the membrane of his right wing, snapping muscle and sinew, before he could react. Pain lanced through him in undiscovered delights. Another wooden missile, and then another, narrowly missed.

Ramulus realized he had a choice. He could either accept his fate, thus ending thousands of years of life. It was a tragedy but he was always curious about what the next world held. It also meant freedom from the tyranny of the dark Mage. That in itself was a most precious gift. Honor demanded otherwise. He was a scourge of the skies. These filthy Elves must pay for their brazen assault. Ramulus decided to press the attack. A pair of bolts caught him square in the chest. They drove into his scales, going deep into the soft organs and flesh of his torso. He heard bones breaking. Felt the agony of his vitals being skewered. Ramulus knew that he was going to die. The great wyrm fell from the sky, out of control.

Faeldrin rolled to his feet and ran for his life. Sixty tons of dragon came crashing down on top of him. He ran until the force of impact pitched him through the air. Unconsciousness took him. Ramulus hit the ground with the speed of a comet. Dirt, rock, and dust exploded. Greenish flames burst from the tears in his body. Heavy winds knocked everyone and everything down that hadn't been fast enough to take adequate cover.

The Elf Lord regained consciousness and struggled to stand. Every inch of his body hurt. His breath came in ragged gasps. He choked on dust. When he finally turned to face the dragon, his heart raced. Elf and dragon stood twenty meters apart. Faeldrin stared into the ice-colored eyes. Walking on unsteady legs, he got close enough to touch the dragon.

Ramulus was still alive, if barely. The light was fading from those jewel-like eyes that had seen the birth of the world. The dragon was not ashamed to die. He had fought hard and regained his honor. Now, at long last,

Ramulus had the chance to join his kind in the next world. He blinked once and died.

Aleor was the first to reach the scene and was so puzzled all he could do was stare.

Ramulus' death broke the Goblin army for good. Cpur and his Pell Darga broke from their hiding places in full force and decimated the Goblins until only a handful remained to escape into the mountains. The Aeldruin defended the pass long enough to collect their dead and wounded. Faeldrin ordered them back to their camp in Thrae. He wasn't finished in Deldin Grim yet. The toll had been much higher than he anticipated. It was going to take decades to refill the ranks and move past his brave friends who died. Aele, always smiling, would never grace him with his jokes again. Faeldrin and a handful of others watched the rest of the Aeldruin disappear back into the pass before turning north towards Mordrun Bal. He couldn't abandon Dakeb and the others.

FIFTY-SIX

Endgame

"Come here, we don't want to hurt you," Kialla soothingly whispered to the six-year-old boy cowering wide-eyed in the corner of his cell.

The boy curled up behind his knees. His eyes were filled with so much pain. He shivered uncontrollably, as if ghosts had come to claim him. Torment echoed in the depth of his bones. Kialla offered a sympathetic smiled. She crouched down, letting him see her for what she truly was. He huddled further away.

"Hey, come on. I promise not to hurt you. My name is Kialla. What's yours?" she asked with a smile.

Seeing him in such a degraded condition made her want to cry. He was wasting away. Most of the muscle was gone. His skin was taut against his frame. He said nothing, but watched her with eyes too large for his head. Kialla reached into a pocket and produced one of the crude travel rations the Aeldruin provided back in Thrae. Reaching through the bars, she offered it to him.

"Go on. You must be hungry."

Alfen timidly reached out and snatched it from her hand. It was gone in three bites. Crumbs covered his torn tunic. "Thank…you."

Kialla smiled again. Progress. "So are you going to tell me your name now?"

"Alfen."

She turned. "Cron, help me with the lock."

He hurried to her side. Cron swore when he noticed the frightened boy. She shook her head. Frowning, he popped the lock with his dagger. It took their combined strength to open the rusted door. Kialla rushed in. Alfen was almost in her arms when Grelic's enormous framed stepped into view. The boy knew he was going to die.

"What's this?" Grelic asked.

Kialla looked up at him with pleading eyes. "Help me get him out of here."

Grelic bent down and scooped Alfen up before the boy could protest. He eyed the malnourished boy. "Don't fear me, boy."

"This changes things," Cron said.

She glared at him. "We can't leave him here to die, Cron."

He held up his hands in defense. "I'm not suggesting it, but we sure can't take him with us to fight the dark Mage."

Realization dawned on her and her shoulders slumped. She suddenly became torn between missions.

"No, he can't," Grelic said. "Get him out of here, both of you. With any luck, Krek will have held his ground. Once you get out of Mordrun Bal, head for the pass and find the Elves."

"Where are you going?" Cron asked.

Grelic smiled. "To find this dark Mage."

Down twisting passages, flights of stairs, and an endless labyrinth of shadowed tunnels he ran. Pregen knew he was undeniably lost. That didn't matter. His friends were scattered. A lurking deceit cautioned that he might be the only one left alive by now. As much as he wanted to turn and run home, he couldn't. The fat Goblin carrying the crystal was too close. He couldn't let him get away. Pregen chased on, eventually coming into a massive tunnel stretching so far he doubted it had an end. Still he ran on. The walls gradually started to spread out, opening into a cavern. He had come unto the heart of mighty Druem but hadn't seen the Goblin.

Pregen skidded to a halt. The heavy sound of hurried footsteps echoed. Pregen smirked. The Goblin was near. The chase was almost over. He pushed harder. So hard he failed to notice the destructive light show raging ahead. The Goblin was heading directly for the violent struggle.

Twenty meters from the battle Pregen overtook his prey and leapt on his back. Goblin and man collapsed in a tangle of flailing arms and metal screeching across the polished floor. Pregen punched Scourd in the mouth as hard as he could and tried to pry the crystal away. A glint of purple flickered in the Mage-light to entice him. Gnarled fingers closed around his throat, threatening to crush the life out of him. He punched again, and again, until Scourd's hand dropped.

Pregen snatched the crystal shard free and felt true triumph for the time in his life. He jumped away from the Goblin general and noticed Dakeb and Ibram for the first time. What he failed to see was Scourd draw his dagger and plunge it into the base of his spine. Excruciating pain exploded through his body. His legs gave out and Pregen collapsed in a pile of useless flesh and bone. He was paralyzed from the waist down.

Scourd rolled to his feet, kicking his enemy savagely away. The taste of blood, hot and salty, filled his mouth and he spat. Pregen looked up helplessly. The Goblin snarled contemptuously and drew his sword. Tired of the games of men and Mage, he wanted this over. He drove his sword down through Pregen's heart with enough force to plunge into the unforgiving stone beneath.

Many things flashed in that moment. Grelic hiring him. His conversations with the strange Codel Mres in the drunken haze of a tavern. The minister wanted Pregen to spy for him and report everything back. Even went so far as to leave signs and messages on their trail north. He'd taken the job out of greed. The promise of a king's ransom outweighed honor. He'd done his job, but something changed along the way. He realized he was part of something greater than himself for the first time in his life. Despite his constant complaining, he had transformed into the man his father always dreamed of.

Pregen Chur died with a smile on his face, for the last thing he saw was Grelic emerging from the darkness behind the Goblin. Scourd ripped his sword free and spun. Steel clashed in a hail of sparks.

Sidian caught the episode evolving out of the corner of his eye and shuddered. The shard was so close. His robes were smoking, burned in many places. He smelled of burnt flesh. The battle tested him greatly, but he took comfort in his enemies suffering likewise.

"Our little game is over, Dakeb. Your friends are dying. They always seem to die, don't they? The shard is right there. I know you can feel it. Sitting, waiting for its master in the grip of a dead man. You can't win."

Ash smeared his face. Dakeb clutched his friend for support. He hadn't been sure until now, but Sidian had grown stronger since their last encounter. He feared neither he nor Ibram combined stood much chance of beating him.

He called out, "It doesn't have to be like this."

Sidian choked back a laugh. "Oh but it does. You think we betrayed the order of Mages, but it was you who betrayed us. When the darkness rose we at last understood the true meaning to life. Power! How insignificant our lives seemed until the dead reached forth to embrace us. And did any of you attempt to save us? Bring us back from that dreadful place where nightmares become reality? No! Not one of you lifted so much as a finger. You and your kind damned us just as much as the crystal."

"That's no excuse for the crimes you committed!" Dakeb fought back. "All of you could have sought our help but greed and corruption were in your hearts. Damn us all you want for your insecurities, but always remember that you brought about the fall of Ipn Shal. You, Sidian the Silver, betrayed all the races of Malweir with your lust for power. Everything that has happened since is your fault."

Tiny bolts of electricity bled from Sidian's eyes. "My, my. How testy we've become, my friend. I need only one more piece of the crystal, Dakeb. Just one more and the world will be plunged into the madness of the dark gods forever. You can't stop me. Victory belongs to who wants it the most. I will prevail. It's only fitting that Malweir suffers my fate."

"You're overlooking one important fact," Dakeb said. "You have two pieces of the crystal, not three."

Sidian laughed again. "Have I?" He reached into the folds of his robes and produced the chunk of purple crystal. "You've failed again. All those years wasted thinking of the perfect hiding places. Places I'd never think to look. You nearly fooled me with this one, but I still beat you. When I find the fourth shard your failure will be complete. I will rule Malweir with tyranny undreamed of. Good-bye, Dakeb."

Ibram couldn't restrain himself any longer. He looked down at Pregen's corpse, knowing the thief deserved better. The former monk of Harr jumped in front of Dakeb and rushed the Silver Mage. He was determined not to let his friend die at the hands of this madman. Dakeb reached out to stop him but was too slow. Ibram raced towards his foe.

Sidian cocked his head, curious at what the youth intended to achieve. For a moment he debated whether to kill the fledgling Mage or convert him. Either prospect bore measures of enjoyment. The decision took a fraction of second. Mage fire lashed from his fingers, striking the charging Ibram in the chest. He couldn't afford another Mage in the world.

"NO!" Dakeb screamed.

Ibram froze in his tracks. Agony stole into him, ravaging the heart of his soul. He screamed in unimaginable pain. Smoke poured from his ears, nose, and mouth. His flesh blackened. His hair burned and fell away. Ibram tried to resist, but was no match for the overpowering evil before him. Finally, he burst into flames. Ibram screamed one last time before his body became ash. Broken bones crashed to the floor in a cloud of dust. Brother Ibram was no more. Sidian turned his rage on Dakeb, but the old Mage was ready for it.

Bolts of purple Mage fire shot from his hands. They burst around Sidian, hammering him back. Neither one of them had the strength of their youth. Both faltered. Sidian hadn't counted on Dakeb's wrath at the death of his pupil. No matter. He had the shard and had killed a potential rival. Victory was his. He summoned his escape spell.

A shield enveloped him, protecting him from Dakeb's rage. "It's over this time, Dakeb. Perhaps you shall think twice before assuming a new apprentice. I leave you in defeat."

A monstrous figure dropped down from the darkness high above. Dakeb reeled. A Shimmering! He'd thought they were all destroyed during the Mage war. An uneasy feeling settled over him as the hulking brute reached out to claim his master. Dakeb tried getting a better look at the creature but the unnatural glaze surrounding it kept his vision unfocused. Claws, spikes, armor plates. A dozen eyes looking back at him from the seemingly shapeless head. The Shimmering lifted up and bore Sidian away while the helpless and defeated Dakeb remained far below.

Grelic blocked Scourd's swing without effort despite the Goblin throwing everything he had at him. The Mage battle going on in the background bathed the combatants in unholy lights. The sound of thunder battered his ears, deafening him to the sounds of his own combat. Scourd staggered backwards. His arms stung from the shock of his last swing. Grelic knew the slower, heavier

Goblin didn't stand a chance unless he stooped to trickery. Still, it didn't do to take unnecessary chances.

"Come on, maggot," Grelic taunted. "You have crimes to pay for."

Pregen's body lay crumpled against the rock wall, his dead eyes staring at Grelic accusingly. Rage consumed the giant. He hadn't felt so angered since the battle of Kressel Tine when a Dwarf nearly took his head. He charged after the retreating Goblin, driving Scourd steadily back. The force of his attacks kept the Goblin off balance. Bringing down an overhand chop, Grelic ran his sword along Scourd's blade all the way to the hilt guard before flicking his wrist. The sudden shift made Scourd lunge too far and in that instant the Goblin knew he had lost. Grelic's heavy broadsword swung almost effortlessly and severed Scourd's head at the shoulders.

The giant sheathed his sword after wiping the blood on his opponent's body. Bending down, he gently closed Pregen's eyes. A growl got stuck in his throat. This was all his fault. He'd coerced the thief to join them under false pretense and now he lay dead under a smoldering volcano. The weight was much harder to bear for a man used to losing friends.

"Grelic, over here," Dakeb said softly.

He looked up to see the old man kneeling over a pile of dust and bone. He didn't want to ask what happened, though he knew well enough. Dakeb sobbed gently, pausing to stare up at the giant with sad eyes.

"Ibram deserved better," he whispered.

Grelic nodded. There was nothing for it. He only hoped his other friends met with better success in their escape from Druem. "Where's the dark Mage?"

"Gone, bore away by an old creature. He killed Ibram first. The boy wasn't ready for this. I didn't train him. Sidian was too powerful. Brave boy. He tried to protect me. He rushed Sidian when it looked like he was about to escape with the shard. There was nothing I could do."

"So it's over? The dark Mage won."

Dakeb shook his head and withdrew the crystal from his robes. "No. Sidian thinks he has the shard but it was merely an illusion. He escaped with a simulacrum, nothing more. Ibram died for an illusion. Where are Cron and the others?"

"Already on their way out. I'll explain along the way."

He helped Dakeb up and went to collect Pregen's body. He'd be damned if he was going to let another friend rot on a forgotten battlefield. That's when he realized he was still missing one person. "Dakeb, where's Fitch?"

The old Mage looked around. He hadn't even thought about it until Grelic brought it up. Instinctively he knew Fitch was fighting demons of his own.

Thousands of nightmares rolled in different versions of misery. Fitch knew in that single moment that he was truly one of the damned. The Dwim facing him, in testament to maliciousness and cruelty, was his beloved wife. His Shar. Shock robbed his strength. He couldn't move. The love of his life stood before him, twisted and perverted by some dark power beyond his comprehension. He wept.

Fitch blamed himself. All of this was his fault. Shar took a step back and dropped into a fighting stance. Whatever was left of the woman he loved meant to kill him. She was no longer human, instead a manifestation of the very evil they'd come to destroy. Now that he had confronted that evil, Fitch found doubt. He didn't have the strength to kill her, no matter what she was.

"I'm sorry, Shar," he told her.

The Dwim stopped moving and cocked her head in recognition.

"None of this would have happened if I had been a man that day," he pressed. His voice cracked as months of repressed emotions poured out. "It was my cowardice that let you be taken, Shar. Taken and turned into this monster. How could you ever forgive me?"

She shook her head vigorously in confusion. She was a Dwim, a servant to the dark master. His true guidance gave her courage in the face of doubt. She growled softly and flexed her claws.

"You have become evil, Shar. For that I am truly sorry, but not as sorry as for what I know I have to do." He drew his sword. The heavy weapon felt clumsy in his hands. "I can't let you escape. You're not a murderer. You're better than this. I'm going to set you free. Set both of us free."

He took an uneasy step forward. Tears streamed down his face. He trembled, wishing his strength to hold. The Dwim leapt. This was the moment he'd been awaiting since that dreadful winter day his world ended. Fitch had wanted to die then, but Fate saw fit to keep him alive. He didn't know how or why so many others took interest in him.

Here at last, buried under the once mighty volcano that had helped shape the world, Fitch was reunited with the woman he loved and his true purpose in life. He held his sword straight forward and met her assault. Steel pierced wooden-like flesh with a sickening sound. Shar screamed. Her claws raked into him, ripping strings of muscle away as the force of impact took them both to the ground.

Shar fell on top of him, impaled on his sword. She swiped at the side of his neck, tearing open his jugular vein. Life blood flowed away, as if excited to be free of the mortal constraints. Fitch jerked the sword up into her chest cavity and twisted. She started to shake. Her body spasmed as his sword pierced what was left of her heart. Finally, she stopped fighting and lowered her head onto his chest where she looked him in the eyes one last time before dying.

"I love you," Fitch whispered. He struggled to reach up and touch her lips again but never made it.

Fitch Iane followed his beloved into death and a silvered new world beyond. All of his nightmares were finally laid to rest.

Grelic reemerged into the sunlight and instinctively tried to protect his eyes from the menacing glare. He and Dakeb kept moving past the host of slain Goblins until the giant ran out of strength. Grelic laid Pregen's body down and collapsed beside him. Time and age had finally caught up. Dakeb fell next to him and wept a single tear. That was how Cron found them a short time later. Neither had ever been so grateful to see another living soul as in that moment.

"We figured you didn't make it," Cron told them.

Grelic relayed their tale in choppy sentences, for the pain was much too real. Both he and Dakeb learned how Cron led Kialla and the boy through the remains of Mordrun Bal and rescued hundreds of slaves along the way.

Grelic stared at the group of people milling aimlessly about. "What is this?"

"There must be hundreds, of all races," Dakeb added.

Cron nodded with pride. "We found them trying to dig through a lava vein. Kialla and I killed the few Goblin overseers and led the slaves out. The city was deserted by the time we got back to the surface."

"Some good came of this after all," Grelic grunted. He was beyond exhausted. "Now what?"

"I say we wait a day or two until most of them regain some strength and push towards the Darkwall. I've got details scouring every hovel and cave for supplies. Some are fixing old wagons for those too weak to walk. We should make it all right provided there's no dragon in wait."

Dakeb flashed a knowing wink. "Oh, I think we don't need to worry about that. Faeldrin is a most capable commander."

He said no more.

Grelic awoke to the sounds of hooves late in the afternoon of the following day. He and Cron rose and went to greet their arrivals. They passed Krek, who gave Grelic the nod of a complimenting warrior. Grelic returned the gesture and carried on. Faeldrin and nine of the Aeldruin reigned to a halt. All wore genuine smiles.

"What now?" Cron asked.

Grelic felt the weight of the world fall from him. "Now, we go home."

Lost in the maddening shadows of his obsidian tower, the Silver Mage sat upon his throne. Anger twisted and marred his features. In his hands sat the purple crystal he'd taken from Druem. A useless chunk of rock. Dakeb had tricked him! All of his carefully laid plans had gone to ruin, again, because of that doddering old fool. Sidian crushed the false crystal into powder and let the grains trickle through his clenched fist. He had lost this round, but the battle was far from over.

The Silver Mage sat upon his barbed throne and let his thoughts drift off towards the age when the curtain of darkness would forever eclipse the world of Malweir. His wicked laughter echoed through the empty halls.

EPILOGUE

Most the world would never find out what happened in the Deadlands. Rumors of a growing darkness spread across the face of Malweir. Kings spoke of a plot to overthrow the monarchy in Thrae and the failed military coup. Suspicions rose among the ruling houses and caused many needless deaths. For the most part life went on oblivious to the bluster or threat of conspiracy. The enemy plotted through it all from his newly forged kingdom in Gren.

Cron and Kialla were wed by King Rentor in the royal gardens. It was a day-long celebration and not forgotten for years. Both Cron and his brother, Maen, were awarded Thrae's highest medal for valor. Alfen Bew decided he liked his rescuers so much that he wound up being adopted by them. He grew to be a fine man, surpassing his father at every aspect. He died holding the rank of general.

The heroes took Pregen's body to his family home for burial. He was laid to rest beside his beloved sister. Some say you could hear the ground sigh in relief as his body was covered with the soft dirt. To this day the ground remains cold and an eerie light haunts the area during certain times of the year. Pregen Chur was forgotten as a thief and assassin and remembered for a hero. Dakeb never told the others that Pregen had been the spy. Some things just didn't need to be said.

Krek returned to the great cavern city of Malg and won great honor to his family name. His deeds in Mordrun Bal quickly became legend. Minotaurs spoke of him for generations. The memories never left Krek and he used them to carry on. Hundreds of years later he led the Minotaurs into the final war against the dark gods.

The riders of the Aeldruin went back to their home wood, bloodied and abused. Faeldrin discharged those who had had enough of violence and went searching for new recruits to replenish the ranks. That proved no problem. In fact, he had to turn away a great number. Tales of the Aeldruin's bravery at Deldin Grim kept their legend alive by all races until the breaking of the world.

The day Grelic came home to Kelis Dur was the last time he ever held a weapon. He'd been witness to far too many devilries and carnage. He suddenly lacked the stomach for it. He took his leave from his friends and rode off into the forests to enjoy his remaining days. Some say King Rentor was one of his pall bearers some years later.

The brave actions of a handful prevented the destruction of all in the barren wastes of the Deadlands. They preserved peace for the time being but the Silver Mage wasn't defeated. He was beaten for the moment, but it was only a matter of time before he discovered the final pieces of the cracked crystal of Tol Shere and made his war on the world.

And of Dakeb? He went back to Druem to collect the ashes of Ibram and took them to the ruins of Ipn Shal. There Ibram was laid to rest beside Seldis and the hundreds of other Mages who'd died in the defense of good. None of the heroes ever saw Dakeb again, but if you pay close attention you just may catch a glimpse of him shifting through the forests of the world in his lonely struggle to keep the Silver Mage from finding the final piece of the crystal.

END

Half a continent from the sleeping forests of Relin Werd stood the Gren Mountains, the treacherous boundary between Averon and the wicked land of Gren. Here the war was very much a reality, not just mere speculation over a mug of ale and a leg of venison. Soldiers of Averon met the enemy in engagements that no one ever heard. Skeletons littered the rocky pass between kingdoms. Whatever fragile peace the capital of Paedwyn pretended to enjoy was lost in this largely forgotten part of the world.

Strong winds ravaged the rocky terrain, funneling through the mountain passes and picking up speed and intensity before unleashing across the open slopes of the Gren Mountains. Dark skies kept the air damp and dour enough for the intruders to quickly lose hope and return the way they had come except for the three mounted soldiers, who silently rode through the lower foothills of the eastern range. Black and purple skies laden with thunderstorms kept the sun perpetually hidden here. Lightning raked the slopes around them, warning them to beware. A thunderclap trembled the ground.

"We should turn back!" one of the soldiers shouted.

Sergeant Hallis, the scout leader, ignored him, noting how quickly the young and inexperienced trooper was ready to give up. The land of Gren had been besieged by nature since the Silver Mage first took power, over two hundred years ago. It was rumored that Gren was once a gilded land of a different name, but history was forgotten in response to the great evil threatening the world. Hallis himself had joined the army of Averon out of necessity. A flux swept through the kingdom, claiming hundreds, including his parents. Having nothing to keep him at home, Hallis left to join the army.

He reached the rank of sergeant and was nearing the end of his third decade of service. Most of his duty had been spent on the wrong side of the Gren Mountains, scouting and spying on enemy movements. It was a learned skill that was almost second nature to him. He barely noticed the weather anymore. Normally he wouldn't have taken such a green trooper, but there was little choice. Despite years of waiting, the army of Averon wasn't prepared for the war everyone knew was coming. There just wasn't enough time to get ready.

Hallis didn't have the luxury to worry about what was happening back at Paedwyn. Assigned to the garrison at the mountain fortress of Gren Mot, his job was to scout out the enemy and report any actionable intelligence.

"Keep quiet and watch me, Troop," Hallis barked at the lad. He wanted to say more but knew it was useless. This was the boy's first mission and no amount of class work or indoctrination was enough to prepare him for the horrors surrounding them.

Flames pockmarked the landscape as far as the eye could see. Scrub brushes void of greenery were the last remnants of a pristine empire. All of the Fair races fled west after a brutal campaign to oust the Silver Mage was lost. Nothing now grew upon the soiled plains. Nothing lived in the fetid waters. The mountains were filled with hordes of Trolls and worse. Goblins and other foul beings lived in the low country, dwelling in vast underground caverns. Hallis knew his patrol was being watched even now.

Most patrols were fielded with the instructions of monitoring only. King Maelor had been concerned with enemy movements and troop buildups for years now and was eager to learn the disposition of his foe. For Hallis, this patrol was unlike any other. Three separate patrols had been sent out the week prior and none returned. Concern was rising that the enemy was at last ready to move. He'd accepted the task because it was a soldier's duty to follow orders, whether he liked them or not. What he didn't accept were the men assigned to him. His complaints fell on deaf ears and three short days later they were inside the realm of the enemy. The third scout reined in close to Hallis and said in a low voice, "Do you think he may be right?"

Hallis finished a hasty drink from his canteen. "I've been thinking that since we left Gren Mot, Jinse."

Older than Hallis, Jinse offered a weak laugh. "So have I. We shouldn't be on the same patrol, at any rate. What good would it do for both of us to get killed at the same time?"

"Orders are orders," Hallis answered.

His friend picked up on the meaning even as the words left his mouth. They both knew the garrison commander at the mountain fortress was an intolerable man who expected his subordinates to obey his every command without question. Jinse also knew that Hallis had been around long enough to put the lives of his men first. The rest of Averon may still be safe behind the illusion of peace, but combat was very real here on the border.

"We should have seen signs by now," Hallis scowled after they rode another hour. "I don't like this at all."

Lightning and thunder emphasized his point.

"The winds are picking up," Jinse remarked. "This is getting dangerous."

Hallis smiled. "It'll make the ale that much better when we get back."

He was going to say more when they rounded a corner and came face to face with a vast plain, normally empty. His eyes widened in horror at what he now saw. Thousands of campfires and campaign tents stretched as far as they could see and into the darkness beyond. Squat, grey bodies in leather armor blanketed every inch of the land. Hallis just barely made out enormous creatures pulling siege machines closer. He'd seen and fought Trolls and Goblins before, but had never imagined an army so large. The people of Averon long believed the impending war was inevitable. Not even the king's top advisors could predict when though. Hallis stared at the answer and the fear that came with it.

"This isn't good," Jinse said, his throat suddenly dry.

Hallis sat still and watched. He'd already given up trying to count. The rookie didn't fare so well. Barely past his teen years, the trooper was on the verge of snapping. Never in his days did he actually expect to go to war. Yet here he sat, locked on the brink of a fate inescapable. Doom was returned to the world of men. The veterans noticed his wild look and moved to keep him from doing something brash.

A lightning bolt blasted a nearby rock into a shower of sparks and pebbles, spooking all of their horses. The rookie was thrown into a boulder before his horse ran off in the direction of the Goblin camp. Jinse was the first to recover and desperately dashed after the horse before it was too late. Hallis immediately went to his fallen trooper. He was halfway there when Fate intervened.

Black arrows rained down on the fallen trooper, killing him instantly a dozen times over. Hallis snatched his shield in a useless effort, for the enemy was on both sides. The assault ended with a horrible roar from the rocks above. A Mountain Troll burst from cover, mighty war hammer in hand and squads of Goblins at his heels. Hallis was cut off. Jinse wheeled about and drew his sword. The odds were against them and they knew it. Then Jinse did something Hallis didn't expect. The grizzled old veteran roared back at the Troll and charged into their ranks.

"Go!" he bellowed to Hallis.

The last thing Hallis saw was his friend plowing into the enemy. One of them had to live to warn Averon. Jinse chose Hallis. Both men spurred their horses hard; one into certain death and the other back into the mountain passes. Jinse offered the ultimate sacrifice and Hallis would be damned if he let it go to waste. The garrison at Gren Mot had to be warned. He feared the fate of the entire kingdom depended on it.

DREAMS
OF
WINTER
A FORGOTTEN GODS TALE
CHRISTIAN WARREN FREED

It is a troubled time, for the old gods are returning and they want the universe back…

Under the rigid guidance of the Conclave, the seven hundred known worlds carve out a new empire with the compassion and wisdom the gods once offered. But a terrible secret, known only to the most powerful, threatens to undo three millennia of progress. The gods are not dead at all. They merely sleep. And they are being hunted.

Senior Inquisitor Tolde Breed is sent to the planet Crimeat to investigate the escape of one of the deadliest beings in the history of the universe: Amongeratix, one of the fabled THREE, sons of the god-king. Tolde arrives on a world where heresy breeds insurrection and war is only a matter of time. Aided by Sister Abigail of the Order of Blood Witches, and a company of Prekhauten Guards, Tolde hurries to find Amongeratix and return him to Conclave custody before he can restart his reign of terror.

What he doesn't know is that the Three are already operating on Crimeat.

Read Dreams of Winter now and begin your journey into the realm of the Forgotten Gods.

ARMIES
of the
SILVER MAGE

CHRISTIAN WARREN
FREED

Malweir was once governed by the order of Mages, bringers of peace and light. Centuries past and the lands prospered. But all was not well. Unknown to most, one mage desired power above all else. He turned his will to the banished Dark Gods and brought war to the free lands. Only a handful of mages survived the betrayal and the Silver Mage was left free to twist the darker races to his bidding. The only thing he needs to complete his plan and rule the world forever are the four shards of the crystal of Tol Shere.

Having spent most of their lives dreaming about leaving their sleepy village and travelling the world, Delin Kerny and Fennic Attleford never thought that one day they would be forced to flee their town to save their lives. Everything changes when they discover the fabled Star Silver sword and learn that there are some who want the weapon for themselves. Hunted by a ruthless mercenary, the boys run from Fel Darrins and are forced into the adventure they only dreamed about.

Ever ashamed of the horrors his kind let loose on the world the last mage, Dakeb, lives his life in shadows. The only thing keeping him alive is his quest to stop the Silver Mage from reassembling the crystal. His chance finally comes through the hearts and wills of Delin and Fennic. Dakeb bestows upon them the crystal shard, entrusting them with the one thing capable of restoring peace to Malweir.

THE
LAZARUS MEN
A LAZARUS MEN AGENDA
CHRISTIAN
WARREN FREED

It is the 23rd century. Humankind has reached the stars, building a tentative empire across a score of worlds. Earth's central government rules weakly as several worlds continue their efforts toward independence. Shadow organizations hide in the midst of the political infighting. Their manifestations of power and influence are beholden only to the highest bidder. The most powerful/insidious/secret of these, The Lazarus Men, has existed for decades, always working outside of morality's constraints. Led by the enigmatic Mr. Shine, their agents are hand selected from the worst humanity has to offer and available for the right price.

Gerald LaPlant lives an ordinary life on Old Earth. That life is thrown into turmoil on the night he stumbles upon the murder of what appears to be a street thief. Fleeing into the night, Gerald finds himself hunted by agents of Roland McMasters, an extremely powerful man dissatisfied with the current regime and with designs on ruling his own empire. In order to do so, McMasters needs the fabled Eye of Karakzaheim, a map leading to immeasurable wealth. Unknown to either man, Mr. Shine has deployed agents in search of the same artifact and will stop at nothing to obtain it.

Running for his life, Gerald quickly becomes embroiled in a conspiracy reaching deep into levels of government that he never imagined existed. His every move is hounded by McMasters' agents and the Lazarus Men. His adventures take him away from the relative safety of Old Earth across the stars and into the heart of McMasters' fledgling empire. The future of the Earth Alliance at stake. If Gerald has any hope of surviving and helping save the alliance he must rely on his wits and awakened instincts while foregoing the one thing that could get him killed more quickly than the rest: trust.

BIO

Christian W. Freed was born in Buffalo, N.Y. more years ago than he would like to remember. After spending more than 20 years in the active duty US Army he has turned his talents to writing. Since retiring, he has gone on to publish more than 20 science fiction and fantasy novels as well as his combat memoirs from his time in Iraq and Afghanistan. His first book, Hammers in the Wind, has been the #1 free book on Kindle 4 times and he holds a fancy certificate from the L Ron Hubbard Writers of the Future Contest.

Passionate about history, he combines his knowledge of the past with modern military tactics to create an engaging, quasi-realistic world for the readers. He graduated from Campbell University with a degree in history and a Masters of Arts degree in Digital Communications from the University of North Carolina at Chapel Hill. He currently lives outside of Raleigh, N.C. and devotes his time to writing, his family, and their two Bernese Mountain Dogs. If you drive by you might just find him on the porch with a cigar in one hand and a pen in the other.